NOSTALGIA'S BOAT

DAVID MATHEW

First Montag Press E-Book and Paperback Original Edition February 2020

Montag Press
ISBN: 978-1-940233-76-5
Design © 2020 Camilet Cooray
Photo Credits:
Front cover: Keith Brooke
Back cover: Tom Lockington

Montag Press Team:
Project Editor — Charlie Franco
Managing Director — Charlie Franco

A Montag Press Book
www.montagpress.com
Montag Press
777 Morton Street, Unit B
San Francisco CA 94129 USA

Montag Press, the burning book with the hatchet cover, the skewed word mark and the portrayal of the long-suffering fireman mascot are trademarks of Montag Press.

Printed & Digitally Originated in the United States of America
10 9 8 7 6 5 4 3 2 1

BOOKS WORTH BURNING

Montag Press Transmedia Collective
MontagPress.com | @MontagPress

Dedicated to Billy Connolly –

"You pass this way but once."

And dedicated to Master Lucas Kent.

Contents

Strangely, it seems, the things we do not know trouble us more than the things we are aware of. They keep coming back, forcing us to return to the scenes of distress, enticing us to replay over and over again the disturbances that shape our lives.

Stephen Frosh,
Hauntings: Psychoanalysis and Ghostly Transmissions

... we are animated and agitated by a power or program that seems to violate our most intuitive sense of self-determination.

Christopher Johnson,
'Ambient Technologies, Uncanny Signs'

I

'Looky yonder. There's a steamboat who must have fallen on a rock and died in the terrible storm.'

Without saying anything to each other Abhor and I leaped onto our trusty ship and headed right for that wreck. Light from the lightning clearly showed parts of her. A pale green deck. And black poles. Then other parts of her. An old rocking chair next to a steering wheel.

I wanted to get on to that wreck as soon as possible and never leave it. Then soon I wouldn't care about Abhor anymore even though she was as crazy as me.

Kathy Acker,
Empire of the Senseless

The finding of an object is the refinding of it.

Sigmund Freud,
Three Essays on the Theory of Sexuality

Ah, nostalgia! It's not what it used to be.

Old joke

THEN

1

Pointing at the air in his study, Raymond grinned and said: *This, boy – this is Duke Ellington.*

He was referring to the music that came out of two ancient speakers, each of which was taller than me. At the time I was two years old. It is my first memory.

Impossible! I have heard said. No child remembers conversations in such a way, especially when the child has yet to start speaking. But *I* do.

He left when I was four years and seven months old. It wasn't until I was much older, aged eight, that I realised I had done nothing wrong. It took me a long while to stop blaming myself for his departure.

There's something wrong with Uncle Raymond's head, my mother tried to explain. *It makes him do bad things.*

What kind of bad things? I must have asked at least two dozen times, before I knew I'd get no honest answer.

I'll tell you when you're older.

She never did. On one occasion I asked her if she would also do bad things, given that they'd shared an egg in Grandmother's womb. She almost shouted her answer at me, but caught herself in time.

It's something I live in fear of, I remember her saying.

At this point the door to the topic was slammed shut, the keys swallowed.

2

Lorraine was an *au pair* and my first true love. After other *au pairs*, who had wanted to 'take care' of me and 'entertain' me (and all that guff), Lorraine came along when I was eight (eight years and four months) with a fresh agenda. She wanted to put me to bed and then spend the evening talking to her boyfriend on her phone.

She was the first woman ever to understand me, I concluded at the time. I thought of her often, and fondly, while I climbed out my bedroom window and down the side of the garage, into the passage next to it.

You might think that an eight year-old walking the streets at night would draw attention, but nothing could be further from the truth. People turned away. They didn't *want* to see me.

When I returned, climbing up the same side of the garage, Lorraine awaited me. Not once did we discuss the matter. She would simply say: *It's bedtime*, and I would say: *I agree.*

At the age of nine years old (nine years and six months), I said to Lorraine: *We need to talk about secrets.*

She said: *You're right. Where do you go at night, when I'm supposed to look after you?*

That's between me and my Maker, I told her. *I need your help. Will you help me?*

I might. It depends.

And that's when I knew I had her on the team. 'Might' means 'yes' to a child.

I need your help, as an adult. We'll forget about your conversations with Pat Kelly. Do we have a deal?

She waited.

What is it you want? she asked. *Before I spank you.*

Ignoring the reference to spanking (a favoured interlude of mine), I said: *All I want is access to a certain building. Then we're quits.*

3

One sunny afternoon, Lorraine walked me up the hill. We did not hold hands.

The guard said: *Who do you want to see?*

Raymond Cossell, I answered.

And do you mind if I ask who you are? the guard said.

Raymond's niece, Lorraine replied. *It's his wedding anniversary . . . or it would be if Wendy was still alive. We hoped to cheer him up.*

Good luck with that. You'll still need to complete a form, the guard said.

Of course, I replied.

The presence of a child was all it had taken for the man to quash his professional ideals.

We emptied our pockets (I only carried a handkerchief and some prize-winning conkers) and Lorraine had to open her purse for inspection. We walked through a metal-detecting gate; it did not beep. We were shown to a room on the third floor, where a second guard took over.

This second man was larger than the first and wore a truncheon in a long holster on his left hip. He said: *You're relatives of Mr Cossell.*

Yes, Lorraine answered. *I'm his niece.*

And I'm her son, I added.

The guard gave Lorraine a queer look that said *What are you thinking? A child? In here?*

The corridor smelled of poo and of lemon disinfectant. The guard removed a key ring from a second holster, this one on his right hip.

You're aware of his crimes, the guard told Lorraine, while he juggled for the correct key. *He's been good for nearly two weeks. This usually means we're due for an episode. Do not approach him. The line you don't cross is where the wooden floor ends and his carpet begins. Do you understand me, Miss? He can only step four feet from his bed but he's got long arms . . . Are you ready?*

The room was not the cell that I might have imagined, but Uncle Raymond was certainly a captive. He wore a thick brown belt around his waist which was attached to a metal ring cemented into the cream-coloured wall. He would only be able to walk in a half-circle, like a nanny goat tethered to a barn door.

When we entered, he had his broad back to us; he was seated at a small plastic desk. He was dressed in blue, in something between gym kit and pyjamas.

Uncle Raymond? I asked, but he did not turn to greet his visitors. From the corridor we had not heard the music that came from a small CD player. The CD player was also chained to the wall.

I don't need any more medication, Uncle Raymond said eventually. *I'm calm.*

It's me – Lucas, I said.

I don't know anyone called Lucas, Raymond answered.

Turn around for your guests, Mr Cossell, said the guard.

You're fictions. You exist only in my bad dreams and leak out into the real world when I'm pumped with drugs.

Nobody pumps you with drugs, Mr Cossell, the guard replied – probably for our benefit.

Lorraine had never met Raymond, and now that she had executed her task as my vehicle into the institution, I had expected her to remain silent. I was surprised when she said:

We walked up the hill just for you, Mr Cossell.

And two things happened at once.

The first was Uncle Raymond, who jumped up from his plastic chair and strode towards us in four bounds that would have been five if the belt around his waist had not restrained him on its twanging tail.

Professor! he screamed.

Mr Cossell! the guard warned, reaching for his truncheon as Lorraine took a step back.

Professor! Professor *Cossell to you, Madam! And who are you anyway?*

The second thing that happened was this: the guard noted Lorraine's mistake. Why would a niece call her uncle Mister?

I'm Lorraine, my *au pair* busked. *Your* niece, *Uncle Raymond!*

But the damage had been done. Raymond did not recognize my chaperone, and he had scarcely glanced at me.

Please take a step away, Professor Cossell, the guard instructed calmly. *You've just said you don't need more medication. Don't make me insist you're wrong.*

The guard and Raymond engaged in a war of eyesights. Uncle Raymond turned from us. He moved towards his desk, saying: *Go. Please go . . . Just leave me alone.*

The guard said: *Miss? I think we should respect Professor Cossell's wishes.*

He did not say *Your uncle's wishes.* Questions would follow downstairs, I was sure.

So I plucked at a memory and said: *This, Uncle Raymond – this is Miles Davis. The tune is 'Freddie Freeloader'. From the* Kind of Blue *album.*

Raymond sat on the end of his bed. Then he stood up and pressed PAUSE. He ran his left hand through what survived of his hair. It was grey; it grew in patchy clumps, like weeds.

Lucas, he remembered.

Yes, Uncle Raymond.

He looked at me for the first time in four years and eleven months.

You shouldn't have been allowed in here, he said wearily. *I'm a danger to humanity, didn't they tell you?*

. . . Aren't you pleased to see me, Uncle Raymond? I asked.

Those are two different issues . . . A meniscus of unshed tears in his eyes, he blinked at me. *I thought you were dead, boy. They told me I killed you when the explosive went off.*

What? said Lorraine.

You didn't kill me, Uncle Raymond! I'm alive!

I can see that, boy.

Raymond turned to the guard and demanded: *Why did you tell me I killed them?*

I said nothing of the kind, Mr Coss – Professor Cossell.

Not you, Uncle Raymond answered. *Your kind . . . The psychiatrists,* he spat out with indignation.

The guard seemed both confused and keen to re-establish order. *Say what you wanted to say,* he told either me or Lorraine.

Uncle Raymond said: *Thank you for walking up the hill to see me.*

I wanted to put a name in his head, and I added: *Lorraine was waiting for a letter too.*

Sorry, Lorraine, said Uncle Raymond. To the guard he continued: *Might we be allowed a few moments of privacy?*

That all depends, he was told. *Are you going to stay seated?*

I assure you. I will not twitch a muscle on my gluteus maximus.

The guard considered the verbal contract. *Five minutes,* he promised us. *I'm outside if you need me. And you move not an inch further forward than you are now. Is that clear?*

As clear as day, Lorraine replied; and in a matter of seconds the three of us were alone in Raymond's room.

I'd offer to shake your hand, Madam, said Raymond, *but my hands are tied . . . A little joke.*

I made my point immediately. *They told me you did bad things. What bad things did you do?*

Let me look at you, boy. You've grown up quickly. Are you shaving yet?

Uncle Raymond, I'm nine!

Are you married?

No!

What car do you drive?

Oh, Raymond! I replied, registering the attempts at humour. When he held up his arms, as he had when I was young, I ran to him before Lorraine could put a hand on my shoulder to stop me. At the end of his bed we embraced.

Lucas! Lorraine called.

His aroma was different from how I remembered it. They had not allowed him to smoke – or he had quit. *Oh Uncle Raymond*, I began.

Here, Lucas! Now! said Lorraine, as if she was talking to our dog, Narna the Third.

I've missed you so much!

Lorraine, listen, said Uncle Raymond quickly, *before he comes back in . . . Can you act?*

Can I what?

Act! Can you act, girl? Act!

I don't understand.

Have you ever told a boyfriend you loved him when you weren't sure you did but you knew it was what he wanted to hear?

I said to Raymond: *She tells her boyfriend that on the phone when she thinks I'm not listening. His name is Pat Kelly.*

Does she now? And do you mean it, girl? Do you mean you love him?

I don't know, Lorraine protested, flustered.

That's called acting, said Uncle Raymond, *and that's good enough for me . . . I'll ask you to act now. I won't hurt a hair on the boy's head. Are we clear?*

Uncle Raymond? I asked. *What are we playing, please?*

Raymond smiled into my face. *Do you remember when you were the wolf and I was the goat? Do you remember how you scared me?*

The memory was bright. We were in Raymond's study; he was taking a break from teaching me Charlie Mingus.

Yes of course!

Both of us on our hands and knees, crawling; the wolf chasing the goat up against one of those tall speakers. The wolf eating the goat.

Well this time I'm the wolf, said Uncle Raymond. *And I'm going to eat you for my supper!*

Lucas! Lorraine hissed.

The door opened – and the guard said a naughty word when he saw me in my uncle's arms.

Give him back! the guard insisted.

But instead of giving me back, Uncle Raymond held me tighter with his right arm and reached for his desk with his left. From its surface he collected a small pill bottle and shook it; there were tablets inside.

You think these are my blood pressure meds, don't you, sir? Well, they're not. And I've just asked the boy to swallow one. In a matter of seconds he'll go into anaphylactic shock.

Pretending to be the terrified goat, I wriggled and whimpered.

What are they, Professor? the guard asked calmly, stepping over the threshold.

A slowly-acting poison, Uncle Raymond told him. He stood up. *And the only chance he's got of receiving the antidote is if my exit from this building is completely unimpeded, sir.*

Straightening his shoulders, the guard said: *You won't get as far as the front door.*

Then he'll die, Raymond said simply. *Imagine the media attention! And all on your watch too!*

Raymond bent down and I wriggled some more. Into my ear he whispered: *Art Tatum. The* Art's Art *album.*

Wooo! I answered affirmatively; then I bleated like a goat.

Track 4: 'Get Happy', boy, he whispered.

What are you saying to him? the guard wanted to know.

I bleated again.

Play the piano solo, Uncle Raymond instructed me, his lips tickling the top of my ear. Immediately my arms shook, and I started to tickle imaginary keys. With the benefit of hindsight, it must have looked like I was having a seizure.

The guard said a different naughty word from the one he'd used before.

That's the shock kicking in, said Uncle Raymond. *You'll notice he's lost the power of speech, and the shakes will only get worse unless I give him the antidote. So what's it to be, sir? Will you toss me your keyring and then stand aside and let us walk out while he can still control his legs? Or do you call for back-up . . .*

Raymond rattled the pill bottle once more.

. . . leaving me to swallow the antidote pill before you cosh the back of my skull?

At the end of the corridor, Raymond whispered: *I'm going to eat you, boy!* – responsively I squealed – and he added: *'C Jam Blues' – the Oscar Peterson version. On* Night Train.

Immediately I changed the tempo and range of my fingers in mid-air. Even *miming* 'C Jam Blues' is an effort, and the spasm of my fake piano solo was enough to get the door unlocked.

4

Outside the asylum, the sun was hot; no breeze assisted; and Raymond and I began the long descent down the hill.

Are we going home? I asked hm.

Not yet . . . Now we're both the goats and everyone else is a wolf. Do you understand me?

I do not know how many people followed us. If I had turned around to look, I would remember; but I had won my uncle back and was not interested. Even Lorraine, who had served her purpose, and with whom I had been in love a day earlier, was not in my thoughts.

Not more than halfway down the hill, we turned left onto one of the roads that leads to the plumbing warehouse where Dad used to work and where he cultivated his hernia. I didn't ask if we were going to see Dad, or if Dad could help us, because I knew Dad was with the angels, looking after Narna the Second.

So where were we going?

Beyond the industrial estate was a swimming pool used by the synchronised swimming team that hoped to represent us at the next Olympic Games; the abandoned Happy Cow Dairy; a sawmill, a white goods factory, and a place that produced photographic solvents and chemicals.

Are we going to the fields, Uncle Raymond?

The fields belonged to a farmer; it was where I'd learned to fly a kite and identify insects. Although there was a nostalgia about those acres, I did not think we would go there now.

No, boy. Do you remember when you asked me about buildings' interiors? Uncle Raymond asked.

I was three years and ten months old, I replied. *You told me, when people are inside buildings, they take journeys. They dream about the past if they don't like their jobs. They predict the future if they do . . . The buildings they work in are like boats.*

That's right, boy: like boats. An occupation is a voyage. It takes us through time, do you understand?

Yes.

But I had it the wrong way round. I think they dream about the future *if they don't like their jobs. They predict the past if they do.*

My legs began to tire. My uncle had never been one for concessions for younger minds; he was not one for concessions for younger bodies either.

Not far away, a siren sounded. Someone had called the police.

Your father, said Uncle Raymond – *my brother-in-law – well, he hated his job selling toilets and taps and shower fittings. He dreamed of other things. He was a man who believed in the curative powers of mortal terror. He thought it healed the soul. And as part of his plans for the total breakdown of society – when the viruses win and take over – he prepared something for his loved ones. A place to hide. And that's where we're going now.*

Are you talking about Dad's Ark? I asked my uncle.

Raymond laughed. *Good. He let you in on our secret . . . Yes, boy. Your father and I built an Ark. For after the bomb.*

5

We turned right, heading for where the plumbing warehouse had stood. It was a paper mill now. WHITE AND DALEY, a sign read. PAPER PRODUCTION. A few cars were outside, and a large distribution lorry with the same name in big letters on the side. A driver climbed up into his cab.

We *were* going to Dad's old workplace! Although nostalgia might seem an inappropriate emotion to attribute to a nine year-old boy, it's the best way I can think of to describe how I felt at that moment. I felt nostalgic.

After hours, during the weekly stock-take, Dad would let me run around the displays of baths. I would hide inside shower stalls and pull the doors closed, the better to leap out on unsuspecting imaginary opponents in my ongoing game of war; and the better to snipe down soldiers of a different stripe, as my shower-cum-tank drove me over the enemy line – and pulverised the fallen bodies of dead or wounded combatants.

The siren was closer now – a street or two away, at the most – and people behind us were calling our names, and I said: *You made an explosion, Uncle Raymond.*

I did, boy, yes.

Why did you do that, please?

Because I wanted to destroy something bad. I had bad thoughts in my brain. I wasn't as forward-thinking as your old man. I thought it was all over for the human race . . .

We entered by the front door.

. . . and I thought if I bombed the government, the government couldn't bomb our neighbours overseas . . . Mr Latham, please, he added to the young man who had walked over to assist us.

I'm afraid Mr Latham doesn't work here anymore, the young man told Uncle Raymond. *He retired last year.*

But we were already walking away from the young man, deeper into the paper mill. *Never mind,* said Uncle Raymond. *We'll browse.*

Again, we walked briskly.

I'm afraid we close in fifteen minutes, the young man called after us.

Raymond said: *What did Robert tell you about the Ark? Your dad, I mean, tell you . . .*

We could wait for the clouds to lift. The land would be a different colour. We might be the only ones left, I answered . . . *Who's Mr Latham, please?*

Another I'd've liked to save, but not to worry.

Ignoring the stares of the few employees still working, Uncle Raymond led me to the far right of the inside of the building, next to an office that resembled a reptile house at the zoo, encased as it was in glass. Inside it, two men typed and a woman did sums on a calculator.

Uncle Raymond stood next to a huge set of metal shelves that reached up to the high ceiling. Every shelf was stacked with boxes of paper.

Just enough room, my uncle muttered, squeezing his body between the end of the shelves and the wall. Then he started to touch the painted bricks. I could not decipher the pattern of Raymond's massage on the wall. I turned around.

The pursuers had followed us this far – the third floor guard in the asylum; some other of that institution's employees (identical uniforms); some of this warehouse's staff; and Lorraine had followed us too.

Run to me, Lucas! she shouted.

That's ticked the box, Uncle Raymond said clearly . . . and I heard a noise of groaning that was not born of any human voicebox.

A section of the wall was moving. Uncle Raymond had touched bricks, I assumed, in a very specific order – perhaps with a specific pressure – and now a section a foot up from the floor, two feet wide and two feet high, rolled backwards on squeaky hinges and sighing hydraulics – deeper into the wall – leaving a hole from which came a smell of damp and that of a mechanic's garage.

Come on, Lucas, said Uncle Raymond. *The next chapter of our adventure awaits!*

His body was large for the square hole that his ministrations had produced, but he fit. There was something about the fact that he had gone first that made me trust him even more.

Hearing my name bouncing off the back of my head, I dived at the hole in the wall. It was very dark inside; darker still as I moved away from the gap, which was something over which I had no control. I had landed on my stomach on a chute, pointed downwards like a slide in the playground. Up ahead I heard Raymond shouting *Wheeee!* – and I slid down, chasing his unseen body.

How far we fell I do not know; without a visual set of references, it seemed like our descent was for miles – much further and faster than we had walked down the hill from the asylum.

But in time, the angle of the chute became less steep (I could feel momentum tugging at my gut), and the slide levelled out, to a horizontal departure point.

Uncle Raymond asked if that was fun and I said yes.

Either his arrival into the chamber in which we stood had triggered the lights to come on, or they had burned for a long time with no one here. The chamber was the size of my parents' bedroom, and was illuminated by four electric bulbs, hanging on bare wires from the low ceiling.

We have to be quick, boy, said Uncle Raymond. He held his right hand to a panel on the far wall of the chamber.

From the chute I could hear the vibrations – and the material resistance – of someone's approach.

The panel read Uncle Raymond's handprint. Something inside the door buzzed; three locks clunked, one after the other, and at great speed Uncle Raymond pulled open what looked like a heavy metal door. The door was a foot thick and lights were on within the box it revealed.

Dad's Ark! I realised aloud ... And Uncle Raymond, standing on the threshold between it and the chamber, now beckoned me inside – at the same time as the guard from the asylum crashed lumpily to the end of the chute.

Get inside, boy! said Uncle Raymond, reaching for something within the Ark – something on a shelf by the door.

It was the first time I ever saw a gun. In this case, a sawn-off shotgun. And the first time I ever heard a gunshot as well. My ears tingled as it echoed off the chamber walls, the sound searching for a home to roost.

Uncle Raymond had fired at a point over the guard's left shoulder.

Two choices, Uncle Raymond announced.

I hear you, Mr Cossell, said the guard. *Professor Cossell,* he corrected himself quickly. He had reached up his arms; he could nearly touch the black ceiling.

Call me Raymond, my uncle told him. *Formalities don't matter much at this instant. What's your name, sir?*

Lovell, sir.

Your first name.

. . . Danny.

Danny, these are your choices. One way or another, Lucas and I are going in there and locking the door. That's a fact. You have the choice of, A: going back up the chute and finishing your day safely, albeit with a ream of paperwork to complete; or B: getting shot in the face if you try to stop us . . . You've got five seconds.

6

Uncle Raymond did not need to shoot the guard. The door locked us into the Ark with three satisfying clunks. It was at this point that Uncle Raymond relaxed. A broad smile helped his features, and he knelt down for a hug.

Were you really going to kill him? I asked. *If he was naughty.*

Yes, boy.

I've always admired honesty from adults, so I nodded and looked at where I'd found myself.

Approximately the size of the six-berth caravan that Dad had hired for our last family holiday (when I was seven years and nine months old), the Ark was well-lit and roomy. Shelves groaned under the weight of tins. Floor space was devoted to vast blue kegs of drinking water.

There's enough food here for a long time, Uncle Raymond said.

Where do I poo, please?

Uncle Raymond showed me the latrine.

How long's a long time? I asked him, settling my buttocks on the oddly-warm plastic of the chemical toilet.

About two years.

I nodded. *And do you not want to go back for two years?* I asked.

I'm not sure I can, he replied.

And will I stay with you for two years?

Would you like to?

Mum's going to be home from the university soon . . . She's bound to be cross.

Raymond chuckled. *Knowing my sister as I do, I think you're right.*

Where's the toilet paper, please? I asked.

In the box to your left. Put it in the box on your right when you're done. It composts it for energy.

I see . . . Uncle Raymond? I asked. *Did you hurt many people with your bomb?*

I thought I had, including you. They lied to me, Lucas.

Who did you want to hurt, Uncle Raymond?

The government, he answered fiercely. *Those guilty.*

. . . Uncle Raymond?

Yes, boy.

Do you have more jazz for me to learn?

The compost machine sucked away my soiled paper.

I thought you'd never ask, he told me.

7

We stayed there for the next four months.

We stayed there while the radio squawked; while drills were ground blunt on the metallic shell. Outsiders pleaded and threatened. I was told that I was a prisoner. My life was worth more than this . . . What no one acknowledged (out loud) was the fact that I was happy with my uncle. At last I had him back where I wanted him.

A so-called hostage expert asked me if Uncle Raymond had hurt me . . . or touched me in any way. But of course he had touched me! Uncle Raymond and I were fond of hugs.

It was the noise that hurt me – the reminders of what occurred outside the Ark. When the tools were silenced and the radio was turned off, I was calm. Even Uncle Raymond said that he wouldn't need his pills in such an atmosphere of tranquillity.

I asked him if he'd liked the idea of hurting people. He considered his answer for a long time.

Sometimes, boy, he said slowly, *circumstances allow you no alternatives.*

One morning he asked me: *Do you know what an Ark is?* We had just finished our exercises and I was towelling off his shoulders.

This is an Ark! I replied.

Yes. But do you know what it is*?*

It protects people, Uncle Raymond.

Protects them from what?

From the bad things, like the Flood.

Yes. He weighed my answer solemnly. His recent refusal of his anti-depressant tablets had coloured the atmosphere a darker tint. *Your father and I shared a realistic tendency*, he added. *A recognition of when the time's up.*

But we have lots of food! I protested. *Enough for two years, you said.*

The wolves are at the door, boy. What happens when wolves meet goats?

They eat them.

Good. I'm a goat, boy, and a wolf has to eat to survive. I don't want you to think there's anything strange about it, do you understand? I will give you strength.

8

The next morning, he would not wake up and his pill bottle was empty. After a couple of minutes, I knew that he'd gone to meet Dad – and Narna the First and Narna the Second.

So I ate him, as he'd instructed.

I put on *Kind of Blue* and used the saw to remove his left arm. I baked it in the pan with dried rosemary, olive oil and pepper. I had to cut it into sections and the blood had an unfamiliar smell. It crisped. Smoke was everywhere.

Uncle Raymond's left arm tasted delicious. It gave me strength (as I'd been promised it would). I ate it with rice and grilled peppers.

And I wondered where the Ark would take me next.

Although I wanted to go home, I knew I had a journey to fulfil. An occupation takes you back in time or forward, depending on whether you like it or not.

I liked mine. But Uncle Raymond's changing of the descriptors had left me confused. Was I supposed to go into the past or into the future?

There would not be much longer, I understood. The outsiders would understand that Uncle Raymond had joined sides with Dad and Narna the Second. Teams would fight their way in.

I remembered the years when Uncle Raymond had been away. I longed for that sense of yearning once more, which was difficult to conjure up while his body lay in the kitchen area.

9

It took me nine days to eat him. That's a lot of protein for a nine year-old boy. I boiled his heart and spine and made a curry with the flavoured water.

I turned off the radio. When the outsiders came knocking, I wanted it to be a surprise.

After four months and six days, they entered. I was fat and they asked me where Uncle Raymond had gone. I told them I'd eaten him. It took a while for them to believe me.

Sometimes, when I sail Nostalgia's Boat back to my Ark – when our ships meet in the night – I think of Uncle Raymond, and of all that he and I left behind.

Miles Davis can take me there, especially the *Kind of Blue* album. In four days it will be my eighteenth birthday, and I like the fact that my room is just down the corridor from Uncle Raymond's old room.

I understand some of his illnesses now; some of his obsessions.

We are still together.

NOW

1

Standing adjacent to the security cabin at the entrance to the business park, Billy Alfreth experiences a wave of *déjà vu* as strong as an urge to sneeze. In his mind he repeats the three words that he spoke aloud in a room full of other nervous young people, exactly a year earlier.

Scared as fuck.

This time he is about to begin his second year at university. The nerves feel no different: he is close to entering a new environment. The presence of the security cabin has stopped him in his tracks, and now he moves to its side, by the eight-foot tines of the metal perimeter fence, and bumps a cigarette from its box.

Telling himself to calm down serves no purpose. Beneath his suit jacket and beneath the expensive shirt that he has bought for this very day, he sweats like a hog. It didn't matter that he had visited here two months earlier, for the interview. The interview was a prefatory matter, nothing more. Today he is due to start work at the biscuit factory and his skin feels awash with slime.

On completion of his cigarette, he worries about the disposal of the smouldering nub (a concern that would not have crossed his mind even yesterday), and when he thinks no one is looking he drops it beneath his work shoes (as new as his shirt) and performs a version of the moonwalk in an attempt to obliterate it that is visibly over the top.

Then he returns to the security cabin's window.

The man inside looks up from a newspaper and asks him how he can help.

"I start work here today," Billy answers, "at Coronet Confectionaries. I'm doing a year's placement as part of a Business degree." He gives his name.

The man inside has a wide face and greying eyebrows. When he speaks, Billy smells tobacco on his breath. "Do you know where to go?" the man asks, flipping sheets of paper over the binding clasp on a clipboard.

"Yes. I had an interview a few months ago."

"So did I, funnily enough," the man replies. "Alfreth, you say?"

"That's right."

"Alfreth, William. Gotcha. You're an hour early, sir. I was told to expect you at ten."

"I thought I'd show willing, sir."

The man smiles. "It's very kind of you to call me sir, sir, but *I'm* the one who gives out the *sirs* around here. Call me Danny. And welcome. We're two new boys together."

Danny reaches to his right and produces a badge on a thick red lanyard. "This is your pass to the business park," he explains. "You'll almost certainly never be asked to produce it. Will you be driving here ever?"

"I don't have a car."

"Well, if you decide to – or if there's one of my colleagues here who might not know you – it might be a good idea to keep the pass with you for that sort of thing. Display it near your windscreen. Other than that, they'll give you a badge at Reception. They're strict about staff wearing them."

Danny looks left and right in the confines of his box.

"God knows why, if you ask me. Mean, It's only fucking *biscuits.*"

*

A small man in his late twenties, in a skinny grey suit, meets Billy at Reception.

"Terry Bates. Nice to know you."

"Likewise, Terry. But I recognise you, don't I? You drink at The Anchor?"

"I do indeed, mate. Drink and slink. Duck and dive."

By half past ten, Billy has his security pass (this one on a blue lanyard) and has been shown his desk. He has a laptop, a phone and a ring binder stuffed as full as a *calzone*. Only once during the morning does the thought cross Billy's mind that there was a time when he would have taken the electrical equipment and gone to see a fence named Glacier, to see how much the bundle would fetch.

"Meeting at eleven," says Anne-Marie, the big-boned, fiftyish team administrator. "Will you be using Powerpoint for your presentation? I can load it up if you give me your stick."

"Will I *what*?" Billy asks.

"I'm teasing you. You get to enjoy the Powerpoints of your colleagues instead. All seven colleagues and four hundred slides between them. If you stay awake till the end you get a cream bun."

*

"Billy Alfreth. I'm doing a four-year Bachelor's degree at the university, as a mature student. This is my work experience year; thank you for having me."

"Two sugars in mine, Billy," says Terry Bates.

The laughter that follows is threadbare, but Terry seems pleased enough with his joke. He leans back in his chair and looks as though he has completed his day's work.

Pat Kelly is the man in charge. He wears a good grey suit and his fingernails are manicured to resemble polished ice. "Don't worry, Billy," he says, "we won't be asking you to make tea and do all the photocopying." He leaves a pause. "That's Anne-Marie's job."

Another ripple of mirth ensues, and this time Billy smiles along. It's just banter; it's team-building – no different from what used to happen at Dellacotte Young Offenders Institution, all those years ago.

When Pat Kelly grins, the sides of his moustache rise in an asymmetrical way, the right side higher than the left. Billy guesses that the man has had a stroke or a Bell's palsy in the past. Odder still is the fact that the moustache sports wings of two different colours. The left is a mercury silver, but the right is tinged with the tulip infusions of persistent and one-sided nicotine abuse.

"Many a true word is said in jest," Anne-Marie mutters. She is the only one not playing along. So far in the meeting she has typed notes and not said a word.

"What's your background, Billy?" asks the man sitting next to Terry Bates, whose name Billy has unfortunately forgotten. He knows that there are two Duncans present but he has already forgotten which one is which. Billy blinks. He focuses on the man's coffee mug: on the words I FUCKING LOVE MEETINGS, ME! on its side.

"I was a bit of an underachiever at school."

*

Scared as fuck, Billy reads that night. He is reading a diary entry that he made a year earlier.

My first day at university. I'm in a queue. We are lining up for our timetables for the following academic year – and the girl in front of me is Jemima.

The phone on his pillow diddlydees.

"Like you're reading my mind," Billy says. "Just thinking about you. Or reading about you, I should say. How's your day?"

"Reading what?"

"Diary. *Jemima Sange. Eighteen years old from her d.o.b. Marine Biology, subject of choice.* You were holding out your paperwork. Are you coming over?"

"It depends what else you wrote about me. Did you meet my dad?"

"No. I was with the Marketing team all day. I go to Quality next week . . . Shall I read?"

"Yeah, go on then. I'm waiting for the bus," says Jemima.

"*I am focussing on her because I'd rather not think about timetables.* Well, that was in keeping, I suppose. *Jemima is fidgeting with the various cards in her auburn purse.*"

Jemima laughs. "I miss that purse!"

From elsewhere in the house comes a sudden barrage of music dense with drums and electric guitars, played now at a crucifying decibelage. The walls shiver.

"Can you hear that?"

"Metal Mickey's doing?" Jemima guesses.

Michael is one of Billy's three housemates. From the volume at which he shares his beloved heavy metal, it is easy to surmise that he believes it to be his gift to the world.

"She turns on her heels and says: I'm Jem . . . I can't help thinking I've forgotten something."

"The bus is coming," Jemima tells him. "I'll see you after my piano lesson."

*

Though tempted to knock on Metal Mickey's door for the six thousandth time to tell the twat to *keep it down*, Billy descends the stairs instead. In the empty kitchen he steals butter from Mercy's part of the fridge and constructs a banana and sugar sandwich, using the last two slices of a loaf that was past its best three days earlier.

Outside, night has fallen; the air is as wet as an otter's armpit. Billy clutches his coat halves together, his fingers forming a makeshift clasp to substitute for the broken zip. Three quiet streets from his front door, he meets Mercy and Ross.

"Evening, Billy," Mercy offers. "Who's home?"

"Just Michael. It's Anthrax Night tonight."

"Oh, goodie!"

Mercy has not adopted her forename. There is not a bad bone in her body; not a bigotry or negative feeling to which she will confess. She loves everyone and likes everything, even the household's unrequested lessons in heavy-, death- and speed-metal.

Billy has got past the urge of wanting to slip Mercy a length, but he still likes her. And he certainly enjoys flirting with her in front of Ross, who is as prim as a starched collar.

As he moves on, away from the shared house, the roads climb and rain starts to fall. Bells clang from inside the church: the campanologists practise on Monday nights. Billy reaches The Anchor, where he'll stop for two pints of lager and four cigarettes.

Inside the warm establishment, he is battered by music once more. This time it is a rendition of 'I Will Survive', sung to a karaoke backing track by a rugby-playing feminist named Noel who works at the service station and sells Billy his pies and smokes.

Billy nods to Terry Bates, who is seated with a small group. Although it seems that Terry takes a while to comprehend where he knows Billy from, he nods back – and even raises an empty glass in greeting. Billy's intention is to walk to the house of Jemima's piano teacher after he's finished in The Anchor. He will invite her for a drink. After all, it's been a year that they've known one another, and this feels like an anniversary.

We're in the same Student Halls, he reads. *We're more or less neighbours.*

Jemima had waited for Billy to sign his own paperwork; she'd invited him for coffee when they'd discovered the coincidental proximity of their rooms.

What have you got on for the rest of the day? she asks me. Not much, I tell her. We've finished her horrible coffee and it's three o'clock in the afternoon.

We emerge from her bed an hour and a half later, sapped and stupid.

"Thought I'd go out to a pub. Get some early dinner." I pull up my socks off and start to untangle my boot-laces. I had simply ripped the boots of when she'd wriggled out of her bra.

*

By the time he reaches The Scarlet, still in plenty of time for the end of Jemima's piano lesson, Billy has thought more about his first day with Jem than he has in months. At a corner shop he has purchased a small box of chocolates.

HAPPY ANNIVERSARY! he texts from pub's garden. Under an awning, he places a cigarette between his lips. MEET YOU IN THE SCARLET WHEN YOU'RE FINISHED TINKLING. Send.

Immediately he regrets the word *anniversary.* Jemima is not his girlfriend – not exactly – and although Billy is certain she will understand the reference, she is not always predictable with her responses.

*

Darryl Carbrini is a martyr to his teeth; his left molar pulses.

His doorbell sounds. His lesson has shown up on time.

'My Funny Valentine' is variously stumbled over and butchered for the following hour. Carbrini wants to put his student's head in a tin bath and then beat the sides with a wooden bat.

Once the lesson has departed (fees paid, arrangements cemented), Darryl Carbrini is preparing for a bath and wishing that there existed a bath for the *gums*, when the doorbell summons him once more. With the aroma of frying garlic in his nostrils, he walks through the narrow hall and opens the door.

"I'm sorry to bother you, Darryl. I'm Jemima's friend – Billy. I thought I'd surprise her."

"You've got the wrong day of the week. My lesson tonight wasn't Jemima. She wasn't here."

*

"Where *were* you?" Billy asks.

"Don't be boring, Billy . . . I was sucking off a sailor, of course."

Billy snorts. "You could've had some chocolates if you'd been here half an hour ago."

"Why, did you eat them all?"

"No, I gave them to Mercy and Ross. I was angry."

They are in Billy's room. Billy sits on the inflatable ball that he uses instead of a chair (to improve his posture and core strength) and Jemima is supine on top of the duvet. Both of them remain dressed. Jemima explains.

"On an unconscious level you hate something in your own personality – in your psychic foundations, if you like – but you can't admit that thing, so you project it onto me and make me your villain. But just in case it's slipped your mind, Billy, we're not together and you don't own me. One of the nice things about you was you never tried to be too possessive. It was touching."

"I was *worried*, Jem," Billy tries. "You said: I'll see you after my piano lesson."

"I *changed my mind*."

Billy hasn't told her that he went to Darryl Carbrini's house. "Forget it. Budge over." He negotiates his way out of a tight plum pullover that he put on when he arrived home.

"You can do this one, Billy," Jemima says, her tone goading. "Item one: my wet hair."

"It's raining."

"Item two." She points at the piece of luggage that she has left near the plug points next to the radiator. "A rucksack. And item three: a faint whiff of chlorine on my skin, which you'd have noted if you'd bothered to greet me with the simple civility of a peck on the cheek instead of strutting around with your feathers puffed out and your wings wide."

"You've been swimming," Billy deduces.

"Give that man a banana."

"Well, why not just *say* that? We could've avoided this song and dance."

Jemima unbuttons her blouse. "You're a much better lover when you're being repentant . . . Now open my bag. Go on." She removes the blouse. "Take out the champagne I bought us. We'll drink it from the bottle, like the old days. It doesn't matter you've had too much already. If you can't get it up, you can use your mouth."

*

Why did she say a piano lesson, Billy wonders, *if she meant a swim?*

This is the thought in his head when he wakes up around two in the morning.

Jemima murmurs in her sleep. "What's wrong, Billy?"

It must be the job that's making me edgy. Jemima's done nothing wrong.

Residual analgesia in his blood stream from the booze . . . it leaks sleep into the rear of his skull. On waking at six-fifteen, however, Billy has doubts in his head. They smoulder. He tells himself that he can't call in sick on his second day at work. He showers and gets ready. Jemima is still sleeping when he leaves the house.

2

"He thinks I should change my name. He says Carol isn't classy enough."

"What does he suggest?" asks Dr Bruce-Sange.

"*Lamella*, believe it or not. It means a layer of bone tissue."

"I know. It also means something psychoanaly-tically. The undead-indestructible object. What Jacques Lacan, if I remember correctly, called the organ of the libido – the organ that exists in the body that has no need of such an organ."

Carol folds her arms. "I'm even *less* flattered now!"

"But what do you mean by change your name? Change it *legally*? By deed poll? Change it for the hour you're with him? What?"

"Legally."

"And you're considering it? Ask yourself why Andreas's request has played enough of a part in your week you'd bring it to me."

"I'm not in love with him, if that's what you're suggesting."

"I'm not suggesting anything, Carol. Why do you mention love, do you think? It's the question you can take away with you. Until next week."

*

The industry is as old as mammals – but careers within it burn bright.

Carol Hayes is one of the lucky ones. Having passed her thirty-fifth birthday, she is two decades into the game, and longevity in any industry earns benefits. One of these, for Carol, is financial stability: this she has achieved via the establishment of a reliable client base, and long gone are the days when she was obliged to work more than two appointments per evening. As time has moved on, Carol has felt confident in the escalation of her hourly rate; more sure of herself when no means no; and convinced of her skills and abilities, as all good professionals must be.

"It was me, by the way," Scottish Tony tells Carol. "The one who recommended Giorgio to you. Or you to Giorgio, I should say."

Carol is rinsing the taste of his penis from her mouth. At Scottish Tony's insistence, she keeps a bottle of mouthwash at his flat for this purpose. She has ceased believing that he will drug it between appointments. He doesn't need to. Carol is already hooked on his cash.

She spits. "Who's Giorgio?"

"The European. The musician."

"Oh, *Andreas.*"

Scottish Tony laughs. "That what he's calling himself, aye? *Andreas,* if you'd be so kind. About as Greek as whelks and cockles, though. From further east'd be *my* bet."

Carol returns to the bedroom. Scottish Tony lies supine, wet with her spit and sick. "Recommended me how?"

Scottish Tony needs vodka before every appointment. Ordinarily this is not a problem. Now he slurs: "Met him at the gym – we got talking. Man's rich as an *actor*. You should be saying thank you!"

"I *am* saying thank you. I didn't know you were acquainted, or I would've said it earlier."

"Does he still have that funny wee purple beard?" Tony continues, his words merging together.

Carol is not sure if she has heard him correctly. "The funny *what*?"

"Or did he shave it off – maybe he shaved it off when he moved to town." But by now, in addition to the uncertain speech, Scottish Tony is mumbling and not making any sense.

"I'll see myself out," Carol informs him.

Curious about the Andreas/Giorgio name change, Carol takes the night bus home. The smoothness of the journey feels awkward and oppressive; it feeds the headache that has grumbled for several hours, and makes it grow. Back at home, as ever, she bathes and scrubs herself, inside and out. She is two hundred pounds richer, and sadder.

*

If Carol is not in love with Andreas, she is certainly fond of him. Apart from anything else, he makes business a pleasure. With his quirky European accent and infrequent failures with English grammar, his longish white hair, his tough fingertips and his whisky paunch, Andreas is somewhere in his mid-sixties, looking good for his age. Often when Carol visits, she will linger a few seconds on his doorstep and listen to the music that he plays on the piano in one of his back rooms. Other times, her ringing on the doorbell interrupts a recital.

She wonders if Andreas might be trying to improve her mind. During her third visit, when a pattern had begun to develop (a pattern of sore knees and two pieces of gum on the night bus home), Carol had asked him what the music was that had played throughout. He told her Mahler – "Mahler's final Budapest triumph! *Don Giovanni!*" Standing up from her nest of cushions on her fifth visit, she wiped her chin and told him: "I recognize this! It's Mahler!" And Andreas smiled so beautifully, so kindly, that Carol almost invited him to keep his money.

Andreas pours Carol a glass of peach schnapps.

"Thank you. The Shost, by the way, before you ask."

"Excuse me?"

"Our musical accompaniment is Shostakovitch: *Lady Macbeth of the Mtsensk District.* 1936, I think. You played it to me three weeks ago." Carol sips her schnapps. "The Shost fell from favour as a direct result of this. It put him under pressure to simplify his *groove.*"

Andreas stares at Carol for so long that she suspects he might be offended. Then he laughs so hard that his penis bows in appreciation.

"*Bravissimo!* You've done some *research*," he says.

"I went to the library – the first time in five years. I checked it out and played it at home."

"Ah!" Andreas sits down beside her; they are comfortable together in their nudity and the temperature is pleasant, even with the patio doors slightly ajar. "I've been thinking about the matter we discussed last week."

She interrupts his flow of thought. "So have I . . . Andreas." *His* name merely sounds ludicrous. "I'm not comfortable with Lamella."

"No, not that." Andreas swats the idea from the air. "What would it cost me to make you give up your other clients?"

Carol flinches again; disguises it by transforming it into a cough. "What do I earn, you mean."

"Precisely."

"Fifteen hundred a week. Cash."

". . . I have money."

"Is that an offer?"

Andreas turns away and teases his moustache. "It's a proposition," he replies. "Eight thousand a month and you don't see anyone else. If I find out you've betrayed me, I'll say you burgled me after I'd fallen asleep. Your fingerprints are all over the place."

Feeling inexplicably let down on some level, Carol says, "You don't need to play rough, Andreas. The threat is totally uncalled for." She wishes she had a robe or something to wear: something to pull tighter across her chest to show him how he'd upset her.

"Do we strike a deal?"

There are bound to be ramifications to the new arrangement, Carol knows; but for the moment, all she can see is a life without visits across town every evening; a chance to see the world before midday; a lunchtime catch-up with friends . . ."We do."

*

Carol sits down outside a café at twelve-thirty. Her lunch date is Lorraine, a friend of nearly a decade's standing, and Lorraine is a few minutes late. Carol orders a blackcurrant tea and watches the world as it falls past . . . As a late teenager, Lorraine had escaped the care system (and an unpleasant incident about which she refuses to speak); and started out in the industry. Now, in her early forties, Lorraine claims to be mended, body and soul, her teeth as flawless as a dolphin's, and in love with an American businessman named Den. He is fifty-two, visits Europe for work appointments, and has a desk in the Capital. Lorraine likes to joke that his nickname is Den of Iniquity.

Eventually, Lorraine orders an ice cream sundae. It is topped with a diadem of pitted cherries. Eyeing the dessert with something akin to disgust, Carol sips her blackcurrant tea and says, "Don't tell me. The doctor says you're not lactose intolerant after all."

"You could have had one, Purple! I offered!"

"I don't *want* one! Not one that size anyway."

"They come in Thin Bitch varieties as well – you saw the menu." Lorraine sucks her spoon clean. "I hear you've found a provider. Spill."

Carol smiles. She doesn't ask how Lorraine knows: the streets between Andreas's house and her own flat are not tar and stones – they are a network. Secrets last no time at all in their profession.

"His name is either Andreas or Georgio. We're not big on names." Carol shrugs, wrapping her hands around her mug. "No, that's not true. Actually he wants me to change mine. He says Carol is not fitting for a muse." She smiles again. "He's a musician, you see; a composer. Piano."

Lorraine nods. "So I hear. Change it to what?"

"Lamella." Carol cannot shake the sensation that this has happened before. Then she makes the connection. "My psychoanalyst tells me it's *pertinent* that I'd bring something like this to the session. It says more about me than about Andreas."

Lorraine looks sceptical. "And what's *his* name?"

"I told you. Andreas."

"*No.* The psychoanalyst."

"Oh. No, it's a she. Her name is Chaz – Charlotte, presumably. Chaz Bruce-Sange."

Lorraine blinks and pauses. For a second it seems she is struggling for something to say, but she recovers. Carol is well aware that Chaz Bruce-Sange is an odd name, but Lorraine's reaction is more than she would have expected.

"There's a brass works the golf club bars," says Lorraine, sucking her spoon clean once more. "*She* caught a dose of lamella the other month. Tell him no. Names are different."

"Says *you*, who still calls me Purple after ten years!"

"Purple Hayes," Lorraine replies deadpan, "you're in my brain . . . Do you want some of this? I'm starting to feel sick. My eyes are bigger than my belly."

Carol is happy to change the subject. "Which seems to be bigger than I remember, if you don't mind me saying so."

"Seventeen weeks. Hence the sundae."

"Ah! The old eating-for-two excuse."

"For three, actually."

"*Twins?*"

Lorraine nods. "I won't say I'm unhappy about it . . . but it wasn't planned. Especially at *my* time of life." She shrugs. "He'll have to put a ring on it *now*."

"Or buy you off," Carol adds – there is no room for sentimental falsity in their world.

"Or buy me off. Will you be moving in with him?"

"I hope not. Intense is not the word, babe!" Carol smiles fondly at a recollection. "And then he can be a real sweetheart. Calling me his muse, that kind of thing." She wants Lorraine to pick up on the muse reference.

Lorraine lays down her spoon, defeated by half a pint glass of remaining ice cream and diced bananas. "My advice? Buy him the occasional gift with what he's paying you. Don't go mad, just show gratitude. What's he into?"

"Classical music. Mahler. Shostakovitch."

"Try to find a rare recording. Or get him tickets to a performance. Something off the beaten track. Unusual . . . and special."

Carol cannot wait any longer. "He says I've inspired him to compose something new," she announces. "The first thing he's written in twenty-five years."

*

"I want to learn about classical music," Carol announces.

"Well, you've come to the right place," says Darryl Carbrini, behind the counter at Octaves. They are surrounded by musical instruments and by racks of CDs and vinyl copies in square transparent sheaths. "Do you have a starting point?"

"I know Mahler – and the Shost."

Carbrini fingers his blue bowtie; the smirk on his lips appears superior.

Specificity will help them both, Carol reasons. "I'm trying to impress my new boyfriend. What he doesn't know about music you could write on a cornflake."

"A present. Your estimated price range being?"

Carol has used the Internet for some light research. The figure seemed outlandish but she vocalises it anyway. "Up to five hundred."

Delightedly smirking, Carbrini strums his bowtie once more. "I'm seeing Elgar." Italicised by this fresh mission, he abandons Carol and forages among the racks, his plump backside swollen in beige slacks. As far as Carol is concerned, it is all the man can do to suppress a howl.

*

Carol has received enough surprises in her life (and work) to be cool towards their dubious appeal. She comes right out and describes what she is handing to Andreas.

"I've bought you some Elgar. A rare one from 1967."

"Elgar? No, I never had the pleasure. Shall I do the honours?"

"Please." *Never had the pleasure of what?* Carol wonders.

The opening bars of *The Enigma Variations* sound. As is customary, Andreas stands close to a waist-high speaker near the drinks cabinet. Carol settles on her knees and opens her blouse and Andreas's dressing-gown.

She is in the bathroom when she hears him play. Although she cannot know that this is the piece that Andreas claimed he had composed with her in mind, it is nimble and sprightly; it feels flattering to have inspired such a prance. Not even Lorraine's sugar daddy has given her a piece of *music*!

Pleased that Andreas has enjoyed the gift, Carol dresses in the lounge and joins her benefactor in his music room. There is a three-quarters sized piano and a bank of recording equipment in here.

"A question if I may. Who have you told about me?" Andreas asks.

"My psychoanalyst, for one."

"Ah! I've tousled with Sigmund in my time, I can tell you."

"Sigmund?"

"Sigmund Freud. Golden Siggy, his mother called him, the spoilt bastard. Almost totally unmusical, or so he claimed; but I happen to know he could squeeze out an ounce of enthusiasm for *Don Giovanni* and *The Marriage of Figaro*. He's an interesting man."

"I think my analyst's a Jungian, I'm afraid."

"Oh." Andreas's fingers trip over a sequence. "Never knew Jung." He stands up and pulls his dressing-gown cord tighter. It is apparent that he wishes Carol to lead them out.

"You never *knew* Jung?" Carol asks.

"No. It's time, Carol."

Because Andreas has already had his second helpings this evening (he is never good for thirds), she assumes that this is her cue to walk to the bus stop. Before she opens the door in the hall, she hears him mumble something behind her back. When she asks him to repeat himself, he says, "Katalina. What do you think of the name?"

Carol riffles through the possibilities. "For me, you mean? It's better than Lamella."

"Which means you'll consider it?"

The evening has been pleasant. Why leave on a curdled note?

"Of course I will."

"That's my muse."

She steps outside into the early morning air. A cat prowls the wall at the end of the short garden; at the sight of Carol it turns tail and runs away, spitting curses over its furry shoulders.

*

It is while she floats in an overfilled bath, an hour later, that Carol wonders if Andreas has slipped something into her drink.

She feels odd: overwhelmed by light-headedness and euphoria . . . Is she *ill*? Well, if she is, it is not like any indisposition that she has contracted in the past. It is pleasurable, she feels young . . . She swears aloud and sits up quickly, crashing waves up and over the bath's slopes. She breathes deeply.

"No. No I won't have it. *No*."

She does not fall in love anymore: it is a rule; she is immune. In the same way that she doesn't catch chickenpox or mumps.

I knew them all, Andreas's voice says into part of her brain.

Am I dreaming? she asks herself. She splashes water into her face; she sits up straighter, her spine as stiff as the head of a rake. Her heart pounds.

I was there, inspiring them . . . Do I surprise you?

Surely standing up will break the spell and shut him up, Carol reasons. She must have dozed off in the water – dangerous business – but then she hears her own voice answering him.

Not at all.

Carol stands up, knee-deep in hot soapy water, and the drama in her skull has not faded out.

I was present at the birth of some of the most important music of all time. I was a muse. I helped them get what they wanted . . . and they all betrayed me.

*

Andreas is in high spirits, the next time Carol pays a visit. "Do you know what this is?" he asks her, his voice slurred.

"It's a CD."

"Containing what, do you imagine? Take hold of it. And this."

Andreas hands her a pen.

"I'm told this will write on the material the disc is made of. I would like you to write the word *Lapsus* on it, and then my name."

Biting hard on the urge to ask him the obvious question, Carol repeats what she assumes is the work's title. "Lapsus?"

"Yes. The return of the repressed."

"Spelt?"

"*Spelt?*" Goodwill seeps from Andreas's features; a smile decays on his lips. "I have just composed my first new work in nearly three decades, and you ask me to *spell. I can't write.* We didn't learn in those days."

Andreas has spun on his heels – the pirouette so melodramatic that Carol would have sniggered, if only she could edit out her sudden fear – and now he stomps away from her.

Feeling foolish, Carol stands her ground with the CD and the pen in her hands. The least she can do is write LAPSUS: unless it has a double P in the middle, it is simple enough to spell, isn't it? And who cares anyway? Andreas has just confessed that he is illiterate.

In the music room he strikes a chord on his keyboard, and Carol follows him along the hallway, intending to say sorry.

He does not look up from his fingers when he speaks.

"All of the great composers needed a muse," he says. "Shostakovitch – the Shost – had a woman named Katalina. Mahler was in love – chastely so – with the infant daughter of some well-to-do neighbours . . . None of these facts will you find in the biographies."

Carol recalls the weird vision she'd had in her bathroom. A premonition? "Well, how do *you* know?" she asks, stepping closer.

"I was there. In spirit, you might say. I was to Mahler and the Shost – and a host of lesser-known names, talented mediocrities as the past has judged them – as you are to me: as a muse."

Carol is getting sweaty. "I still don't follow. When you say you were *there* . . ."

"I inhabited the space between Katalina's mortal breaths. I created the smiles on the little girl's face; I deepened her dimples and made her cuter. I made those composers love something in those females – a quality that would inspire them to create wonder."

As a fantasy, Carol supposes, it is harmless enough. Andreas wants to take credit for some of humanity's most enduring classical music. Let him have the last word. Egocentricity is not a crime.

"I helped them create masterpieces, and what did *I* get? A soldier's wage, a servant's wage – whatever job I happened to occupy at the time. But I wanted to *write*. I gave them tunes and melodies and the best I received was a bit-part in their dreams. Well, I've waited a long time for my turn – and then I found you. And I promised myself I would never treat you in the way they treated me. They didn't even know my name!"

Perhaps it will help to anchor the conversation down to the now, to the present – to this room. "What is it, by the way?" Carol asks. "Your real name."

"It's whatever you want it to be. I owe you that much."

"What's the name on your passport? *That's* what you owe me."

Andreas looks confused. "I've had many names. You choose it," he offers.

"No, that's not good enough. Who is Lamella?"

"Pardon?"

Carol takes two strides to the piano. As hard as she can she slams the keyboard lid down on Andreas's fingers. His immediate scream and her ferocious demand – "*Who is she?*" – are of an equal decibelage.

"The little girl Mahler thought inspired her. *But it's me!* The little girl is just the human form. *It is me in his head*, in his hands."

Carol does not understand but she lifts the keyboard lid. If she hasn't broken one or more of the man's fingers it will be a miracle. What has she done? This man has volunteered to take her away from a tough life, and she might have crippled the only tools he uses. She has not even thanked him for the CD that she has apparently helped him to create.

She crawls under the piano, thinking of two things. The first is that she only knows one way to apologise – only one way to do most things, it seems – and when she drops her lips into his lap she hopes he will play the tune of his forgiveness.

If this isn't love, she thinks, *I don't know what is.*

She needs to be punished, she understands. By cancelling the weekly appointments with her clients, she has missed out on their unvoiced resentment; she has lost their anger, which she has taken a long time to build up. Too much happiness is a poison.

It is in the following moments that she realises that his money is not enough. She longs for bad nights and disappointment.

She loves her European; his name is not important. When he starts to play a piece of music that she does not know, she is sure it is *Lapsus*. It is her tune.

3

It is Darryl Carbrini's habit to walk through the botanical gardens twice a day, morning and evening, in the belief that it short circuits any stress in his system. After bathing in the gardens' energy, he sits in a coffee shop and wrestles with a paragraph or two of his manuscript. This is the norm. Today, however, his toothache has reached a constant hum that is punctuated only infrequently by stabs that feel like hypodermic needles deployed in a sawing motion along the length of his gums. He will have to see a dentist, and he knows it. He is frightened of dentists.

He is also frightened of the homeless men and women that he encounters on his travels every morning. They are usually huddled around something hidden by their bodies. They resemble a murder of crows, by the war memorial or proximate to a random recycling receptacle; sometimes near the shop that he opens every morning at eight o'clock. In Darryl's mind, these tramps are hatching something; plotting and waving their drunken arms, regardless of the hour; trying to stick the boot into the fat pigeons that navigate and strut the bins' circumferences; comparing tattoos and teasing scraps of edible matter from one another's beards.

And that's just the women, Darryl deadpans to himself.

This morning is cool and the walkway is slick from the night's rain. While Darryl ploughs towards a crowd of these destitute scumbags, he notes, as usual, their conspiratorial huddle, but what is peculiar is the muted timbre of their voices. Ordinarily, some of the individual members compete for top volume; today there is something more sombre and less defiant about this murder of crows. Thinking little more of this anomaly, however, Darryl is prepared to pick up his velocity as he moves past them; but he looks up at the challenging cry of the word "Sir!"

"Sir!"

"Sir!" says a third voice – it is broken by experience, levelled down an octave or two. It is a woman's voice – a woman has called out to him, and he turns his head.

Instinct informs Darryl that what is about to unfold is more important than a beg for a quid, or an appeal for his purchase of a copy of *The Big Issue*. For one thing (crucially), there is a body on the pavement, curled up like a piece of seaweed. For another, the murder of crows is staring in Darryl's direction.

The woman occupies an age zone rather than a specific age. She could be forty; she could be sixty. Unless she is an actress of remarkable acuity, however, the distress on her smudged and lightly bruised face is real.

"Please would you consider using your mobile phone," she implores him. "We've found our poor friend in this condition this morning."

Though Darryl has never thought of himself as brave, he steps towards the murder of crows, unconsciously tightening his arms to his torso for fear of being robbed of his wallet.

"We'd be obliged if you called an ambulance."

"I will; but what happened to her?"

The woman on the floor is dressed in the abundant layers of those around the world who do not live under a roof. There is something arresting about her appearance. It takes Darryl several minutes to quilt together a few of the visual clues, and by this point he has exited the scene.

"Was it drugs? Drink?"

"Lorraine was tee-total," Darryl is told with a note of pride. "Your phone, sir, if you'd be so kind. The sooner the authorities are informed, the better the chance we have of saving her, if indeed the poor woman might be saved."

Although appalled by the notion that no one has thought to check her vital signs, Darryl is unwilling to get any closer to her body either. It is not simply her association with the homeless diaspora that holds him back (because something still niggles in the back of his brain); it is more that this woman on the pavement seems different from those around him. She is not as rough, not as beaten, as the rest of this murder of crows.

Without another word, Darryl dials the three nines. He gives details of the incident's location. Because Octaves is only two hundred metres further on, he is able to give the telephonist a specific post code.

A man with long grey hair shuffles aside, away from Darryl. It is too soon for the medical services to be arriving – the only person approaching the group is in a tidy dark blue suit, swinging his arms in a pleased-with-himself fashion – but the atmosphere has changed.

Then Darryl hears muttered the word *biscuits*.

At the man's continued approach, there is something about the group's reaction that is akin to how village serfs would react to the arrival of the prince. Although Darryl has seen this man on the street from time to time, walking to and from work (he has assumed), he has no idea who he is. Darryl waits for someone to doff a cap or tug a forelock when he hears the word again, this time in a context that is inexplicable.

"Here's Lord Biscuits."

He's in his forties, Darryl reckons; a professional demeanour, a fondness for grooming. Immediately he takes charge, dropping down onto his haunches and placing two fingertips to the side of the woman's neck.

It is not humility that Darryl experiences: it is simple masculine aggression – annoyance that this new guy has become the scenario's alpha male, without so much as saying a single word. "I've called for an ambulance," Darryl tells him as he walks away.

It is only while moving in the direction of his day's work that he realises what had bugged him before. The victim had been *too clean*. Her mouth was open and her teeth were neatly set and pearly white. Most interesting of all was the ring on her finger, which had looked authentic and expensive.

*

"Here Billy," says Terry Bates, "you got a bird?"

In the same way that Billy knew that Jemima would ask him, eventually, about his time in prison, he has known that someone at Coronet Confectionaries would ask him about his current dating status.

"Jemima. It's sort of on-off, but yeah. Jemima . . . Do you know Kieran Sange?"

"The Biscuit Inspector? Of course I do, mate."

"His daughter. We met on our first day at university last year. It's her I have to thank for getting me this work experience."

Terry sips on his cigarette. "Do you like your chicken *phal* with extra Tabasco as well?" he asks.

"I'm not with you." Billy lights his second cigarette of their break.

"You like a risk. Sange is one of the company directors and you're a new boy with snotty nostrils. And you happen to be banging his offspring."

Terry exhales fiercely, in an exaggerated manner designed to imply restlessness against a tight deadline. In the way that Billy has already become used to, Terry has changed the subject.

"If there's one thing I love," he says, his voice textured with sarcasm and anger, "it's scummy bastards who leave me the present of *their shit* in the bowl. With a few leaves of bumwad on top of it for *ironic measure.* So I made this. Look." Terry hands Billy the A4-sized card that he's been carrying in his left oxter. "I laminated it in Repro," he adds with a note of pride.

> IF YOU'RE IN DOUBT, FLUSH IT ANYWAY
> YOU FILTHY PIECE OF WANKERDOM,

Billy reads. "You can't be serious."

"Why not? You can't be *pleased* seeing another man's waste."

"Well, no I'm not."

"*This* way," Terry adds, "I'm telling whatever fuck it happens to be, they can *fucking do one.*"

"But you're suggesting putting it up in the Gents' toilets," says Billy.

"No, I'm thinking of putting it up in the Prayer Room. Where *else* but the loos?"

Together they leave the Smokers' Area – the Cancer Cottage (as it's been dubbed) – and return to the office, in disagreement but in good spirits. Although they have only been gone for ten minutes, the air is different when they arrive back. There's a cloud in the office that has nothing to do with one of Pat Kelly's tantrums.

"Anne-Marie's had to leave," explains a Duncan. "Her sister was found dead this morning. She was living on the street, by all accounts, and it finally caught up with her. The poor girl."

Billy says, "Oh my gosh. How did she find out?"

"A policewoman came here. She might want a word with you."

"With *me? I* don't know anything," Billy answers.

"Woah. I only said *might.* Cool your boots."

*

He is not aware of the sobriquet Lord Biscuits, but Kieran Sange knows that he is referred to as the Biscuit Inspector. The Biscuit Inspector's official job title is Director of Quality Control. His role is to coordinate standards in a portfolio of comestibles that includes the Jelly Zinger, the Mayflair Mellow and the Orange Crackle. From time to time, when he can scrape his self-esteem up off the floor – and on the rare occasion that he is invited by anyone to explain his job – he will joke that it is his responsibility to eat biscuits for a living and say that they are nice, at which point a further four million are produced and packaged. In fact, the Biscuit Inspector is now so high up on the company scaffold that he rarely has to put biscuit one to his thin lips: he has a team to do this – a team of four people to eat biscuits all day, every day. Earning as he does, four times more than the average salary, the Biscuit Inspector feels hollow and unfulfilled in his role, and greets his half-yearly bonuses and incremental pay rises with a mixture of suspicion and dread.

Two years earlier, the Biscuit Inspector had decided to eschew the chauffeured drive to and from Coronet Confectionaries and had started walking. When it rained he felt pleasantly guilty: bad weather was something that he ought to endure. Although he left the house at 6.35 a.m. (after the Radio 4 news headlines), word had long since gone around the small community of homeless people that at this time every day strolled a man who seemed hellbent on giving away pockets of change. The Biscuit Inspector tips every comer, young or old, not a princely sum per person, a pound or a two-pound coin, but for those prepared to ask nicely it is regular income. Nor is this the extent of the Biscuit Inspector's generosity. On a monthly basis, vast direct debits catapult chunks of his accumulated wealth in the directions of fifteen national charities, the better to ease his emotional burden with the notion that his contributions are helping the futures of blind children, rhinos and brain or heart surgeons, among many other donees.

The Biscuit Inspector is a boring man. He even bores himself. Although he has plenty of money to take up a hobby that might, in the fullness of time, colour in some of his soul's etiolation, the problem is that nothing grabs him. In the past he has enrolled on college courses in Film Studies and Radio Production, on the lookout for a spark of recognition in his consciousness – a sign that this was what he'd been seeking – but found nothing apart from another certificate of completion. His one and only parachute jump ended well. He landed, inexpertly but safely, and rolled up the chute's fabric, then waddled to the side of the field, to the waiting off-road vehicle, a little chafed in his personal undercarriage, but otherwise healthy and unharmed. He reads novels and scores his verdict in a diary from years earlier that he did not fill in at the time. His scores are in the form of stars that he carefully draws with a heavy fountain pen that he bought in an antiques shop on a whim, which he had hoped to use to compose his memoirs, before he recognized that he had nothing to say for his forty-four years on the planet.

He vowed to change. It was clear that if others found him pleasant in the short term and boring after any length of time, the trick would be to keep it brief. Whatever it was, keep it brief, and do not repeat yourself with the same person.

Once, on a flight home after a holiday, enjoying an almost-unknown fourth glass of champagne in Executive, the Biscuit Inspector removed his socks and waited for someone – air staff or civilian – to challenge him on the foot stink that he had been cultivating for the previous four days. Disappointed by the silence, he pulled a blanket over his lap and freed his penis. Feigning sleep felt delicious. The Biscuit Inspector pulled gently at the edge of the blanket, an inch at a time, to the point where gravity took over and the blanket fell to the floor of the aisle. What the cabin crew saw, therefore, was a man in a tidy suit in Seat 5B, fast asleep and snoring, with his slim penis flat against the breached fly. Had the Biscuit Inspector been the kind of man to make notes, he would have recorded the cabin crew uttering such gobbets as: "*I'm* not touching it!" or "Someone should wake him up and tell him" or "Why don't you put the blanket over his lap?" But no one put the blanket over his lap, and the Biscuit

Inspector feigned sleep for another half an hour, even searching for sexual imagery among his memories to make it grow (though this did not work). During this happy half-hour, the Biscuit Inspector understood that the strange or not-welcome could be made ignorable or even invisible to people whose chief instinct was to want not to know.

Setting foot on the High Street on his return to work three days later, he was encouraged to acknowledge the approach of a homeless man named Frank. The Biscuit Inspector had been giving Frank two or three pounds a week for the past fourteen months, and Frank's face was smiling and his long grey hair neatly combed. When he asked the Biscuit Inspector if he could spare any change, the Biscuit Inspector told him that there had been some alterations to the arrangement. At first, Frank assumed this to be a joke; when the Biscuit Inspector told him to follow, he did so.

They walked away from the High Street, into an alley by the side of a vegetarian restaurant. At the end of the alley was a small courtyard, full of bins and a scattering of rat-traps. *Your payment today is five pounds*, Frank was told, *provided you eat that*; and the Biscuit Inspector pointed at a trap that had caught and all-but trepanned a small female rat. Perfectly understandably, Frank showed signs of perturbation. Nevertheless, the Biscuit Inspector was adamant about these new conditions. He was close to ambling away when Frank made a step towards him and claimed that he could, as an alternative, simply take the money anyway, there being no cameras behind the restaurant to capture an act of violence for future evidence. If Frank so much as breathed too closely into his face, the Biscuit Inspector would go back to being driven to work every day, meaning that none of the other beggars would receive an additional penny. Furthermore, the Biscuit Inspector would make it clear that Frank was the sole reason for the cessation of his generosity.

The word circulated that the Biscuit Inspector had got stricter; that the gravy train had been derailed. To say there was a sense of disbelief was an understatement. The beating he received was sturdy and heartfelt; apparently it was also instantly regretted (it was not only Frank who had a tear in his eye as he aimed kicks at the Biscuit Inspector's head).

After a few weeks of fiscal stalemate, during which despondent threats of further assaults were half-heartedly made and rebuffed, the word went around that if acts of self-debasement were what the Biscuit Inspector demanded, then perhaps they should agree. Some went so far as to state that they owed it to the man. It was Frank himself who greeted the Biscuit Inspector one morning with his customary smile, and a dead grey rat in his left fist. Apologising for their earlier misunderstanding, Frank raised the rat's head to his own mouth and said *Bon appétit.*

During the months that followed, the Biscuit Inspector was treated to an ever-worsening display of pre-arranged defilement. Soon gleaning the man's peccadillo and his preference for watching them eat the customarily inedible, the coterie busied itself by imagining foul things to put into its collective mouth.

At work, the change in the Biscuit Inspector's demeanour had been noted, and not always positively. He was asked if he was having any personal difficulties, and these enquiries persist to this day, albeit less frequently than before. Each well-meant enquiry is met with an assurance that everything is well and that the Biscuit Inspector has never been more content. Enigmatically he might add that he no longer feels like a boring man. When he joins in on a tasting – it is rare but it happens – there is a gleam in his eye sometimes, as if he is thinking of something else.

*

He's thinking of something else, Billy believes once he's been in Kieran Sange's office for less than five minutes. He is distracted – irritable and queasy-looking. Believing the man's reaction to be connected to the young woman that they share, in one way or another, Billy sits still at one end of a chaise longue, his knuckles intertwined tightly, with blood-draining vigour, on his lap. Sange himself has only stopped pacing in the last few seconds. Now he sits at the other end of the chaise longue, plucking at non-existent stray hairs that are lapping at his left temple.

"You'll have to forgive me. I don't know if you've heard the news but a woman named Lorraine was found dead this morning. She was Anne-Marie's estranged half-sister."

"Yes, Kieran," Billy answers, relieved to have something to talk about. "Did you know her?"

"No. But Anne-Marie has worked here for a long time, like me."

That'll explain it, Billy concedes. *Workplace empathy and all that.*

The Biscuit Inspector gives himself a shake. "But to business," he announces. "You don't want to hear my war stories, do you, Billy?"

"No, I suppose not."

"You want to know about Quality Control. Who wouldn't? Probably as much as *I* want to know how your relationship with my daughter is being viewed by her husband of five months."

Shifting uneasily, Billy clicks his tongue. He tries a smile on for good measure. "Jemima and I met at Registration a year ago."

"This much I know. How do you think her new husband," says Kieran, "reacted to your back story? And how did *you* feel when she told you she'd be married at the age of nineteen?"

"Can't deny it took me a bit by surprise," Billy confesses, ignoring the first part of the question. *Is this relevant?* "But she's always been a woman who knows her own mind, as far as I know."

"*Feisty* I've heard. So how was your first week at Coronet Confectionaries?"

Billy nods his head with intensity. "It's given me a glimpse into the working world at a higher level than I've known up to now. Most of my work has been low-paid, unskilled labour."

"You'll be with me for two weeks. My plan was to have you work with the tasters the first week, starting today. They're the team that checks the products for flavour, consistency and texture."

"Sounds good," Billy tells him while pondering on what the difference might be between texture and consistency. "I know there must be more to it than eating biscuits, but . . ."

"No, not really," Kieran interrupts.

"Excuse me?"

"No, there's not more to it than eating biscuits. You eat biscuits. Then you tick a form and add comments in an open-text box if you are so inspired." At which he frowns briefly – a sign that he has changed his mind that to Billy appears overdone. "Well, I say *eat* biscuits. You don't have to actually *eat* them, of course. That's between you and your conscience and how you feel about waste. And your waist*line!*' Momentarily pleased with himself at the coincidence of the homophone, Kieran grins. "Some people treat the tastings like you see on the telly with wine tastings. One slurp and a spit in the bucket, only in this case it's one nibble – *at both ends of the biscuit, Billy!*" he adds with comically heavy emphasis, "then you digest or discharge, as you prefer. I'll show you the vomitorium when we meet the team."

Billy pauses. "Did I hear you right, Kieran? The *vomitorium*?"

"Yes Billy, this isn't the 1980s and the greed-is-good bullshit. Nor do we throw our half-mangled dove bones over our shoulders like Henry the Eighth. If you feel a bit queasy from all the sugar, as you're bound to at first, there's a room where you can go to be sick."

"That's gross."

"*That's biscuits, Billy,*" Kieran informs him, with semi-pointless savagery. "It's not about dunking a digestive *at elevenses*. This is filthy business, my boy. This is *war.*"

By the time Billy leaves Kieran's office a half-hour later, he is reeling from the bad odours of unwanted information. *Who'd have thought,* he'd offered in a ruminative manner, *the biscuit industry would be so cut-throat?*

Kieran had nodded slowly. *In the last five years alone, we've had three suicides here – one of them actually in the building, the other two colleagues who took their angst home and were unable to contain it. The one in the building was a hanging; the other two were wrist-slitters. Don't believe anyone who says that biscuits is a comfortable commodity.*

Billy slopes over to Cancer Cottage after two mouthfuls of his sandwich. Inside the smoking area, Billy is pleased to rendezvous with Danny Lovell, the security guy.

"I bet you're having a better morning than I've had," Danny states up front.

Billy snorts gently. "Do you know, I'm tempted to take that bet."

"Well, I bet you haven't had to deal with vomit and a trapped dog."

"Not exactly. Vomit, yes, indirectly like. So what are you saying?" He rolls a cigarette into the left side of his mouth. "You had to clear up some dog sick?"

Danny chuckles. "They don't pay me enough. No, it was two separate incidents. Like . . . I'm doing my rounds of the car parks – checking for passes in windscreens and the like – and I see down the side of this new aubergine QashQai, *the most humungous* streak of puke you've ever seen."

"Jesus. What's *wrong* with people?"

"My sentiments exactly. And you wouldn't believe the bloody paperwork. Incident at work form. Then I have to let my manager know because I'm new and I want to make sure I fill it in right. Then I have to find the car owner from the records and let him know. Unbelievable."

Billy waits for a second, puckering on his cigarette. "Do you happen to know Kieran Sange, the bloke they call the Biscuit Inspector?"

"I've heard of him. Story goes he walks here every day – here and back. He was mugged by a bunch of tramps on the High Street. He stopped giving them money and they turned on him. And after the assault he changed. Became nice in a *forced* kind of way."

Nodding his head, Billy says, "You could have been in the room with us . . . Tell us about the dog. You mean a dog in the car park?"

"Yeah. A dog in *a car* in the car park, with the windows right up! And I know it's not exactly flaming June right now, but the poor thing's got no ventilation. He's pining in there, giving me the sad eyes – one of them Labradoodles – and there's no bowl with a bit of water. Nothing . . . I've been back to the car about five times, trying to catch the owner so I can have a word."

"The registration plate's not logged, I take it."

"Nothing so nice and easy. I've been to all the Receptions and asked them to put calls out and All-Staff emails, to say there's a dog dying in the back of a Volvo." Although his cigarette is only half-smoked, he crushes what remains of it in the heavy plastic ashtray. "Have you got a few minutes?"

The two men walk towards the far left corner of the car park. Danny leads them to a red Volvo that is parked askew, at a defiant angle to the painted white lines on the ground. Billy does not need to know that a dog has been left inside: he hears the creature's whines as they get closer.

Something about the way the car has been parked bothers Billy. Back in the day he had seen cars parked like this all the time. Usually they'd been stolen and abandoned.

"You've never seen this before?" Billy asks.

"Not to my recollection."

"You don't think it's been left here, do you? Joyriders, I mean."

"With a dog?"

"I don't know. Maybe they didn't know the dog was in the back," Billy reasons. "Maybe that's why they ran away, if they did: the dog was asleep and then it woke up . . . I'm just guessing."

Danny leans his face to the rear offside window. The dog within - a pitiful sight of badly-kept fur and sapped energy - starts licking at the glass between them. Silently Billy seconds what Danny has already said: that unless this dog is released it is going to die.

Danny says, "I thought of an abandoned vehicle myself. If it wasn't for the dog I'd say a joyrider, no question, but I'm wondering why a dog would be in the back of the car in the first place, when it was stolen. It doesn't make sense."

"I don't suppose breaking a window is a good option."

"No it's not. But I've considered it," Danny answers.

*

Ordinarily, Danny's working day is complete at six p.m. – as the day's light leaks away.

Today, however, is not an ordinary day.

When Roger reports to the cabin to take over for the evening shift (some of the buildings stay open until midnight for international trade), Danny lingers. They have a plastic cup of tea each, the steam from the tall dirty kettle filling the physical environment. They talk about a win that Roger has had on the horses.

Emitting an exhalation that is part whistle, part sigh, Danny delineates the events of the previous hours. "I'm going over there now," he concludes, referring to the badly-parked Volvo. "If that dog's still alive I'm breaking the window."

"They'll lock you up, mate," Roger assures him.

The possibility fails to make much impression. Crossing to the far corner of the car park, Danny thinks back to the incident that enforced his retirement from psychiatric security. The memory returns with the force and combustive quality of a nightmare. The boy and his uncle in that bunker; the sawn-off shotgun that Professor Raymond Cossell had pointed . . . Despite everything he had seen as a psychiatric officer – the episodes of insanity that he had umpired, the rages that had stormed in his direction – the altercation with Raymond was the only occasion on which he'd felt sprinkles of urine trickle down his knees. And something about the dog trapped in the car reminds Danny of the boy in that Ark.

It's the helplessness, Danny interprets. *The connection is the victims' utter helplessness.*

He arrives once more at the Volvo, in which the Labradoodle strikes a more woe begotten figure than ever before. So parched, scared and lonely is the creature, so stricken by asthenia, that it cannot raise its head off its forepaws.

Enough is enough. Three strides take him to one of the raised beds of flowers that surround the business park's acreage. This far from the buildings, the display of flora in the bed is far from majestic and well-maintained. In among the soil, some discarded chocolate bar wrappers and the faded colours of a Coke can, is a small collection of rocks. Danny chooses one, and then swings it at the car's front passenger side window.

The glass does not break. A fierce spasm of something that feels like electricity runs up his right arm and settles in his shoulder.

The dog has stood up. It patrols the back seat in a solemn and weary panic.

Danny swings the rock at the glass once again . . .

. . . *and the memory of the boy Lucas returns with passion – a memory that won't be ignored – and he remembers how Professor Raymond Cossell could have killed him.*

Inside the Volvo, the Labradoodle barks feebly.

He could have *killed me,* Danny recalls with fierce resentment, striking at the window for a third time. This time the pane cracks.

Frightened by the noise, the Labradoodle barks. Danny thrusts the rock at the window in anger, another three times . . . and the glass gives.

The window implodes with an ugly thud.

Sweating and cursing, Danny smashes at the remaining glass, clearing a space for the dog either to be lifted or to climb through. Splinters tear into his hand's flesh but he scarcely acknowledges the pain. From inside the car escapes a mingled stench of dog and what a dog leaves on the grass.

The dog yelps. And then there is another sound. A voice.

"Come on, boy," says Danny, well aware of how scary he must seem to this abandoned animal. "I can't help you if you don't help me." Bending at the waist, he leans towards the space where glass had been held in place a few minutes earlier. He is as careful as he can be not to cut his nose or forehead on what he hasn't managed to clear away.

The Labradoodle takes a cautious step in his direction on the back seat. Though the inside of the car stinks, Danny stays in his position, his lips clenched in an aggressive mimp.

"Don't make me beg."

"*You fucking bastard!*" someone shouts from behind. "*What are you doing with my car?*"

Danny hears this. Still, he maintains his position, coaxing the dog with treats that can only be verbal. He has nothing to offer the animal to tease it out into the open air.

Footsteps. Someone running in Danny's direction.

"*Leave my car alone, you thieving prick!*"

Stepping back from the Volvo and straightening up, Danny turns to the man who is approaching with quite a lick of speed for a short fat guy. If the man's hollers had remained unheard, Danny would have known his intentions by the expression on his puce-coloured bovine features. He is clearly as livid as Danny was while he broke the glass.

"There's a dog in there," Danny replies, matching the car-owner's mood. "You left your dog in there to die, and I'm not about to let an innocent creature suffer."

"I'll make *you* bloody suffer, mate!" The other man is no further away than five metres by now, and his pace is decelerating. "You'll be paying for that for starters!"

With a yelp that at least sounds triumphant, the Labradoodle springs at the open space, sensing freedom. The next yelp that the dog proffers, as a result of landing its belly on the horizontal frame (and presumably on some toothy shards of glass), is anything but triumphant. It sounds agonised. While Danny winces at the animal's discomfort, the dog scrambles for purchase and after a few seconds, it manages to wriggle free. Claws tapping on the Volvo's paintwork, the dog launches itself out of its prison and it flumps to the ground, panting and wheezing.

Danny points at the creature. "What were you *thinking*?"

"It's not mine!" the other man protests. "He must have climbed in!"

"You've given him a full set of keys then, have you?"

"The door's aren't locked! It's open. I've been waiting for the bloke who works at my garage all afternoon. There's something wrong with the engine. When I phoned him he told me to leave the car somewhere conspicuous, away from all the other cars. Leave the doors unlocked and the key in the ignition."

Danny cannot meet the car-owner's eyes. He looks at the wounded dog, which has started to limp away, dripping blood. "Then where is he?"

"He couldn't come. His little girl's sick. I was coming over to lock it up."

For a few seconds of silence the two men watch the dog as it hobbles in an uncertain direction. "*God* knows how it got in there," the man tells Danny.

Understanding that he has made an error, Danny wants to try one more thing. The car door opens . . . and Danny knows that it has been unlocked all day.

"See? Now. About the damage."

The dog will have to fend for itself, Danny realises. He walks away, nursing his wounded hand with the healthy one. "I'm not giving you a penny," he states clearly. "I've been to every building on this business park today. I've tried to find you to rescue this poor dog."

"*It's not mine, you thick twat!*"

"Doesn't matter. All you had to do was come out and check your car."

"I was in meetings all day . . . Where do you think *you're* going?"

"Home."

"No you're not. I'm calling the police. You're going to prison."

Danny snorts. "I've had worse than prison in my time," he tosses over his shoulder.

4

Although Frank and Finley have occupied the same body for the last three years, both men are keen to keep their identities discrete. Apart from the physical they have little in common, after all; their ways of life are worlds apart, and if the one enters the consciousness of the other, the two minds can agree on one matter: that they don't like each other very much. As a result, they regard one another from a distance, like people at a zoo, standing a respectful two metres from the wire-mesh, even though the wolves within can do no harm.

Because of The Project, the man has been Frank more than Finley in recent months; but tonight will take the form of a train journey north, and as the tracks clack, as they tick off the miles to his ex-wife's door, Frank will fade slowly and become diaphanous; Finley will condense, the edges of his imagination first curdling (as he sees it), before setting hard as a screed. Finley will be remade. And he will note, as he always does, that he is not the same – not exactly – as he was the last time that he used these bones, these lungs; that most people fail to identify their own alterations, because they have no alter egos to use as controls that recalibrate the scales.

Frank and Finley awake from a slippery doze and listen briefly to half of a conversation. The man in the seat behind them is summing up his luck in love. "I've had it with Thai brides," the man says. "I've been married four times – five including the English one – and I've been fleeced every time. No, Giles. From here on in, it's strictly Brazilian ladyboys for me."

Taking the conversation as a sign, Frank and Finley lift their shared body off their own cramped seat. In the small toilet cubicle on the train, Frank begins the transformation. Removing the wig of long grey hair reveals a scalp shaved down to what resemble iron filings, stained a pomegranate hue in the insufficient light. His face appears fuller (Finley is a chunkier man than Frank's street-leanness) and a number of years float away from his features.

The sapor of dead rat has lingered on Frank's tongue for four weeks. In the intermingling handover of their minds, both men hope it can be killed by coffee and by the doughnuts that Frank purchased from a van near the station. While washing his face in the tiny basin, Frank scoops some water into his shared mouth, even though a sign is present to warn users of its unsuitability for drinking. The water's flavour – vaguely ammonia, oilily perfumed – is no more successful at shifting the taste of rodent than alley brandy, rollups or dustbin chilli have been.

The make-up bristles are washed from the man's face. They peel off the squat blemish that is worn above their left eye (a gesture of authenticity that once seemed cautious and canny but now seems overwrought, and quite honestly a difficulty to remember and maintain); and then, once clean (with the basin as smudged as an ashtray), the men climb out of Frank's dingy clothing. Finley experiences a now-commonplace sense of inordinate self-disgust, as if he's done something scarcely legal but cannot recall what it is.

Finley's clothes are in Frank's tattered bag. Pulling them out is like unwrapping a gift at Christmas, and Finley wears them proudly for a moment – until someone knocks on the door on the other side.

"Are you okay in there?"

Finley's attempt at an answer is little more than a glottal-stopped grunt: after leaving Frank behind he is often afflicted by at least half a minute of stunned aphonia, and true to form, he cannot speak properly now.

He coughs loudly. In something of a panicked funk – a second knock on the door sounds louder than the first – Finley accelerates, stuffing Frank's stinking clobber into the briefcase that he removes from Frank's bag.

"Come on, mate – people waiting out here!" the voice continues on the other side of the door.

"Just a second!" Finley croaks while he folds up Frank's bag as small as it will go. The bag he also crams into the briefcase; then he leans on the lid, perching the case on the toilet's yoke, and manages to click it shut, finally tumbling the security lock's numbers with a sigh, and wiping clean the basin with an ebullient flourish.

To the sound of the toilet's flush – a terrifying hydraulic gulp – Finley opens the door to a besuited thickset man in his early thirties.

"Sorry," the man offers. "Thought you might be in trouble you been so long."

"I was. I've had an upset stomach all week. I'd give it five minutes if I were you. *At least* five minutes. And send a canary in first."

*

Although plenty of cabs are available and it has started to spritz, Finley walks from the station. The walk will do him good; and he's early anyway. His mind chatters like a toddler learning language, playing catch-up with his renewed persona. He thinks less of a dead rat than of a dead woman – the woman who died on the street – and he views her with a fresh perspective, determined to remember (if the knowledge is in Frank's head) if he has ever known why Lorraine had been in that crowd in the first place. Given her appearance – the cosmetic dentistry, the ring on her finger – she had clearly been cut from a different bolt of cloth.

Was she doing the same thing that I am? Finley wonders.

When he gets to the house, his daughter is outside, standing close to the road, finishing a phone call and smoking a cigarette. They embrace, and Finley says, "Happy birthday, sweetheart."

"Thanks, Dad. And thanks for the vouchers – they arrived yesterday. But why didn't you bring them with you?"

Finley shrugs. "I wasn't sure how close your mum would let me get."

"On my birthday?"

"Well anyway. I'm here now, on time. How is she?"

"About a four: not bad at all, considering. She's nearly finished."

"Third draft?"

"No, further. She's reading the galleys . . . You've not been around for a while."

"I've been busy. Sorry."

"Still deep undercover?"

For a second Finley believes that she knows what he has been doing; he can see her, in a memory as false but as strong as spirituality, standing in the kitchen of a vegetarian restaurant, watching through a window as the man in the suit points to a dead rat in a trap on the ground. He can see her watching Frank refuse the man's demand to eat it; then the scene shifts, and Tamara is floating above Frank and the gang, a witness to the pounding they gave him . . .

"Just work stuff," Finley answers. "Maybe a book of my own at the end of it. We'll see . . . Who's here already?"

"Uncle Bill and Aunt Jodie. A few of my friends from Club. And Mum's got a new boyfriend."

"Yeah, she told me. What's his name?"

"Seriously? You didn't get as far as his *name*?"

"I wasn't concentrating when she told me." (*I was Frank*, he doesn't say.) "What is it?"

"Frank. Frank Tucker."

"Brilliant: another Frank. He's here as well?"

"Yep. He's always here . . . What do you mean, *another* Frank?"

"The first to arrive, eh? Keen?"

"No. He never leaves, is what I mean. He's moved in."

Finley pauses. "Well she doesn't waste much time, I'll give her that. What does he do?"

"Something at the uni. If it makes you feel any better, Dad, he's older than you."

"And richer, I hope."

"Why richer?"

"Well. If he's got my house, he can have my mortgage as well."

"Dad. It's my birthday. You promised."

"So I did. Let's go in and meet Frank. See what we've got in common, apart from the obvious."

*

The birthday celebration is the predictable admixture of joyful cake-cutting and ditty-singing, and the awkward self-defensive indignation peculiar to any gathering to which ex-spouses have been invited. Once everyone has had a drink, however (or a *further* drink, Finley notes, in the case of Frank Tucker), the cogs of conversation are oiled more efficiently. A gin-and-vermouth deep into the first hour, and Finley is even close to a state of pleasure.

It is close to eight o'clock (and Finley is perusing his fourth gin, holding the full glass like an actor's prop but not actually sipping its contents) when the scientific law of bodies moving slowly in a confined space dictates that he will have to speak to Frank Tucker. He can avoid him no longer.

"Tamara tells me you work at the university," Finley says to open the first conversation that the two men have shared since they shook hands an hour earlier.

"I run the Masters in Public Health," Frank informs him. "Epidemiologist by background."

Unaware of how much Louise would have mentioned her ex-husband, but alive to the fact that she can be self-absorbed while working on a new book, Finley names the university that employs him, nearly two hundred miles south of where they stand chatting.

"Psychology, Senior Lecturer," he adds. "I'm on a sabbatical; investigating role changes among the physically chemically addicted in under-privileged social settings. Group dynamics and hive-mind internal goal settings in the country's non-classes."

Although Finley is simply paraphrasing the abstract of an academic paper that he has almost completed on the subject (with one career eye on a conference appearance in the future to present his eventual findings), he is pleased with his gobbet.

In fact, he hopefully expects the concept to be lost on Frank; but Frank merely nods while Finley speaks, and slurps at his half of bitter.

"You're talking about tramps," Frank translates. "Pissy tramps with small rodents in their beards. Tamara mentioned something about your stint undercover."

It is at this point that Finley decides categorically to hate Frank. Not just now, and not just for the duration of the man's relationship with Louise, however long this turns out to be, but forever – with an energy ever true. Although Finley's work involves being noticed by his academic peers, he does not count Frank among their number. He dislikes the way that Frank has decoded his professional intentions. He already shares half of his mental and physical existence with Frank the Homeless: the incursion of this second Frank feels like a dilution too far.

"Yeah," says Finley, finally deciding to embark on that fourth gin that he's gripped for ten minutes. He rolls the liquid around his tongue in a mouth washing action; he is even tempted to *gargle* with the gin, right here in front of the Frank that he will make pay his share of the mortgage. "I'm writing about tramp life."

"Good for you," Frank tells him. "I read an interesting paper the other month, about homeless life in Peru. It turns out that where you'd expect illness, liver complaints, sexually transmitted diseases and the like to be sky-high, in fact among that group, the general condition of health was robust. It was a fascinating insight, Finley. I'll send you the link."

"Thanks," Finley replies, though he wants to instruct Frank not to patronise him a second longer than he feels he must. With a second swig he cleans his glass of clear liquid; this time he swallows it in a gulp – it descends the chute of his upper body like a hardboiled egg, still in its shell and scalding hot to his oesophagus's touch. "But I've read it already. I was asked to contribute an expert's opinion via a video conference. We had a good session."

"I'm pleased to hear it. I wonder why the author didn't cite you in the References – or even in the Acknowledgements."

How would you remember that? Finley demands in silence. "At my request." His eye line wanders to the kitchen, which he hopes Frank will interpret (partially correctly) as a sign of impatience for more alcohol. Although Finley does not want to get drunk, he very much wants to be away from Frank's presence, and a trip to where a makeshift bar has been set up on the surface next to the fridge is the only way that he can think of to do so, short of leaving the house.

When the iPod's shuffle function abruptly silences Bruno Mars and introduces Abba, Finley senses the opportunity for a spell of one-upmanship. "From what I've discovered so far, Frank," he almost lectures, "the health benefits of life on the streets in *this* country have yet to be quantitatively proven, anyway. Only yesterday – an intriguing glimpse, I believe, Frank . . . a woman died of organ failure, right there on the passway. She wasn't a heavy drinker." Finley pictures Lorraine, sitting with the group and declining her mouthful of Super Strength Cider when the three-litre brown plastic bottle came to her. "So, try telling me, *Frank,* that a woman of mothering age's premature *death,* is any way *indicative* of a healthy lifestyle among homeless people in this country."

Throughout Finley's lecture, Frank's features have not moved. Now he asks: "Are you aware that you've raised your voice quite considerably in the last half a minute?"

If not for Tamara moving closer and saying "Dad?", Finley might have rebutted the implication in the question with a modelled and qualitatively-studied *Go fuck yourself, Frank.* But Tamara has sensed the rot in her birthday party's atmosphere. "Time for a fag break."

Tamara and Finley leave the house via the kitchen, where Finley fishes a can of Tango from the sink, which is full of melting ice and crammed with cans of pop and bottles of lager and white wine. For now, he has decided against a fifth gin-and-tonic.

Judging by the way that Tamara leads them beyond the patio and on to the grass, her movements stiff but just a little unsteady (her heels sink into the waterlogged lawn), she wants to be a distance from the house. Halfway down the fifty-metre garden, Tamara stops at the pond and takes a seat on the stone bench. Finley is a few strides behind her; with his daughter's back turned to him, it is impossible to deduce how infuriated she is, and it is only when he draws alongside Tamara that he sees she is crying. She stares at the surface of the pond, her back bent, her shoulders twitching.

"Darling, I'm sorry," Finley offers, "about my minor disagreement with Frank back there."

Tamara is removing a cigarette from a box that she has damaged out of shape in her right fist. Her gaze still fixed on the water, she says quietly, "My *birthday*, Dad. You promised."

"I'm really sorry."

"My *twenty-first* birthday, at that," she continues. "The one we remember for the rest of our lives, some say. The one I could have spent with my friends in a bar and then gone on to the gay club and danced safely until two in the morning. *That* birthday."

Maintaining a two-metre buffer from his daughter, Finley weighs up his options: to sit by Tamara on the stone bench; to sit by Tamara on the stone bench and put an arm around her softly heaving shoulders; to *ask to* sit by Tamara on the stone bench; to *ask to* put his arm across her shoulders; to repeat his apology; or to explain his reasons for the altercation.

"He was winding me up," Finley tries to explain.

Tamara looks his way and blows smoke into the dark air. "Well of course he was! That's his job. That's the whole frigging point of Mum inviting him and you into the same space. It was *your* job not to rise to his taunts, Dad, whatever they were . . . You've disappointed me."

Nothing feels worse than being made to feel small by your offspring.

"Do you want me to go?" Finley asks her.

Suddenly he thinks of Frank – the other Frank, the Frank who shares his consciousness – and he remembers how he and the others in the group had set upon Lord Biscuits; how they'd knocked him to the ground and cleaned their boot-tips on his scalp. The rage in which Frank had shared and participated – it climbs up through Finley's torso, and the taste of the rat that their shared mouth had accepted is as bitter and vile as it ever was. If Frank the Tramp could turn a situation around and make himself the top dog again, why can't Finley? Finley is the one with the PhD and the education. Yet he cannot think of anything to add to the silence.

"Yes Dad," Tamara finally answers. "I think you should leave."

*

Finley heads for the B&B that he usually books whenever he travels north. Carrying his bag stuffed full of Frank's life, he greets Glenda, the evening Receptionist, with a familiar smirk and a question about how she has been since he was last in town.

"We don't have you," Glenda tells him. She types with the blood-red tips of her pointlessly long forefinger nails. "You're not in our system."

Finley answers her with the steel in his voice that Louise had always loathed. "I booked a fortnight ago. Finley Reardon."

"You booked online?"

"As always, yes."

"We had a big system crash about then. It doesn't look like your booking went through."

Finley sighs. "Not to worry. Any room'll do."

"I'm afraid we're fully booked. Everywhere is, apparently: it's the farm machinery trade fair this weekend, just up the road."

Contemplating the hypothetical conundrum of how this evening can get any worse, Finley asks, "So what am I supposed to do? I've already paid."

"We won't have taken your payment if you're not on the system," Glenda tells him. "But I've been on the phone all evening. Everyone says fully booked."

When Finley steps outside, a cold rain has started to fall. Given the way that things have gone so far, Finley half expects a sky cracked by lightning, a timpani roll of thunder, a plague of amphibians. The street is quiet – no people, no traffic – and he counts his options. The first is to make it back to the train station and to buy a new ticket and reverse the journey, south and home again – an eighty-quid return fare for a whistle-stop tour of his daughter's birthday emotions. Or two: to embark on a tour of other places that might put him up for the night . . . though if Glenda was speaking the truth, there is little chance of finding a warm bed and a shower in the area, and it is already close to ten p.m.

The third proposition manifests itself as an unpleasant taste in Finley's mouth. A few seconds pass before he realises that the flavour is not the four gin-and-angers that he imbibed at Tamara's party. He remembers the rat that he ate while he was Frank. And the total of Frank's physical belongings are in the bag that Finley carries: why not look upon the cards that he has been dealt as a chance for some unplanned research? In a matter of minutes he can be Frank once more.

The gates to the park near the B&B are closed and padlocked. Finley knows, however, that on the park's far side is a covered bus shelter made of brick (and bedoodled with graffiti). It is unlikely that there will be many buses dropping off and collecting at this time of night, and it is towards this shelter that Finley heads to change.

*

"I'm not sharing," the man with the mauve beard declares. "If you think I'm sharing, you're a penis."

"I'm not asking. It's your sparkling company I'm after," says Frank.

The man harrumphs. He and Frank are seated on a bench no more than three blocks from the train station, where the rain seems fearful to tread.

"So what do you get up to of an evening?" Frank wants to know. "Going anywhere nice on your holidays?"

"Piss off." The other man swills from a three-litre brown plastic bottle that once contained supermarket cider. He puckers his lips and bunches his knuckles, like a wine connoisseur scenting shiraz perfection.

"Where do you spend your night?" Frank asks.

As though scenting the air for competition, Mauve Beard weighs up the pros and cons of answering.

"Behind the old stables they closed down," he answers, "on the Fullwell Road."

"I need directions."

"It's on the outskirts." Mauve Beard points his finger. "There's a building site there but it's been abandoned. The developers ran out of money." He shrugs. "It's where we doss down." He takes a sip of his concoction. "If you're lucky you get one of the horse's stalls or a worker's hut, but the competition can be a bit saucy."

Sleeping in a horse's stall! To Frank this sounds perfect: the lovesick worried groom and the ailing mare . . . Determined not to sound too desperate, Frank leaves a second's pause and then asks, "May I join you?"

"It's a free country."

"I'm not sure it is," Frank prods. "May I *join you,* you filthy snail?"

"Fucking join me. See if *I* care. But you're not having any of this."

"As I said already," Frank reminds him, "my Earthly Delights are your company alone."

The other man pulls a gulp from his homebrew. Wipes his whiskered lips with something close to satisfaction. Remains silent on the matter.

"Tell me, Mauve," says Frank, "if you'd be so kind. Have you ever eaten a rat?"

Mauve Beard sniffs orchestrally. "Eaten a *lovebird,*" he tries to compromise.

"But that's not what I said. Have you ever eaten a *rat*?"

"Welll of course not! What do you think I am, a bloody animal?"

"*I* have. And that's why, if I don't get your respect in the next thirty seconds, I'm going to take that bottle of hooch and remind you why the anus is an outy and not an inny."

*

Not for one instant does Frank believe that he has tormented the mauve-bearded tramp into a condition of obedience. While it is true that Mauve leads Frank to the group, there is no sense that Mauve is under Frank's influence. Indeed, there is no sense that Mauve is as much as aware that Frank is on his heels.

A fire trickles into the black and heat-distorted air; the conflagration is a mixture of red, white and blue – a Union Jack of corroded flame, fuelled by White Spirit and the remains of desiccated fashion magazines, littered on the building site nearby.

Heads turn at the odd couple's approach . . . then turn back to what they had seen or not seen a few seconds earlier. The climate is one of end-approving silence. No banter. No words and no arguments. Just the movement of arms; the tilting of bristly and buxom throats. Once Mauve Beard and Frank have infiltrated the ill-defended outer limits of the small camp, it is as though they were never apart from it.

Minutes gluey and unfinishable float past. The blaze crackles. A middle-aged old woman wearing a cowboy hat starts to talk about her Persian cat. A young old man begins to recite football scores and team positions in a league that might or might not have once existed.

Someone mumbles something about nostalgia not being what it used to be . . . *Bull by the horns time*, thinks Frank. "What do you remember, my friend?" he asks.

Nine people are present. All but one is suddenly alive, scraped from a coma with fingers and toes twitching. The ninth remains asleep with her eyes open, blissed on a current of meth.

"I remember the flood," the man states clearly.

Frank pictures the nearby canal. Most of the time, the canal is a duck-infested vein of caramel sludge; Frank has never heard of it flooding before . . . but he knows that he is sharing Finley's memories, and that man should never be fully trusted.

"What happened, friend?" Frank asks.

The homeless man grunts like a moose. "What do you think happened? *Destruction* happened, son! Waves like you never seen! *Obliteration.* Bloody God. Giving it the Big I-Am. Thinks he's Charlie Conkers, the cunt. The Big Banana." The man's sniff and expectoration are epic. "If I had *my* way . . ."

"With God?"

"Yes-with-God!" the man answers angrily. "It takes people to stand up to a bully – a concerted effort. Put our heads together. Hit Him where it hurts!" The man turns to Frank with a timid smile peeping through his silver beard, which is dyed a kaleidoscope of yellows and browns by the flames. "Can I count on your support, pal? Are you with me?"

Frank inhales. "You're not talking about a flood at the canal, are you?"

"What canal?"

In the space of a few spoken sentences, Frank had written the man a sketchy back story. Not only had he referred to a flood at the canal, he had also pictured his caravan damaged by the water. Circumstances had led him to his existence on the streets . . .

No.

"You're talking about the flood in the Bible, aren't you?"

The man's response is unequivocal. "Pah! The *Bible* he says! Load of bloody hacks, you ask me . . . *Scaremongers*, the lot of 'em. God flicking bogeys and wiping his fingers on entire civilisations – and *expunging* them from the pages of history? To the notion I say *bollocks.* The flood wasn't two by two and that play school nonsense, son. Do you think I took my place next to a sodding *yak*?"

"I guess not, no."

"No. Of course not. The flood wasn't *literal*."

Even the woman asleep with her eyes open has woken up, or at least regained a variety of consciousness, and everyone looks the way of Frank and his new BFF.

"You mean the *water* wasn't literal?" Frank persists.

"Leave him alone," a man orders – a man of uncharacteristic personal bulk in such a setting. "The man's got his problems." The accent is subtly European – maybe Polish. "It's up to us to respect his thoughts. Don't badger him."

"My friend," Frank protests, "I'm not *badgering* . ."

"And I'm not your friend. Who *are* you, anyway?"

"Yeah, who *are you*?" a woman to this new speaker's left demands to know.

"I came with . . ." Pointing at Mauve Beard, Frank realises he did not ask the man's name.

Threatened me, he did!" is Mauve's sullen contribution.

The new speaker stands up. He is dressed in layers of motley shades and hues; his back is bent, his hair cropped back to a scalp that wears scars and blemishes like tattoos.

"Oh, did he now? *Who invited you?*"

And he takes a few steps away from the crate on which he'd perched, reaching backwards to hand his bottle to his female companion.

"Go on, Malcolm!" she says. "Show him who's boss around here!"

As the paltry fire flickers, the man called Malcolm steps around it, thereby awakening the curiosity – and the blood lust – of the other people present. Animal instinct is roused in Frank's system: he must make his exit. He of all people knows the dormant power of street people with nothing to do who are suddenly offered a bit of gravel theatre – especially if there's liquor in the capillaries already.

Frank jumps up to his feet, clutching at the bag in which his change of clothes is safe.

"I didn't mean any offence," Frank says. "I was just making conversation. I'm sorry."

Malcolm's female friend is also on her feet now, goading her man along. "Show him, Malcolm! Coming to our fire and taking our heat! *Show him*!"

The fist fight between Malcolm and Frank does not last long, but it doesn't need to. Malcolm has seven other people on his side who are willing to lend a hand. Or in this case, a foot. Before seconds have elapsed, Frank is curled up tight in the dirt, and kicks are aimed at his body. Phlegm is spat at his face, despite his howls of protest – or perhaps because of them.

The only two people who abstain are Mauve Beard and the man who talked of the flood. The rest take part in Frank's murder. He dies as a result of repeated insult to the head; and when he's heaved his last breath, the communal wisdom is to try to cremate his body, to get rid of the evidence. It is left to Malcolm to go through Frank's bag to see if he has anything that will ignite.

Four of the people present start a game of tug-o'-war with Frank's warm corpse. When his joints start to crack, Malcolm orders them to stop. It is time for the midnight funeral.

5

Every industry has its stories, and Carol knows many of the actors in these tales, at least by name. To make sure that she stays on top of what is going on, approximately twice a month she meets a fiercely determined gossip named Roberta, for an hour or so in the fading afternoon.

"I still can't believe it," Carol says. From the other side of the beautifully manicured room, Roberta hums her nicotine-deepened concurrence. Dressed in a flamingo-print pink silk kimono, Roberta cuts every bit as striking a personal figure as her lounge does. While Carol continues to talk – "She was living a double life. Whenever I met her she was respectable, Robbie, but she also spent time on the *streets*, hanging around with the *homeless*" – Roberta pours scalding water on two spoonfuls of green tea in a Japanese infusion pot.

"I'll just let that brew," Roberta decides. She rejoins Carol on the nine-grand sofa.

Carol is agitated. "She told me she was pregnant with twins. I mentioned she'd put on a bit of weight . . . Christ. Are you sure you only want tea? I'd be happy to stand you a drink at The Scarlet."

Roberta smiles. "Not before the sun's over the yardarm, darling, you know the rules. The tea, by the way, is from a private non-commercial farm in Mozambique of all places. I pay five hundred pounds a packet. It gives you strength."

"At that sort of outlay, I'd expect it to give me life insurance."

Late-fiftyish (Carol imagines), broad in the beam, Roberta is the owner of a large collection of wigs, a colossal accrual of jewellery, and even when alone, her face is a cosmetic masterpiece of misdirection, disguise and sleight of glands. She looks good. It is only when she speaks that one can hear the decades of ignited cigarettes . . . and one might form the distant suspicion that Roberta had once been – or remained – a man.

Roberta is the proprietor of three establishments in the area. Two of them offer what are euphemistically termed *assisted saunas*, and they hide behind a key-cutting shop front and a shop called Octaves, which sells sheet music, instruments, CDs and vinyl. The third business has no reason to be so coy: it is located in a private house.

"Do you think she lied?" Roberta asks from her own suite of rooms in this very same third business establishment. The top floor is Roberta's own; access is via a locked door.

"About the twins?" says Carol. "I have no idea."

Roberta returns to the Japanese infusion pot and pours two small cups of liquid that by appearance might be diluted pea juice; her kimono swishes. The other sound that enters the room is a squeaking of bedsprings, from below.

"Who's working?" Carol asks. "Thanks," she adds, receiving her drink.

"Clarissa. Earned her salary this week, that girl has." Roberta's voice sounds complimentary. "Gave a *two-hour* blowjob to a bloke called Ross. Couldn't bring him off and he kept offering a half-hour extension fee. Two hours! Her jaw's like a Halloween pumpkin."

"Ross? Mid-twenties? With a do-goody girl called Mercy?"

"The very same. You've had the pleasure?"

"Couple of years ago. Same old song. *My girlfriend doesn't do this. My girlfriend doesn't do that.*" Carol shrugs and sips her green tea. "What have you heard about Lorraine?"

"Maybe it was the sugar daddy, is what I've heard," Roberta answers. "Though I don't like it much at all, but there you are. The wealthy American in the Capital. Maybe he liked the sugar part but didn't fancy being the daddy – the nappies and the sleepless nights and the colic. Maybe he bid her fond adieu."

Although it's a reprehensible suggestion, it is not a new arrival in Carol's mind. In fact, it was one of the first things that she had considered. "I wish I could do something," she says.

"You did do something. You were her friend."

"Well I *thought* I was. Why would she lie to me like this?"

"Sweetie. Did *you* tell *her* everything?" Roberta asks.

"Of course not. But *I'm* not the one without a suicide note, cold on a slab somewhere."

"It was organ failure, darling. Her liver gave up. Her kidneys gave up. Ultimately, darling, her heart gave up. Lorraine was *ill* – she might not have known."

"True enough." Carol decrypts the signals of warmth that the green tea sends out to her bones. She feels displeased. Internally she queries why none of this is enough, why Roberta's words sound like a jigsaw puzzle with a corner piece missing.

Roberta leaves a pause and then says, "Talking of sugar daddies . . . How's it going with Andreas and your pocket money allowance?"

"It was weird at first. I'm used to working. So I've been learning about music in my spare time. I go to Octaves and spend some of my not-hard-earned money on classical CDs. It's been a real education, and Andreas loves it when I tell him something obscure about Stravinski or Berlioz."

"And who's your teacher?"

"Young kid named Darryl who works there. Wears a bowtie. He's sweet."

"Apparently he hums Beethoven's Fifth when he's about to finish."

The inference that Darryl is a patron of Roberta's brothel is vaguely disappointing to Carol. "He thinks of me as his muse," she tells Roberta. "Andreas, I mean – not Darryl."

It is at this moment that Lorraine – dead Lorraine – walks into Roberta's room. She opens the door and strides in with her old confidence. The temperature rises.

There is nothing transparent about Lorraine's appearance. She is wearing an attractive ensemble, purple and cream, with a wide-brimmed matching hat and dark brown designer sunglasses with large oval frames to contain the tinted prescription plastic.

Someone's remembering you, she says. *You can change what people remember . . .*

Carol is on her feet, her heart pounding. Roberta does not move a muscle – not even in her face – and much later Carol will think of her as someone who receives visitations on a regular basis. Either that, or Roberta is paralysed by panic and perplexity.

"Lorraine?" Carol says. "What are *you* doing here?"

You can change what people remember, Lorraine repeats . . . and around her edges, as if the short speech has rendered her exhausted, the purple and cream colours fade. She is vanishing before their eyes. She looks peaceful. She looks like a dream.

Ask the doctor, Lorraine suggests as her spirit bids her friends farewell. *Ask Chaz . . .*

Lorraine leaves them as suddenly as she arrived. For her final scene she does not make use of the door; she slips away into the air, her reminder the scent of the perfume that she'd worn when she was alive. It lingers like the cool breath of a storm. The temperature in the room lowers back to what it had been before Lorraine had put in her appearance.

A minute passes . . . two minutes. Finally Carol asks if Roberta saw what she saw, her voice breathless and patchy, and Roberta confirms that she did.

"What do you think she meant?" Roberta wonders.

"I've just seen my first ghost," Carol answers. "It wasn't a dream, was it? You really saw it."

Roberta nods her head. "I really did. But not *it*. I saw *her*. I saw Lorraine, large as life."

*

Cacidrosis in her nostrils from the final patient of the day, Chaz Bruce-Sange is on the brink of playing Shostakovich or Mahler (the soubriquet *The Shost* pounds hard against her eardrums, thanks to Carol Hayes) when the phone rings, and she answers an officer named Bark.

Identities established, Police Constable Sharon Bark tells the Good Doctor, "It's about the note we found."

At rest, without any internal or external stimuli, some people are naturally happy and some people are naturally sad. Chaz Bruce-Sange is naturally impatient. It is ironic (she believes) that she works as a practitioner in a field in which results are so slow that service user progress can take years.

"What about it?"

"You're named in it, Doctor," answers WPC Bark. "The deceased had something to tell you."

*

"I suppose you heard about the woman who died up the road the other day."

"I did. I was there, actually."

"There where? When she *died*?"

Darryl Carbrini nods his head. "Or when she was discovered, at least," he answers, flicking through a rack of CDs. "One of the least pleasant things in my life so far, I must say."

Carol Hayes asks what happened and Darryl explains. At the same time he manages to find the recording by Shostakovich for which he's been digging. "Eureka!"

"What is it?"

"The Jazz Recordings. Riccardo Chailly in the crow's nest, as it were." Darryl gulps; he seems to be quite overwhelmed by his own discovery. "A masterpiece if ever there was one."

"I'm game."

His back to the woman who will pay him for his expertise, yet mindful of the three other customers browsing in Octaves, Darryl stands erect so abruptly that a joint pops in his back; he flinches with the future memory of further back pain. At the same time, the bad tooth in his mouth is like a jungle drummer, beating a solitary bongo all night and all day.

Carol has knowledge that Darryl doesn't know that she owns. Roberta had said that Darryl went (at least once) to one of her brothels. There is something more than an element of teasing in her mind when she asks, "Did you know her?"

"The dead woman?"

"Her name was Lorraine. Did you know her?"

"No. What makes you say that?"

Carol shrugs. "Small world, small town." She leaves a pause. "*I* did."

Darryl ambles back across the shop and round the other side of the counter. Wordlessly Carol asks him why her confession has led to his inability to meet her eye. She has become used to a certain shyness about Darryl but this seems different.

"Have I upset you?"

"No." Darryl looks up from his perusal of the CD's artwork. "You've confused me, though."

"My connection with a woman who gave every appearance of living on the street," Carol elaborates. "I can see why that would be confusing."

"Not that it's any of my business, of course . . . Shall we play it now?"

"Yes, please . . . It's your business if you've got a genuine query. Allow me to explain, Darryl. I'm a woman who sells sexual favours . . . and so was Lorraine. This I knew. The part I *didn't* know about was the fact that she also spent time with the town's homeless community. And if you think *you're* confused, I bet I can trump it. She had a man who showed every sign of loving her – she had money. She wasn't rich but she was doing better than many. And yet she chose . . . for all I know, she *chose* . . . to frequent with tramps and squatters. What was wrong with her?"

Darryl Carbrini blinks. "Is that an honest question?" He rotates his head on his neck to take in the whereabouts of Octaves' other three customers. One is heading for the door, his browsing over. Darryl hopes that the man has not chosen to leave because of the conversation with Carol.

"No, not really, I'm being hypothetical."

"It's upset you more than you want to admit, Carol."

"I think it has."

Carol pays for her CD and tucks it into a pocket of her new beige handbag; she zips it up.

"Just for the record," Darryl says to her back when she is halfway to the door.

Carol turns, an inquisitive expression on her face. She watches his features as he chooses what to say next. More than ever before, it seems that she and Darryl are flirting.

"I think you're brave, doing what you do."

Deciding to play along, Carol keeps her distance from the counter and smiles. "There's nothing brave about it, Darryl. In fact, there's nothing more ordinary than the job you've done for nearly two decades. It's the air you breathe. It pays the mortgage."

"I didn't mean the tricks," Darryl counters. "I mean the way you've put the rest of your customers on hold. That's very brave. That's chancy economics."

For Carol, this analysis is like a paper cut: she knows exactly what Darryl means, and she agrees with him. What hurts is the fact that someone from outside of that part of her life has pointed it out.

"Tell me something. If a great opportunity came your way . . . say you're offered a lead part in the National Orchestra. What's your favourite city?"

"Vancouver."

"You're offered a dream gig. You can play the solos to a packed house in Vancouver every night for a month. The compromise is, you have to shut your shop. Wouldn't you do it?"

Carol returns to the counter.

Darryl smirks; the temporary expression drops years from his already youthful features (and decimates his IQ, it seems to Carol). "Of course I'd take it," he answers at length.

"Well, this is the nearest comparison I have. I'm earning more than I ever have, for less work. And be honest, Darryl, you're wondering what it would cost to outbid the European and have me to yourself, aren't you? The problem is . . . if I go behind Andreas's back, there's no guarantee you won't tell someone, and then that would be it as far as my working relationship with that man is concerned. He's made that clear. But I do like you."

Darryl nods his head. "I've touched a nerve," he realises.

"A bit. The only way you'll see me naked is if I choose to sleep with you, where no money changes hands. Where you'll be – I hope you don't blush or find this too cloying – my *boyfriend*. And if that happens – if I make that decision – I promise I won't be shy."

The door at the front of the shop opens; an old-fashioned bell above its frame tinkles. An older man in a full-length sheepskin coat walks in, removing his trilby as he crosses the threshold and shaking raindrops off it onto the pavement outside.

Carol turns from Darryl again. "This will be a lesson in self-control and patience, won't it? I'll visit Octaves and buy music and tease you by seeming not to give you the time of day. And then one day I'll ask you to lock the front door. What's out back?"

"Small relax area. Kettle and a fridge."

"Chairs?"

"Two kitchen chairs and a small sofa, rather beaten up."

"Then it might be there, you never know. I'll see how I'm feeling. Until then . . ."

Carol returns to the front door, passing the older man and offering him a smile. As she exits the shop and receives her first wind-driven slap of rain to the face, she experiences a proud glow.

*

Dear Chaz (the photocopy of the letter reads),

At the very least I owe you an explanation. Over the last four years I have visited your office, two or three times a week, and I've sat on your couch and spilled my secrets. And I know I haven't always been easy. You were right to think there was something in my past that hurt me and scarred my psyche.

I told you I was a babysitter for a boy called Lucas when I was a teenager. But as far as I know, I never told you the full story.

You know he raped me. I have never made any secret about that – not to you. I was scared of him . . . and yet I went back to the house to babysit, time after time. You hear of murderers who return to the scene of their crimes.

We're drawn back to places that are painful. We return in order to improve on what happened last time, or the time before that. I was a fifteen year-old girl, having a sexual relationship with a nine year-old boy. Did I convince myself he was violent every time? Do I remember it correctly?

So far, the tight, controlled script has reached near the end of the fourth side of a collection of eight sheets of lilac paper. The remaining space on the fourth side is a dense black rectangle of crossings-out and inky obliterations. Lorraine had tried to articulate something else but had been unhappy with what she'd composed.

"She was frightened of what she'd composed," Chaz says into the microphone that protrudes from a headset she is wearing. Software takes her words and reproduces them on the screen.

"Perhaps she was under the influence when she wrote the part that she has destroyed . . . Note to self. Ask WPC Sharon Bark if I'd be allowed to view the original. Failing that, ask if there'll be any attempt made to decipher what she crossed out.

"Question. When did she write the letter? It's not dated. How long before she died did she put pen to paper? Question. How did she know she was going to die if she died of natural causes?"

The fifth side of paper returns to the theme that Lorraine had not finished dealing with.

Even when Lucas was eight, nine he was a big boy – very strong. Built like a rugby player. And I was only sixteen. I didn't know nine year-olds even had those desire!

I don't know if I encouraged him. I don't even know that I didn't like it much. My face burns with shame while I write this, by the way.

Did he know what we did was wrong? It wasn't once. It was more than twice.

And now I've seen him for the first time in twenty-five years, I know I am still scared of him. Which I'm quite sure is what you've been waiting for, Chaz.

Here, Lorraine had drawn a smiling face.

Less than a fortnight before the day I'm due to die, I saw Lucas coming out of Octaves, the music shop on the High Street, with a bag in his hand. He was buying CDs. And I remembered what he used to tell me about jazz.

I almost died there and then, I reckon – but that was never the deal. He used to tell me he would make me lose my life less than two weeks after I'd disappointed him for the final time.

He was nine, right? Do you really think I took that kind of talk seriously? But as soon as I saw him coming out of Octaves, I knew my days were numbered.

I didn't think he saw me . . . but he knew I was there. He could smell me. Sense me.

It was like a pact. I knew I had agreed to die when he saw me next. The only part I didn't know was what next actually meant. After twenty years plus . . . well, you might say I'd rested a bit. I'd learned to take the rough with the smooth.

Lorraine has left a line in the narrative.

Please go to Den for the other half of the full story. And then find the Biscuit Inspector, at Coronet Confectionaries.
All my love,
Lorraine xxx

*

Chaz Bruce-Sange is appreciative of coincidences. She understands their importance in the psychic lives of her patients, but she welcomes them when they arrive in her own life as well.

It is nearly two years since she learned of the coincidence of two of her patients knowing one another as friends and colleagues. Carol had mentioned Lorraine in a session. She'd been describing a dream she'd had, saying, "I'm at a huge wedding celebration. There's food everywhere and I'm trying to eat. My friend Lorraine walks past and I ask her where she's been all these years, since we were kids – even though I didn't know her when we were kids."

The psychoanalyst doesn't ask her patients to describe their dreams. Sometimes they do without being prompted; this one had intrigued Chaz Bruce-Sange. "Who's Lorraine?" she'd wanted to know.

"She's a worker."

Could it be the same Lorraine? Chaz had wondered. "Whose wedding was it?"

"I don't know. I'm not sure if I'm invited or not."

*

Carol Hayes crosses the familiar carpet in the familiar office. "I would like to talk about one of your other patients, if that's okay with you."

"You know it's not, Carol."

The patient sits down in the armchair set at an obtuse angle to the desk. Occasionally she uses the sofa, but today she wants to see her psychoanalyst's eyes. "Patient confidentiality," Carol says. "Except, what if that patient is dead? And what if you – you – might hold a key that unpicks the lock of the mystery?"

"What mystery are you referring to?"

"The *mystery* of my friend Lorraine – or your patient Lorraine, depending on how you want to look at it. The woman with money from an American benefactor, who nonetheless chose to spend time with the homeless."

Chaz Bruce-Sange answers her coldly. "I've explained I can't talk about a specific person in my care."

"She told me you'd help me find answers," Carol states.

"You seem shaky, Carol. Have you been ill?"

If the doctor says *You look like you've seen a ghost,* Carol will leave the office . . .

"That's one way of putting it," Carol admits. "Do group hallucinations count as illness?"

The two women view one another with guarded respect and fear. Ten seconds pass . . .

"Do you believe in ghosts?" Carol asks.

"No."

"I'm surprised you answered that. I thought you'd say: *it depends on what* you *believe, Carol. Define your terms about the word ghost, Carol.*"

"Well I didn't."

"No, you didn't." Carol sips her water, determined not to let Chaz see her glass-holding hand vibrating. She fails to do so. "I'm talking about an occasion – recently – when I saw Lorraine with another woman – a mutual friend – present."

"And what's odd about that?"

"Lorraine was already dead at the time." Carol bites her bottom lip and explains – or unpacks – the experience, using simple vocabulary. *"Someone's remembering you,"* Carol recites. *"You can change what people remember."*

*

Carol chooses to walk home from her appointment with Dr Bruce-Sange, and not only because the next bus is not due for another twenty minutes. She fancies the exercise – and a clearing of her head.

On the High Street, she takes her place at the back end of a short queue that leads to a refreshments van. When it is her turn to order, she changes her mind at the last second and eschews her original plan for a caramel coffee in favour of a mulled wine. Although the fresh air tastes rainy and cold, this is not the reason for her decision: she likes the idea of strolling slowly and watching her breath condense in front of her face while the wine warms the bones beneath her coat.

The botanical gardens are busy, despite the inclement weather. Two artists sit on benches almost opposite from one another; for a moment Carol imagines they are each sketching the other, from either side of a wide bed of hardy perennials. She is tempted to wander around to test her theory. Almost as an afterthought, she notes that both women bear resemblances to Lorraine.

It only takes a few minutes to finish her paper cup of mulled wine; Carol does not pause to sit down – the wooden benches appear damp. The last thing she wants is to catch a cold. Instead, she dumps the cup in a waste bin and strides from the gardens.

Inside the building that she approaches on foot, men and women will step into a square called a ring, with boxing gloves on their hands . . .

Crosstown Trainer is the name of the business. As soon as Carol enters the premises, she can hear the whirr of exercise bike wheels turning at speed; the amplified but muffled voice of a teacher giving her students their instructions. In rooms not visible from this Reception area, weights clank; and from the kiosk in front of Carol, a woman's smile asks if she can be of assistance.

"I wondered if I could have a quick word with Scottish Tony, please. Is he available?"

Carol gives her name and is invited to take a seat over by a water cooler and the receptacle in which people dump their damp towels.

From Scottish Tony's expression it is clear to Carol that he has not appreciated being disturbed while at work. As he sits beside her, he asks her quietly, "What are you doing here?"

"I have a question."

"Not about gym membership, I'm willing to bet."

"About Andreas the European. You said I should be grateful to you because you'd pointed him in my direction, as a customer. You met him here in the gym, you said."

"So?"

"Two things. You said something like: *Is that what he's calling himself these days?* You said you knew him as Giorgio. What *I* want to know is where you know him from. Because I don't imagine for one *second* that the man I call Andreas ever visits a gym."

"Carol – with all due respect – that's none of your business."

Carol has anticipated a show of resistance such as this.

"Tell me, Tony. Does the girl on Reception know you asked me to keep a toothbrush at your place? I wonder what I'll say if anyone asks me what I do for a living."

"Don't play hardball with me, darlin': it doesn't suit you. It's *none of your business*. You can tell *who* you like *what* you like; but don't forget who pays who in this transaction, even if we *are* on a hiatus. One word with a couple of the steroid-and-coke-heads here and they'll be tapping your postcode into a navigation device. The only place they'll stop on their way to yours is the petrol station, to pick up a couple of gallons of unleaded to use on your furniture. Do you *feel me*, Carol?"

"I'm sorry. Did you mean he changes his name a lot?"

"Well, I couldn't tell you *a lot*. I first knew him as Giorgio. He was busking in the Capital. I was doing some business there on a regular basis and I'd see him playing a keyboard, making up tunes on the spot about the people who walked by or sold hot peanuts.

"One day I got talking to Giorgio. He spun me this line about wanting to settle down somewhere else – somewhere away from the Capital – and did I know of a nice town where a musician could compose uninterrupted. He wanted to start again. Said he wanted to inspire and be inspired, but in the Capital no one noticed him. And if I'd help him buy a property, he'd see me all right for a few pounds. He didn't want to tell me why he couldn't approach an estate agent directly – but he made it clear he was a cash buyer.

"Naturally, I thought it was a scam. But I can't say I wasn't impressed by the bare-arsed cheek of the man, so I thought I'd stay on the ride. Then the next time I saw him, a few days later, he showed me the bank statement for his current account. Not even his *savings* account: his *current* account. A busker he might have been, but a *poor* busker he wasn't. He had nigh-on four million in readies, just sitting there. And I'm a businessman, right? *Of course* I was going to lend a hand helping him buy a house where he could play his piano loud."

The scale of Andreas's wealth makes Carol say "Wow." It also makes her feel slightly wobbly; it is a good job that she has remained seated.

If the man is rich, what on earth does he want with me?

"Am I free to go about my day's work, Carol?" Scottish Tony wants to know.

"Nearly . . . If Andreas wanted your help in securing a home, I assume it's not his name on the deeds. So whose name is it?" A second passes; Carol reconsiders. "No. I've asked the wrong question – the name's not important. The important thing is, he wanted to *change* his name. He was Giorgio in the Capital – and when he moves to town, he becomes Andreas. He's running from something."

Scottish Tony shrugs. "Or someone."

Carol nods. "Do you remember, when you told me about him, you tried to ask me something about his beard? Or I *think* that's what you asked."

"No, I don't remember – but Giorgio had a purple beard when he busked. Tidy, neat; and purple. Maybe to attract attention from passers-by; I couldn't tell. I probably asked you if he had his beard on or off when you saw him."

"Yes, quite likely; but what did you mean, *on or off*?"

"Oh, I see. Well, I started to think the man had two faces. Every time I saw him in the Capital – tidy purple beard. In town, here, no beard – and, as it turns out, a different name. So I probably wanted to know if Andreas has a beard when you pay a call."

"No. He's always clean-shaven," Carol answers. "He had a moustache once but not now."

"Then one day, a day after he'd viewed a property here – not the one he ended up buying – he had a chin as smooth as a baby's bottom, as usual. But *literally* the next day I saw him back in the Capital – and the beard was back in place. And no one grows a purple beard overnight."

"You mean it's a fake beard, depending on place? That might not be the most eccentric thing about him."

"You're right. It's the voice, right?" Scottish Tony says. "Two faces – well, *at least* two faces – and at least two voices. Bog-standard Capital accent *there*. Weird Eastern European accent *here*."

"You mean his *accent* is fake?"

"I mean *one* of his accents is fake. It must be. A man has only one face and one accent. Everything else is for someone else's benefit."

6

Saturday.

Billy has been shopping for shirts – three pricey gifts to himself, now that he's had his first payslip from Coronet Confectionaries.

Towards the end of the afternoon, Billy returns home to a house oddly phlegmatic and subdued. Neither the soul-conjoined emotional hydra of Mercy and Noel, nor the meatily aromatic Metal Mickey, occupies the kitchen; furthermore, the latter's clamorous music is conspicuous by its absence. It is like walking into a show home ... until he views the sink. Soiled plates and utensils have been stacked inside it, which is unexpected.

Metal Mickey is a slob but he always completes his washing-up within half an hour of eating, fearful (as is Billy) of one of Noel's admonitory post-it notes. Besides which, there are four plates in there, and Metal Mickey has no one over to share a meal, ever. It is utterly unthinkable that Mercy and Ross have forgotten to do the washing-up – not unless they were called out of the house on an emergency. The only other possibility is Joshua Thou, who rents the converted attic space at a knock-down price but is rarely present.

Having stolen a carelessly unprotected cooked sausage from Mercy and Noel's section of the fridge and collected a can of lager from his own, Billy ascends the staircase. He is just about to holler up to the attic – yell "Holier!" or "Holier Than" – when he spies a piece of paper. The note blu-tacked to Billy's door is written in Mercy's confident, lavish hand:

We're having a house night out at The Anchor. Band playing – Floored Masterpiece. One of Michael's faves, apparently.

The implication is that Billy should join them, and though he longs for a reason not to – a planned phone call to Mumsy, an expected visit from Jemima (some hope!) – he's got nothing in the excuses tank. A callithump evening of second-grade heavy metal it is likely to be, then – with Billy fully aware that if there's one thing worse than heavy metal music, it's *amateur* heavy metal music.

He has a quick wash and then slopes out to The Anchor.

*

The pub's as full as a train at rush hour; bodies are pressed tight against one another. Inside, it is as warm as a llama's tongue. Tables have been moved to the sides to accommodate more punters; a boisterous and noisy parade of tenner-waving customers are lined up four deep at the bar.

Considering ordering two drinks to save time later on, Billy joins the queue while he has no choice but to absorb the din crashing out from the small stage to the right. Occupying the stage is the five-piece known as Floored Masterpiece: two electric guitars, a bass, a drum kit, with the lead vocalist remaining instrument-free and hence able to flick devil's-horns and shake fists at the vengeful Lord of his vocal impoverishments.

Mercy, Ross, Metal Mickey – and even Joshua "Holier Than" Thou – have scored a space near the wall on the left, adjacent to the lavs. Billy joins them, a pint in each hand. Metal Mickey wears a grin so close to imbecilic that Billy wonders if the man has received a blow to the head since the last time they conversed. Metal Mickey is *capitán de navío*, navigating his battered vessel through a storm of hot noise. He even has his right hand on his belt buckle, fingers noodling, and his left arm extended as he plays an imaginary guitar.

"Evening, wanker," Billy says to Metal Mickey.

A lodestar of sartorial bad taste, with his long convex body and his dark hair slicked into fully tumescent spikes that could have someone's eye out (not to mention the meaty aroma that swarms around him like a halo), Metal Mickey is erinaceous in appearance. The fact that he habitually wears matador boots, with iridescent socks and a matching shirt, often with daffodil yellow chinos so tight about the crotch that you can deduce his religion, does nothing to dispel the hedgehog comparison.

"What was that?" Metal Mickey shouts.

"I said: All right, Michael?"

"Yeah . . . Aren't they brilliant?"

The band is competent enough, Billy allows, but it's not his type of music. He prefers something with less angst driving it (he's had enough *angst* in his twenty-nine years). However, this is one of those rare house nights out and he wishes to savour his dislike of it for some time yet, so he goes in slowly. "Yeah, they'll do," he answers.

Predictably enough, it is Ross who looks the most out of place and miserable. *I've just eaten one of your sausages, mate,* Billy thinks as he pays attention to bellowing hello to the man and asking him at the top of his lungs how his day has been. He is more than usually pleased with the expression of grumpy discomfort that Ross exhibits.

Meanwhile, through the heat and the fracas from the band, Mercy grins like a schoolgirl on a stage herself. In the past, more times than several, Billy has wondered if there is anything on Planet Earth that upsets her. From the gentle trickles of music that sporadically leak from the room she shares with Ross, Billy has inferred that her preferences lie with energetic gospel, occasionally a ration of Bob Marley or Peter Tosh. So how can she be so cheerful in the presence of *this* cacophony?

"What are you doing on Bank Holiday Monday, Billy?" she asks.

"Why?"

"We're all up for it, the rest of us: a gardening day. The back garden's a bit of a mess."

Billy doles out a smile of contentious provenance. "Fine. I'm up for it too. Bagsy the lawnmower."

"Michael has already bagsied it. He made a joke about heavy metal and he made me laugh."

Yeah, I bet he did, the acrid little twat. "That's okay. Put me on secateurs duty. I'll trim the bumfluff off the bushes. It's no problem."

Gardening days are an ordeal for Billy. While he understands that the housemates have to keep the back garden tidy for the landlord, he would rather that they all took turns than the entrapment of being all together, clipping things and binning things and using blunt tools from the landlord's shed to hack at weeds and remove the calcified portions of pigeon- and cat-crap.

"Ross has voted for the secateurs," Mercy replies.

"So what's *my* job?"

"Cleaning the path, stones." Mercy shows no sign of requiring any lip-reading skills. It's as if Floored Masterpiece is a riverside chamber orchestra, pleasant and non-distracting.

Brilliant. *On my knees for three hours with a washing-up bowl of suds and a scouring brush.*

"That sounds great!" Billy says.

When Floored Masterpiece brings to a raucous close a song that seems to be called "My Sputum Blues" and introduces

"Hammering the Glans", an increase in energy is palpable – both among the band itself and among The Anchor's customers.

Billy steps outside for a smoke and to phone Jemima, who is . . .

*

. . . less than two miles away from The Anchor and not within aural distance of her phone's chimes.

"I thought I might stay in tonight," Jemima announces.

"Why? It's not my birthday," her husband replies. "Why change the habit of a lifetime?"

"Or I could go to my piano lesson. I haven't been for a couple of weeks."

Lucas's reply is both weary and subservient; but first he sighs. "Do as you wish, Jemima. I won't fight it." He leans over and prods at the car's engine with a spanner as large as a policeman's truncheon. There's a clang of metal on metal, short-lived but blunt enough for Lucas to make his point.

"Don't forget, Lucas. I *never once* said I'd be a stay-at-home wife."

Lucas straightens his back quickly, waving the spanner like a weapon. "*What,* Jemima? If someone put a knife to your heart *right now* and demanded to know what you wanted out of life, what would you answer?"

Sometimes she cannot understand that she is married; it seems like a joke whose punchline she cannot fathom. She looks back on her first year at university as on the precise movements of water in a geyser or a whirlpool.

Pausing briefly in the hallway of the house that he'd moved her into, Jemima examines the simple but beautiful ring on her left hand. She remembers the summer's day and the gorgeous beige dress that she'd worn, the olive green suit that Lucas had donned. Tipsy on sparkling wine, after the service and when the guests had started to drift away, Lucas and Jemima had returned to this very hallway. In the hours since they'd left the building, Jemima had been given a new surname; she had been awarded a duo of syllables to annex to her existing Sange. She had become Jemima Sange-Reardon. Although the name had seemed unwieldy, Jemima had been adamant that she would not give up the *Sange*.

Jemima collects her lilac handbag from under the hallway table. She closes the door gently as she exits, feeling wistful – almost romantic. She closes the front gate behind her and walks onto the darknened street – and steps straight into a meniscus of rainwater collected in a broken paving slab. Water leaps up her leg and drenches her tights.

Marvellous.

From inside her handbag, her phone rings. Jemima entertains a brief moment of hope: that the call will be from Lucas, begging her home. No, *ordering* her home. *And I mean now, Jemima, or you won't know what's good for you. Get back in this house.*

Oh, please don't be cross, Lucas, Jemima wheedles.

Never mind cross, her husband demands. *It's now or I'm locking the front door. You can sleep in the front garden – or with your boyfriend – but don't darken my doorstep again, I'm telling you.*

But the phone call isn't from Lucas, of course.

"Hi, Billy." Sometimes she enjoys impersonating the prison slang and accent that he never appears keen to teach her, saying that some of those old times were scary business. "*Wogwun, blood?*" Jemima half-asks and half-greets.

Billy snickers in her ear. "Allow it, ting. Are you listening?"

"I'm listening."

"Man in yanker rudeboy visit anna ting."

Jemima hesitates. "No, okay, you got me on that one. What did you say?"

"I'm in The Anchor. Do you wanna come over for a drink?"

"I'll see you there in a bit," she says with a hint of sadness.

*

Floored Masterpiece beats up the air again, this time for the encore to their set.

Billy Alfreth is outside for a smoke. "So I can't help but be curious," he is relieved to be able to say in his normal voice at its normal volume. He sits on one of the parched picnic tables. The smokers' area is grey with moonlight. He is with Mercy. "Did you have guests for dinner tonight?"

"No, Billy. Why do you ask?"

"The plates in the sink."

Mercy gives Billy a look. "No plates in the sink, Billy, not with Ross on crockery patrol."

"Now I feel like a snitch. It must've been Holier Than."

"We all left the house together, Billy."

The band leads a chant that sounds like "sweaty anïi"; to Billy's ears it is uncharacteristically melodic – in fact, the best thing they've played throughout their set.

Billy shrugs and says, "Well, they're not mine, so no one can ask me to wash 'em up. I wonder if Norman's been round."

Norman is their landlord.

"Why would Norman dirty our dishes?" Mercy asks.

By the time that Jemima arrives, Billy is a fuzzy bundle of rage. "I called you an hour ago!"

They stand outside.

"Patience is a virtue, Billy," Jemima retorts.

Billy has had four pints; he is in *no mood.* "I'm serious, Jemima, I was worried. You said you were coming and I've been sat on my tod for over an hour! You could've *called.*"

Jemima frowns. "*I don't want to be worried about.*"

Billy's sigh tastes of lager and nicotine; there's a salty residue at the top of his epiglottis. "What are you doing? I don't mean right this minute. I mean, with your life and mine? What's in the bag?"

"I thought I'd stay over if Your Majesty obliges. I've bought us a bottle of brandy. Some cooked chicken, crisps and dips. I thought we might have a midnight party."

*

The weather on Bank Holiday Monday being cool but fine, the housemates are all in the back garden. Billy is dressed in his oldest clothes, on his knees on the path, with a scouring pad in one hand and a bucket of steaming water by his left hip. It is his task to clean the path. They've been working for two hours and the garden doesn't look any different.

Why did you marry him? Billy had asked Jemima once, not long after she and Lucas had honeymooned. (The honeymoon had hurt him like a hair-vest. The ten days had passed like sessions of soul torture.) And then, there he was, less than a week after her return, enquiring after her *modus operandi* while the sweat cooled on their chests, in his bed.

Picking a hair from between two teeth, Jemima had considered Billy's question with sincere self-reflection. *He's financially stable and he doesn't try to boss me around,* she'd said.

He's your dad, in other words.

So what? All women marry their fathers in one way or another.

Billy walks back towards the house but does not enter via the kitchen. Instead he heads down the passage and tangos his way past the trio of colossal rubbish receptacles that block his path. On the street in front of the house, he sits on the wall and watches the traffic. While lighting a cigarette, he looks up to his left – and his arm freezes halfway to his mouth.

A dog trots in his direction. A Labradoodle, without an owner.

Although Billy is no expert when it comes to dogs, his instincts tell him that this is the same animal that was trapped in the Volvo in the business park car park.

Billy raises his buttocks from the brickwork. "This can't be happening again," he says to the dog when it stops a metre from him on the pavement. The dog is trailing no leash – it has not escaped from an owner and run away. "You've come to see me, haven't you?"

The dog nods.

"What's your name?"

"Narna . . . Thank you for setting me free."

The words were never designed for a mouth belonging to any species but *homo sapiens*. The dog's jaws move in what appear to be painful contortions. The words are slurred and include glottal pauses for gulps for air; a thin wheezy whine accompanies their production.

Checking up and down the street for pedestrians, Billy asks, "Were you human once?"

Narna the Labradoodle shakes his head and body with vigour, as if displacing raindrops from his fur. "Have you got any food?"

"Are you real?" Billy asks.

"She has *no piano lesson* to go to," Lucas answers . . . then sprints away.

*

Billy wakes from a terrible dream.

He was riding a horse in a desert – a horse with his mother's facial features. The horse was called Mumsy. The sky was the colour of toffee; a bracelet-shaped moon swivelled fast among clouds that resembled yoots he'd once known at Dellacotte Young Offenders.

His old friend Ostrich had squeezed himself out of a cloud and glided down to the desert floor on wings made of diamonds. "Wogwun, blood," Ostrich said.

"Allow it."

"Tell me, Billy. I got a question for you – are you listening?"

"Man listening," Billy answered in the vocabulary that had once seemed natural.

"What's the name of man's town?"

"*Allow* it, Ostrich-fam man!"

"Point blank, blood. Where do Billy *live*?"

Billy flounders among the memories that have shifted over into the world of his desert dream. He cannot remember the name of the place where he lives. There is no word.

On waking, he cannot remember the word either.

*

Tuesday after the Bank Holiday, and it's the beginning of Billy's fifth week at Coronet Confectionaries. Disturbed by the dream, and having overcome a scrotum-tightening fear of going into work at all, Billy walks up to the security cabin and bids a good morning to Danny Lovell.

All is well until 11:46 by the clock in the corner of Billy's PC. It is at this point that Anne-Marie moves over to his desk in the open plan office and bends slightly at the ample waist.

"When you've got a minute, Billy, Pat's asked to have a word."

Anne-Marie gives Billy *that look*: the one he had all but got used to before she went off work on compassionate leave after the death of her half-sister.

"Anne-Marie, I just wanted to say ... "

"Thank you, Billy – but don't. The funeral's next Wednesday. I appreciate your concern for my wellbeing," Anne-Marie adds, "and for once I'm not taking the piss."

Billy and Pat share a sofa in the latter's office. Pat begins by explaining that Billy is not being singled out and that all men will be asked a similar question until the culprit is found. Pat would like to make it clear that he does not honestly believe that Billy would have gone to such silly lengths as to produce the offending item – and here he hands Billy an A4-sized laminated sheet – but that it wouldn't be fair to exclude Billy from the investigation. In big bold letters, the sign reads:

IF YOU'RE IN DOUBT, FLUSH IT ANYWAY
YOU FILTHY PIECE OF WANKERDOM

It's the sign that Terry Bates created. Knowledge of the perpetrator puts Billy in an awkward position, and he is forced to lie when Pat asks him if he knows who made the sign. When Billy leaves Pat's office, he is angry that he should have been put in such a position ... but ludicrously, he is also protective of Terry Bates.

Billy finds Terry easily enough: Terry is rushing pell-mell down the corridor – in the direction of Pat's office – towards Billy. Billy holds up a hand and says, "Wait!"

"Mate, I can't!" Terry protests. "I've got the turtle's head! It's a race against *time*."

Making a snap decision, Billy turns on his heels and follows Terry in the direction of the Gents' toilets. One of the Duncans has a place by a wash basin and is busy rubbing ink from the palm of his left hand. Otherwise, the Gents is deserted.

"Run for your life, mate," Terry warns the Duncan. "I'm touching cloth." He slams the cubicle door shut from the inside (it rattles on its hinges) and Billy is able to hear the warble of panicked whining from Terry and the rustle of the lower half of his body's clothing as it finally slumps to the ground.

"I need to talk to you, Terry," says Billy.

Terry's response is a plaintive anal exhalation. "Not *now* for fuck's sake! This cunt's the Second Coming! Gunna need a *blood* transfusion."

"For what we are about to receive," Terry grunts – and the Duncan leaves the Gents with an expression on his face that speaks clearly of consternated bemusement. "Take cover! Incoming!"

"It's just that Pat Kelly wants to know who did the sign," he says. "He's on the warpath."

"I'm lightheaded, mate," Terry answers (and his voice does indeed give Billy the impression of someone on the verge of authentic cerebral collapse). "What sign are you talking about?"

"The one you put in here – the one about flushing the toilet."

"Mate, I haven't . . . Hang on."

The sound that reaches Billy's ears is like oil bubbling, followed by that of a small car landing in a river; throughout these sound effects, Terry maintains the pained or jubilant yodel of Tarzan, swinging from tree to tree. Billy holds the heels of his hands to his ears, but only for a few seconds, because he then needs one hand to pinch his nostrils together.

In due course, Billy observes Terry's emergence from the prison cell of his own toilet cubicle. It is abundantly clear that Billy's work colleague has done hard time on the porcelain torture unit. Terry's face is alabaster.

"I suppose I'd better wash my hands," he concedes.

"I suppose you'd better flush away your timebomb as well," Billy advises. "It doesn't work by magic, you know."

"Silly me." Terry steps back to the stall and presses the silver button. "Good luck to it getting rid of *that* python," he adds with a smirk. "Now, you were saying."

Despite the sentences that they have already shared, Billy experiences the urge to recapitulate. "When I first started here, you showed me a sign you'd written – or printed. About people should flush the bog when they've finished." Billy even adds a half-hearted interrogative inflection to the final clause. But all he faces is Terry's blank stare. "Don't tell me you don't remember! How can you forget something like that?" he asks with anger.

"Because it weren't me, Billy-Boy!" Terry retorts. "Shall we go for a post-fecal fag?"

"No we shan't, Tel. We can go for a smoke when you've *admitted* to me you produced a sign you were going to hang in the Gents' because someone was abusing the facilities."

For the first time in the exchange, Terry sounds riled. "It weren't me. You've mixed me up. And now, if you'll excuse me, I have some work to avoid while I go for a cigarette."

Dutifully, Billy steps aside, his mind a choked nest of disparate strands.

After Terry has left the loo, Billy remains where he's been stripped of his dignity and composure. *It's happening again,* he thinks. *After all these years . . . it's happening again.*

7

After the Bank Holiday weekend, when the Biscuit Inspector gets ready for his walk to work, a corner of his mind is occupied by thoughts of Jemima. He is not sure why he was so surprised when she phoned him on Saturday night, but he supposes it was because he always assumes his little girl to be otherwise engaged on a Saturday night (for example, in a crack den some-where) and that he would be a cosmic distance from her im-mediate thoughts. So engrained has this conception been for so long that when Jemima *did* call, the Biscuit Inspector's first thought was that she must be in trouble.

"Do I want the good news or the bad news, as the saying goes?"

"The bad news won't be bad for you, don't worry, Dad," Jemima answered. "But it's made me a bit sad and confused."

"Go on then – bad news first," the Biscuit Inspector said.

In truth, he had felt far from resilient at the time. Seeing Lorraine's body on the High Street had shaken him, there was no doubt about it. The Biscuit Inspector has purchased her time on a dozen or so occasions, to complain about aspects of his life – such as why his daughter rarely called him, ironically enough. Once the Biscuit Inspector had come to terms with who was lying on the High Street, and once he'd given his instructions on how the matter would be handled, he had managed to continue his stroll to work, feeling sick, and had intended to make the vomitorium at Coronet Confectionaries his first pit stop of the morning. He hadn't got that far. Sensing the urge to vomit, the Biscuit Inspector had tried to find a secluded place to do so, but had ended up regurgitating down the side of a poor sod's brand new QashQai.

Jemima hesitated.

"Are you pregnant?" her father asked.

"No. And before we get any further into the *obvious* ones, no I'm not doing drugs either. I had a shock, that's all. One of the lecturers at Uni was found dead up north. He was murdered."

"One of *your* lecturers?"

"No; but I saw him around the corridors and in the coffee shops. I knew who he was." Preparing for something else, she paused. "These tramps kicked him to death, Dad!" There were tears in Jemima's voice. "And it made me think of when they attacked *you*. We could've lost you . . . and I think it took his death to . . . to make me realise how lucky we were."

"Oh, darling," said the Biscuit Inspector.

"And do you know the weird thing? He was *dressed* like them. He had a long grey wig on, make-up stubble . . . He was trying to fit into their clan. And his life was ended because of it."

Now, as he leaves the house and begins his walk, he is not sure if he was successful at soothing his daughter's troubled mind. Something about what she'd said had troubled his own: not the murder *per se,* or its resemblance to the kicking that he had received himself, but the identity of the murdered man. The Biscuit Inspector had not liked the description of the long grey wig one little bit . . .

He had asked the name of the man who'd been killed. With his forefinger trembling slightly, he touched on his phone's tiny keys to search for FINLEY REEDON MURDER NORTH ENGLAND. And although he'd misheard the surname that his daughter had provided, and although she'd been sketchy on the county, the search engine had performed admirably.

And there was a photograph.

The Biscuit Inspector had used his thumb and the same forefinger to expand the picture as wide and high as it would go in the phone's frame.

He is on the High Street now. He takes deep breaths and his legs feel heavy, even though he has not exercised over the weekend. If the man called Finley really *was* the man the Biscuit Inspector calls Frank, then why would he have been in the north of the country, in his guise as the latter?

"What was his name?" the Biscuit Inspector wants to know. "*I* knew him as Frank – which seems ironic in the circumstances – but he was Finley to some people. So, what was his real name?"

"Frank," say a trio of the group.

"Finley, it must have been," a woman with pockmarks on her cheeks disputes. "I mean, it has to be the name he had in the working world."

The Biscuit Inspector is curious and he cocks his head. "Why's that?"

"Because *their* world has more weight than *ours,*" she answers.

The Biscuit Inspector starts doling out pound coins, one each. On this sad day – sad for them and sad for him – he asks for nothing in return. He is almost speechless. It is not until he has reached the business park and has said good morning to Danny Lovell in his cabin that the Biscuit Inspector is able to read the scribbled handwriting of his emotions. First the group lost Lorraine and now Frank, but *so did he* – and the loss is brutal. The Biscuit Inspector imagines himself falling over the edge of a cliff; he is sweating by the time he reaches his office.

I'm in mourning, he tells his computer screen. *So this is what mourning feels like . . .*

He is sluggish until lunchtime. Knowing that something should be done does not help because he doesn't know what the something is. He is bothered and bewildered. He is angry.

It takes the Biscuit Inspector until after a lunch (a sandwich from the van that visits the business park on Mondays and Wednesdays) to understand that he wants revenge. He wants to avenge Frank's death – and to do this, first he must comprehend it.

*

Danny Lovell has been dreading the rolling-around of Tuesday morning. All through the elongated Bank Holiday weekend he has been worried about what will happen when he gets to work. In his focus-free dreams he sees the dog that he freed from the back seat of the man's car. Under its meat-coloured breath, the dog mutters out a guttural stream that sounds like profanities but is not.

"Don't remember me," the dog repeats. "I don't want to be remembered."

Deliberately, consciously, Danny chooses to park near where the dog-prison car remains parked. On leaving his own vehicle, he locks up. He gives the Volvo the once over, but there's nothing strange about it, other than its actual physical presence (shouldn't the breakdown service have towed it away by now? he wonders). And half expecting the dog to be circling the vehicle, now that he knows it's not inside, Danny is both relieved and disappointed to glance no creature on such a scale. The only living animals on the scene are bluebottle flies. Two of them in particular dart close to his head; they swim the air in hexagonal circuits.

Danny unlocks and opens the Security cabin. He uses the ten-gallon drum of water on its tripod perch to fill his kettle; flicks the switch. When the water inside the kettle gives off sounds of early agitation, he begins to feel a bit better; he tries to concentrate on his morning routine. But his thoughts are as jumbled as linguini, and he cannot stop thinking about the dog.

Among other matters. While he listens to the water boiling in the kettle, he thinks of when he had emerged from the bunker underground – the Ark as it had been known – and he had wanted to get back to more mundane work. On reporting for duty, however, he was told that he needed time off: paid leave was authorized for a block of two weeks, with the assurance that the fortnight could be the first of many. For Danny it had felt punitive, as though he'd done something wrong; he had taken it as a criticism of his failure.

Why didn't he shoot me? Danny wonders.

Unnoticed kettle steam curls up into the cabin's top corners. The noise of water boiling does not jab holes in his reverie. If anything, the steam and the bubbling water help to blur the present; to create a frame of mind that will lend weight to the fantasy.

And then a face appears at his open window.

"Remember me, twat?" says the man who owns the broken-down Volvo.

*

A letter has arrived on the Biscuit Inspector's work desk. This missive is unusual because it is sealed in an envelope with only his first name on the front, below an underlined gobbet in capital letters that reads 'DELIVERED BY HAND'.

The Biscuit Inspector tears the envelope open. He drags free two pieces of standard white A4 paper, with an unpredictable and inconsistent scrawl scratched thereon. The ink is dark blue, a fountain pen ink, much the same as the ink that emerges from the pen that Chaz bought him for an anniversary present, seven years earlier (although the two of them had been divorced by that point). The thought enters his mind that it was Chaz who delivered the letter; however, Chaz writes with confidence; whoever has written this lacks both confidence and the skill of writing with a fountain pen.

Dear Kieran,

Surprise surprise! It's Lorraine speaking . . . or writing. No doubt you know I'm dead. No doubt you won't be shocked by my death, either –

That's not fair, the Biscuit Inspector interjects silently. I *was* shocked.

I thought about a way to explain to you that you wouldn't be in any doubt about.

I'd like you to think of a packet of biscuits – the Mayfair Mellow, for argument's sake. And imagine you open the packet . . . and every single biscuit is broken! What would you do? Take them back to the shop? Complain to the manufacturer?

Try to piece them back together, one by one?

Well, consider my death and this letter as an appeal to the jigsaw puzzle-solver in your soul. I want you to put me back together again – to glue my story into a tapestry.

When I was yet to escape the prison of my teens, I suffered an experience that might have sent others packing. But I want you to know that I did not commit suicide. Lucas killed me.

"Who the dickens is Lucas?" I hear you ask. "Can she possibly mean my son-in-law?"

Allow me to elaborate. The experience in my teens involved babysitting a young boy named Lucas. Not to put too fine a point on it, he went mental. He was obsessed with his Uncle Raymond, who was in the funny farm for what I thought at the time were violent crimes – bombs, for example.

When Lucas was a boy – and I do mean boy – he either raped me or I raped him. I keep getting this wrong, as soon as I've fixed on what it was. I think I raped him.

But that doesn't mean I believe him.

It is not true to say that the Biscuit Inspector thinks back on his own encounters with Lorraine at this point, although the memories of her body drift in and out of his consciousness. It is more like the letter – and the physical holding of it – are Lorraine herself; Lorraine as the Biscuit Inspector knew her, but a Lorraine far wider than this narrow focus.

She knew she was going to die, the Biscuit Inspector tells himself. *She had time to write me a letter.*

I knew he would find me eventually . . . though I wasn't hiding. I've come to learn – already – that we are being remembered, like nostalgia. But we don't have to be remembered the way we are if we don't want to. We can change the way people remember us. I don't know that this is what Lucas's reappearance is meant to have shown, but it showed it anyway.

Nostalgia is a bringing or binding together; a conjunction of either happy memories or of a large mosaic memory, shared by many, of something that happened in the so-called good old days.

It is not about me and what I remember.

It is not about you and what you remember.

Nostalgia is a clue that it's time to challenge what we think we remember. The most startling thing about my teenage years (to put it mildly) was the incident in which I took Lucas to his Uncle Raymond's room in the asylum. Things happened on that day that do not compute. They are false. And it's not for me to tell you what to think. It's for me to tell you to think.

Find Mr Latham. Find Lucas.

Believe it or not, all my love,

Lorraine xxx

P.S. You'll be wondering who I convinced to deliver this letter to you by hand. The answer is no one. I delivered it myself. I walked past your colleagues and no one said a word to me, though some turned their heads in the way that animals on the mesa might turn their heads, fearful of an unseen predator. One or two of them knew I was there . . . but they didn't see me. Or to put it another way, perhaps, they didn't want to see me, and so I passed through like a current.

Which in turn will make you ask how I knew to write this bit before I walked a letter through your offices and corridors. The answer is: I didn't. I wrote this here. At your desk. You'll recognise the ink if you compare it with the ink in the fountain pen you have in your Nick Cave mug.

*

Such is his fear of the sadists and weirdos who occupy the position of *dentists*, that Darryl Carbrini cannot so much as book an appointment to have the pain in his teeth checked, let alone walk into a clinic or a surgery. What he *can* do, however, is investigate his symptoms on the Web. Two words have snagged on his attention, and both of them start with the disgusting prefix *gomph*.

The first word is *gomphiasis*. It means a looseness of the teeth, which Darryl is convinced he will suffer with before long. The toothache to which he seems set to be martyred is not as bad as it's been, but it has accomplished a fuller reach across his gums. This morning, strolling as usual through the botanical gardens, he had glanced up into an *eau-de-nil* sky . . . and the clouds had resembled teeth in the jaws of the heavens.

It had scared him something rotten.

The second word that Darryl has learned is *gomphosis:* the growth of teeth into the bone cavity. Try as Darryl might, he cannot believe that this option represents a much better proposition for a healthy and pain free lifestyle in the near future.

Awakened early by pain (and by a pre-dawn dream concerning Carol Hayes), Darryl had left the house before his usual time, slightly tripped on a build-up of codeine pills that have been in the kitchen cupboard for nearly three years, since they were prescribed by a doctor after Darryl hurt his back on a sponsored cycle for charity. Since self-medicating on this old stock at the commencement of his various toothaches, he has been vaguely high on occasion, and his belly has been troubled.

As is his way, he stops in the botanical gardens for what he predicts will be his customary ten minutes of loose meditation before ambling on to Octaves. He sits on his usual bench. Birdsong sweetens the air; insects buzz and hum in the organised blooms. The day is at rest and will shortly become busy, but there is always tranquillity in the gardens. He is not certain if his head is swaying slightly or if this is an effect of his self-medication; either way, it is not unpleasant. His thoughts turn to Carol and what she'd said about having sex with him on her terms. Then he thinks about the dream that he'd had of her ... and he frowns.

It had not been a loving dream; not a sex dream either. In the dream, Darryl had floated in a bubble filled with a liquid through which he could breathe. Carol was outside the bubble, a conductor's baton in her right hand. She led an orchestra that Darryl could neither see nor hear. With a flick of her wrist she controlled the bubble and made its vibrations more intense or less so. It was then that Darryl had started to panic. He knew that if Carol could control the bubble then she could also conduct his *teeth*.

Darryl's teeth resembled pebbles as they fell, one by one, from his mouth. They slid over his lower lip and he tried to protest. A tooth came loose and Darryl tried to put it back in his mouth; but another one slipped out when he tried! His teeth came free and floated in the balloon's fluid.

Without knowing he's doing it, Darryl raises a hand to his jaw and rubs his cheek, as if for assurance. His teeth are still in his mouth. With his other hand he starts to fiddle with his bowtie. His tongue finds a tooth that he hasn't brushed adequately, way back on the upper left – a molar. The tooth is as rough as builders' sand. Darryl knows that he'll worry about this tooth for his entire working day; that he'll be unable to stop his tongue prodding it.

When he looks up and to his left, Darryl observes a woman approach. She is in her late thirties or early forties; and although the sun remains low, hindering a reasonable visual assessment of her appearance, Darryl is certain that she is expensively dressed. It is only when she has walked closer, however, that he is able to see who it is. Such is the extent to which his breath catches that he is unable to make his brain drag his tongue from the bad tooth.

It's the dead woman on the High Street.

In her purple heels, her business suit, her threadbare pancake and with her hair done up and resisting gravity . . . it's the woman that Darryl saw lying dead surrounded by the town's tramps – the murder of crows with their stolen prize possession.

"Won't you invite a dead girl to sit down?" Lorraine asks.

It's the medication, Darryl counters silently. *The medicine's made me barmy.*

"No it hasn't," Lorraine informs him as she sits down. "Touch me if you want to check."

Darryl smells her perfume. He also notes that the temperature has risen in the previous few seconds.

"In the absence of your greeting," says Lorraine, "can I at least confirm you remember me?"

Darryl has shifted slightly away from Lorraine, towards the end of the bench. He nods his head slowly.

"That's something at least," Lorraine tells him. "Now, some people are faces people and some are names people. Pretty clearly I can remember your face. Your name's a blank."

"Darryl Carbrini."

"Darryl'll do. This isn't a job interview. Darryl. And what's mine?"

"*Lorraine.*" Darryl rallies and takes stock. Phrasing himself with immaculate precision, he asks, "So what brings you to these gardens – and to me?"

"A favour. Though you don't owe me a damn thing," Lorraine explains.

"Go on."

"I'm on tour," Lorraine tells him. "I'm going around the people I know or knew. I have a teeny tiny task for you, if you're willing to accept it."

*

"My name is Chaz Bruce-Sange. I was Lorraine's psychoanalyst for a number of years."

Den has been drinking bourbon, Chaz suspects. He stands like a guard in front of his five-bedroom mock-Georgian home.

"I wondered if I might have a word," Chaz continues, standing on the path that leads from the quiet road to the eye of Den's grief. "Lorraine left me a letter and she hints in it you might have one too. I think she intended for us to put our minds together."

"You'd better come in."

8

It is the day of Lorraine's cremation.

Early morning cloud cover colliquated hours earlier and now the mourners swelter in dark clothes under a pulsing blue sky. Ambling breezes pass infrequently, and many a forefinger is swiped around the inside of a tight shirt collar. Even when the group is invited to enter the chapel at the allotted time of eleven-fifteen, they find that the service's official – the life celebrant (so called) – appears hot herself in the cooler white. Her upper middle-aged face, heavy with jowls, is red and sweaty at the hairline.

Thirty or forty in number, the mourners take places in the pews. Among them is a psychoanalyst, Chaz Bruce-Sange, and a good number of Lorraine's work colleagues and her associates from the street-life part of her snuffed existence. A policeman is sitting at the very back of the congregation, in uniform. Once they have taken their seats, Carol asks Robbie who the policewoman is. "She's on the case," Robbie explains. "That's Sharon Bark."

Sex workers, the homeless and the law: quite likely the most unusual service that Carol will ever attend.

When the life celebrant starts speaking, she introduces herself as Cecilia Hatton. Carol is four rows from the front, staring at the woman and trying to place her accent. The woman's voice is plummy but with unexpected dips and rises in pitch; she makes Carol think of someone who has suffered a stroke and has learned again how to talk.

"I would like to introduce," she says, "the concept of psychomachy – the conflict between the body and the soul."

Wait a minute, Carol thinks. *Cecilia Hatton.* She remembers a girl from school called Cecilia; in an attempt to stop people singing the Simon and Garfunkel song at her, the girl had started to call herself Cilly – "Silly with a C", she'd explain. What if the life celebrant also goes by Cilly when she arrives home to her plump husband? Cilly Hatton. *Silly hat on!* Carol is able to avoid laughing by dipping her face into her joined and cupped hands, pretending that she is stifling tears.

Concentrate! What's wrong with you? she demands, as if to a second person.

The answer is simple, of course: she has come to the cremation service but she does not want to listen. She does not want to know how this woman at the front of the chapel has decided to decode and fragment Lorraine's life on the planet. She does not want to know how other people think Lorraine lived.

"It is fair to say, I believe, that Lorraine spent difficult years among us . . ."

You didn't know her, Carol thinks. *It's not fair for you to reinterpret her.* Carol wishes that she had said yes when Lorraine's half-sister, Anne-Marie, had offered her a five-minute slot to read a tribute as part of the proceedings. Carol had cried off, pleading fear of speaking in public; and although this happens to be true, she wishes that she had confronted those fears. No one would have blamed her if she'd welled up or forgotten her place in whatever sketchy script she had rustled together. She is not an actress.

"Now we will play a favourite piece of music of Lorraine's," Cecilia Hatton announces, "chosen for us by Anne-Marie. And while we hear this selection, I invite you to think of Lorraine and to remember her in a way that is appropriate for you.

Anne-Marie has asked that we not sing hymns because Lorraine did not share the faith that shapes my own life, which is her prerogative."

Just before the music begins, Carol thinks what an easy job it must be, being a life celebrant. How many services do they get through in a day? What do they earn? And all we have to do is listen to a bit of music . . . easy money! On recognising the opening bars of Shostakovich's Tenth, Carol smiles.

Of all composers – now at this point, at this event – Shostakovich!

Fate's playing games, Carol voices carefully inside her head, suddenly convinced that Lorraine can hear her thoughts from within the soundproofing of the dark wood coffin on its marble plinth. *Or is it you, Lorraine?* her mind asks as loudly as she dares it to.

If Lorraine can hear her, there is no sign of a successful transmission. The air is full of sound, with the contrapuntal additions of mourners' sniffles. Apart from these noises, all that she is aware of is the buzzing of a fly that weaves towards her, time after time. As a girl she had been convinced that flies wanted to land in a child's eyes and eat her from the inside out. It takes perseverance to lose some of our juvenile beliefs, and to this day she hates flies buzzing close; her fingers swipe at the air before her face with circular motions.

Given everything that she has seen, Carol wants to believe that the fly is Lorraine – her new shell. With her left hand she reaches out to take Roberta's right. They do not look at one another.

Shostakovich's Tenth is granted three minutes of air-time.

Cecilia Hatton brings the ceremony to a close; more tears are shed while the mourners watch the curtains close in front of the coffin. The mourners spill out into the heatwave.

Carol leaves disappointed that Lorraine has not shown her a fresh sign. She thinks of the celebrant and of how she hoped that Lorraine would rest in peace.

"No rest for the wicked," Roberta announces; but Carol is not sure what she means.

Or who.

Memory constructs the past, and reconstructs it. This is not a question of revising the facts but, as with the modifications in neurological pathways, of placing experiential information in new – sometimes larger and richer – contexts. In that sense, the past changes under the pressure of the present, as well as vice versa.

Eva Hoffman, *Time*

Sweeter than the flesh of hard apples is to children
The green water penetrated my hull of fir . . .
. . . And at times I have seen what man thought he saw!

Arthur Rimbaud,
'The Drunken Boat'

Our minds manipulate our recollections, to tell us things about ourselves we don't otherwise know, and can't know, because they are painful, or dangerous, or at odds with other important ideas we have about ourselves.

Matthew von Unwerth,
Freud's Requiem

LATER

1

Derek Latham has worked on the railway for most of his adult life. He has seen it all, he believes – until this morning.

Checking tickets on trains all over the country, he has seen the drop-down drunk behaving outrageously on late journeys from the Capital; seen disagreements and fist fights (he was once attacked himself while trying to intervene in an altercation between a young man and his girlfriend – they had both turned on him). More than a few times he has chanced upon a couple kissing with heat; he was once present for the conclusion to a solitary handjob, and seven or eight times he has viewed the act itself, right there across a double seat, the woman with her bottom up for grabs and her partner galloping hard against her hips. However . . .

He has never seen anything like *this*.

Before the sight greets his eyes, it is the impact of the aroma that must be endured. With his ticket machine on a strap around his neck, Derek moves from Carriage B to Carriage C and announces "Tickets, please" – when the stench assaults him.

At first he believes that it's the mass of people crowded into this carriage, irrespective of the fact that the majority of them are dressed in suits and smarts for their trip north. He frowns. Why are so many pressed into this carriage anyway? From the driver's cab he had watched the passengers on the most recent platform embark. There hadn't been more than twenty, and yet the aisle is chock-a-block, the vestibule crammed.

It isn't until Derek has checked his fifth ticket (while wondering if the toilet up ahead is blocked and should be classed as out of order) that someone tells him that it shouldn't be allowed.

"What shouldn't be allowed, madam?"

"Them manky tramps," the woman answers, tossing her retro bouffant in the direction of Carriage D or beyond. "It's not *their* bloody train – and I bet they ain't got tickets!"

"We'll see about that," Derek tells her with a stern nod. "How many tramps are we talking about, madam?"

"About ten. Stunk the bloody carriage out. That's why we're all packed in here like bloody sardines. I pay five grand a year for me season ticket! I've got used to not getting a seat but I shouldn't have to deal with a load of bloody pissheads on the morning commute!"

"I agree," says Derek. "Leave it with me."

With many an excuse-me as he shuffles his bulk along the aisle past disgruntled commuters, Derek contemplates calling the Railway Police. The smell of soil, dirt and the great unwashed intensifies as he approaches Carriage D. Moving through the thronged vestibule, he scans the seats ahead. There is indeed a collection of down-and-outs, scruffy and whiffy, taking up most of the carriage. The only people who have braved the scent in the seats around them are four younger people and two older, at the far end of the car, with hankies or scarves to their nostrils.

Apart from one man . . . There is one man, dressed smart-casual in dark clothes but thoroughly presentable. Not only is he sitting among the homeless passengers, he is actually conversing with them! *Laughing* if you please!

"Tickets, please," Derek announces.

Heads turn to face him. *This is going to turn ugly*, the ticket inspector decides.

The man who is seated with the group, however, reaches into his shirt pocket and proffers a clutch of orange tickets. Then he says, with uncertain weather in his eyes, "Here you go. Twelve returns for my guests. I apologise for the scent. We seem to have cleared the place out. Perhaps it was better in the old days, before air conditioning, when you could open a window."

A woman with dirty features cackles like a pheasant. "Good old Lord Biscuits!" she shouts. Then she raises the bottle of port that she carries and sucks on it with fervour.

Lord Biscuits? wonders Derek Latham, feeling helpless.

There is nothing he can do. They have tickets; he cannot ask them to disembark – not on the strength of their hive perfume, at least. They've done nothing wrong. They are not being unruly, and there's no guideline in the rule book about consuming alcohol.

"Thank you, Lord Biscuits," says Derek Latham.

You aristocratic silly cunt, he adds silently for the benefit of the story that he'll tell later.

*

For the first time since Kieran Sange became acquainted with what he used to call tramps and dossers, he knows the individual names of the people that he leads; and he does not call them tramps and dossers anymore. He calls them an army. *His* army.

Lord Biscuits' Army.

The army disembarks at the town where their friend was murdered by a group of tramps and dossers who are not (firmly *not*, in Lord Biscuits' opinion) an army.

To Lord Biscuits it stands to reason that this group must be punished.

He leads his army from the train station (where their individual tickets open the turnstiles' jaws, to the silent but visible surprise of the uniformed attendant patrolling nearby). Proud of the army (seven men and three women that he has paid to command), Lord Biscuits consults the map of the local area that he printed off at Coronet Confectionaries.

Aware that an army runs on its stomach, Lord Biscuits has ensured that his followers are good and *pissed.* Before they left their home station this morning, he entered a corner shop near the botanical gardens and bought eight four-packs of super strength lager, at outrageous markup. Proud of his team's intentions (and even its raucous beauty), Lord Biscuits sat with them while they consumed a can or two each; the remainder of the booty he confiscated, with the promise that he would dole out more to those who wanted it on the train. He made it clear that everyone could also bring what they wanted to drink on the way.

Stumbling like zombies and profaning like Marines, the men and women move through the streets surrounding the train station. Lord Biscuits is in his element. When rain starts to fall, he is pleased with the deterioration in the climate.

It feels like good slaughter weather.

*

In the middle of a road, Lord Biscuits stops walking.

He raises his right hand, a sign for the army to stop moving as well. The soldiers await his direction. A car horn sounds, the driver unable to pass on his way.

"Is anyone frightened?" Lord Biscuits enquires.

The chorus of *Nos* is emphatic; a few members of the army spray spittle through the gaps in fudge-coloured teeth as they hiss derisive laughter at the very notion of fear.

The man in the car honks his horn again.

Lord Biscuits turns in the direction of the impatient driver. The car is as red as its owner's rage; the vehicle is nearly new, roomy, expensive – the sort of car that Lord Biscuits had once been driven to Coronet Confectionaries in every morning.

"Get off the sodding road, stupid!" the driver shouts.

Lord Biscuits closes his eyes, the smile on his face fading and being replaced by something akin to bliss. "Show this man no fear, my beautiful army!" he commands.

The men and women move swiftly towards the red car; some run. Light on the windscreen obliterates the driver's features, and it is impossible for the army to see the panic in his flesh.

His shoving of the gearstick into reverse creates a deep crunch. As the car spins its wheels, gains traction and screeches a path backwards, the first member of the army, lighter on his feet than many of his number, has reached the driver's side window and has thrust his arm inside the vehicle. He has grabbed hold of the lapel of the driver's jacket . . . but the car's reversal wrenches the driver out of the soldier's grasp. Curses fly like bullets in a different altercation. And it seems that the impatient driver will get away from Lord Biscuits' revenge . . . until the red car makes contact with a Range Rover that is arriving behind it. Their bumpers thud together (there's a tinkle of light reflectors shattering) and both vehicles are halted.

With a drunken roar, so colossal and distorted by fury that it fails to resemble words, the soldier strides up to the side of the red car. The window rises; the soldier is able to clock the distress on the driver's face. A corrupted smirk writhes across the soldier's features.

The Land Rover driver hollers in frustration, but no words are necessary. The soldier thrusts his denimed arm into the dwindling space between the rising glass and the rubber at the rise of the aperture. Though the glass soon pinches into the underside of the soldier's arm, his hand is able to reacquaint itself with the driver's lapel. He tugs.

Other soldiers in the Biscuit Army have caught up. One of them – a woman in her mid-forties – throws open the driver's door. In doing so, once again, the original soldier is pushed away from the driver, and the contact between them is broken. He yowls in a voice and lexis less than human.

It falls to the woman and the man to drag the driver out of the car and onto the road. Greedily they begin to stamp on his body: it's a case, almost, of finders keepers. Only reluctantly do they step aside for other members of the army to have a turn at aiming kicks and conducting their foot-stamps on the driver's nose-bridge.

Lord Biscuits and three members of his army stand close to the Land Rover's door. The driver of this vehicle is unlikely to exit; too much is at stake. For this reason alone, the Land Rover driver and Lord Biscuits *et al* observe the murder of the man in the red car.

"Take a hand or a foot or an eye if you want a souvenir," says Lord Biscuits. "But no bickering or squabbling. There's more to come."

*

The approach to the land shared between the empty stables and the abandoned building site is a rutted lane of longitudinal humps. The ruts sport successive monks' tonsures of grass growth.

A woman named Pony is on the ground, struggling to get up. Her movements are jerky and uncoordinated (Lord Biscuits remembers seeing her downing brandy on the train) and she is almost crying with humour.

"*ElpmeeAP ya cants! ElpmeeAP! I pissed meself!*"

The soldiers around her laugh – laugh too much for Lord Biscuits' liking. If he is not careful, this will turn into a game; they will stop taking the pilgrimage seriously. And yet . . . he is certain that if he starts talking tough, someone will turn on him – and then, in turn, the army will do the same.

Lord Biscuits looks deep into himself, and rallies. He holds up both hands.

The sounds of laughter dwindle around him. Precisely as he has predicted it would happen, he is earning – or *re*-earning – their awe and admiration; maybe their fear as well.

He waits a few seconds more than he needs to, for effect. Not a word is uttered around him; he hears a rustle of clothing that he takes to be Pony as she climbs to her feet again, possibly aided by her paramour, Catso. And then he lowers his arms and breathes out, as though in meditation.

"We are close," says Lord Biscuits, "to where Frank was killed."

The army murmurs; a few people nod their heads.

"I want you to show no mercy when we arrive. Ask no questions and accept no excuses. Be as ruthless as the scum who murdered Frank were to our poor old friend. And whoever – listen! – whoever causes the most mayhem and damage – for I'll be watching carefully – I will give fifty pounds to as soon as we arrive back home. Fifty pounds!"

Lord Biscuits bows slightly when he receives a round of applause.

*

Homeward bound, back on the train heading south, several hours later, Lord Biscuits is subject to a host of conflicting emotions.

Along with his army he won the battle against the other group of rough sleepers – the group led by Malcolm; the group that had killed Frank – and Lord Biscuits had cried with unchained pride. On what had become the battlefield, he had surveyed the spoils through eyesight rendered dreamy with tears.

It had all been over quickly; but *no one fights so dirty as the dirty*, as Biscuits had internalised the blood-messy view. An entry, perhaps, for the diary that he could never see the point of completing, what with every workday being so similar and with some of his outside-work activities revolving around coercion and criminality.

("Tickets, ladies and gentlemen, please," Lord Biscuits hears from somewhere behind – possibly the vestibule before the carriage proper.)

Outside the train windows, fields are plump with a crop that Biscuits cannot identify. Concentrating on its burnt-amber colour, he thinks of rats out there in the stalks, attempting to find food. He tries to imagine what his walk to work would be like if he was himself a rat.

These are not the thoughts of a victor, Lord Biscuits tells himself. He faces forward; he makes a steeple of his fingers on the table in front of him. Although there is blood under several of his fingernails, he makes no effort to hide his hands.

Pride and fatigue both jostle for his attention. In a moment of epiphany, Lord Biscuits understands that he will not brag about the victory that he orchestrated. He also understands two further related opinions.

The first is that he has no one to brag *to*, for who would believe his story?

The second is that eventually he will have to answer questions about the bloodbath that occurred. Technically, even this soon after the last ring fingers, ears and noses were removed for souvenirs, Lord Biscuits is about as *wanted* as a man can be *in potentia*.

"Tickets, please," says Derek Latham, in the aisle behind Lord Biscuits's head.

Biscuits turns slightly at the shoulder. Three tickets for travel are in his right hand. "For me and the two . . . " He indicates to the adjacent table and the two men sleeping soundly on either side of it. The rest of his army had either decided to remain in the north for a holiday or had been too wounded or too dead for an immediate return journey.

"Thank you, sir. And hello again," Derek offers. "I hope you had a nice day in the north with your friends."

Lord Biscuits smiles. "Very useful indeed," he replies, not entirely answering the conductor's implied question.

2

Although the working day at Coronet Confectionaries is done, Billy Alfreth leaves the building with neither light in his heart nor a spring in his step. The day has been troublesome.

The previous eight hours had simmered with joylessness, and Billy had felt subtly *unwelcome*. Conversations that he walked towards suddenly stopped. Colleagues had clicked their mouses to change whatever had been on their screens, as soon as Billy had stood up.

Alone, he crosses the car park to the business park's entrance. No one has left Coronet Confectionaries at the same time as Billy, and now he tries to convince himself that his solitary exit is not a further part of an as-yet-unvoiced plan against him.

There is usually enough time to smoke two cigarettes before the bus arrives. Longsufferingly sighing, Billy lights the first of his post-work treats, recalling that even his cigarette breaks in Cancer Cottage had been solo endeavours today. Even his favourite smoking buddy, Terry Bates, had not reported for work this morning – Billy had assumed the man had called in sick.

Four drags into the cigarette, and Billy looks up at the approach of a low-slung Honda as it pulls alongside the bus stop.

Its engine rattles faultily, but this is difficult to hear beneath the rumble of the modified exhaust. This ride has been pimped – expensively and compre-hensively so: the tyres are fat; the skirts are low; the italicized font on the front registration plate is surely cop-bait.

The Honda breaks with unnecessary violence. (Billy tenses and drops his cigarette.) The tinted passenger window slides down; straining against a seat belt, the driver has leaned over into the passenger's empty space.

"Get in the car, Billy," the driver instructs.

Bent at the waist, Billy clocks the driver's aviator shades (wholly redundant in the evening's gloom) and his pepper stubble and sophomoric pout; furthermore, he sniffs the unmistakeable waft of cannabis from inside the vehicle.

"All right, Terry?" Billy asks.

"I *said*: get in the car, Billy. I want a word."

With an exaggerated movement that seems immediately overdramatic, Billy wriggles into the passenger side, both confused and emotionally poised for conflict.

Terry shoves the gearstick into first as though he is trying to move furniture. The engine roars; they speed away from the bus stop, with Billy viewing the space between the lens of Terry's sunglasses and the man's eye. Terry squints.

Billy turns to face the front. Meanwhile, the road pounds towards them as the Honda gathers uncalled-for and perilous velocity. The speedometer trembles around the fifty mark, and they have yet to leave the feeder roads surrounding the business park.

"Do you wanna catch me up?" Billy suggests. "What's going on?"

"We need a quiet place," Terry replies, tugging the gearstick into fourth.

"We're in the middle of the countryside, Terry. This is about as quiet as it gets."

The comment is intended as lighthearted; however, it is not taken in this spirit – Terry weighs Billy's words carefully before replying.

"Somewhere with no cameras, I mean," he says; then he floors the accelerator and risks a manoeuvre to pass a motorcyclist who is following the middle of the lane and obeying the speed limit.

Billy is relieved to see the motorcyclist shake his leather-gloved right hand in the traditional "wanker" gesture. The man has remained on the bike.

"Slow down a bit, Terry, would you? You almost hit him," Billy says, performing his torso-twist in reverse and facing the road ahead once more.

Terry is unrepentant. "The bitch should've moved aside," he states, his voice slurred. It is not the first time that Billy has been in a speeding car with a drunk man at the wheel, but it's the first time it's occurred for a good few years.

"Yeah, you're brilliant," Billy tells Terry. "If you'd knocked him off and killed him, that's four years for dangerous driving. And that's *before* they take the cannabis and booze in your system into consideration."

Terry sniffs. "A custodial sentence don't scare me. It's not like I've got a job to go back to."

"Have you been sacked?"

"Like you don't know!"

"I don't, actually," Billy replies, his voice on the petulant side. He makes a mental note to discuss Terry's nonchalant acceptance of a prison term at a later date.

"Pat Kelly gave me a bollocking, Billy," Terry explains, "after an anonymous tip-off. He said I was selling heroin and coke."

Billy has not seen this coming. "And are you?" If Terry has also snorted cocaine this afternoon, it might explain the hell-for-leather dash away from the business park.

"Well yes," Terry admits, "but that's not the point." Terry stares through the dust on the windscreen and through the grey approach of early evening.

Billy stares at the side of the man's head. "You think *I* told him?" he demands. "No wonder he was so odd with me today! Well, I didn't say a word, Tel. I didn't even *know* until this second."

"He mentioned Jem."

Terry pulls the car off the road and brakes with unnecessary violence in a diner's car park. The two men sit silent for a few moments.

Billy feels as though something is missing; that he has turned over too many pages at once, by mistake. What does Jemima have to do with any of this?

Perhaps the pungent air in the car is muddling his thoughts. Billy opens the door to let in something fresher. The air around the diner stinks of cooking oil, incinerated steaks, and the whiff of a distant bonfire.

"Oh my God," Billy whispers. "You're selling to *Jemima*? I didn't even know she was into that shit. What does she do?"

"H, mainly."

"For how long?"

Terry shrugs. "Six-seven months."

"What did Pat say to you?"

"He said you basically have two choices. Do nothing at all, and he would inform Kieran Sange – then I could argue the toss with the Biscuit Inspector and Human Resources. Or he'd keep his mouth shut if I left immediately."

A stream of air leaks through Billy's teeth in a hiss. He unfastens his seatbelt and climbs out of the vehicle; his work shoes scratch in the gravel.

"This is a lot to take in," Billy tells Terry after a few seconds.

The latter has also exited the vehicle. "Understatement of the year," he replies. He leans his back against the upper frame of the driver's side; the door remains open and Terry's arm rests along its top, as if he needs its physical support to stay upright. The effort he then spends on lighting a cigarette appears gargantuan.

"But he gave you no indication of how he came by the information," Billy states, lighting a cigarette of his own. "That suggests he might be protecting a source."

Billy considers a patchwork quilt of conversations that he's had with Jemima, on the subject of Lucas. What if the spineless foal had developed a backbone? What if he'd told her that Class A narcotics were the final straw?

Terry closes the driver's side door and walks around the back of the vehicle. Billy tenses. He is certain that a fight had been on the cards five minutes earlier; but surely the two of them have moved beyond that.

"Could you close the door, Billy?" Terry instructs. "I'm gonna buy you a burger to say sorry. I shouldn't have suspected you."

"Thanks. I need to call Jem."

"Well do it quickly. I've been smoking all afternoon and I've got the munchies."

"All right. But one favour, though, eh?" Billy asks.

"Just name it."

"Take the sunglasses off, you silly bitch. We're not in Milan."

But where are we? a voice asks at the back of Billy's mind. The voice sounds like Ostrich, from the prison days; but the face that Billy imagines is that of Narna the Labradoodle.

3

His eyes are of such varying hues that even a colorimeter would struggle to submit a definitive conclusion. Comate of cheek and chin (the hairs like rats' tails), the man perches, skew whiff, on the side of a supermarket trolley that has been abandoned or dumped on the building site.

He has not foregone his suspicion of his well-dressed visitor.

The well-dressed visitor has not dressed well for the specific purpose of this meeting. The well-dressed visitor is wearing the slacks-and-jacket combination that he dons most days that he cycles to the university where he works. To have put on anything different this morning would have alerted his grieving partner that there was something different about today.

Frank Tucker had not wanted Louise Reardon to know that he would be doing anything other than going to work. Louise would not have approved of Frank's intervention.

But.

*

Tape flutters in the breeze; the tape reads CRIME SCENE DO NOT CROSS.

Frank Tucker's interlocutor is an old man – unutterably filthy, run down, his features busted by experience and intoxicants, his nose a crimson knuckle of alcohol abuse. He looks up at Frank's arrival and says clearly, "I'm not sharing."

He's referring to the three-litre bottle of something (whatever it is) that he now clasps to his pigeon's chest. "If you think I'm sharing, you're a penis."

"I don't want anything," Frank attempts to assure him. "Apart from information – about the man who was killed here recently."

The old man swigs from the three-litre bottle and then wipes his lips on the sleeve of his jacket. "Are you a Hebrew by any chance?" he asks.

"No, my ancestry is Scots-Irish."

The old man nods. "The universe, as conceived by the ancient Hebrews consisted of a flat disk-shaped habitable Planet Earth, with the heavens above and Sheol, the underworld of the dead, below. So-called *science* would have us believe that my forefathers were chatting shit on the subject, but we don't know." He takes another drink. "Because it's not for us to decide. We do not have *the full range of facts* . . . What's your name, son?"

"Frank Tucker. *Dr* Frank Tucker."

"Do spare me your *engorged* sense of self-righteousness, boy," he says. "There's no one but me and the maggots to impress with your *prefix*. Everyone else's dance-card seems to be marked this evening. They've obviously gone to one of the other dancehalls in town."

Frank is surprised to acknowledge a sense of shame. Nearly twenty years earlier, when he had first been awarded his PhD, he had insisted on being called *Doctor* at every happenstance. For the purpose of veracity, he had amended other people's contributions to a discussion in their mid-sentence, his motive always having been a sense of pride in the recent awards ceremony at the university that still employs him. However, it has been some time since Frank has played the "Doctor" card for the purpose of putting a speaker *in his place.*

"I remember when I used to do that," the old man offers.

"When you used to do what? Insist on *Doctor*?"

"The very same." The old man burps.

"You." Frank points a finger at the other man's chest – so much less threatening than at a man's face. "*You* used to ask people to call you Doctor."

The old man shifts his position on the upturned crate. "As a matter of fact, I insisted on *Professor*."

"You were an academic? You were a *Professor*?"

Again, the other man chuckles. "There's no need to use the preterite," he protests, a grin on his features. "Use the present tense simple! There's no *age limit*."

"What?"

"I *remain* an academic, boy – despite everything. You could call me Emeritus Professor, I suppose, but I was never stripped of my achievements. I *am* a Professor, to this day."

As the self-proclaimed Professor takes another drink (even the plastic bottle gulps, as if in incredulity), Frank Tucker acknowledges a sense of inadequacy in the presence of an intellectual superior.

"Professor Raymond Cossell, in old money."

Frank knows the name from somewhere; indeed, its mention elicits a scintilla of nostalgia. Just as Frank starts to assume that Professor Cossell is undercover with the homeless in the same way as Finley had dived into a set of research outcomes, the good Emeritus Professor speaks again.

"Frank, you said? Frank Tucker?"

"That's right."

"Frank for truth; Frank for honesty . . . and Frank the embodiment of God-like coincidence. Except there's no such thing as coincidence where God's concerned. Coincidence is what happens when God wants to remain anonymous . . . which He does a lot of the time, these days. Used to be the Big Man, did God. Bit of a *celebrity*, you might say. But these days? Bit of a *poodle*."

Frank laughs. "That's one way of putting it, I suppose."

"The Earth, the Underworld and the heavens above," Cossell says, his eyes beginning to water, "they were surrounded by a chaos sea – a sea of *chaos,* mark you – protected by the firmament, which was a transparent but solid *dome* . . . resting on mountains that ringed the earth."

Frank sits down after upending a plastic crate that had once transported milk bottles. His throne is not entirely robust; it threatens to collapse beneath his weight, so Frank keeps his legs wide and his feet as far apart as they can go. "You certainly know your Bible," he says.

"The Bible is a corrupt dossier," Cossell counters coldly. "If you want to know about Noah's so-called Ark, ask some poor bugger who *lived* through it."

Frank pauses. *Through* is an unusual adjective here, he thinks. "By which you mean you."

The old man nods his head and takes another drink.

"By which I mean me. Among others, of course. What I witnessed here," the old man continues, "was nothing short of that same sea of chaos. It's where the Earth, the heavens and the underworld collided. It was carnage."

Frank leans forward; the plastic beneath his rump shifts unsteadily. "You were here when the man from the south was murdered."

"And when his *compadres* exacted their revenge."

"Are you prepared to tell me about it?" Frank feels a mild exertion in his chest, as if the air has changed and it is suddenly difficult to breathe.

"My diary seems to be empty for the day. Come back with a bottle of good brandy and you've got a deal. But I'm telling you now, I won't be sharing it with you."

"I could give you twenty pounds right now. You might be able to get *two* bottles of brandy if you're prepared to leave your spot."

The old man shakes his head. "For one thing, no one around here will serve me. Been caught too many times with tins of stew down my Y-fronts. And two bottles are no good to me. Can't protect myself properly."

"From whom? There's no one here."

"Not from whom, son. From *what*. From Nostalgia's Boat. It's on its way back to us."

*

"It started when Louise and I were in our mid-to-late-twenties and early thirties," says Raymond Cossell. "A group of us decided to test a theory we'd had about how to protect people – the young, in particular. My twin sister had a son with her first husband, and my brother-in-law and I doted on him, even though he was a complex boy – and often a long way from happy."

"Are you suggesting your sister *did not* love the boy?"

"I suppose I am in part," Cossell answers. "At the time we were both newly-qualified with doctorates from the same university. Louise, Anthropology; and me, Psychology with a leaning towards Criminology."

For Frank, the coincidence manifests as a pinching sensation at the root of his throat: not painful exactly, but insistent. However, he tells himself to keep a grip. Louise is not an uncommon name; Anthropology is not an uncommon subject for an undergrad to study for her Bachelors.

"Are you with me, son?" Cossell asks.

"Yes, I'm with you, Professor."

"For the sake of the story, I want you to be clear on how *unnaturally close* we were, my sister and I; though we ignored that sort of comment at the time. People would talk, obviously. And think we couldn't hear them, presumably. It didn't matter. Twins are probably as close as two people can get, and we lived up to that particular cliché. Right the way along to sitting our respective PhD Vivas within a month of each another, years later."

Frank smiled. "Who was a doctor first?"

"My baby sister was! And fair play to her. After her Viva, she had some minor modifications. Mine were more serious – some structural flaws. But she *lived* her PhD, did Louise. Totally immersed . . . and that was the story of her life. Anthropology.

Ethnology. *Action research*: becoming – essentially – one of the tribe, in order to record their behaviours."

Now that the coincidence of forename and academic calling has been established, Frank can smile at how well it seems to be continuing. He has always been interested in the phenomenon known as *déjà vu.* He likes to be in its arms, in its embrace: to see how long the experience will stretch, and to try to mark the moment when the world divides into two once again – the 'then' and the 'now'.

It's not the same Louise, he reminds himself . . . but the links are striking.

"I suppose," Frank continues, "you'll tell me you both got jobs at the same university."

"We did. And it *still* didn't strike me as too close or too cloying."

"I won't claim to be any expert on twins, but from what I know, what you've described is true of many. You and your sister were close – a bit more than many pairs, I suppose, but I don't really see what the problem is . . . or was."

"Well, let's just say it set scenes for what was to follow."

*

"Things were mostly okay with our closeness – with our *proximity,* Dr Tucker – until Louise had her son with Robert. As the song says, that's when all our troubles began – though they didn't at first."

"What happened?"

"In a word? *Jealousy* happened."

"You were jealous your sister had had a child first?"

"No, not that. I was pleased for her, in fact. I'd never wanted a child – an heir, or even a companion. The thought had never entered my head. My new nephew – Lucas – was adorable, even if he was challenged in a number of ways. His dad and I used to talk about how we'd protect him from a world that mightn't understand the boy's different way of thinking."

"I'm not sure I understand."

Not-quite-sighing, Cossell replies that he is not sure that he understands either. "But Robert and I knew we had to protect the boy – from *what* exactly, we hadn't quite decided. From life, I suppose. From the future. So we took it upon ourselves to teach him all we knew. Why? Because knowledge and self-awareness are the rivets that hold a body of armour together – or so we thought at the time. Little knowing the boy's mother resented our combined intervention."

". . . It was *Louise* who was jealous."

"Habitually so, Dr Tucker – though as I say, I didn't know it at first. Not for a long time. Perhaps if I'd known, I might've had the consciousness to withdraw a little bit and let them get on with being a family. But I was in. I was a fixture – in the family, but more importantly, in the child's life and plans for the future. It gave me something to think about other than work – other than tenure at the university and grading undergraduate submissions and reading journal articles."

"How did Louise's jealousy manifest itself?" Frank Tucker asks.

"To be honest? Silently; and without sign language, either. It was a long time before I even knew there was a problem; and Robert was the same. Not once can I remember Louise so much as voicing a concern that her husband and I were doing things to protect her boy. And why would she seek out signs to suggest this anyway? Doesn't it seem to you like a strange thing to object to: the *protection of your son*?"

"Am I right in thinking your sister had something to do with your – what shall we say? – your fall from academic grace?"

Cossell grins.

"All his dad and I wanted to do was to *save* the boy – against the wishes of his mother, who did not want anyone interfering in what she saw as a child's natural progress through life. Whatever format that journey might take."

Without a word of explanation, Cossell stands up and sidles off to the right, with the effortless charm and dexterity of an ice-skater. Frank takes it as a compliment, the fact that the man leaves behind his three-litre bottle without having asked if it was okay for Frank to mind it. From this, it seems, an imago of trust has developed between them. From within surrounding darkness comes the sound of impatient and copious micturition.

Two quandaries occur to Frank during this breathing space.

The first is a question, aimed at his own head – like an arrow – that enquires how he is going to write this up for his own future publications.

The second is a question, aimed at his own head – like an arrow – that demands how he is going to explain all of this to Louise on his arrival back home.

A matter of seconds before Cossell returns, Frank Tucker hears commotion somewhere behind him. "People are coming," he announces when Cossell re-emerges from the gloom.

The Professor's message is simple. "It's you who should think about a hasty retreat, not me."

"Because I'm an interloper. Like Frank was – the man who was killed."

"Partly. But also, that evening was strange. Have you got a few more seconds?"

Not entirely speaking the truth (and feeling fearful), Frank answers: "As long as I can get out of here safely, my time is your time. What's on your mind?"

"A name," Cossell answers. "The name of Malcolm – the ringleader who killed the man whose death brought you here, Frank. And others followed him. Angry as a wasp around lemonade."

Frank starts to wriggle. So uncomfortable has he become with both the conversation and the noise of people getting closer that he decides to stand. His legs feel heavy. He walks closer to Professor Raymond Cossell but maintains a respectful distance.

"Who *is* he, Raymond? Who's Malcolm?"

"I suppose that's the point. *No one knows*. I'd never seen Malcolm before a week before the fight. Neither had anyone else. He was a new boy. And do you want to know the truth? If my memory serves me well, so-called *Malcolm* arrived just in time for a violent fight in which people . . . shall we remind ourselves . . . *died*. So. My question would be, *who put him there?*"

Frank is nodding his head. "Are you suggesting that Malcolm was set up by someone?"

"That would be my guess."

"But who would've hired Malcolm to cause damage? Who would've wanted to create trouble? Who *had it in for* Dr Finley Reardon? And how would anyone have known that Finley – as Frank – would have *gone there?*"

"You took the words right out of my mouth, son," says Cossell. "Now you should leave. Before you encounter a frontier party with pitchforks. I wouldn't want to feel responsible for another murder."

Frank stands up.

"*Another* murder? How were you to blame for Finley Reardon?"

"I *spoke* to the poor bastard," Cossell answers. "I'll have that on my conscience until I break bread with my Maker."

4

"Before I arrived here – on my way over," says Chaz Bruce-Sange, "I wondered whether I'd treat our meeting in a professional or a personal manner."

"And what would the difference have been?" asks Den of Iniquity, returning to his armchair.

Raising both her left eyebrow (minutely) and the fat glass tumbler to her lips to sip, the psychoanalyst considers the question.

"I wouldn't have accepted your very kind offer of a bourbon, for one thing," she replies. "And usually, when I'm working, it's me who asks all the questions. I don't know if it's the drink or the fact that I'm answering – but I must admit, I feel perfectly comfortable at the moment."

"Discussing your dead patient," Den reminds her.

"Yes. And your dead girlfriend."

The word *Lorraine* is in the air, as a musical note that both of them can hear but to which neither knows how to respond.

Chaz decides to override the plan that she had formulated on the drive over here to the expensive part of town. She had convinced herself to elicit from Den all that he wanted to proffer; to treat their meeting, in fact, like a therapy hour session. But now she is not so sure. Den of Iniquity is not a compulsive talker, and his responses so far have been guarded.

"I'm assuming you didn't know she liked to sleep rough," says Chaz. "You didn't know she had a life away from you."

Ambiguously, Den nods his head.

"You *did* know?" Chaz asks.

"No, I didn't know. I was agreeing with your assumption." Den leans forward and places his tumbler on a low table; despite what Chaz believes he drank before she arrived, he has only sipped at the bourbon in his glass while in her presence. "I thought I had bought her away from her old life, I must admit," Den continues. "But I can't say I didn't have doubts. I work away a lot, as you probably know. I'd come home from a business trip and she'd not be here. Nothing's been touched in the fridge; the same amount of water's in the kettle. So I'd ask her, 'Why don't you stay here while I'm away?' She tells me, 'A girl gets lonely' and stuff like that. I don't force the issue: I've never tried to hold her in one place. I say to her, 'Just promise me you're not selling yourself again – that's all' – and she would smile so sweetly and tell me not to worry."

"She wasn't lying."

Den rolls his shoulders backwards; the sockets pop in tension-relieving bursts.

"Technically no," he agrees, "but what was her life away from me instead of the game? She mightn't have been selling her body but she was still *deceiving* me."

"Was she? What did she say she got up to?" asks Chaz.

"Oh, *girlfriends*. Coffee shops. Catching up with friends . . . I still can't quite believe it. I mean *vagrants* of all things! *You're* the one with the window into her mind, Chaz, not me. What do *you* think she was doing?"

Chaz has been waiting for something like this: for a request for a diagnosis. What she hasn't expected is for Den to acknowledge the presence of the psychic ball-and-chain known in her industry as *patient confidentiality.*

"I mean," Den adds quickly, "I appreciate you're not supposed to talk about a client, of course, but now she's worm food and there's no legal investigation, I don't really see how it hurts."

Den retrieves his tumbler from the table. "Besides, you didn't come here to *share fond memories.*"

"You weren't at the funeral, I noticed," Chaz replies.

"Guilty. I couldn't face it," Den tells her. "Do you know what I dreaded? I thought some of the homeless people she hung around with would show up. And that would've been like meeting her other boyfriends or something. I didn't think I could face that – or what they were thinking."

"About you? What *would* they have been thinking?"

"They'd think: *what a gullible sap.* Giving her a decent life and some spending cash – while all the while she's playing away from home with a group of bums."

"She wasn't punishing you, Den – or I don't think so anyway. She was punishing herself. She was saying, girls like me don't deserve guys like you." Chaz points at Den with a lightly curved middle finger. "My professional opinion is, she was doing more than reminding herself of the world she'd left: she was abasing herself because she couldn't accept she'd earned your love and goodwill."

"I was too good for her, you mean," says Den.

"So *she* thought – at least on an unconscious level," Chaz informs him.

Having rolled bourbon around his gums, Den grins and stands up. "And what about you, Doctor? Do *you* think I'm too good for her? Or do you believe it's the other way around?"

"I am sure you loved each other – it's not for me to judge how you lived. Or live."

After a short pause Den asks: "Are you married?"

"Divorced. One daughter at university." Chaz is aware that this might be the most she has talked about herself for years. On one level she feels that she has lost control of the therapeutic hour; on another level, she is surprised that she doesn't much care.

"Would you like something to eat, Chaz? Grief has made me peckish."

Chaz nods her head. "Shall I follow you through?"

"You might as well. That's where Lorraine's letter is, pinned to the board."

*

Neither of them has ever been on a blind date: this is one of the findings of the following hour. Nevertheless, both of them – Chaz and Den – agree that what happens next causes feelings similar to those that would evolve if a blind date should be foisted upon them.

Chaz is thinking of Lorraine – of how Lorraine has set them up, her and Den of Iniquity. *She wanted to get us together,* Chaz says to herself.

"Why what?" Den asks.

"I'm sorry?"

"You said *why.*"

"Did I?"

"Unless I imagined it, of course."

Chaz holds in her left hand the letter that had been pinned to the cork message board in Den's kitchen. "She used to pay me in cash," Chaz tells Den. "After a session."

Uncertain where Chaz might be going with this, Den offers: "Maybe cash I gave her. I used to give her a stipend. Bit of pocketbook money."

"Which means," Chaz continues, "she did not write me a cheque – and I have never dragged myself up to date with regards a credit card franking machine – and *certainly* not touch-pay. I wouldn't know where to start."

Seconds earlier, Den had returned from an old-fashioned sideboard in the lounge, where drinks are clustered on a large pewter tray. He had poured himself a bourbon (Chaz had declined his invitation to join him for another). Den sinks that double – possibly triple – bourbon in one fell swoop; now you see it, now you don't.

"Apologies if my drinking's making me slow," Den says; "but I don't see what you're getting at, Chaz. Have I missed something?"

"Not for sure. Just a question. Are you certain this is Lorraine's handwriting? I've never seen her handwriting – not on a cheque, not on anything."

"Well, who else's would it be?" Den replies.

"That's not what I asked."

Den pauses.

"Truthfully? I wouldn't swear on my mother's eyes. It *looks* like it. But we're in the digital age, Dr Bruce-Sange. I hardly write much more than a postcode myself these days – you know, on a sticky note, to take to the car for the SatNav. We just don't use pens as much as we used to. And I'm *ancient*."

Chaz smiles. "You're not ancient, Den."

"But what are you saying? Someone else faked Lorraine's note to me?"

"Again, not for sure. I'm playing records, Den. This is no more than my Possibilities Jukebox. Who can tell what's coming up next? As far as I know, Lorraine left you and me a kind of not-quite-suicide note. In which she claims she foresaw her own demise, if we can put it like that."

*

Chaz will ask herself questions in the days that follow.

Did Lorraine write letters? And if she did, how did she get them delivered to their destinations? And if she *didn't*, then what was going on? Who had written letters in Lorraine's name?

Somewhere in her studies, Chaz had read something about willed hallucinations. Here, she is thinking about the fact that both Carol and Roberta had seen Lorraine, shortly *after* Lorraine had passed away. Was it Freud who had suggested that two likeminded individuals, with sufficient reason to do so, could conjure up a member of the dead, back into life?

It's the equivalent of two kids, Chaz will type into her diary, *who are committed to being scared by a ghost on a family holiday – or a school trip – in a new place. The being-scared is its own objective. It doesn't actually matter, scared by what or whom.*

What did Carol and Roberta really see? What does a dead friend's ghost look like?

Chaz will pause before typing the next two questions. Her fingers will crab above the keyboard and she will consider her actions for a second or two. Then she will type the following:

Was Lorraine ever alive in the first place? Maybe Lorraine didn't exist – she was what held the others together, she is in their memories. Their belief is what makes her real. Lorraine is what stands in place of something far worse in the collective memory.

Shortly after contributing these sentences, Chaz will delete them – with an anxious and self-criticising shake of the head. And yet ...

The thoughts that led her to typing these gobbets will persist.

*

"Think back on the happy times in your childhood," the American invites Chaz Bruce-Sange. "What makes them so happy? Well, for a start you've filtered out all the bad shit."

"I'm sorry, I beg to differ. I can certainly remember some unpleasant events in my childhood."

"Name one thing you'd answer if I asked you to explore your demons, as it were. Give me an example."

"I broke my arm when I was six. I fell off my bike."

"What happened? The specifics."

"Leonard Cowie's parents were having an extension built on the back of their house. There was a load of extra sand knocking around so we formed a massive pile on a patch of grass they had at the front, between the garden and the road. Basically a ramp. And all the kids in the neighbourhood were flying at this mound of sand as fast as they could, and jumping."

Chaz shrugs her shoulders.

"It was all but inevitable someone was going to fall off. That evening, that someone was me."

"Was anyone killed by a serial predator?" asks Den of Iniquity.

"In my neighbourhood? No."

"Then I'd say you had it lucky, wouldn't you?"

"Wait. I might have had a drink, but if I recall your invitation correctly, you asked me to name something negative in my childhood, to show it's not all filtered out."

Den is smiling. "Which you singularly failed to do."

"What do you mean? It was the first thing I recalled."

"Exactly."

"There were other examples I could've chosen."

"*Exactly.*"

Chaz frowns. "This is getting on my nerves, Den. What do you mean, I failed?"

"You told me about an event that probably made you into a bit of a heroine among your peers for a while. It's hardly having your soul trampled on by a pederast."

"Christ. No. Well . . ."

It is not often that Chaz experiences a loss of control over language – but this is indeed one of those occasions. Nor does it occur to her to blame the few drinks that Den has been kind enough to provide. She is not drunk. But she is weary in her bones; exhausted in her fibres.

Attempting to recover, Chaz sits up straight.

"Your earlier point," she says, "was that people sieve through their memories and protect themselves against the darker material, whatever that darker material might be."

"We did not in fact get to the point I was about to make."

"Then perhaps you could make it now: because we *do* remember what happened – the good *and* the bad stuff."

"The mind has a self-protective function: *that* was the point, in brief. When you discussed the fall off your bike, you did not even mention the pain you endured, which I don't doubt was probably serious."

"You wanted to hear about my pain. I can't remember it."

"I probably shouldn't say this," Den continues. "But I've been thinking about this a lot. And my best guess? Sit tight; you're not likely to believe this. But I reckon we are someone else's nostalgic memories. Someone is remembering us right now, and by keeping us alive in the memory, we are kept alive in our bodies . . . if 'alive' is even the right word here. We and everything around us – everything we see and feel – is the memory of someone trying to keep pieces of his or her past alive."

For Chaz, this is nowhere near the most outlandish statement that she has heard during a therapy hour. She will not dismiss the man's conjecture. Nor will she endorse it.

"Nostalgia is what Sigmund Freud called a screen memory," she says, "a lightly poeticized and sweetened representation of something that did not happen."

She is aware that she is leaning on the delivery of a previous lecture. In fact, she is succumbing to nostalgia, in a sense.

"A tapestry of idealised parts of the past, stitched together with the less pleasant segments cast aside or corrupted into something beautiful." In precisely the same way as she has smiled at this point in the past, she smiles now. A denouement looms. "The good old days, in other words. Experience viewed through pink-tinted spectacles."

Den nods. His eyes are closed but he is listening.

Chaz throws out her summary line.

"Above all, it's a lie we can use to assuage guilt or pain."

"Or maybe just boredom. Nostalgia edits out the bits that were dull. It leaves us with a cleaner picture. It vaselines the camera lens."

Chaz plunges. "What can you tell me about her secret hurt?" she asks.

Den sighs.

"I don't think I can tell you a single thing about her secret hurt, Doctor. I didn't know she *had* a secret hurt. As far as I knew, she had come to peace with herself. I believed I was helping her to do that. Perhaps I was – perhaps I wasn't; but I flattered myself that Lorraine was happy with me."

After inhaling at length, Chaz exhales a tide of bourbon-scented breath.

"Allow me to say one thing, Den. I have absolutely no doubt she was happy with you. But I don't think she was happy everywhere else. *That* was the problem."

5

It takes a few attempts before Jemima will accept Billy's phone call. From the way she says *Hi, Billy*, it appears that she knows that he knows: her tone is weary but relieved.

"Where are you?" Billy asks.

"At the swimming pool. Do you wanna talk in the sauna or jacuzzi?"

"Why there?"

"Because that's where I am already. I can get twenty lengths in before you arrive."

When Billy arrives at the swimming pool, he shows his membership card to the girl behind the plastic screen at Reception, and the hip-high gate swings open for him to enter the premises. With his little-used gym bag over his left shoulder, Billy walks into a corridor of snacks and drinks machines. Then he enters the changing room. He strips down to the bathing shorts that he has on already and pummels his belongings into one of the thin chest-height lockers. All he carries with him, from the changing room to poolside, is a large orange towel, rolled up.

On his way to the far end of the pool, Billy spots Jemima in one of the bubbling hot tubs. She is not alone in the frothing spume, but Billy imagines that her companion might be a stranger to her. At first glance (as he approaches) there appears to be no conversation between Jemima and the large grey-haired woman. Indeed, Jemima has her head back over the lip of the tub, her eyes shut.

Just for a second, Billy wonders if she's still alive.

He places the towel on a white lounger nearby. Temporarily cleansing his mind of tension and perturbation, Billy watches the seven swimmers in the pool. They are executing lengths at varying velocities; the water is an erratic lacy knit-work of froth and enthusiasm, the noise being somewhere between drone and sizzle.

When he returns his attention to the hot tub, Billy notices the large woman looking at him. In his wilder years, before prison, he might have dipped the waistband of his bathing shorts and showed her what a man looked like; but now he merely feels self-conscious and embarrassed. Very briefly he wishes that his tummy was as tight as it used to be.

Cross-footed and careful, respectful of the wet floor, Billy approaches the hot tub. "Room for a small one?" he asks.

Jemima opens her eyes and says, "Welcome!" – though any attempt at a smile seems cauterized.

Cautiously, Billy steps down into the tepid, gargling water.

The other woman in the tub has brightened up; if her smile is anything to go by, she is happier to see Billy than Jemima is. It occurs to Billy that she was sizing him up.

"Can I introduce you to Roberta?" says Jemima. "Roberta – this is Billy."

"Call me Robbie."

Billy is trapped; he feels bamboozled, he feels small. Not for some time has it occurred to him to wonder why confident women concern him so, but he considers the question now. It seems obvious, as he settles in the water, that Jemima and Robbie have been talking about him, and he does not appreciate playing catch-up. The sensation that has bothered Billy all day – that of somehow missing out on the rumour, or worse, of being the subject of that rumour – is no less exaggerated in the warm effervescence.

What a weird day, Billy reflects, having no way of knowing that it is about to become stranger. For now, all he can think is that Robbie's presence is a hindrance – an impediment to the accusations that Billy would like to put to Jemima. Of all unexpected things, it appears that he will have to employ *small talk.*

"How do you do, Robbie?" asks Billy.

Although he hears Robbie's response – "Fine, thanks" – the simple words take a second or two to register. This is because Billy's other senses are assaulted at precisely the same moment. First, a sudden repugnant taste manifests in his mouth; temporarily, this stalls his other thought processes, apart from allowing through one word, which rings in his mind. The word is *sapor*. In a flash, Billy is aware that *sapor* means something to do with a foul flavour.

"I've heard a few nice things about you, Billy," Robbie continues.

Sapor.

The sapor of dead rat, thinks Billy, in a convincing instant of clarity. *What is* that *supposed to mean?* And what has he eaten for his taste-buds to react in the way that they have?

"Are you okay?" Jemima asks him.

"I don't want to be crude. Just something I ate."

"You don't feel you're going to be sick, do you?"

"No, no – I'm okay. Bad taste in my mouth."

"Bad day at the office?" Robbie asks.

Despite everything, Billy smiles. "Something like that," he agrees.

"Robbie and I were just discussing my career options after I graduate," Jemima continues.

Trying his best to ignore what his mouth and mind want to tell him, Billy says, "Oh, really? And what is it you do, Robbie?"

"I run three brothels."

"Yes, of course you do. Why wouldn't I have guessed that?"

"You sound like you don't believe me, Billy."

"I totally believe you, Robbie, because this one here . . ." He indicates Jemima. ". . . seems incapable of knowing anyone *normal*, with a *normal* life and job. Not one single individual."

"Like attracts like, Billy," Jemima replies. "And do you include yourself in that group?"

Robbie shrugs. "Define *normal*."

These push-backs are inevitable, Billy knows; he has spoken in haste and in anger. He leans back in the water and tries not to think of the taste of a rat in his mouth (if this is indeed what rat tastes like); not to think of words that intrude upon his conscious thinking with the subtlety of fog-horns; and not to think of talking dogs. He tries to recall a time when he had been in charge of what he thought about; a time when he had been the boss of his own mentality.

Does he include himself in the group of abnormals who know Jemima?

Very much so.

I need help, Billy admits. *I'm not coping with this at all.*

When he closes his eyes, he is both surprised and not surprised to feel tears in them. He senses Jemima sliding closer to him; and from what she says next, it is inferred that she has also noticed Billy's crying.

"It's okay, Billy, I didn't mean I was going into Robbie's *industry*. We were talking about my career choices in general. I didn't mean to upset you."

"What about becoming a mule?" Billy asks.

He opens his eyes to find Jemima even closer to him than he'd imagined. He uses the proximity to whisper in her ear. "I met Terry Bates today. I suggest you tell whoever you need to tell quickly, because the man's been fired and he's probably not going to stay quiet for too long."

With this piece spoken, Billy stands up. As water crashes off him, the bad taste in his mouth dwindles. By the time he gets back to the changing room, his anger is as frothy as the waters he has left behind, and the filthy flavour on his tongue has vanished completely.

Most important of all, he has made a decision. By hook or by crook he is going to get to the bottom of all that confounds him. He has grown sick and tired of feeling confused.

He vows to talk to as many people as he needs to in order to get gain an insight into Jemima's world – her proclivities and her failures. After all, *someone* must know: and this someone is likely to be her husband, Lucas. And this someone is likely to be her father, Kieran Sange. And this someone is likely to be her mother, Chaz Bruce-Sange.

One by one, Billy will speak to them. This nonsense has gone on long enough.

*

When Lucas arrives home from his work at the florist's shop, he finds Jemima in the kitchen, typing on her laptop at the kitchen table. Although she smiles on acknowledging her husband's presence, it is clear that she has a sentence she wishes to complete. Lucas waits on the threshold for a second or two; then, realising that he might be here for the duration of the composition of a paragraph, he moves past her quietly and flicks the switch on the kettle.

By itself his wife's presence is enough to make Lucas suspicious. As the water starts to warm in the kettle, Lucas tries to remember the last time he saw Jemima writing. For a long time now, she has tended to confine her studies to the Silent Room at the university, or allow herself to read expensive academic books in the bath or while sunbathing semi-naked in the back garden during the warmer months. How long has it been since Jemima opened her laptop lid for anything other than shopping or social media?

"Aha!" Jemima cries. She finishes the bit that she's been writing and slams the lid shut.

Lucas asks if she would like a cup of tea.

Without answering her husband's question in words, Jemima shakes her head and says, "I've been making notes. I started with a pen on paper but found I couldn't keep up with my thoughts."

"What's the essay about?" Lucas asks.

"Oh, it's not an essay. It's a set of prompts, so I don't forget what I've planned to say to you."

Inwardly, Lucas jolts. It seems apparent that his ongoing fear of divorce proceedings is about to be realised. By way of coping with this inference, he turns his back on Jemima and starts to prepare a cup of tea . . . On his walk home from the shop he had been happy. He had taken orders for three funerals and seven birthdays. Passing trade had been enthusiastic; he'd had a good day. Now, he wishes that Jemima had stayed away from the house – gone out with one her boyfriends, or gone to the Student Union for supper, or stayed in the Library to work.

He is certain that Jemima is staring at his back. After only a year of marriage, he feels able to divine more than where she is in the house: he also knows – or *believes* he knows – what she is thinking; what she is feeling. Sometimes he also likes to imagine where she is in the town, during those days and night when she goes missing in action.

Having her here and present is worse than her absence can ever be.

*

"I imagine conversations," Jemima tells him slowly, "in which you make me promise I won't see Billy anymore. You force me to be a good wife – or at least *try* to be a good wife."

"Why only Billy?" Lucas asks. "Is he my only true rival? I very much doubt that, Jemima."

"He's not your rival, Luke. I married *you*, remember, not him."

"Only because he didn't ask. Besides, if you recall, it was *you* who made *me* make a promise, Jem. Have you forgotten that?"

"How could I?"

"Well then. Careful what you wish for: you might just get it."

For a second or two, they both seem stunned by the cliché. Lucas is about to apologise when Jemima speaks into the gap.

"I asked you not to fence me in and to let me breathe," she says slowly, "if we were going to have a chance of making a life together. I didn't ask you to *ignore* me – or pretend we're siblings. A query about how I'm feeling wouldn't go amiss. A bunch of *flowers* for Heaven's sakes! You work in a florist's! You could even bring me what you're going to throw out with the trash!"

"You hate flowers. They give you the sniffles," Lucas protests coolly.

"The sniffles aren't the *point*, Luke. Sometimes I think I'm invisible in this house – do you know that? I feel numb. I feel *anaesthetised.* I have meaningless sexual encounters simply to provoke my husband into taking an *interest* in me. I try to convince myself it's because I'm impulsive and a *bit of a one* – as my dad would say – but if I'm honest with myself, I do these things because it's better to feel disgusted with myself than to feel nothing."

"Is that why you've started taking heroin?" Lucas asks.

If the effort of confessing so much to her emotionally absent husband was not sufficient to silence Jemima, the question he has now posed is enough to slap the wind from her lungs. Indeed, it takes her a few seconds to recover. Although she is proud of the way that she manages to keep her mouth closed, she is not proud of anything else, right now. Nor is she falsely defiant. She does not embark on a heated denial; she does not so much as shake her head to feign appalled acceptance.

"I didn't know you knew about the heroin," Jemima answers.

"By my reckoning, it stared about six weeks after we were wed. Does that sound about right?"

"Yes."

"Six weeks after I had invited you to share my home for the duration of our married life together. I wasn't *bowled over* by your sense of gratitude, Jemima."

"Marriage isn't supposed to be about being grateful!"

"Not entirely, I agree; but an *element* of it might feature, from time to time."

"That's what I was saying! About a *gift* every now and then! It doesn't have to be anything flash."

"I meant, in the form of a reduction in the number of your extramarital affairs, for example."

"They're not affairs, Luke. There's nothing as important as an *affair* in my life. Even Billy's not an affair – they are just . . ." Jemima falls silent.

"Ways of filling the aching void I've introduced you to. None taken, I'm sure."

"I was the same before I met you, Luke," Jemima argues.

"It's a bit late to get defensive *now,* isn't it?" Lucas interjects.

Responding to the effect that she is not being defensive is a classic way of being defensive. Jemima says instead: "I used to drink too much. I stole things from shops. I thought about suicide."

"You still do. Drink too much and steal, I mean. And if heroin isn't suicide on an instalment plan, then I don't know what is."

"I haven't stolen anything for months."

"Well done. Maybe you'll avoid prison, in that case." For the first time since the conversation started, Lucas's face shows an emotion. The frightening thing for his wife is that she does not know which emotion it happens to be. His lips stretch . . . but it's not a smile exactly. "I have only one question," Lucas adds. "The heroin, my darling. Where in this town would one go about the purchasing of *heroin*?"

Jemima looks away for a few seconds. While it seems obstructive to hold anything back from Lucas at this point – after all, she has elicited a response, an actual, healthy, emotional, adult response, which is just what she had wanted – it also feels worse than obstructive. It feels *silly.*

"There's a guy at Coronet Confectionaries," Jemima answers; "he gets it for me. He's been dealing for years. Half the Marketing team are on smack this year, he tells me. He's had to downscale on cannabis to the guys in the warehouse, just to keep up with demand."

"And this guy at your dad's workplace, selling his daughter Grade A narcotics right under his nose – does he have a name?"

It is not even worth asking why Lucas wants to know. Whatever he does with the information is his own affair: and Jemima is suddenly extremely tired.

"Terry Bates."

*

"Your wayward nature was part of the reason I asked for your hand in marriage," Lucas tells Jemima later. "I was convinced you'd bring trouble. But also fairly convinced it was trouble I needed."

The admission surprises Jemima. She asks her husband to explain what he means.

"I mean . . ." Lucas pauses. Jemima watches him as he works something through. Her mother had told her (often enough) that the strongest and most versatile tool a psychoanalyst possesses is her hearing. In this conversation with Lucas – a sharing of feelings that feels emotionally stormy, fraught and frightening – Jemima takes after Chaz Bruce-Sange more than she might wish to admit.

"I thought . . . having trouble as my wife would stop me dwelling so much on troubles of my own – or on the troubles I've caused others, it might be better to say."

"I was your distraction, you mean? Well, I'm sorry that didn't work out for you." Jemima's voice sounds more than a trifle bitter.

Lucas nods his head. "Maybe distraction's the wrong word. Maybe counter-balance is better – a counterweight of some sort."

It would take a more observant man than Lucas to note that tears have started to shine in Jemima's eyes.

"You think of me . . ." says Lucas, "as *inconsiderate* in some ways. If I don't ask you where you go then I can't care. Something like that."

"Yes, something like that."

"Then how do you imagine *I* might feel, your older husband, when you don't ask me anything at all about the life I led before I met you."

"But you *did* tell me, Luke. You told me you were in an asylum."

"But not why. And the word *asylum* is misleading: it was a high-security psychiatric clinic for private patients, at the top of a hill. The fees were exorbitant, apparently."

Jemima has swapped feeling sensitive for feeling guilty. "Did you want to *talk* about being inside the clinic? My God, Lucas! I thought I was being *supportive* – by staying quiet about those dark days. I didn't think for a minute you'd want to rehash that stuff."

"I expected to be asked," is Lucas's enigmatic response. "I'd prepared a story for you. I thought – if I had one story ready, I could tell you once and you'd be unlikely to ask ever again. It didn't occur to me you'd imagine I might've been locked up for *depression*."

"Be fair, Lucas. This is the first time you've mentioned locked up . . . or maximum security clinic, for that matter. How was *I* to know?"

"You could have asked. You didn't. So the story I knew when I was eighteen is the same one no one wants to know about. Can you imagine how that might feel? That story's been trapped inside me for fifteen years! As trapped as I was."

"Okay. When you say *story* . . ." Jemima prods, ". . . do you mean a lie? Or what do you mean?"

*

"I had an uncle with what are now called *mental health issues* – which never seems to do the subject justice if you ask me, but there you go. The term certainly doesn't do justice to my *uncle's* problems. Uncle Raymond. He disappeared when I was a little boy, and no one would tell me why. All I'd hear was, he had a problem with his brain, and it made him do bad things.

"I'd ask what kind of bad things – but no one talked about it to a child, of course. It wasn't until years later that I found out, and by then, to be honest, I was too in love with him to be shocked by the crime. I remember I asked my mum once – she and Raymond were twins – I asked her if she was worried she'd also do bad things, given they'd shared an egg and all that. She told me the idea terrified her.

"I loved him dearly, and I thought I'd done something wrong, to make him go away like that. It turns out . . . he was sent to the funny farm. That was what I was told when I was a boy."

"By who? By your parents?"

"By my mum, at least. My dad I can only remember as a washed-out, rather henpecked man – talked over and I have to say, rather *laughed at* by Mum and my Uncle Raymond. The two of them were twins – thick as thieves. I think I remember Dad being a bit of an outsider, even in his own home."

"What happened to him?"

"To who? Uncle Raymond or Dad?"

"I think you're getting to your uncle without any help from me, but the only time I can recall you mentioning your dad is very early on for us, well over a year ago – I asked you if you knew where he was and you said Yes. So I asked if you'd invite him to our wedding and you said No."

". . . I was always *distantly disappointed*," Lucas admits, "that you didn't pursue that line of questioning." He waves a forefinger between the two of them. "Assuming we're finally being honest, of course, Jem."

Is there a note of sarcasm in what her husband has just said? Jemima is not certain. Although she longs to encourage Lucas to speak the truth, the sentence rubs her up the wrong way. She gives herself credit that she keeps a vice-grip on her temper. After all, has she ever assumed that this conversation with her husband was going to be simple?

Patiently she explains: "Yes, Lucas, we are finally being honest. *Both* of us. And I'll pursue the line of questioning, now, that I thought you wanted me to strangle at the time. Why *didn't* you want to see your dad at our wedding?"

Lucas pauses.

"Now that you've asked me, I find it hard to talk about," he tells Jemima. "Several reasons. The first is, I didn't know how he'd be after our long silence. He'd not only left me and Mum, he had achieved a real escape velocity away from his entire life. He'd started what you need to start to be recognised as a woman, for one thing. Mum and Ray, I think, had even bullied him out of his *gender*. And did I want a man I hadn't seen for years arriving at our wedding as a woman *no one else* had seen for years? Well, call me a coward, but no I didn't, not particularly. Not *because* Dad had wanted to be a woman – but because a marriage ceremony was not the place to reconcile us, perhaps – not to mention the fact that Mum wouldn't have wanted him there anyway."

"But Lucas, your mum didn't join us either!"

"No, she didn't; but I honestly thought she might. Despite everything. After I went through the brain-work and heart-work needed to send her an invitation, I expected her to bury the hatchet."

Jemima shakes her hand. "I still don't understand, Luke. You're suggesting she was angry with you; but *why* was she angry with you?"

"She was angry with everybody."

"Okay – but why *you*?"

"Because I abandoned her – as far as she saw it – in favour of Uncle Ray and Dad. I *adored* them; but I didn't hate Mum or anything like that. It was a long time later that I discovered how jealous she'd been through parts of my childhood. So much so – I see now, and I've known for a long time – she even set to polluting my mind and memories of them both. But subtly: never overtly – never anything I could have . . . *refuted*. Exhibit One of this particular conversation, of course, being Uncle Ray's time under psychiatric care."

Now that Lucas has fallen temporarily silent, Jemima watches his face and infers that he is mining for the relevant words and the right way to piece them together.

"Earlier," Jemima tells him, "you said he was sent to the funny farm, and then you said something like: *That was what they told me when I was a boy.* It suggests you learned something to the contrary later on. *That's what they told me when I was a boy but I found out different later on*: something like that. So *did* you find out something different later on?"

"... I did, Jem."

"Don't clam up on me, Luke. Did your Uncle Ray or *didn't* your Uncle Ray spend time in a secure psychiatric hospital?" she asks.

"He did; just not in the way I thought when *I* was in a psychiatric hospital," Lucas answers.

*

One does not need to have a psychoanalyst as a mother to be aware that people are not detained for their own good without first having done something – or a series of somethings – unpalatable.

Jemima is not shocked that her husband had once suffered from a mental illness (she has suspected as much from before their wedding day, in fact); but the news that he had been hospitalised comes as a hard blow. It is difficult for her to hold her head up in this fresh and troublesome storm.

Hold her head up, however, she must.

While attempting to remember what her mother has ever told her of the psychoanalyst's trade, Jemima invites her husband to tell her what he remembers.

"I will, Jem; but you should know, I've waited a quarter of a century for someone to ask me to do this. Some of my skills of recollection may well be rusty."

"It doesn't matter," Jemima replies, feeling closer to Lucas than she has since their wedding day. In the seconds that her husband needs to marshal his thoughts, Jemima wonders if this might be the obstacle that they had always needed to hurdle: this *confession*; this clearing of the airwaves. Perhaps – despite everything and after all – they *would* go on to be a normal married couple ...

*

"The only way I know to tell it is to say there are two stories – at *least* two stories," Lucas begins.

"I was a complex child, I know that. I have vivid memories of very specific times of my childhood. My very first memory is Uncle Ray saying: *This, boy – this is Duke Ellington!* And he pointed at these speakers that seemed massive to me at the time, because I was two. We were in his study and he was teaching me the finer points of jazz."

"Two years old?" Jemima sounds sceptical.

"I know. It's impossible to remember anything from that early on; and I seem to have been quite defensive about my abilities to do so, when I was still young. It was only much later I understood I'd been given a lot of the detail by my mother."

Lucas sniffs the air, like an animal at the waterhole.

"*Force-fed* by the woman, more like, I should say," he continues.

"Lied to?"

Lucas nods his head. "Lied to and *convinced.* She had me think it was all my fault. Her goal was to punish me and Dad and Uncle Raymond – for the simple reason she couldn't find a way into our shared life. And when others got involve, things got worse."

"I'm not sure I can take this all in, but what *others*?" Jemima asks.

Lucas shakes his head slowly, saying, "No. No, I want to keep it all in order if you don't mind."

"What happened next?"

*

What happened next?"

"It's a good question," Lucas admits. "My instinct is to blurt it all out. I mean, I know what happened, don't I? I know the *order of service* . . . Well, believe me, I'm not sure of anything. Once upon a time, I could have told you to the *month* what happened – to the month and year. Would you like an example?"

Jemima tips her head onto her left shoulder. "Yeah, why not?"

"Starting at the age of two I received jazz lessons from my Uncle Raymond. At eight years and four months I met my new *au pair*, Lorraine . . . I could continue. Does anything strike you as peculiar?"

Jemima waits a second or two. "The precision, I think you mean."

"Yes. The precision is *exactly* what I mean. Why would I say *eight years and four months*?"

"Unless what? Unless you're reading a *script*?"

"That's it. I might have gone with something like: *been exploited by a decade of emotional abuse and conditioning.* But *script* is good."

"I wasn't trying to diminish it, Luke," Jemima is swift to add.

"I didn't think you were; not at all. In fact, the more I think about it, a psychological script – provided by my mother – is jarringly accurate." Lucas sounds amused in a bitter way. "She's the ultimate screenwriter, you might say."

Jemima pauses and lets the information dissolve.

"If everything is true," she says next, adding quickly, "and I have no reason to *doubt* anything, the obvious question has to be Why? What's *in it* for her?"

"Her academic career is what's in it for her! Just about everything revolves around her work," Lucas tells Jemima. "Once an ethnographer, always an ethnographer."

"No, that doesn't do it, Luke. The university has Ethics Committees, at the very least!"

"Not if you're writing a book that doesn't need ethical approval."

"Have you ever read one of them?"

Lucas smiles. "No, I've never felt that brave. I couldn't even tell you how many she's published. I think it would be like seeing myself on television. And *that's* not going to happen either."

*

"I remember a relationship with an *au pair* called Lorraine – a temporary marriage of convenience, you could call it. You could even call it a business set-up, in the sense that money changed hands.

"She died a few weeks ago and I wanted to feel anything but numb. I adored her for a while when I was a boy. I could tell you what she *smelt* like if there was a way of translating aroma into words as a universal language: her scent is still familiar.

"Well. Uncle Raymond had been away in the psychiatric home for years and I decided I was going to pay him a visit. I don't think it had occurred to me to do this before then, but Lorraine was my passport inside that building on the hill. She was the first *au pair* who hadn't tried to take care of me. She was just there for the money – and I respected that. Her only responsibility was to put me to bed and then spend the time Mum was away for the evening talking to her boyfriend on the phone."

"Not really an *au pair*, as such. A babysitter; and not a very good one."

"You're right. And that's why I loved her. We suited each other's needs perfectly. She could talk to Pat Kelly on the phone, safe in the assumption she couldn't be heard. While I could sneak out the bedroom window and roam the streets at night. It was perfect."

"Weird coincidence," Jemima interjects.

"What is?"

"At the place where my father works, one of the other directors is called Pat Kelly."

Lucas smiles broadly (for his wife, this is a most pleasant expression to behold).

"Oh, I very much doubt it's a coincidence. In fact, I've lost faith such things even exist. It's all *connected*, in ways we sometimes see but usually don't. Especially in a town like this."

As far as Lucas is concerned, Jemima seems to be on the brink of saying something at this point (perhaps to defend the reputation of the town? perhaps to offer her speculations on the fate of a passed-on prostitute who enjoyed the company of the homeless) but instead she closes her mouth. Lucas has read that expression before. It means: *now is not the right time.*

"A little bit later on, Pat Kelly became one of the men in my Uncle Raymond's Ark-building business; but that's getting ahead of myself." Lucas smiles to himself. When he adds "I did say there were two stories – and *at least* two stories", he seems to be offering - a rebuke.

Feeling the need to take hold of the rudder, Jemima says, "Finish what you were saying about Lorraine, please, Luke."

"She helped me into the asylum. I had a hold over her and I played my blackmail card to perfection. I said if she didn't help me, I'd tell Mum she was a lousy *au pair* and she'd get the sack. So one day, we walked up the hill and talked our way into the asylum to see Uncle Raymond."

"Just like that. I mean, forgive my scepticism, but you don't just walk in even if you're an adult. They were not going to give access to a couple of *kids*."

Lucas shrugs. This is *his* Nostalgia's Boat and he will steer it any way that he wishes. In this moment, Jemima understands that she had not taken control of the rudder a moment earlier after all.

"We pretended to be his relatives – or rather, Lorraine pretended to be his niece and I was her son. We invented a wife called Wendy for Uncle Raymond and made it their wedding anniversary, except Wendy had died. We didn't need to be specific about the years. We were asked to fill in a few forms and were shown to his room."

Lucas pauses. "Your face says it all, Jem."

"I'm sorry, but you can see this simply couldn't have happened. You wouldn't be allowed to visit like that, even back then."

"You should park that thought," Lucas advises. "It's about to get even *less* believable."

Jemima holds up the palm of one hand while she reaches for her mug of what by now must be citrusy tepid water. "Just before it does. You had an *au pair* – or a series of them."

"Yes."

"Which suggests your mum left you a fair bit. Your dad had left home by this point, right?"

"Much earlier."

"So where did your mum go when she left you?"

For the first time since beginning this chapter of his recollections, Lucas appears troubled. The tale-to-be-told (Jemima concludes) had been oddly reassuring. Being wind-buffeted away from the charted course, *not so* reassuring.

"University functions, I imagine," Lucas answers. "With the benefit of hindsight, she might have been going about her experiments with people's lives. Who knows?"

"Okay; sorry to interrupt," Jemima adds – and Lucas thinks she means it.

"When we went in the room, he had a big belt around his waist and the end was fastened to the wall. He was listening to jazz on a little tape player. The guard warned us not to get too close, but don't forget how much I'd loved him when I was tiny and he taught me Jazz 101. Needless to say, I ignored the warnings, and I helped him escape."

"How?"

"We played a game. He told me to mime a particular piano solo he'd taught me. The guard thought I was having an allergic reaction to a pill he'd slipped me – except he hadn't, of course. He bluffed us out into the open air. And we had to move quickly but we *did* get away – albeit pursued. He took us to a place near where my dad used to work."

"And where was that? He sold bathrooms, you said."

"It was on the industrial estate where Coronet Confectionaries stands now. The bathroom showroom was gone and there was a paper manufacturer – White and Daley. Uncle Raymond pressed some bricks on a wall and a chute opened. We slid down the chute to a heavily fortified chamber. Only one guard – called Lovell – bothered to follow us."

While considering a suitable response, Jemima sinks the rest of her lemony water. She makes a show of considering taking something from the bowl of peanuts. She is far from hungry.

"Do you know what this sounds like, Lucas? It's just occurred to me. It sounds like a cartoon."

"Perhaps I should be annoyed. To me it sounds like a horror story."

"The two worlds are not mutually exclusive."

"No, I suppose not. Then we entered the Ark Uncle Raymond constructed with my dad – a sort of bunker affair. A tough metal casing, resistant to drills and tools. And there I spent the next four months with Uncle Raymond. "It took me nine days to eat him."

6

It will take a short while – no more than a matter of days – before Dr Louise Reardon self-evaluates and remembers something about bad news needing to strike a second time, before the first occurrence can be brought back to life and light and recognised for what it had been.

However, if the job of the second instance is to recontextualise the first (Louise wonders), what is the job of the third or fourth similar instance?

Although Louise has been completing the third draft (the submission draft) of her book, today has made her consider the other writing that she has been completing. This side project has mostly taken the form of sentence-length gobbets about her marriage to Finley; or statements of confession that amount to how she has known for a long time that the past would eventually punish her.

As an example of one such moment of full disclosure, Louise has written: *It has taken them twenty-five years to find me. But every game of hide and seek must end at some point.*

If the news of Finley's murder is the first strike that Louise had no choice but to endure, then tonight (she believes) is going to be the second. The idea that there might be a third, hard on the heels of these two examples, has not really crossed her mind, although she knows (more generally) that justice has a way of locating the one who is guilty.

The fact that tonight, this second bad-news arrow should be fired from the quiver and bow of her partner, Frank Tucker, is greatly disturbing. More so, when she comprehends that Frank has stumbled onto something like the truth without even knowing what he has been doing.

*

"May I ask you where you've been?" Louise says to Frank Tucker.

Louise has spent the better part of the day alone, what with her partner inexplicably elsewhere and her daughter, Tamara, out with friends for a weekday matinee, cocktails and then a meal at a restaurant named Profit – an event in honour of the twenty-first birthday of one of Tamara's friends. Louise has remained in her office for the previous six hours. This solitude is not a destination that Louise would have chosen. It does not matter that she is nearly at the end of the submission draft of her latest manuscript – on the subject of autoethnographical approaches to qualitative studies – she does not want the house to be completely empty.

"You sound cross," Frank tells Louise. "I'll say up front I'm sorry I sneaked away. But I'm reasonably confident you'll thank me in a minute, when I explain."

Louise twists in her office chair and crosses her arms and her legs. To both parties present she appears as tight as a coconut; and to both parties present the smile on her face seems false and strained. "Then please explain."

"I went out to where Finley met his end," Frank replies. "I got talking to a man who used to work as a Professor in a university in the south. Do you know the name Raymond Cossell?"

The pause is infinitesimal; Frank does not clock it. He had been of two minds as to which of two possible opening gambits to deploy. The other question that he might have asked would have gone something like: *I know about Finley Feardon . . . but were you married before Finley? Were you married a long time ago, when you were in your twenties?*

"Well, not in an academic sense," Louise answers, a trifle miffed with herself for allowing her fury to dissipate. She leans forwards slightly, now gripping her left wrist in her right hand, in a gesture that both of them know denotes nervousness.

"So in what sense?" Frank wants to know. Uninvited, he steps into Louise's study and takes a perch on the battered faux-leather two-seater that takes up the space between an overcrowded bookcase and a 1980s stereo system that has tiers including a cassette deck, a radio panel and the turntable for a vinyl collection that includes several signed sleeves – scrawled upon by Paul McCartney, Barbra Streisand and Nick Cave.

"In the sense of . . . ripples," Louise replies, sounding vague and undecided. "Do you recall when that colleague of yours was called to do jury service, and got herself in trouble with the police?"

"Sure. She was told not to say anything about the case and she blabbed on social media. She was arrested and questioned."

Louise nods her head. "You know what it's like in academe," she says. "Word spreads like a weather front; and I can vaguely recall the name Raymond Cossell – there was a scandal, I think. What did he do? Was it something to do with a bomb? He blew something up."

"He tried to, at least. But he told me he thought he was doing something positive. He *believes* he was doing something positive."

"Well that's all right then. What did he actually *say*?"

*

Louise is not certain how long Frank has been speaking before she holds up her left hand.

"I beg you, Frank – please."

"What?"

"Stop." Louise waits a few seconds. "I have something important to say to you."

She studies her partner's face – but for only a beat or two. It is all she can stand. While turning aside, she says, "Please forgive me for the barrier I erected earlier. For *barrier* you might read *lie.*"

"You lied to me?" Frank wishes to confirm.

"And I regret to say, not for the first time."

"You'll understand I want an explanation."

"I will. And *you'll* understand I'll find it difficult to offer one. Give me a moment, would you?"

Frank is not so much angry at what has happened; he is frightened. "Are you angry I wanted to know what happened to Finley?" he asks.

"I am, as a matter of fact; but that's not what we're talking about now," Louise replies. "Frank. Up front, I don't want to shock you; but I've waited to say something about Raymond for twenty-five years. I've been hiding something important . . . It's difficult to talk about."

Frank frowns.

"For crying out loud, at least *try*. I think I know what it is, but I still want you to say it."

Louise bows her head. "Have you guessed what I've been hiding?" she asks.

"I was *told* what you've been hiding. My question is, why hide it? My second question is, why hide it for a quarter of a bloody *century*? And my third question is, why hide it for a quarter of a century and then hide it *from me*?"

Louise's head remains bowed.

"Academically, this is an experiment, Frank; I am part of my own ethnographic study, and I have been for decades. I am *still* involved in my action research project – close proximity to others' pain and loss of control."

She looks up; not only are there no tears in her eyes, a staunch defiance has been etched into her features.

"And what about on any other level but academically?" Frank demands. "What about life *outside* of the manuscript you happen to be drafting?"

"I've wanted to be caught for *years*," Louise confesses. "I've wanted to *express my findings.*"

Although Frank is frowning, his voice mellows. "Why not tell me," he suggests, "as if I don't already know? Why not tell me as you would tell a police officer?"

He waits a second before adding: "Dr Louise Reardon, we insist on knowing the truth."

"It's time to try," Louise admits. "Professor Raymond Cossell is my twin brother."

*

"We should probably inform the police for real. What do you say?" Frank asks.

"But tell them what? You went to a hobo jungle and a drunk rough sleeper told you a story about Finley's murder? You'll be asked – at the very least – why you went there in the first place."

"And I'll answer truthfully: to investigate the murder of the ex-husband of my partner. Isn't that good enough a reason?"

"Well, for *me* it might be. I'm not so sure about the police. You should be prepared for an accusation of vigilantism."

Frank protests. "It was hardly *that*, Louise!"

"But weren't you, though? Hypothetically – what if someone there had said: *yes, I did it. I killed Finley.* What would you have done? What if Raymond *himself* had confessed?"

By now, the two of them have moved out of Louise's study and are seated in the lounge. Although the house is not cold, Frank has started a fire in the log-burner. The flames are comforting.

Unable to think of a good way to answer his partner's question, Frank sips from his glass of wine. "I also don't think he was drunk – Cossell, I mean. He sounded perfectly lucid."

"I'm not saying anything to the contrary, Frank." Louise pauses. "I'm not exactly sure what I'm thinking, to tell you the truth. I've got the book to finish. I've got Finley to mourn. And for a while now I've felt like a rope has been tightening around me." She looks into Frank's worried expression.

Frank asks: "I'm not stifling you, am I?"

"No, it's nothing to do with you. I have a question. Have you ever attached future meanings to any particular ages in your life?"

Frank nods. "I'm sure I did – I must have. Eighteen, twenty-one ..."

"No, I don't mean the usual ones linked to laws of the country. Did you ever tell yourself you'd go through a life change at the age of thirty-three, for example?"

"I don't think so. Did you? You did, obviously."

"Not thirty-three ... though my dad died when I was thirty-three. It was looking forward to forty-seven. From the age of about thirty-six I imagined that something life-altering would happen to me when I was forty-seven."

"And did it?"

"Yes! I moved to this job. I published my first book. Finley and I got divorced."

"All right," Frank replies. "I won't argue it was a big year for you. I don't mean to sound brusque, but what of it?"

"I look back on that year with a fondness that couldn't possibly have been the case. I mean, the divorce was hardly a bowl of cherries."

"Publishing a first book's a big thrill."

"Yes, it was; but when I think back on that particular year, I experience a sense of nostalgia for a past that can't have happened."

"Why couldn't it have happened? I'm not sure I'm following you."

"Because that year has a certain feel to it in my memory; and when I try to explore it beyond the events I mentioned, it's like a Siberian wasteland. Like nothing else happened ... but how can that be? I feel a sort of *tightening* and *tension* in my head .. . which is where I was going a moment ago – it's like I'm being drawn to something – to those memories."

"Are you sure you're not being incredibly hard on yourself? I mean, you ask me about when *I* was forty-seven and I'd have to consult a calendar or something – it's all fuzzy."

"For argument's sake – just for a second – try. Do you remember what you were doing when you were forty-seven?"

"Well. I haven't had that many jobs, as you know, so that's easy enough. I think I visited Japan for the first time when I was forty-seven. But it's hazy."

Animation floods Louise's features. "Exactly! Surely *that's* more normal than being defined and delineated by a selection of events at a particular time."

"I'm still not sure what you're suggesting," Frank tells her. "You're wearing rose-tinted spectacles? You're nostalgic?"

"It sounds crazy. You'll think you're in a relationship with someone certifiable."

"I already think that." Frank smiles.

Decisively, Louise shakes her head. "I'm being serious, Frank. This has frightened me – this feeling I get that I'm being drawn towards something again."

A second earlier, Frank had been about to confess that the fear his partner is experiencing is a fear that he shares. However, Louise's facial expression has chased from him any notion of unity-through-honesty.

"Darling, *tell* me," he half-asks and half-orders.

Little though he knows it at the time, it is the use of the term of endearment that unlocks Louise's store of panic. A sob punches a hole through a membrane . . . and suddenly Louise is crying properly. Frank moves closer in an attempt to console her by using a physical code that they have never learned wholly for one another. Neither of them favours the casual hug; indeed, it is a sign to Frank of how deeply run Louise's scared feelings that she allows him to embrace her at this moment at all.

In this instant of intimacy, it is all that Frank can do to remain silent; he longs to say something encouraging – something to elicit his partner's elucidation of the point. However, for the moment Louise remains equally as silent – and apparently content to be held.

When she feels able to talk again, she is still in the embrace. She says, "It's like it's not me remembering those things. I don't feel . . . " She waits; she prepares it. "Sometimes I'm not at all convinced it was me who put some of the nostalgic thoughts in my head. It's as though I'm *meant* to think of certain life events, rather than choosing to."

Still, Frank chooses not to respond. *Allow her to get it out,* he thinks. *We'll talk about it when it's all on the table.*

But Louise stops talking. In the ensuing seconds, Frank is nearly convinced that Louise has fallen asleep in his arms.

Not so.

"What if I'm *supposed* to remember certain things?" she asks quietly. "Nostalgia is what we call the sewing-together of random impressions and conversations: *I feel nostalgic.* But what does it mask? What really happened?"

"Something duller?" Frank ventures.

"Or something worse – something much worse."

Warming to the theme, Frank busks: "Or maybe nothing at all."

"I would definitely put that in the 'something worse' category."

"Nothing at all?"

"Emptiness; banality. Yes, I would. But I don't think it's that," Louise tells him.

It takes her a few seconds to release herself from Frank's cuddle; her skin is hot where it had communicated with his.

"I think someone else is remembering things for me and storing them in my head – to protect me from knowing something worse. There I've said it."

Louise waits and then adds, "Good. You didn't laugh."

"It's the last thing I'd do," Frank attempts to assure her. "Assume I concur . . . *Who* is doing this? Or *what* is doing this?" At the same time, he tries to rationalise what Louise has said up to now. The woman is clearly exhausted.

"It's definitely a who."

"Then who?"

Not answering the question, Louise tells Frank, "I try to find him sometimes. I hadn't properly realised until now . . . how to interpret some of the searching feelings I get, that I translate into wistfulness or even loss. But I'm sure I'm *searching* for him . . ."

"Christ, Louise! For *who*?"

"It's a boy called Lucas."

Frank waits. The explanation is sure to follow, but the thought of the most likely possibility is sufficient to ignite a bloom of heartburn in his chest; it makes him wince – and he sucks in a breath. It has been a long time since Louise brought up the name of Lucas.

Frank senses Louise as she holds her breath; he does not need to see her – he can feel her tension through the space between them, her emotion riding molecules of darkness in the chasm.

"The boy I gave birth to," Louise clarifies. "Lucas – my son."

*

There are moments during the conversation that Louise has with Frank that makes Frank wonder if strange things collect together, like creatures huddling for warmth on the prairie. Surely his visit to hear Raymond Cossell's story should have been plenty of strange; but Louise had decided to up the ante on him. What had started with a thought about Finley Reardon had ended in a most peculiar place. And now Frank is uncertain how to proceed.

Louise is similarly confused. Her partner – with whom she shares a house, a bed and a life – had asked her outright if she had heard of Professor Raymond Cossell . . . and her response had been a lie. A flat-out fib. She had made up a story about rumours spreading efficiently in academic orbits, but had not said: *Yes, he's my twin brother.*

Why did I lie? she asks herself.

There are moments during the conversation that Louise has with Frank that make Louise think of much earlier conversations with Finley; moments when she glimpses her ex-husband's features in her partner's face, smoothing Frank's contours and bumps ideally flat, and the then growing new shapes before her eyes. Louise is reminded of a passenger flight over hills, with the terrain as changeably fluid as November weather. For Louise, the morphing that she witnesses – the liquid shuffle between Frank and Finley, Finley and Frank – is oddly soothing. It's a source of calm to have two of the men she has loved in her life, in the room together; and not only physically present but seemingly comfortable – in a manner that had not been true in life, as events at Tamara's birthday evening had demonstrated. At one point Louise is conscious of her own grin; though she forces herself to rinse the dregs of humour from her soul, the sight of Frank co-habiting in Finley's face, and vice versa, is like watching one of those cute videos of cats and dogs primping one another's fur with their tongues. Only when she glances at the black window and takes a mental stab at the hour of the evening does Louise abandon the idea of suggesting that the three of them wrap up warm and go out for a walk together.

It does not feel like the end of the day, but it must be getting there; they have talked for a long time. Unburdening some of her memories and fears on Frank has had a livening effect, despite the hour; but Louise knows that she should fill Frank in on the parts where she either lied or did not mention the subject.

Evidently the same possibility is also on Frank's mind. "I think I need to know about Lucas," he tells Louise softly. "We've covered a lot of other ground, and I think I've not wanted to ask, but I've known it was there."

"It still is," Louise replies. "My first husband Robert and I had Lucas, and we loved him. But there were problems from the start. Lucas was a very serious little boy. He hardly ever smiled. We would ask him all the time if he was okay and he'd always say yes, but there was something not quite right about him."

"Give me an example," Frank says.

Louise nods. "He used to count obsessively. He had to know how many baked beans were on his plate – or how many cups were on the draining board. He used to arrange the towels in the airing cupboard so they were red, cream, red, cream – that kind of thing."

Given everything that has happened and been aired, Frank is aware of plucking his words from his store with caution.

"Is it possible," he ventures, "he was on the autistic spectrum?"

"I think it's almost certain; and if things had wound up different, I dare say we would have taken the tests eventually and got a diagnosis. But it wasn't to be."

"No." Frank waits. "So if I may . . . how did Lucas die? What happened?"

Louise's face is millpond-still. "Lucas didn't die, Frank. He lives half an hour from here. He got married last year to a girl called Jemima. He works in a florist's shop."

Frank's facial expression is not so much a frown of displeasure as the depiction of a factory collapsing, as rendered by a melancholic mime.

"I can't believe I had this so wrong. Why didn't I know this?"

"You sound hurt, Frank. I don't like to talk about him."

"Whyever not? Why would you hide him from me?"

"I'm not sure I did. It feels more like I've hidden you *from him*," Louise answers, having taken the accusation seriously. "I can't be sure but I think I did it to protect you."

"From what? From *Lucas*?"

"It's all so blurry, Frank. It's like it was a different lifetime. But I'll try . . . even if it's like looking through a different person's diary . . .

"My first husband was named Robert, as I mentioned. One thing I should say about him straight away is, he was mad about jazz music – if *mad* even does it justice. Lucas was almost named Miles, after Miles Davis. He would have been if Robert had got his way, but I said no. And I said no to Ed, after Ed Thigpen, the jazz drummer; and no to Art, after Art Tatum, the pianist."

"Yes, I get the idea," Frank tells Louise.

"In the end we compromised on Lucas – after Reggie Lucas, the guitarist, but nobody ever needed to know that."

Frank remains in a state of spinning motion from learning that Lucas did not die tragically as a boy of nine, which is the impression he has nurtured (and shied away from) for the duration of his relationship with the boy's mother.

Louise chews her bottom lip. "Do I mention the jazz connection now, I wonder, so early, because it foreshadows future activity? Or do I mention it as a way of filling you in on some background, because I'm feeling guilty or think it might help a bit?"

"Perhaps your own motivations are not the crucial element right now, Louise."

"Perhaps not," she agrees. "Robert and my twin brother Raymond used to instruct Lucas on all matters jazz. And I mean obsessively. I think they regarded it as something of a mission: to train this intense child in something worthwhile."

"They taught him to play?" Frank asks.

"Nothing so useful! Neither Robert nor Raymond could play a note. They were admirers."

"So what did they do? Play records to your son?"

"Exactly that . . . but with a lecture thrown in, each time. As young as two – I swear – or thereabouts, Lucas was taught modal scales and stride piano. He became their *project*."

"They taught him things about jazz. Forgive me, Louise," says Frank, "if I seem dim. If Lucas was not bothered by this dad and his uncle, and if he's living close by . . . then what happened? Why is tonight the first time I've learned anything about any of this?"

Louise falls silent. When eventually she speaks, she says, "I don't know if I've blocked it or if it never happened in the first place."

"Even roughly, Louise! *Something* must have happened!" Frank is becoming angry. It's impossible, he reasons, that if something serious enough for a mother to turn her back on her son has taken place, that same mother will forget what it was. The human brain is not a sieve, keeping only the good bits and allowing all of the bad experiences to be rinsed away like specks of dirt.

Perhaps a change of tack is needed. Modifying his tone as well as he's able, Frank says, "You haven't said much about Robert. If it's relevant, perhaps you might carry on from that angle instead."

"I haven't spoken to him for years. Not since he went through a change . . ." Louise laughs. "To put it mildly!"

For Frank, it is good to see his partner slip into a more light-hearted spirit, however temporary this status turns out to be.

"What do you mean? A change of fortune? A change of job?"

"Both! And more! Robert decided that the masculine life was not for him. He did it properly: the hormone replacement; the surgery; the counselling. And lo and behold, Robert was reborn Roberta. But not only that!" She holds up a hand to silence Frank's budding objection. "He set about proving that the oldest profession is one of the most stable . . ."

"The oldest profession? As in: prostitution?"

Louise nods her head. "My ex-husband Robert, the seller of bathrooms, became Roberta, the well-to-do madame and pimp."

"Wow. Talk about a career transition."

"As I say, I've scarcely spoken to him since those days."

Laughing briefly but genuinely, Frank asks, "I'm not dreaming this, am I?"

"Not unless we both are, Frank. Later on, she – Roberta – married a man named Derek and they adopted a daughter named Lorraine. I don't know how *officially*; but I know the girl was well-known (as they say) to the care services."

"Surely it can't have been official."

"Maybe not," Louise concedes.

"The adoption services would have looked into what the parents did for a living. They wouldn't have allowed a child to grow up in a world of prostitution."

"You're probably right. I'm not even certain if the marriage was official. It might have been a common-law arrangement – or you know when people say *married* but they mean *committed* – it might have been like that. But Roberta and Derek became Lorraine's guardians, in whatever state of legality. And guess what."

"My instinct is to say the girl went on the game."

"Your instinct serves you well."

"Gosh." Frank pauses before continuing. "And to think, when I was young, my Uncle Charlie went to prison for six months for fiddling the books where he worked. And we thought *we* were a dysfunctional family!"

Although Louise registers the attempt at humour, she does so with a fragile and exiguous smile. Blink, and you would have missed it; as indeed Frank does miss it.

7

From time to time, especially on some of the longer journeys north, Derek Latham will take a moment away from checking tickets and announcing the next station stop, to gaze out of the window and invite nostalgia and reverie into his life. He imagines a much older train on which to travel. Hears the clack-clack-clickety-clack of steel wheels on railway lines. Even the hissing bellow of steam's release into the air outside unnameable industrial towns.

He believes in a different experience – that today's train travellers have grown soft. On quieter journeys he yearns for noisier journeys, simply because (in his opinion) the etymological link between *travel* and *travail* should never be forgotten. To move any great distance, in the not-so-distant past, requires fortitude and resilience. The idea of 'stepping on' a train should still seem . . . magical.

If he ever gets around to drafting his memoirs, reference will be made to the perils of travel. Then again, Derek's memoirs have been in conceptual draft for the better part of two decades, and the only things of which he is certain are the title (*Station to Station*, even though David Bowie used it first), and the fact that an entire episode will have to be expunged. It is not his wish to return to those days – not even if (as now) recent events have opened a crack in his memory's walls; and not even if Derek can sense this part of his past almost scratching at those walls for a weak point of ingress.

He has discovered that having had some of those thoughts awakened after years of their suppression, he can keep them under a semblance of control by bringing to mind the traumatic incident involving Lord Biscuits and his followers that had stirred thoughts of his earlier days in the first place.

Ample opportunity to reflect on the events of that day have visited Derek Latham ever since. One of the most notable was a request to discuss the day with a policewoman named Sharon Bark. In uniform, Bark had arrived at Latham's home one early evening.

"I think I recognise you, don't I?" Derek had asked her. "From the business park car park? You visited me in the security cabin."

"That's right," Bark had replied. "I took the dog away after you rescued it from the car."

"After I broke the window of a car that wasn't locked."

"Well yes, that as well," Bark had agreed. "The dog is at the rescue centre now. Can we talk about the people on the train, please? The group travelling north to fight."

Obligingly (and simultaneously nervous, appalled and flattered), Derek had run through the little he knew. He called to his mind's eye a reasonable physical description of Lord Biscuits. And he mentioned to WPC Bark that he could recall the stench of the carriage that the travellers had occupied on their journey north. How Lord Biscuits had produced a valid ticket for each and every one of his compatriots.

Sharon Bark had described the fight between the two groups of rough sleepers. Probably as discreetly as one can in the midst of such a description, she had also mentioned the murders that had ensued. To this day, a week later, Derek hopes that he managed to convey the appropriate degree of shock at Bark's news. Certainly, his combined feelings of being nervous, appalled and flattered had deepened. Derek had wondered how best he might help solve WPC Bark's weird gangland homicide case. Since then he has even begun to wonder how he might write it up for *Station to Station*.

Towards the end of the twenty-minute interview, WPC Bark had asked Derek Latham something that he still does not understand.

"Do you think you will remember that day?" she said.

The question had arrived out of nowhere; Derek had replied that he suspected so, why?

"Because there are things that we don't expect to forget but do forget," Bark had answered.

Derek had stayed silent; Bark had smiled. "But I suspect you might be one of life's rememberers," she had added. "I'll show myself out in a moment. First, I'm afraid I have another matter I must discuss with you. A piece of bad news. About someone you know."

*

His shift completed, Derek Latham drives his off-road vehicle the three miles from the station where he usually begins and ends his day's work to the pleasant one-bedroom coach house that he owns on a new-build estate close to the canal. He cannot stop thinking of the people on the train that morning – the great unwashed, as it had seemed. Something about the encounter is slow to leave him, and it is not the collective aroma that was in evidence in the carriage. Nor even the compounded disbelief that he had been forced to work through: one batch of disbelief, first, that the group of what he took to be homeless scruffs would be travelling anywhere together; and then a second bath of disbelief at the man who had produced valid tickets for travel for the entire ensemble . . .

And there was something, Derek realises at this moment, *about that leader* . . . He inserts his front door key slowly, just in case it is haste that ends up souring the memory and ruining the chances of making the relevant connections.

Stepping into his hallway, he smells the musty aroma of a chain of takeaway evening meals this week, the foil dishes awaiting his attention in the kitchen sink upstairs, and an overflowing basket of dirty clothes.

When the telephone rings in the lounge, Derek strides purposefully to take the call. Although he feels excited at the thought of talking to someone on the phone, he is also nervous. For a second he believes that it will be the man on the train who is contacting him.

As always, Derek answers by saying his own name, albeit in a querying tone.

"Derek Latham? Hello?"

"It's me." The caller waits. "It's Robbie. How have you been?"

*

"I can't say I *expected* you to get in touch," says Derek, a minute or so later, "but I must admit I expected *something*. The last couple of weeks have been weird."

"Consider me nodding my head," says Robbie. "We are both in the presence of the peculiar, I reckon. The question might be, whose version of peculiar is the *right* version of peculiar?"

Derek smiles. At first he is not sure how to respond; then he interprets that the smile and the fact that he is not sure how to respond – when combined – are a way of offering a reply.

"One of the things I missed when we divorced was your unique phrasing," he tells his ex-wife.

"I have some bad news to tell you, Derek. About Lorraine."

"I already know, but thank you, Robbie. A policewoman told me the other day. We were talking about something else and she slipped it in as she was about to leave."

"It wasn't Sharon Bark, was it, by any chance?"

"Yes it was; why do you ask?"

"Because she seems to be all over *everything*," Robbie replies. "You might think the police force have no other officers working their shifts at the moment. She was even at the funeral."

"*Lorraine's* funeral? Why?"

"She was on duty; I have no idea. But it seems like you only have to throw a pen out the window and it'll be returned to you by WPC Sharon Bark."

"Yes . . . *About* that funeral, Robbie," Derek prompts.

"I knew this was coming. I'm sorry: I should have called you. I thought about it for days . . . Would you have gone if you'd known about it?"

"And I knew *this* was coming. I don't know, is the honest answer. I have a lot of unfinished business," Derek replies. "Now destined *never* to be finished."

"True; but you turned your back on us a long time ago, Derek, don't forget that."

"I've spent a quarter of a century running away, Robbie. I hadn't spoken to Lorraine for nearly twenty of those twenty-five years. And you ask if I'd gone to her funeral if I'd known about it? The simple answer is probably not. But I'm not sure we're at a time to think simplistically. So maybe."

Robbie laughs into his ear. "Well, that settles *that* then."

Derek smiles. There follows a pause. Then Robbie's next question arrives out of the blue.

"Do you think she would have gone to *your* funeral, if *you'd* died first?"

This time Derek laughs out loud. "That's a question I could probably only answer if we were in the same room," he tells his ex. "What do you say to a drink? For old times' sake."

*

"I was thinking in the cab on the way over," Robbie tells him. "Maybe I got things muddled, but you mentioned – I think – that Sharon Bark told you about Lorraine; and you said you were discussing something else and she slipped Lorraine in as she was about to show herself *out*."

By now they are in The Scarlet. They agreed to meet with what will seem to both of them (in the future) a surprising lack of suspicion or foreboding: as if the rendezvous has always been on the cards and inevitable. In addition, they had both imagined the same pub in which to meet.

"Yes. I gave a statement about something that happened that led to a series of murders. She came to the house to take down what I had to say in evidence."

"Gosh. A *series* of murders?"

"Kind of. Almost like a gang thing. Basically, I was at work and one of the carriages had been stunk out by a group of pissed-up tramps – all apart from their leader. They called him Lord Biscuits. He was sober as a stone; and he had a full set of their tickets."

"Well, what about them? Being smelly isn't a crime."

"They travelled north by train to a *different* group of homeless people and basically kicked the shit out of them. There were deaths. All because, a little bit earlier, one of the *original* group had been killed by someone in the group up north while he was visiting."

"And what did Bark want of you in particular?"

"Just to describe what I'd seen and heard – which wasn't much, truth be told."

While Roberta sips her drink, little frown lines appear on the bridge of her nose.

"And she *told* you all that – what you've just told me?" she asks.

"She was surprisingly open about it all, I must admit."

"While in your house – as opposed to at the Police Station."

"Yes, I suppose that was a bit unorthodox," Derek admits.

"Why are you frowning?"

"I suppose there was something else odd. Bark used a laptop. And I remember thinking: whatever happened to a police officer taking notes with a pen and a little notepad that fits in the pocket, until I realised I was probably thinking of episodes of *Columbo* from the Seventies. She sat there typing, looking me in the eye – touch-typing – while I gave her what little I had to start with."

"I agree with you: that's unusual," says Roberta. "I don't suppose she showed you her credentials, did she?" At the end of her question is a giggle that sounds forced and nervous.

"Now that you mention it, I don't think so."

Roberta sips her drink again.

Leaning back slightly into The Scarlet's background sounds, Derek closes his eyes and tries to recall anything more about Sharon Bark's visit. He hears a female voice ordering drinks at the bar. Commentary on a football game from a screen in the far corner. Pool balls clicking.

He almost starts his next sentence with the words *Am I . . .* but corrects himself in time.

"Are we cooking up a conspiracy, do you think? It *does* seem our Sharon's jurisdiction is rather wider than you might expect."

"It does," Roberta agrees. "So what are we saying? She's not a real police officer?"

Derek leans forwards, returning to their table's orbit.

"We've managed to avoid the past for a long time, Roberta, but look what we did to that boy. And now Lorraine. Look what we did *in the name of protection.*"

"I know." Roberta drains her glass, and immediately wonders what the drink had been – she cannot taste anything. "We might hate the situation, Derek, but we *are* the parents – adoptive parents or not."

Derek nods. "We *are* the situation."

"Exactly. We have a responsibility. We have a *conscience.*"

"It chills my bones to say this . . . but what if Sharon Bark is part of our punishment? And if you tell me right now I'm being stupid, I will actually thank you. I want to be wrong."

Without acknowledging Derek's plea, Robbie continues to speak.

"I wasn't sure I'd ever hear from you again, Derek," she says.

"Did you want to?"

"I suppose I did. Just when you start to think you've got away with it, is the point when you're made to understand you haven't. Complacency's the problem . . . I saw her, Derek."

"Yes, you said – at the funeral."

"Not Sharon Bark. I saw *Lorraine.* After she'd died. In my home. With a witness present who saw the same thing. Lorraine wandered in, large as life, and my friend Carol says: *What are you doing here?* And Lorraine says something about us being able to change what people remember."

"The chance would be a fine thing!"

"We watched her colours fade – purple and cream. She looked peaceful. And then she asked Carol to ask Chaz – her therapist – but that hasn't come to much because of patient confidentiality. Then she slipped away, leaving nothing but a trace of her perfume."

Abruptly, Derek straightens his back. "Christ, that's it!" he says, placing his glass on the table too heavily (a few people turn their way to check the scene). "I *knew* there was something else!"

"What?"

"When Sharon Bark came to mine, she wore the same perfume Lorraine used to wear. I thought it reminded me of something but I didn't know what – I hadn't seen Lorraine for so long. Or reminded me of *who,* I should say. *Christ.*"

"It's a big leap, Derek; are you sure?"

"Well, as sure as I can be after twenty years. And yes, I know perfume isn't sold to only one person either – it could be a coincidence – but I couldn't think why Bark seemed *familiar* in some way."

"*Someone's remembering you* – that's what Lorraine said to us. Or to me. *You can change what people remember . . .* I have those words down cold. As soon as she drifted away, I wrote them down. The question is, what did she mean by them?"

"Well, partly. The other question is, how did Sharon Bark arrange for the ghost to appear? I don't doubt you and your friend saw *something*, but it was an illusion, Robbie. Ghosts don't exist."

Roberta and Derek fall silent. Seconds pass in which they are content to be surrounded by normal pub sounds; now that they have both swallowed what had been in their glasses, they are comfortable with drinking in The Scarlet's noises of normality.

"But we did our best, didn't we?" Derek protests against an accusation that only the two of them can silently hear. "We took Lorraine in and we kept her close to us. We even got *together* so we could keep her close. It was *me* who couldn't hack it. It was *me* who left and got a job on the rails."

Roberta nods her head. "We tried hard, Derek – we really did; but the damage was done a long time ago. We should never have got involved with that boy Lucas. Now we've a price to pay."

8

"Are you free for a minute, Chaz? There's something I think we should talk about."

It is three-fifteen on a weekday afternoon, and Chaz Bruce-Sange has answered the phone on her desk. Her patient, Carol Hayes, was due at three, and is usually punctual. Chaz has expected a call from her to explain her absence. She always mutes the phone's volume when a patient arrives for the therapy hour.

"This is about me, Chaz – about something I've done."

Chaz attempts to recall what assumptions she makes in the seconds that come after the words *something I've done.* She has been a psychoanalyst for three-quarters of her working life; in this time she has heard some outlandish confessions, and her guesses are usually accurate. She can tell a weekend transvestite, say, from someone lost in a Steinian psychic retreat. She can spot someone living with the after-effects of childhood abuse, sometimes as soon as that person walks into the room. But an admission of guilt – offered without warning – by one's ex-husband is a curiously different matter. Even as she utters the words "Okay, I'm listening," she cannot tie a notional crime to Kieran.

Perhaps he has been reckless with a financial investment . . . Perhaps he's getting married, she reconsiders (with something of a shock) a heartbeat later.

"You'll have a word for me," Kieran Sange informs his ex-wife, "professionally speaking."

"You're stalling, Kieran. Are you sure you want to tell me this?"

"Yes, I want to. The *how to* is the tricky part. What do you advise your clients when they find it hard to talk?"

"It won't help you. I don't advise anything at all. Sometimes you can learn as much from silence as from the words chosen."

There is something about her own response that disappoints her. Despite anything that she might have felt (or experienced) in the past, today's pastures are new, and the old lines, for once, are not the best.

At the other end of the line, Kieran sniffs. Chaz is not sure if the sound signifies laughter or a condescending form of dismissal.

"Are you *reading* me now, Chaz?"

"I'm trying to. I'm not getting much."

"Allow me, then, to be more specific . . . Isn't it odd that the one time I phone you at work is the same time your client doesn't show."

It is not perspiration that rolls down Chaz's spine; it is a sense of uncanny dread. Not for one instant does Chaz like it that Kieran has given voice to an aura of foreboding of which she was aware but had been oblivious of how to *cathect*.

"That doesn't *sound* very specific, Kieran. What's up?"

She rallies. Perhaps she has misunderstood up to now. With a degree of hope she adds: "Do you want to meet? Is that it? Do you want to discuss something you've done?"

Her left arm lifts the glass of water to her lips, and almost misses. Liquid dribbles down her chin; she gets approximately fifty per cent of the sip onto her tongue. Meanwhile, her right hand grips the phone with such tenacity that a new pulse originates in her wrist.

Kieran says: "I'm setting a scene, I think. You'll be able to remember the whys and wherefores of where you heard me say what I'm about to say."

At least it's not Jem, Chaz reminds herself. Jem is safe.

"I'm addicted to power," Kieran tells her. "I make people do horrible things, and I watch. It has only this second occurred to me I might have filmed what I orchestrated, but I didn't."

The next question is important, Chaz understands.

"What *kind* of things?" she asks, her voice as neutral and cloudless-sky as she can make it. "Do you mean sex things?"

"No. No, I mean violent things." Kieran sighs – and by doing so (in Chaz's estimation) he opens the chapter. "I once forced a tramp to eat a dead rat. That's the level of the starting point."

Chaz knows better than to test the silence with any further interruption.

"And that was bad enough," Kieran concedes. "But more recently I started a war."

Eventually, the silence seems to ring with a sound buried deep within it.

"Tell me everything," Chaz decides.

Eventually, Kieran obeys the directive; but not at first.

*

"She told me about a lecturer at the university," Kieran answers. "He was murdered. She was a little cut-up about that. No pun intended."

"I don't understand what you're saying, Key."

Kieran dodges into what seems to Chaz to be a painstaking silence. Professionally, Chaz is attuned to silence; she relishes it when it spreads between her and a paying customer – generally speaking, it means that a search for words or a plan for atonement or a longing for comprehension, are floating around the customer's conscious thinking. With this crucial element of her training and experience in mind, Chaz prompts herself once more to give Kieran space to find the means to divulge what is either on or underneath his mind.

"Do you remember," Kieran says, his voice lower in volume, "when we were first courting, we used to play games – conversational, get-to-know-you games."

He waits for an answer.

"Yes, Kieran – of course. Favourite this; favourite that. Politics. Music."

"And we talked about how much we could forgive about the other person, if you recall." Kieran's voice remains subdued; if it is not precisely a monotone, it is not much more animated than this.

"You asked me," Chaz recalls, "if I could forgive you if you killed someone."

When Kieran says "And what did you reply?" she swears she can hear him smile.

"I said . . ." Chaz has stood up with the phone in her hand. She walks around the front of her desk, to where the patient either reclines or sits down. With her less confident left hand, she lifts the jug of water from the tray. Pouring herself a glass is not as straightforward as it should be: a gulp of water from the jug's lip does more than miss the rim of the waiting glass – it misses the tray, and even the desk, and falls to the carpet with an inaudible impact.

Her right hand grips harder on the phone, as if to squeeze answers out of the connection – answers to questions that Chaz has yet to pose but must.

"And have you done that, Kieran? Have you killed someone?"

"More than someone. More than one," the Biscuit Inspector replies.

Injecting a note of authority into her voice, Chaz says, "Tell me. Tell me now, Kieran. Do I need to inform the authorities?"

"No. You need to listen."

Chaz waits a beat before venturing one step further. "For you, would it be better to meet face to face?" she asks.

The response is immediate – and unexpected.

"It really doesn't matter, Chaz. On the phone, in person. On *videoconference*. I did it. I took a group of people to fight a different group of people. I even got involved. And I enjoyed it. The violence was like a cold glass of water, to be honest. Now I have to think of a way of salving my conscience. You used to call it the post-traumatic depression."

"I still do. That's what it's called," Chaz replies.

She hears her ex-husband sniff. "How I miss your sense of fair play and decorum," Kieran tells her. "I miss the *calibration*. I don't have any of that now."

"What do you have instead?"

"The id roaming rampant. And what good will *that* ever go towards?"

"No good whatever. But tell me anyway."

Kieran pauses long enough for Chaz to believe that she has hit at least one target. When next he utters anything, it is in the form of an invitation.

"I take it back," he tells his ex. "It would be lovely to say what I have to say to you in person. What's your diary like? How busy are you?"

"Right now? Or during work hours?" asks Chaz.

"Well. If you're talking about now, I could get a taxi. The old place?"

Almost in spite of herself, Chaz seeks clarity. "The Anchor, do you mean?"

"How soon can you be there? I can finish early and walk there in forty minutes."

"Well, *I* can't, Kieran. My three o'clock appointment hasn't turned up but I have a four o'clock scheduled and then my notes to write up."

When Kieran suggests "Five-thirty, then?" Chaz is just about to accept; then she remembers an idea that had occurred to her when she'd been heating a can of soup for her lunch.

"Make is six-thirty, Kieran. I have something to do after I finish work."

*

Her day's work completed, Chaz's preparations are no more complicated than pulling on a scarf. Her coat is already in the car (where it always stays). It is almost as if she has been ready for years.

Without warning him that she is heading in his direction, Chaz drives over to the house of Den of Iniquity, in the expensive part of town. On her arrival, she parks in one of the visitors' bays, next to the space with the wheelchair painted inside it. She hopes that it is not an allocated space, and that she will not return to an angry resident.

Her mobile phone rings as she opens her door.

"Hi, Jemima," Chaz says. "Are you okay?" – the standard Mother's Question when a call comes in at an unexpected time, perhaps.

"I'm not okay but I have a question. Do you have a second?"

"Sure. But what do you mean, you're not okay?"

"Mum, I said *I* have a question. Can jealousy be treated?"

The identity of Chaz lock-and-loads efficiently into the identity of Dr Bruce-Sange. She collects to mind some research that might answer the question.

"Nasio believes so," she answers.

"Now imagine you're not at a conference and you're talking to your daughter."

"Sorry. A psychoanalyst name Juan-David Nasio – I was reading him recently for a case and I liked what I read. He talked about jealousy being *soothed* – and I like the word *soothed* here – if the person can be taught about the roots of his anxiety in childhood. He advocates seduction – constant and repeated *seduction* of one's partner. Trying to keep in mind the first date and feelings of trust that were created ... Does that answer your question?"

"Partly. What if it's siblings? Twins, specifically. What do *you* think?"

"I think the principle is exactly the same, obviously without the romance."

Jemima pauses and Chaz wants to the fill the space by asking her what is wrong. She tap-dances on this precipice for long enough to imagine the fall below if her daughter were to end the call in protest. Has she not just mentioned the word *trust*?

Allow her to chew, Chaz thinks. *Den can wait a few more minutes.*

"And what if there *was* a romance?" Jemima asks.

"Between the twins?

"Why else might a sister decide to destroy her twin brother? I mean, utterly *destroy* him? Set fire to his academic career. Belittle him on a career-wise scale. Make him homeless."

"Let's be clear," Chaz states, stretching her legs (her feet depress the pedals beneath her, to no effect whatever as the engine has been stilled). "Are you suggesting an incestuous relationship between a brother and a sister?"

"Not exactly. I'm *suggesting* I can't think of anything more applicable."

"*Which* brother and sister?"

"Lucas's mum and her brother – his Uncle Raymond."

Although Chaz had not announced to Den of Iniquity that she had planned to visit, she remains aware of her internalised daily diary. Has she time for this right now?

Probably not; but where would she be if she abandoned Jemima at this moment?

"Are you saying you know this for a fact?" Chaz wants to know.

"No, Mum. I'm saying I can't think of a better reason for a sister's actions against her brother."

"Than what?"

"Than habitual and wholehearted attempts . . . at personal and professional bullying."

"I see. But darling, there's a leap you've made there, between sibling rivalry – however serious – and a sexual crime. I'd need to consider at least *some* sort of evidence."

Jemima sniggers. "The evidence is surely my husband!"

Chaz reaches into the volcano's lava.

"Are you suggesting that Lucas is the *result* of an incestuous relationship?" As she asks this, she tries to count the number of loose ends that such an historical nightmare might tie up. "I take it you've discussed this with Lucas himself. What did he have to say?"

"He is *firmly* of the opinion that Louise has tried to control and then ruin his life. Not to mention the lives of his dad and his Uncle Raymond – among others, no doubt. He thinks it's her work and her life combined. Auto-ethnography. Being a part – an indispensable part, at that – of *everything* you observe. Of *everything* you witness others witnessing."

Mesmerised by the porch lights outside the house, Chaz nibbles gently on her bottom lip while conducting clerical duties on the material that Jemima has provided.

"I have to go," Jemima tells her mother, suddenly.

*

"This must be my lucky day," Den tells her, having opened the door. "Not one but *two* visitors. Two lovely ladies, no less."

"I don't mean to intrude," says Chaz. "I know I should have called ahead."

"You're not intruding. Why don't you come in?"

"You have company. I only have one question."

"At least into the hallway," Den replies. "I'm letting the heat out."

For the second time ever, Chaz Bruce-Sange steps into Den's property – into the hallway of the five-bedroom mock-Georgian pile.

"Would you care for a bourbon?" Den asks. "The bottle's open already."

"No, thank you – I have to drive."

"You had to drive the other day as well. You still had a few glasses with me."

"And I called a taxi to get me home," Chaz counters. "And there's somewhere I have to go shortly. That's not what I'm here for. I've wondered from then until now why neither of us mentioned the pregnancy – Lorraine's pregnancy. Did you know about it?"

The question seems to slap Den across the chops. "Did I know *what?*"

"That Lorraine was telling people she was expecting twins. By which we should assume *your* twins, Den. And yet – when I was here the other day, you didn't even mention your children."

"I had no idea – that's why. Who told you Lorraine was pregnant?"

"A policewoman named Sharon Bark. And Lorraine herself, of course."

"Lord Christ. I wonder if this can get any worse."

"I'm afraid it can," Chaz tells Den. "You have the perfect right to tell me to mind my own business, but I'm going to ask it anyway . . . You've got a few bob in the bank. You could attract a lot of different women, so why concentrate on a woman who was a prostitute, who escaped the care system? Help me understand. You obviously liked her, but what did you like?"

Den waits a few seconds.

"Mind your own business," he tells Chaz Bruce-Sange.

Suddenly, Chaz wants to know who is already present in Den's house.

"Chaz. My girlfriend died of organ failure on a street in this town, surrounded by a group of homeless people she regarded as her friends. To the best of my knowledge, there were no children – otherwise, why wouldn't I know this before now?"

Chaz notes movement to her right, at the end of the hallway. Someone approaches from inside the lounge, on a gentle wave of Miles Davis's *Kind of Blue*.

"I *thought* I recognised your voice, Chaz!" this other visitor announces.

"Carol. What brings . . ." She stops herself from posing the question. After all, why *wouldn't* Carol Hayes know Den of Iniquity if Lorraine had known him? They had worked in the same industry. It is she – Chaz Bruce-Sange – who is the outsider; and the time has come to vacate the scene.

"Carol and I were discussing my limited options," says Den. "I've begun to picture a future Lorraine and I will never share. That includes the holiday on the country's canals we won't go on. The narrow boat I won't steer through the locks. The pubs we won't stop at for lunches."

The hallway feels too small for this breadth of acceptance.

"I loved her, ladies," Den tells Carol and Chaz – and himself. "I wouldn't have made her an offer if I didn't believe in it. I'm very far from being a rock star, but I earn a decent Capital salary. If I hadn't loved Lorraine, I could have found a romantic solution in a different way. And I *did* want to spend the next chapter of my life with her, irrespective of anything else."

*

Along with the instincts to reflect on one's behaviour and to challenge one's own beliefs, a fundamental job requirement for the psychoanalyst is what Chaz Bruce-Sange has always regarded as a sense of self-preservation, tied to a knack of divining when something unfamiliar is approaching, possibly with menace on its mind.

She is reminded of this opinion again tonight.

Years earlier, at a conference in the Capital, she had startled and confused a workshop audience of supervisors, PhD candidates and Masters students with what seems (in retrospect) far less risky a comparison than it had at the time. To a certain extent, reducing some of her decodings of the work of Wilfred Bion to a handy soundbite, Chaz had said:

"To analyse a person (let's not worry about terms such as *client* or *analysand*, let's keep it human, on the human level) is to drink at the muddy edges of the watering hole, convinced there is prey nearby, and getting closer."

Dr Bruce-Sange's workshop had followed the theme of the weekend's conference: the nuances and interlocking links of intersubjectivity and recognition theory. As if on wings of song, Chaz had led the room through low clouds of puzzlement – and up! up! – into the thinner, chillier air of understanding and fulfilment. Academic eagles to a one, they had soared together for the two hours allocated to the session. And although not much about the conference as a whole has remained within her memory's grip, Chaz is able to hold onto how she had felt during the workshop that she had led, and not least because she had set herself a new challenge of how to describe her work from that off-the-cuff moment onward.

In the intervening years, she has never managed anything that has felt so accurate as the waterhole simile. Unexpectedly, it returns to her now, in a beam of yellow light, as powerful as that from a fireman's torch.

Keen but unable to process what she had discussed in the home of Den of Iniquity, and then with Kieran in The Anchor, Chaz has returned home emotionally breathless – a tad vulnerable, even. She requires a spur to fresh thought; intellectually, she has much to chew through. Although she has dressed for bed, complete with a generous application of night-time face moisturizer, she has put her feet up in her office and not in her bedroom, having chosen for her lullabye reading a well-thumbed copy of *Beyond Doer and Done To* by Jessica Benjamin.

Mere minutes into her re-reading of a favourite chapter, and a sentence trips her brain up. Not knowing that she is squinting in the insufficient desk-lamp light, Chaz Bruce-Sange straightens minutely, a frown on her face. Then she reads the sentence again, this time aloud to her audience of shy ghosts.

"There may be no tenet more important," she recites slowly, "to overcoming the shame and blame in analytic work than the idea that recognition continually breaks down, that thirdness always collapses into twoness, that we are always losing and recovering the intersubjective view."

Her breath has stalled, a faulty engine. In deliberately short flashes she thinks of Den and Lorraine; it is as if, by thinking quickly, she might collide their images or words together, like the clicking of pool balls, the better to create unexpected angles of trajectory and reach. *What am I missing?* Chaz asks herself through the flickering kaleidoscope of their untouching bodies.

"We have to keep reminding ourselves," she continues reading from Benjamin's book, "that breakdown and repair are part of a larger process, as concomitant of the imperatives of participating in a two-way interaction."

For Chaz, the workshop that she had led, and the creature-at-the-watering-hold recollection, both arrive in her head in a nostalgic gulp. Looking up from the text, she peers into the room, almost daring Lorraine to appear for her as Carol Hayes had claimed that she had wafted in for Carol and Roberta.

Show me, is the sentence that Chaz forms in her mind. Then aloud she adds: "Give me something about you to believe in."

Only silence speaks back to Chaz Bruce-Sange . . . except it is not quite silence. The air sounds faintly of ringing, in the way that her hearing has droned and tinkled during moments of high pressure, for decades. It means nothing by itself, she knows . . . and yet . . . hadn't Carol mentioned that directly before Lorraine had put in her appearance the air had grown hotter? And here it is, at nearly ten in the evening, when the air should be nippy, a certain *blush of temperature* in the day's fading hours. Absent-mindedly, Chaz wipes a thin patina of sweat from her forehead.

"Am I ill?" she asks aloud.

No, I am not. I am drinking at the watering hole, surrounded by dry land.

Chaz sits up straight; her spine clicks. What form will her predator take? The shape of Lorraine herself? Lorraine dead or Lorraine alive?

The threat is not what's in the muddy water. There is no boat in there – no crocodile either. The threat can see me but I can't see the threat.

When the telephone rings, Chaz almost jumps out of her chair.

She drops *Beyond Doer and Done To* onto the carpet; the negligible impact is muffled. All that Chaz can do is go over to the desk to pick up the receiver.

*

The voice at the other end is playful.

"It's Super-Supe!" the voice informs Chaz's left ear.

For Chaz it is to be an evening of firecracker reminiscences. If the powerful memory of the workshop she had orchestrated at the conference had not been enough to convince her of chains that grow invisible with age but never snap, the voice and the academic pet name adds evidence to the hypothesis.

"Louise?" Chaz asks – but of course it is Louise.

If Chaz remembers correctly, a matter of months before the conference, Dr Louise Reardon had called her out of the blue, ostensibly to enquire after her general academic and physical wellbeings. The other reason that Louise had phoned was to pick Chaz's brain on a question that the latter cannot specify, other than to say it had referred to one of Louise's academic monographs.

Hearing Louise's voice right now makes Chaz believe that her former PhD supervisor has another set of questions for her. The fact that the hour is so late is not enough – not immediately – to crumple the notion underfoot.

"What ails you?" Louise wants to know.

Recalling the routine, Chaz smiles; a portion of tension lifts from her left shoulder, where it had built while listening to her ex-husband's confession in The Anchor, though she had not been aware of it acutely until now.

After the obligatory term as a PhD candidate's second supervisor, Louise had displayed the correct credentials to be a first supervisor. This part of her career had been launched by supervising a thesis by a Psychology Masters graduate named Charlotte Bruce. Chaz could remember Louise joking that she – Chaz – had developed her own name as she'd developed the drafts of the chapters.

"You're a super supervisor," Charlotte had told Louise in one of the university's cafeterias, after a supervisory hour.

Louise's response had been playful. She had even frowned a made a show of flexing her muscles in imitation of the Hulk of the Lou Ferrigno era.

"Me a Super-Supe," she had replied. "What ails you?"

"Nothing," Chaz answers – as she'd answered at the time, at the inauguration of one of the pair's longest running routines.

Louise had grinned (as Chaz imagines her grinning right now, at the end of the phone line, wherever that happens to be). "If nothing ails you . . ." Louise's voice taunts.

". . . then what is the *point* of you?" the two women say together – a punchline that neither has heard for several years, nor even read in the occasional catch-me-up email or Yuletide card of goodwill.

A few seconds elapse while they laugh. Then it seems to Chaz that the shadows lengthen – not necessarily in a physical sense, but maybe that too.

"I'm sorry," Louise offers, "I know it's late." She sighs into Chaz's ear. "I've been travelling. I mean tonight. I left home after dinner, at about eight o'clock. I had dinner with my daughter Tamara and my partner Frank. Then I told them I needed to work – I'm working on a new book. I ran a bath. I even took that bath. Then I entered my study . . . and crawled out of the window when I was certain Tamara was on the phone and Frank was watching a documentary."

"You climbed out of the *window*?" Chaz repeats. To Chaz, Louise's short speech has about it a slight whiff of overpreparedness – of trying a tad too hard. One of the things that Chaz had loved about having Louise as her PhD supervisor was the other woman's freshness and ability for an off-the-cuff delivery. The stiltedness in Louise's lines elicits worry in Chaz's brain. She has tensed without knowing that she's done so.

"Louise? Friend to friend. What ails you?" Chaz asks.

"I travelled to see you tonight. I sneaked out of my office window and across the garage roof. A woman of *my* years!"

"To see *me?* Where are you now?"

"At a pub called The Scarlet," Louise tells her. "I took a train south."

"To see *me?*" Chaz repeats.

"Partly. Also to face a demon or two. I've been sitting in the smokers' garden since I got here. Saw my first ever real-life *rat* tonight. It moved between two bushes, not three feet from me."

Chaz is not sure of the thread that runs through Louise's statements, if indeed one even exists. She frowns. "Where are my manners? If you've travelled to see me – even as part of something else – the least I can do is invite you over. Which one's The Scarlet? I'm sorry – I'm not one for pubs."

"I'm about six streets from your warm embrace," Louise answers; "and for the first time I think I've understood the full implications of the phrase *freezing my tits off.*"

*

"I'm going to assume you have no idea about my ex-husband," Louise says, "otherwise I'm sure you would have said something." As Chaz shakes her head, Louise explains. "He was murdered. By a group of rough sleepers near where I live."

"Oh my word! My own ex-husband told me about this only a few hours ago. I can't believe it. I mean, I had no way of knowing who he was. He worked at the university here. That's all I knew."

Louise sighs.

"As far as I know, Finley was living a double life for academic purposes. He was pretending to be a homeless guy named Frank, around here somewhere. When he visited the house for our daughter's twenty-first, he got into an argument with my partner – also named Frank, just to make things more complicated. Tamara asked him to leave – and instead of going somewhere safe, like a hotel, like a *normal* person, he decided to get into character and hang around a gang of tramps."

"As Frank?"

Louise nods her head.

"Like a busman's holiday. I think he was either writing something – or researching to write something – or he was building material for case studies to use with undergrads. Can you imagine how his twenty year-olds would have loved his efforts on their behalf!"

Chaz leaves a beat. "You sound bitter," she tells Louise.

"About my ex-husband's murder? He was set upon by a pack of scum. They kicked him *to death*, Chaz."

"No. About Finley's appeal to his undergraduate classes," Chaz clarifies.

Louise sniffs into a tissue that she has produced from the left-arm sleeve of a peach blouse with a honeysuckle print motif on the front. She squeezes her nostrils rather than blowing her nose.

"I think you imagine I'm accusing Finley of trying tactics to get into his students' best books and thereby their knickers. Well, it's possible. I honestly don't know. As far as I know, there was one twenty-four year-old called Lorraine, years ago – the affair that didn't exactly end our marriage, but it made me question certain truths about Finley."

The word *Lorraine* is like a ricochet of syllables these days. *But it's just a girl's name,* Chaz attempts to convince herself. *It's not the same woman. It can't be.*

Except she was *a prostitute* . . .

"Is it my imagination," says Louise, "or do you currently sport the expression of one in receipt of a *wet fart*?"

"So I'm clear. Your ex-husband once had an affair . . ."

"A fling, really."

"A fling, then – with a woman named Lorraine. A student at the university."

"Correct. But it was donkey's years ago. I'm not angry."

"Could you describe her?"

"Physically or emotionally?"

Chaz recalls something that Louise had repeated during the PhD years. "Interpret the question any way you want to," she advises her former supervisor, with the growing pains of a smirk on her face.

Louise copies Chaz's expression.

"Well okay. I can't do the physical resemblance – I never had the pleasure of her company, thank God. What do you say to the student – even if she's a mature student – who doesn't care if your marriage ends or stays together?"

"That's fair. I don't suppose you remember her surname, do you?"

"I doubt I ever knew it. But I remember – when it all came out, with Finley – he said something like, she's trying to better herself. She'd escaped the care system and her mum managed a brothel, of all things. *What ails us?* you ask. She told Finley there was something pitch black in her teenage years – something happened."

Louise pauses.

"To put the matter at its most specific, something happened when she was a babysitter for our son Lucas, when he was eight and nine and Lorraine was sixteen."

"I'm confused. You just told me you couldn't describe her physically . . . yet you're saying now she was your *babysitter*?"

"For a little while; yes," Louise tells her.

"I know I'm tired, Louise, but please help me with this. Why aren't you interested in why I'm interested in Lorraine? Why haven't you queried anything along those lines?"

"I'm not at all sure what you're suggesting, Chaz."

"It's almost as if you've assumed I know who Lorraine is. Was."

"You were the one who mentioned her!"

"No, Louise – that would have been you. You brought up the subject of your ex-husband's fling and I can't help think you led me into the discussion."

"Chaz. Are you *analysing* me?" Louise seems to find the notion amusing.

"It's late. What brought you here, really?"

"Would you mind if I left you with a cliffhanger? It's late, as you say, and I'm tired. We can pick it up in the morning."

Although she resents the assumption that Louise has made – that a room is available for her to sleep over – Chaz cannot feel bad either about going to bed now or about talking more in the morning. She has not so much as started to process the information that Kieran had told her in The Anchor, about coaxing groups of homeless people to fight one another. Today has been a day of massive communicative traffic, all of it on its way to Chaz's head.

"What's the cliffhanger, then?" Chaz asks.

"Do you remember what you wrote about Carl Jung and the imago?"

"In the thesis? Seriously?"

"I assure you. You don't forget the good ones."

Despite everything, Chaz smiles at the flattery. "The good theses or the good students?"

"Both." Louise appears deadly serious. "You wrote something like, Carl Jung coined the term imago to describe a way that people form their personality by identifying with the collective unconscious."

"That sounds about right. It's a bit of a distant memory, I must admit," Chaz replies.

"What about this? What if Lorraine was a part of the lives of so many people we have in common that she might as well have been a part of the lives of *everyone* we know?"

*

It proves difficult for Chaz to remain asleep. Although she is able to drop off quickly, she wakes several times before dawn, damp with bad dreams and an insistent bladder.

On the third of these internal wake-up calls – on the landing, while tiptoeing past what she will always refer to as Jemima's room – she holds her breath for a second, curious to know if Louise is a snorer. Momentarily it disappoints Chaz not to hear snoring but to hear, instead, the gentle rhythmic pads of nails on laptop keys. Although the sun has yet to rise, Louise is working. Chaz wonders if she should offer her guest a cup of tea through the door.

Chaz is convinced that she has been worked. Manipulated. But what she cannot see is why Louise would have chosen to do so.

Late last night, when Louise had retired to Jemima's old room, Chaz had returned to her office to peruse her collection of books by Dr Louise Reardon. Louise's area of interest is now autoethnography; it has been for some time. This means that Louise likes to dig in. She likes to be part of the show and not simply a reporter.

If Louise is working the room, then I am also in that room. Being worked.

Chaz goes down to the kitchen and brews tea.

Louise joins her twenty minutes later. "Sorry if I kept you," she offers; "I think I mentioned I was close to the end of a book."

"You did. What's it about?"

"Oh, the usual, to be honest. Being part of the study you're observing. Living in the tribe you're interacting with."

"And who are the people you're observing? What is the tribe you're interacting with? What is the book actually *about?*"

Louise makes a show of sipping from her juice. She announces that she is struggling with the book; and although Chaz hears the words, she is not sated. Being told that the book is proving difficult is nowhere near the same as explaining the book's general theme.

I'm being lied to. Why is she lying to me?

9

Darryl Carbrini settles back into the gentle incline of the bath-tub. The water is as hot as blood.

After his ablutions, he ventures downstairs and tries to take stock. Uppermost in his mind is the intertwined image of Carol Hayes and Lorraine. As he pours himself a drink and puts on a CD, Darryl finds it difficult to distinguish between the two women. He also senses their combined imago climbing down from a ledge in order to smother him.

Unexpectedly, next, he thinks of Jemima Sange – specifically of Jemima and her boyfriend Billy. With his skin remaining hot from the bath, Darryl stretches out at a right angle from his couch, his bare feet, steaming, on a faux-leather pouffe, his dressing-down wide open in order for his body's pores to breathe. In the log-burner next to the television, three dried arms of wood crackle contentedly in a mauve-and-orange gentle blaze.

When the front doorbell rings, Darryl rises to his feet with the glass of whiskey still in his hand. The whiskey is good for his ever-loving toothache. However, it is not so good for his general balance and sense of composure. Darryl stumbles to the front door, not angry at the intrusion; merely prematurely drunk – and a good portion sad.

Who else is likely to visit him after nine o'clock in the evening, after weeks of subtle flirtation? It is bound to be Carol Hayes, who has visited Octaves time after time to discuss recommendations for presents for the Sugar Daddy in her life.

Smiling broadly, Carbrini opens his front door. His visitor is not Carol Hayes.

"Hello, Jemima. Is it a piano lesson night I didn't know about?"

Darryl steps aside to allow her access.

"I have some piano lesson in my bag," she replies. "Be my teacher again, eh? Won't you?"

*

The two of them sit in Darryl's living room. Not a word is shared between them. With great concentration on her face, Jemima cooks heroin in a spoon over a naked candle flame. Darryl watches – with hunger and a degree of greed.

"Darryl, sterilise the needle, would you? We're nearly there."

Darryl moves into the kitchen and boils the kettle again. He holds the needle of the syringe that Jemima has brought with her near the spout, where scalding steam forms drops of water against the plastic and drips away onto the chopping board.

"Hurry up, Darryl!" he hears. "We have the opening bars!"

He calls back: "Strike up the band!" Then he hurries into the living room with his dressing-gown wide open.

"You're first," Jemima tells him. "My gift to you – my thank you."

"For what?" Darryl asks.

"For not asking questions like *For what*? Which arm?"

She and Darryl watch the liquefied heroin move through the barrel and into the narrow point. While leaning back into an armada of cushions and throws, Darryl acknowledges the warm Morse code in his blood; the forward tilt of his head.

Ideally, his mind would be empty; this, however, he is unable to achieve. Doubts ferret along the tunnels and rope-bridges at the back of his mind. But at least his toothache has vanished. His brain rides a wave of euphoria; there is no reason not to share this joy with a loaded sigh.

"Enjoy it," Jemima tells Lucas now. "I'll just watch tonight."

The pleasurable sensation that Darryl has been enjoying is diluted and dimmed. The warmth in his body, concentrated in his arms, heart and bollocks, ducks down a degree or two: to such an extent that Darryl remains happy, but reality has cut through the narcotic surf.

Darryl finds the idea of Jemima's abstinence problematic. He waits for the panic to course through his frame. Jemima has injected too much into his flesh. Jemima has mixed the powder with rat poison . . . Darryl waits to know what to say in order to reflect his own terrors.

Jemima asks him: "How come you've never married, Darryl?"

"I have nothing to confess. Will you speak honestly if I ask you an honest question?"

"Well, I might. You want to know what I gave you. You want to know if there's an antidote."

"Partly. More pressing, though," says Darryl, "I want to know what's in it for you. Why are you doing this?"

While moving to another chair, Jemima sighs as she might at the announcement of a train being late. In her bones there is no trace of anger: there is only disappointment, which she knows she will have to decode for Darryl shortly.

"Honestly? I wanted a reaction from you I couldn't get from my husband. He ignores me."

"You sound petulant. You make my teeth feel better, at least."

". . . Believe it or not, Darryl, that's probably the nicest compliment I've ever been paid. Things are *that* tragic. I make a toothache go away."

"Believe it or not, it's the most positive compliment I've offered."

Jemima prepares another fix for Darryl Carbrini.

While Darryl nods, post-injection, Jemima seeks out a CD to play that she already knows. The cover image being familiar to her, she selects *Kind of Blue* by Miles Davis, and slides it into the tray.

"Don't worry about me," says Darryl, apropos of nothing. "I was only ever supposed to be a minor player in this drama."

He explores the waves of analgesia that wash in and out of his gums; and on tides of discomfort and then bliss, he sails away, in search of a sunset.

*

Jemima is caught between the tugging tensions of contrary purposes.

Stepping away from Darryl's house, she contemplates her walk home to Lucas – and to whatever she might find there – while the drizzling rain is framed in consecutive squares of moonlit attention. She cannot move away from Darryl's front door. She is not certain if behind her back she has abandoned a live man or a dead man.

Reluctantly she walks into the rain.

"Billy," Jemima says into her mobile, "I need to speak to you. I think I've made a horrible mistake. I think I've left my piano teacher dead."

Grinning, she lengthens her stride, suddenly eager to be home.

*

An hour later, and conversation has reached a natural but temporary cessation. Lucas and Jemima have stopped talking. They break from each other, and while Jemima uses the bathroom, Lucas prepares refreshments. When he returns to the front room, Jemima appears poised.

"Have you ever told anyone about this?" she wants to know.

"No. I've always assumed I wouldn't be believed."

"Well, that's reasonable. You have to admit it's farfetched."

"The *furthest* fetched! And yet it's what I remember. As far as I know it's an accurate record."

Jemima leans forwards. By this point they are seated opposite one another, a coffee table between them. For the conversation that was certain to follow, they eschewed the option of alcohol, or even caffeine. Both have a mug of hot water with a slice of lemon staying afloat. Even the bowl of peanuts in No-Man's-Land equidistant across the width of the table has been untouched.

She takes her husband's hands in her own and tries again to articulate her thoughts.

"Except you know it can't *really* have happened, don't you, Lucas?" Jemima does not wait for a response. "Because if it *had* happened, you would have spent a long time in psychiatric care. Do you understand? And however painful that sort of experience might have been . . . "

"That *sort of* experience?" Lucas protests. "Is it not at least *unique*?"

"That experience then: however painful it *was*, it's impossible you would've kept it smothered for so long. So *repressed* for so long," she adds.

Lucas dunks his head under a shower of silence.

"Your uncle . . . Could I ask you to be more specific? I'm not sure I understand what you're saying. What did he *do*?"

Visibly, Lucas winces at the airing of this question.

"He set off explosives in crowded places. But I didn't have any idea of that until much later."

"He was a *terrorist*?"

"He and Dad were *activists*. Others joined them."

"Yes. You mentioned Pat Kelly."

Lucas nods his head.

"Lorraine's boyfriend when she was my *au pair*. He got involved in trying to *protect* me, along with the others, but later. This is when things were blurry. The other was a man named Derek Latham. There were four of them. All obsessed with the idea of keeping me *safe*. And then later, my *au pair* Lorraine safe – even though it was her boyfriend Pat Kelly who pimped her out to me in the first place."

"While you were a *child*?" Jemima sounds aghast.

"While we were *both* children, really."

*

Quite considerably later, but before they have retired to bed, Jemima asks: "Do you think she would still have the same work mobile – your mum, I mean?"

Lucas shrugs. "I can't see why not." Then his face turns curdles – something between a displeasured frown and the expression of a build-up of flatulence. "Why do you ask?"

"I'm going to phone her. Find out what *she* thinks happens to her twin brother."

"You're not!"

"I *am,* Lucas. Don't get all manful and husbandy on me *now* – not when we might actually be *getting* somewhere! And I'm finding it difficult to believe, by the way, this is the first time you might've considered this."

After no more than a few seconds have elapsed, Lucas forms a slow and high-wire sentence. "If you call her . . . " he begins.

"Yes? What will I say?" Jemima guesses.

"Yes. What will you say? She's likely to put the phone down."

"Say she does. What have we lost? Nothing. And who knows? It might be a trigger . . . Mum likes to talk about *closure* in her work. Sealing the traumatic experience, in terms that are at least acceptable if not exactly pleasant."

For the first time in a while, Lucas grins – and to Jemima it seems authentic. Her husband appears truly amused.

"Am I to be one of your mother's case studies?" he asks wryly.

"You could do a lot worse, mate!"

"I *have* done a lot worse! That's why I'm trying to tell you! I ate my uncle!"

Absentmindedly, Jemima thumb-strokes a sequin-sized red dot that is there, as plain as plain can be, in the crook of her left arm. Where the needle punctured recently, an itchy rust of healing skin has developed.

"But you *didn't,* Lucas. Are we not getting anywhere with breaking down this barrier?"

*

"Mum was an academic. She probably still is. The last I heard she worked at a university in the north."

"When was the last time you spoke to her?"

"Actually *spoke* to her, eleven years ago. I called her two days before Christmas and asked if I was okay to call her on Christmas Day itself, just to offer her and her new partner my best wishes for the season. She said it was probably best if I didn't. She even asked how I'd got her mobile phone number – as if she'd told everyone not to give it to me if I ever made enquiries."

"And how *did* you get her mobile number?"

"It was a work mobile. It was listed on her profile on the university's web pages."

"So what did you do?"

Lucas shrugs. "Wished her a Merry Christmas and hung up. What else could I have done? She said goodbye and made it clear I wasn't worth bothering about. And that it wasn't a great idea to try again . . . so I never have. You want to call her, don't you?" Lucas asks.

"Your mother? Absolutely I do."

A sigh escapes Lucas's teeth, like air through a slow puncture. He nods his head briskly. "Then call her. With my blessing," Lucas says. "And I'll just offer you my good luck."

"But I won't call here from here. I'm going out again."

*

Billy Alfreth wakes in the early hours of the morning.

Jemima is asleep beside him, dressed in layers of clothing that is not night-wear. She arrived at the shared door, drunk and inconsolable. Although Metal Mickey had allowed her across the threshold, his expression had informed Billy that Jemima's appearance was not a welcome surprise.

On hearing Billy's offer of coffee, Jemima had simply said, "I need to sleep."

Similarly tired – emphatically too tired to fight – Billy had opened the bedsheet beneath his duvet so that it resembled a boat's sail. Jemima had floated into his bed and picked up the tail-wind of her own dreams. In sleep she had sailed away quickly, but not without a statement to leave Billy puzzling in her wake. Although her eyes had been closed and her breathing had been heavy, apropos of nothing they'd discussed, Jemima had said:

"Nostalgia isn't what *you* remember, Billy. It's not what I remember either. It's what we *all* remember, compressed into something intense and natural as weather."

Somewhere close to three in the morning, Jemima slides out of Billy's bed and opens the bedroom door as quietly as she can. By now, dressed only in one of Billy's t-shirts, she tiptoes down the flight of stairs, on her way to the kitchen, where she knows that a strong phone signal throbs.

"He told me everything you taught him about the asylum and those days," Jemima tells her interlocutor. "Would you mind if I told you I was impressed?"

"That Lucas could recall the details?"

"No. Impressed that you had such a *catastrophic* impact on him . . . You're *good*. I can only hope to be half as good as you."

At the other end of the phone line, Dr Louise Reardon chuckles. "All in good time, I should say. You're doing great, Jemima," she replies.

She lay there sound asleep with her wanderings over and mine just beginning. I have been thinking about this simple event for years now. It stays with me and repeats itself over and over again like a pale marble movie.

Richard Brautigan,
Revenge of the Lawn

Then thoughts of childhood walks with my parents and travels to Nolinga Canyon drift through my mind. "Is that you, nostalgia?" I murmur. I start pedaling faster.

"Don't worry," I assure anxiety. "I'm paying attention to the path."

Soramimi Hanarejima,
'Self, Out of Focus'

It has been noted that society can only choose her masterpieces from works that are known.

David Mamet,
Make-Believe Town

NEVER

1

This is in the Realm of Never, one of his drivers informs him. *There's no Now, no Before, no Later. There's just Never. And unfortunately for you, that's where you are. Because we've never existed, do you see,* Frank? *You were never here. Nor were we. Only your pain is something that can exist here. Your words can't.* Do you understand me?

My name is Finley – Dr Finley Reardon. I am not Frank.

We made you Frank – Frank is who you'll be as far as we are concerned.

Okay, I'm Frank.

*

Someone remembers you, she tells him as he clings to the mast.

He is on a boat, at what he only knows as 'the pointed end'. It is impossible for him to judge the size of the vessel; he believes it is small, rocking as it is from side to side. The mast smells of blood and disinfectant, and he is terrified of letting go of it in case he is tossed over the side. But even if he *is* lobbed overboard, it will not be into dark waves of angry bruised water: no surges or upswells or eddies have the boat in their grip. For this particular ocean does not consist of water . . .

The ocean is made of memories – and made of dreams.

As far as the eye can see, the waves are shambolic and they ramble. The noise is intense: conversations and wars; dream crimes and fantasized sounds, merged together in humankind's collective unconscious. Some thoughts drowned, abandoned on the sea floor; other notions squabbled in the waves, rippling and flowing and climbing the sides of the boat, as if wanting to be caught like strange fish.

When he awakes, it is as if the dream spills into the room; for a heartbeat he rides the rolling surf of what his mind conjured up, as it laps over what the limited illumination offered by his desk lamp defines. Then the wave retreats – and he is alone in a study, surrounded by books and papers.

Are you coming to bed? a woman asks him from beyond the closed door. *It's late. Your Exam Board is in the morning.*

Standing up produces clicks in Frank Tucker's back. *Coming!* And he knows that nothing more needs to be said – he and Louise are both academics, neither of them scared of long working hours – but he wants to explain what he has been doing.

Fresh from a close-to-midnight bath, Louise is wrapped in towels, and her moisturizing night-cream aroma is piquant as she waddles across the landing. Frank follows. Louise whispers: *How did you get on?*

I fell asleep working . . . I have to tell you something, Frank answers.

Before he is five sentences into his account, Louise has stopped drying herself. Sitting on the edge of the bed, she listens to her partner intently. Frank has moved fresh folded laundry off a reading chair; he sits here, leaning forward, his hands a performance of exaggerated mime, his eyes wide but not focused on the present. It is almost like a broadcast from a trance.

And you didn't think to tell me? she keeps asking herself – but silently. She allows Frank Tucker to talk while her skin cools. Night-cream seeps into the lines around her eyes and mouth.

I'm telling you now.

Panic reaches into Louise's ribcage; it gives a squeeze. *What's my ex-husband's name?* she demands of herself.

Frank answers aloud: *His name was Finley.* He has stood up and is now undressing for bed. *But he was not your first husband. You were married to a man named Robert. You and he had a son called Lucas. And you tried to destroy them both – and others.*

Ignoring the accusation, Louise demands: *How did you know what I was thinking?*

Frank continues: *He said: "It's impossible for a journey to be incomplete, son. Even the boat that sinks reaches a final destination – though not the one anyone planned for it, or expected for it. The boat still finished somewhere: it had a starting point and a resting point."*

I'm just tired, Louise tells herself. *I'm in shock.*

But what's the point you're making? she adds. *I'm not sure I understand.*

Louise fights hard to rejoin herself in her own head and body.

I've been working on a theory, Frank tells her. *May I join you on the bed?*

Louise laughs. Has she heard him correctly? *Of course you can. It's your bed as well as mine!*

Well, it was before I died. I wasn't so sure . . .

Before what? Louise answers.

Between two blinks of her eyes, Frank Tucker has morphed into Finley. It is her ex-husband, recently violently deceased, who stands in what once had been their marital home.

Louise considers calling for Tamara. Not only will Tamara know what to do, she will also have a cocky young woman's take on her mother's state of mind. Tamara will burst the bubble – maybe wake Louise up from what must be a dream.

However, the other Louise is speaking again.

Oh, Finley! she says in an amused tone from within their shared body. *It's not like I'm cross with you. We haven't had an argument. Of course you can come to bed.*

Finley lies down next to Louise.

Don't panic, the scared Louise tells herself.

Finley hears her thought but assumes that the words are in response to his question about joining her on the bed. *Okay, I won't panic*, he says.

Together, as if on cue, they wriggle into slightly different positions, the better to see one another; however, there remains a small gap between their bodies – they have not yet touched. Although there is no light on in the room, they can see one another clearly. To neither of them does it seem surprising that they are now naked, with no memory of having disrobed.

You're wondering if your fingers will go through me, says Finley.

Louise takes a deep breath. When the other Louise inside her says nothing, she ushers the dialogue along by asking: *Well, will they?*

I don't know. Let's try.

When they lean up on their elbows and join hands there is a moment of confusion, similar to the first thoughts upon waking – a dislocation that rushes to clear itself. For both of them, the holding of hands is not like skin on skin had once been, but a link is made in their heads.

Are you a ghost, Finley? Louise asks silently.

The man closes his eyes. *I've had such dreams, my darling*, he replies. *I honestly don't know how to answer your question.*

If Louise is disappointed with the reply, she is not disappointed with how her senses clear and settle. No longer can she feel the other Louise; all she can feel is a union with her ex-husband. The *mal-de-mer* nausea has abated.

I am under the effects of shock, she whispers. *But tell me what you saw. Calm me like you used to.* With which she shuffles into an embrace that she will remember with fondness.

*

Hours later, she thinks of a different timespan from that of hours. She thinks of decades; of lives.

What we experience, she decides, *are recollections made much later. What we experience are the memories of dead people.*

When Louise wakes, it is to a room in which no one else is present – not Finley, not Frank, and not Finley's alter ego Frank, either. She is alone . . . apart from in her head. With her inside her head is the face and the voice that had once belonged to Lorraine.

Why are people drawn to people they know will be trouble? To 'tame' the violent rapids of their partners' hearts? Perhaps. Because they are bored with stability and stasis?

. . . *How much* longer *do I have to wait?* Louise asks herself, rolling out of bed.

*

I suppose I have one more thing to say, Dr Tucker – about nostalgia. And this is only my opinion, but based, I think, on quite a lifetime of experience on the subject.

Nostalgia is a way of stitching together one's happy moments and leaving out the dull bits. It's the Ark that collects the dull bits for storage, for when we need them to hide something worse. The Ark sails us through some of the hard times; but it also protects us from remembering some of those same hard times. The Ark did not collect animals two by two, it collected experiences and boredom.

Please give my good wishes to the loved one in your life, Dr Tucker.

2

Their lives take place on a massive ship, someone says. *A ship taking experiences to other universes.*

Billy wakes with the shakes and sees Jemima on the threshold into the hallway. He has no idea of who has given him the advice during the dream-year that has elapsed in the previous few minutes, with his head crowded onto the pillow that he has squashed to his cheeks.

Did you dream of a ship? she asks him . . . but even in these immediate wakeful moments, Billy is not certain that her voice is the right voice.

Where do you go to, my lovely? Billy half-asks and half-sings. It's an old song by Peter Starstedt, a song that Billy has heard recently on a karaoke night in The Anchor, sung by Noel, the rugby-playing feminist. It is also a song that was occasionally sung in the register of high irony during Billy's time in prison. The boys on C Wing used to sing it.

Billy gets serious. *Actually, where* do *you go to, my lovely?* he asks.

I was never here, Billy, Jemima replies.

Her voice has turned into something deeper. A man's voice? Simultaneously, Billy's imagination reins in the Labradoodle in the back of the car. Billy tries to implicate Jemima in the canine abandonment, based on what she has just said. He cannot make the argument swim.

Tell me honestly, Billy calls. *Are you on something right now?*

On something like heroin? You can stop being my over-protective baby sister, Jemima retorts. *I'll do whatever I fancy.*

Billy knows that what she says is true. He must change tack. *Does the name* Narna *mean anything to you, Jem? As in . . . Narna the First. Narna the Second . . .*

To Billy's surprise, Jemima nods her head.

My husband had dogs called Narna when he was a boy, she replies.

The dog in the back of the car was called Narna the Third. It was Lucas's dog! Billy explains in an excited tone. *Lucas is trying to tell me something . . .*

Jemima smiles, backs out onto the landing and repeats something that she has already said.

I was never here, Billy . . .

Walking backwards, dressed in her swimsuit, she continues talking.

But do you remember when we met on our first day at the university? You kept a diary, but I've kept a memory. From the first time I saw you, I knew I was the glue between two stories.

Billy hears her slither down the stairs.

3

Emeritus Professor Raymond Cossell hears his voice spoken through the medium of dream and wakes up to a familiar scene of comfortable despair. This happens often.

In his dream he had lectured to a hall full of undergraduate students. The subject was *Crowds and Power* – Elias Canetti. And the King had been in his counting house: the Professor had flung himself around in the paradoxically limitless confines of his comfort zone. He'd enjoyed the full range of his intellectual swing; and three hundred undergrads had hung upon his every well-chosen word.

Both the dream and recent events have given him back his name. It is not that he had forgotten the respected career in

Higher Education that he had enjoyed; it is more that the caesura between those work years and his current status contains an event that he would prefer to keep secret, even from himself.

"*People* know *the man whose death they lament,*" Professor Cossell quotes from *Crowds and Power*. "*Only those who were close to him, or who know precisely who he was, have a right to join the lamenting pack.*"

Taking in his surroundings this evening, Cossell sees not the vista available to his eyes – a contained but healthy fire; eight or nine of his tribe in various small-group or solitary activities – but the time-lapsed crowd in the university's auditorium. Where his eyes now capture two young men playing cards for matchstick stakes by fire- and moonlight, the Professor's brain chooses to remember the eager faces, the hands moving fast across the page to make notes . . .

This is not the first time that this has happened for Raymond, but it feels oddly poignant tonight, and he is not sure why. Possibly because of the murder of that fellow lecturer, recently – Dr Finley Reardon . . . posing as Frank. And then the visit that Raymond had had from a different Frank altogether.

Possibly? his undergraduates scream in a chorus. *Possibly*?

Yes, possibly, says Emeritus Professor Raymond Cossell, while staring into the blue and orange flames of a fire on a disused piece of land, in a town whose name no one in the clan can even recall, unless explicitly pushed to do so.

Tonight, there is not much noise. Other evenings, the din can suffocate. As a man from the group approaches the Professor, neither of them look into their destination's eyes. Toting a bottle of transparent fluid, the man with a mauve beard sits down on a beach chair within Raymond Cossell's easy orbit.

Before the man with the mauve beard can speak (but sensing that he is about to), Cossell says: *I quote from the source text.* "*The victim is not thought worthy of it; he perishes like an animal, with none of the forms usual among men . . .*"

That's as maybe, Mauve Beard retorts. *But I'm still not sharing this. If you think I'm sharing, you're a penis.*

Then why did you approach me, just out of interest?

For precisely this kind of interaction.

You're an odd fellow, Andreas, and no mistake.

My name's not Andreas when I'm here! I don't call you Mr Cossell, *do I? I say Professor.*

In fact, Andreas, you don't address me by any name, ever. You were Andreas when the Flood began, and to me, you're Andreas until the waters subside.

The man with the mauve beard shrugs. Before he tips the plastic bottle of clear liquid to his lips, he says, *Have it your own way; names are social constructs, they mean nothing more than an emotional response. I was even a* Glenda *once; I was a muse . . .*

And now you have a muse of your own. How is *Carol?*

The other man wipes his mouth and lowers the bottle.

She has rejected my name-change, Andreas the European replies. *I wished to call her Lamella, Professor Cossell, after Freud's "partial object": a human organ that can survive without a host body. The smile in the* Alice in Wonderland *cartoons that exists without the Cheshire Cat's body being present. Lamella. The very* definition *of a composer's muse, wouldn't you say?*

Did you ever explain why you wanted to change her name, Andreas?

No, I did not. I was paying for her time and her body. I confess I thought her name would be the cheapest of all three things to purchase; but it wasn't to be.

Not everyone thinks of names as social constructs, Professor Cossell argues.

I even composed something new, just for her! And how does she treat me!

Without missing a beat, Professor Cossell answers the question by changing the subject. *The same way that we are all about to be treated, Andreas. Nostalgia's Boat is sailing closer, you know that, don't you? Can you feel it sometimes? Approaching?*

The European sighs. *I sense the Flood, Professor Cossell. And I know that we have matters to repent, you and I, that will need much more than an apology.*

4

Darryl Carbrini and Carol Hayes awaken at the same time.

What did you say? they utter in unison. *I was asleep – I didn't catch your drift.*

I said, they offer as a duet, *compulsive talking prevents the threat of annihilation. If we speak, we must live.*

The duet agrees with itself. Two heads nod as one, as if the move has been choreographed.

What if what we're thinking now – and doing now – is what someone remembers? Or what something remembers. We are thoughts. We're the way a special someone saw it at the time. Nothing more than a point of view. We are someone's evocation of the good old days. We are someone's nostalgia. We might be firing in the synapses of One Who created planets.

The duet pauses.

Or we might be wrong.

Or we might be wrong, Darryl and Carol concede, lip-synced – the perfect recital.

*

Carol 'Purple' Hayes does not wake up so much as receive a surge of unexplained energy. She is not in the European's arms – but she *is* in his piano. At some point of which Carol has no conscious recollection, Andreas must have scooped out a grand piano's varnished wires and blocks, all the guts and sinews of which those who do not play may well remain unaware – and he either lifted Carol into her once-musical tomb . . . or invited her to ascend a short flight of foldable steps and said:

Climb for me.

She has entered the body of the piano, where now she regains something like awareness. The piano's lid has been lowered, either by Andreas the European or by Carol herself, while in a fugue.

There is no fear upon her. Still electing not to move a muscle, Carol understands the importance of being trapped. It feels right

– it seems *appropriate,* somehow. If anything, the relevance would seem to resolve around how empty and peaceful the confined space happens to be. And a revelation, of sorts. Perhaps it is the scent of piano polish that has convinced her so readily that she has awoken inside the instrument. She is subsequently aware that she has awoken with new information in her brain.

Her name, for instance. Andreas has won. Carol has changed her name to Lamella.

Synapses click and ignite. The woman who once was Carol remembers that she has not attempted – not once – to raise the piano lid. She smiles. She imagines sitting up quickly and cracking her upper forehead against the aromatic, treated wood.

I wish I could be as angry as you imagine me to be, Andreas had said. *Now that I've recovered somewhat, I must admit there's a certain poetry to this. A beauty, almost.*

5

Kieran Sange closes down his computer. For the last half an hour, he has sat at his desk at Coronet Confectionaries completely naked.

One of the Duncans pays a visit – to ask permission to attend a pastry conference in the Midlands. He views the Biscuit Inspector's pale and sparse chest . . . not to mention the other man's elongated teats, like those of a bitch in a puppy-breeding racket.

I'm by no means comfortable watching your nipples, the Duncan tells the Biscuit Inspector. *Or your alcohol belly, for that matter.*

Why aren't you reporting me to Human Resources?

I am not convinced you are very well, Kieran, the Duncan replies.

I am not convinced I'm even alive.

*

Tonight, they have incinerated four rats.

Not for fuel for the blaze; not even for the rudiments of a meal for a collection of starving bellies. Simply for sport; for a pastime; for something to do to convince themselves that the cold is not creeping closer, in tendrils from the canal.

The third and fourth rat combust in a most ineffectual manner; the paltry flame barely keeps alive the dream of violence in the collective bosom of the group that killed Finley Reardon.

On that particular occasion, Malcolm had been the unsmiling ringmaster, but tonight there is no joy in his contemplation of the carbonised rodents. There is dim recollection of an act of violence spent . . . but he does not know when it might have happened, or to whom – or why. The past is a road blocked by avalanche – mental avalanche – and the sort of debris found in the forensic investigations of a roadside crew in white toe-to-scalp chemical coveralls.

The man who once spoke to the dead man Finley Reardon about the flood once knew about white toe-to-scalp chemical coveralls. In what seems like a long time ago indeed, when he had been known by the title of Professor, he had known colleagues at the university – two corridors along from his long-term office – who had worn such coveralls while teaching their students on the Masters in Crime Scene Investigation, in the Simulation Laboratory.

You didn't kill me, Uncle Raymond! Professor Cossell mumbles. *I was waiting for your letter! I'm alive! That's what he told me!*

Please be quiet, Professor, Malcolm answers. *I was explaining. No, we're not* haunted *by things we cannot remember. We are created* by things we can't remember. *Think in terms of a massive junk pile of forgotten facts and thoughts. They lie in a yard somewhere, just waiting for the person who wants the equivalent of a replacement headlamp for a Ford Cortina.*

It's all there, you see. Available to all, or to anyone with an interest. The wreckage of previous thought experiments – or only thoughts. Hanging in the air like mist. The important thing being, you don't decide. We. We *don't decide. It's all a matter of psychic privilege and smoke and mirrors.*

Professor Cossell raises his hand to speak. Malcolm grants him the privilege.

Once upon a time I created an Ark to protect a child, and I have been punished for it for twenty-five years. I had a respectable job in the academic world.

Please get to your point, Professor Cossell, Malcolm tells him. *We've heard this many times.*

Has Nostalgia's Boat developed a leak?

6

How do you know what you remember is the truth? Jemima asks. *It's only true in the way that a performance you've seen is true. Like when I went to see* The Birthday Party *at the theatre two nights running. I was big into Pinter –*

So my big birthday was coming up – my eighteenth. And Mum and Dad clearly don't bother communicating about something so trivial, and they both bought me two tickets to see the play – by chance on consecutive evenings.

Dad accompanied me on the first night, at my request, and it was brilliant – it's always been my favourite. When Stanley goes mad and beats the drum? One of the most chilling things I've ever seen.

I looked forward to seeing it with Mum the next night, but she had to cry off – one of her patients was in a crisis. So I went on my own – my first time alone in a theatre. And I expected to bathe in the familiarity of the menace, like watching a film you know well for the umpteenth time.

But the audience was different, and people laughed in different places from where they laughed yesterday. Or they didn't laugh at all; or too much. I got edgy and a bit cross.

Even more distressing were the actors. They guy who'd played McCann the night before must have been ill, because an understudy had taken his place. They stressed different words or left longer or shorter pauses. It wasn't the same play!

By halfway through Act One I thought: I'm leaving. *I can't sit through another two-and-a-half acts of these mistakes . . .*

I should add, I was sober on night two. And I thought how unfair *it was, to deliver the lines differently – cheating the audience. I wanted to heckle. I couldn't move. I was in the middle of a row, in the stalls, a couple of miles from any aisle. I was trapped . . .*

And that's how I feel about the truth. How do I know the same actors give the same performances, night after night? I only lived through it once: I didn't get a chance to compare it with a second recital – or a third, or a fourth. So how do I know I'm looking at the right one?

*

I need a moment of your time, Billy says to Jemima.

Yawn. So does everyone.

I want to watch you inject, Billy tells her. *If it's what it takes to keep you, I'll be the one who keeps you safe if things go wrong. I'll watch; talk to you if that's what you want. Just come back to me, Jemima – please?*

Jemima smiles. *You wouldn't want to join me, Billy? Experience it together?*

No, not really. I think I'd be too frightened.

Jemima holds Billy's face gently in her hands for a few seconds and tells him: *Sweet boy. You've joined me and experienced it with me for months . . .*

*

Is it okay to come in? Billy asks the closed door in front of him.

Come into what? he is asked from the other side. *Come into my room or come into my memory?* A man's voice; a voice he knows.

I don't know how to answer that, Billy admits.

Then you are definitely not ready to come in . . .

I feel I am. I just don't know what's on the other side of the door.

What did Derek Latham tell you, Billy? What did Danny Lovell tell you?

Billy is puzzled. *Who is Derek Latham?*

The voice he hears from beyond the closed door is the voice of his manager at Coronet Confectionaries, Pat Kelly.

*

Holier Than Thou had belched.

In my dream, there was a massive boat approaching the shore. Holier Than sits down at the table. *The boat wasn't moving through a body of water – it was moving through time.*

Yes?

And the passengers went in two by two. Is that how the song goes? It was the Ark. And a woman my dream knew as Lorraine disembarked. She grabbed hold of one of her breasts and started to tear herself into two people. I'm too much for one body, she kept screaming, as she tore herself into pieces. And then she said: I'm too much for people to remember. You can't remember me. You've created me. I'm too much for you. I'm holier than thou.

Billy crushes the maggot of his completed cigarette into the same patch of gravel near the bus stop as he has used for precisely this purpose since beginning his work experience at Coronet Confectionaries, months previous.

To Billy's pleasure, Danny Lovell is in his place in the window of the security cabin.

You're back! says Billy. *Were you forgiven?*

Morning, Billy. Forgiven for what?

The dog thing. The car window.

Danny pauses for long enough for Billy to know there is no advantage in maintaining this line of questioning.

I took the wife and kids to Disneyland Paris, Danny tells Billy. *Is that what you mean?* Danny smiles. *We had a lovely time.*

I'm glad you did, Billy volunteers. *Maybe see you mid-morning in Cancer Cottage.*

What's that?

The smoking hut.

Danny chuckles. *I haven't smoked a cigarette for twenty-five years and I don't intend to start again now . . . Do have a good day, sir.*

*

Later, Jemima visits Billy again.

I don't suppose there's any point in asking where you were last night, he tells her, *so I won't. New game. Guess where I was last night.*

He told me, Jemima replies. *You went to see Lucas. Well done, brilliant. Set my ideas backwards in time five years, why don't you? You're a saint.*

See? Despite your sarcasm, Jem, I have literally no idea what you're talking about. What *ideas? And why aren't you spitting if I went to see your husband?*

Honestly? I assure you right away – it won't do your ego any better than my husband's ego has endured over the last year, Jemima replies. *Are you ready for this?*

I even think I know what you're going to say, says Billy.

It's because I don't care about you either.

*

If I promise to stay off heroin, do you promise we might have one day of honesty? Just one?"

Lucas elevates his eyebrows. *Like an embargo?* Then immediately he answers a question that Jemima has not posed. *I'm not sure if* remember *is right because I don't know if it actually happened. But these are the pictures in my head if I close my eyes. They might as well be memories.*

I used to sneak out of my bedroom at night. I can't recall if I couldn't sleep, or what it was, but I know that I would often be awake in the early hours.

Jemima nods her head and tells her husband: *You're clear so far, Luke. Please carry on.*

*

Someone's remembering you.

There is a pause – and then the other person present says: *I don't* want *to be remembered. How can I* stop *being remembered?*

You make the one remembering remember something else.

But how do I do that?

You take a voyage on Nostalgia's Boat.

UNTIL

1

Not without a quantum of trepidation, Carol Hayes reports as usual to the front door of Andreas the European. She has made a decision and her nerves seem as tight as ropes in a fire-fighters' tug-o'-war. Sighing heavily, she produces the key that Andreas had given her. *For the last time?* she wonders.

"The piano is pumped with energy this evening," Andreas calls from the back of the property. "Would you be interested in hearing what the instrument sees fit to offer?"

Carol has made it no deeper into the house than the entrance hallway.

"No, not really," she replies, calling back as she removes her coat. She moves through the ground floor to the music room.

Andreas watches her enter, his expression one of disappointment – maybe anger. Certainly, Carol's declining of the invitation has taken some of the wind from her benefactor's sails.

"I don't understand what you mean," the European tells her.

"No, I don't want to hear what level of energy your piano is possessed with today – or from now onwards, on any other day. I'm sorry, Andreas."

Carol takes a breath that is louder than a sigh and sounds like a hiss.

"I've thought a lot since Lorraine was taken from us," she starts to explain.

"Such a quaint expression," Andreas interrupts her. "We have no equivalent in my mother tongue. But *taken from us*. By whom? For what reason? What could the ones stealing have use of with the mouldering atoms of a prostitute's body?"

"You forget who you're addressing, Andreas. May I sit down?"

"Yes, you may; and no I don't. I *don't* forget who I'm addressing – not for one moment."

"My profession, I mean," Carol adds.

"I know precisely what you meant."

"And the fact that I'm no different from Lorraine. No better and no worse."

Andreas is seated on his piano stool. Carol now takes a place on the sofa, her fingers threaded together and occasionally flexing.

Through a smile the European offers a mild protest of his own.

"Come come, my dear. No better or worse than Lorraine we can agree on. But surely there's a world of *difference* between the two of you."

The idea that Andreas had known Lorraine but had chosen to remain silent on the subject makes Carol's spine tingle. For months she has known of the European's fondness for wordplay and lexical misdirection; indeed, at times Carol had felt like the gullible tourist paying for the cardsharp to turn over one of the three cards lying face down. Furthermore, she had come to enjoy the duping, in its way – or the being duped. There had seemed something innocent about it; something harmless – antediluvian, chivalric and charming. On the level of metaphor, if Andreas had been asking her to turn over the card to expose the Queen – to Find the Lady! – then hadn't she also assumed that her punter had played a similar game for his own benefit? By requesting that Carol saw no other buyers of trade, hadn't Andreas himself turned over a card and revealed a Queen? Certainly he had given the impression that he had found his lady . . . *but whose were the faces on the other two cards?*

"Did you know Lorraine?" Carol asks.

Andreas turns away from Carol and massages the piano keys gently. Next he settles on a few block chords, making Carol believe that he has run out of things to say. After the time they've been together, perhaps she owes the European the courtesy of a student's evidence of adequate tutelage.

"G Minor 7," Carol offers.

Andreas nods and grins. Then he begins to play something else. Understanding that there is nothing he does without a reason, Carol tries to identify the tune. It has not evolved from the piece that he composed for her: it is far too simple.

Why is he playing a game of Name That Tune? is what Carol longs to demand; but what tumbles from her mouth is a different question entirely.

"Is that 'Frere Jacques'?" she asks.

"The very same ... How does it make you feel?"

"I would rather you explained your comment about Lorraine and me being different."

"I am doing exactly that, my Lamella. Delve deep into the memories the music gives you, even if they happen not to be your own."

(*What's that supposed to mean?* Carol does not have the opportunity to query.)

"For the moment I'll ask you to set aside what you came here tonight to discuss with me." Andreas emits a rare chuckle. "That's if you *remember* what you came here tonight to discuss with me! Close your eyes. What do you see?"

There is no doubt that if Carol had gone through with announcing the cessation of the business arrangement with Andreas, she would have missed these parlour games and real-life crossword puzzles. She cannot help but enjoy his company – and this includes his obfuscation.

Her eyelids lower with a feeling located somewhere between sympathy and remorse.

Once again, Andreas starts playing 'Frere Jacques'; his fingertips are caresses on the keys, and he employs the soft and sostenuto pedals with a mixture of generosity and precision.

Carol breathes her way into a memory; or more accurately, a suite of interconnected images, at least at first.

"I think it's Venice," she offers; "but it's not me – I've never been to Italy."

Andreas hums along with the notes that he selects. "It's about a friar who has overslept, I believe. The singer is ordering him to wake up and sound the bells for midnight prayers. The prayers depend on Brother John, Lamella! Can you imagine the sort of pressure he must have been under!"

Carol listens, but Andreas's voice seems like a breeze through a squall of memories.

"We had dinner outside – a restaurant beside a canal, in Venice. A musician played the tune on an accordion. He wandered up and down, but he was employed by the restaurant. He didn't hassle us for a tip."

Through her lowered eyelids, Carol observes the starlit scene as if she is staring at a photograph. The image is of a middle-aged man and a younger woman, both enjoying Italian food in a busy waterside trattoria. Night-time and canopy lighting have rendered the canal a pea-soup hue. The evening temperature is warm: the couple are dressed in summer ware; in the background, a handful of pedestrians cross a footbridge.

"Lorraine was on holiday with her boyfriend Pat Kelly. It was long before Den. She had seafood linguini and some local fizzy wine. An accordion-player serenaded the diners with 'Frere Jacques'."

"And riddle me this, Carol," says Andreas, bringing the music to a halt. "Did she *tell* you this memory? Did she *gift* you this memory? How do you think you come to see what you actually see?"

Carol's eyes remain closed. She has built the European's voice into this specific fantasy. What a second earlier had been a still photograph – with the exception of the musical accompaniment – has now developed into the opening scenes of a motion picture. Andreas's voice – and its questions and suggestions – are now offered by a canal side musical entertainer. The language he uses is not so much important as intriguing. Not for the first time does Carol wonder what country Andreas the European hailed from. Given the man's years – who knows! – perhaps he had been the accordion player!

For Carol, it is an effort to keep her eyelids on the down-low.

"Was it you with the accordion, Andreas?" she asks.

"Do you feel nostalgic?"

Searching for an answer to a question that remains blurry, Carol waits for the accordion player to shuffle closer; it is either

her imagination or Lorraine's memory that gives the musician a modest swinging of the hips and an ankle-to-ankle slow-dance crabwise advance.

"I can see your fingers on the keys and the . . ." Carol does not have the requisite vocabulary; she is not certain what the parts of an accordion are called. ". . . those little buttons. You are right in front of me, Andreas – or right in front of Lorraine, I should say: Lorraine with her boyfriend."

"How did you know his name was Pat Kelly?"

"I have no idea."

"Describe them, Carol," Andreas advises, beginning the tune once more.

"Lorraine is happy," Carol answers, her mouth pausing to smile.

Andreas interrupts her.

"No, Carol. Don't describe Lorraine – or even Pat. Describe the musician's fingers. Tell me what they looked like under the Italian half-moon and the dots of stars in the Occident."

Carol creates a mental performance of folding her available inspirations and clues into a single demonstrable whole. She does not feel confident: the lines and wrinkles of story do not appear neat, but all the same . . .

"Strong hands. Tanned fingers – thick like the necks of geese."

There is a pause.

"*Dormez-vous?*" Andreas prompts.

". . . with ingots of dense clipped hair embedded into the knuckle joints. With crenelated nails like ovals of *flint*."

Carol hears Andreas breathe contentedly along his nostrils. She interprets the sound as one of partial – and no doubt temporary – satisfaction.

"Very beautiful, Lamella." Andreas rises to his slippered feet and tightens his robe. For less than a second, Carol interprets the latter gesture as her invitation to drop to her knees and conclude business in what has become the customary fashion. She has had her audience with the European – and yet she has not even said what she hoped to say: that she no longer wishes to be regarded as Andreas's good and chattels.

"I can understand you were there, Andreas," Carol begins. "Somehow you serenaded my friend – of all the keyboard players in the world, it was you. What I *can't* fathom is how I was there as well. I've never *been* to Italy, let alone shared a meal with Lorraine there."

Andreas steps closer and sits beside Carol on the settee.

"Was I there, Andreas? Did I see what Lorraine saw?"

"Close your eyes again, Lamella. Ask yourself the same question you've asked me." Andreas waits. "Can you see the scene again? Can you *feel* it?"

Carol has closed her eyes on command, and now tries to hunt down the vision that she had viewed a moment earlier. She only squints when the European asks his next question.

"Is it art?"

Is it what? Very little that Andreas says is uttered without a means in mind. Accordingly, Carol sets to the task of decoding.

Is *what* art?

Andreas has returned to the piano and has started to play something much more complex than 'Frere Jacques'. The genre is jazz, Carol is surprised to note. In all the time she has known him she has never heard him play jazz. She does not recognise the tune.

Is Andreas asking her if his rendition is art? Or perhaps he wants to know if the music plus her memory (if *memory* is quite the right word) have created a form of art.

The music accelerates; grows denser, more complicated. While Carol swans along a Venetian canal in the darkness, searching for the relevant restaurant – the one where she had dined moments earlier – the piano-playing tickles at the rear of her memory. She starts to wonder if her initial reaction had been wrong: perhaps she *does* know the tune after all. As slowly as she can she shakes her head; she does not wish to scatter her thoughts widely, like seeds from a shovel. Concentration squeezes her forehead. Never before has she been so certain that Lorraine is trying to send her a message.

As soon as she has reached this conclusion, Carol is convinced that the Venetian canal has gone. She is travelling – slowly – walking now, accompanied by others. It is not the case that the air in Andreas's music room smells different all of a sudden. For Carol, it is more that case that she has learned to breathe in a different atmosphere; accepted a share of oxygen into different lungs – into a body that she knows must be Lorraine's.

The air smells of a combination of words that Carol would rarely use. She visualises a long corridor and hears a boy's voice describe the air as smelling of disinfectant and poo. When she inhales twice with force, she can smell the usual aroma of the European's room, but she can also smell something like a bodily soured hospital building. The temperature rises at least two degrees.

Where am I, Lorraine? Help me – even if it's only a little bit, for crying out loud! I can follow you but I don't know where we are ... Deliberately she converses in full, clear sentences.

Behind her eyelids, the picture coalesces into something identifiable. Although it is not clear if she *belongs* to one of the three people she accompanies along the corridor that smells of disinfectant and poo, Carol knows that she has at least stowed away for the ride. But with whom?

The answer is, a motley crew. A young boy of approximately nine years in Carol's estimation. An older girl, maybe mid-to-late teens ... And then their chaperone: a man in an official's uniform, leading the way down the aforementioned corridor. Such dialogue as occurs is muffled and stifled through this dreamy transmission on the airways of Nostalgia's Boat.

The three walkers (with a spectral Carol in tow), now stop in front of a particular door. Carol takes note of the uniformed man's appearance. He is large; he wears a truncheon in a long holster on his left hip.

You're relatives of Mr Cossell, the official asks – and Carol understands that he is more than a guide: he is a *guard*. His role is to protect these two children from something on the other side of the door where they have stopped.

The teenaged girl turns to face the guard – and thereby turns to face Carol at her most ethereal . . . for Carol is adroit at switching positions between the three visitors.

I'm his niece, the girl tells the guard; and she blinks.

Carol blinks too, almost as a mirror image. *Lorraine . . .* Carol gulps at the realisation that she has travelled further back in time than the decade-consistent décor of a British health vicinity had given her any clues about. In this particular journey on Nostalgia's Boat, Lorraine cannot be more than seventeen or eighteen years of age, and that verdict is if Carol is feeling *generous.*

During the reeling-out of these images, Andreas has played more of the jazz tune with which he had taunted Carol with brainteasers about art. Carol tries again to place the tune; she is now convinced where she heard it: in Octaves, on a shopping trip to buy something for Andreas from Darryl Carbrini. The tune had wafted through the shop . . .

What's the music? Carol had asked Darryl.

Does it make you get happy? Darryl had replied.

I suppose so.

It's called 'Get Happy'; it's by Art Tatum – from a record called Art's Art.

And as the eight-year-old boy in the memory tells the guard that he's her son – Lorraine's son – Carol thinks of Andreas asking if it is art. He hadn't referred to the act of creation; he had been messing with her. He was asking: *Is it Art?* – 'Art' as in the first name of a jazz pianist, Art Tatum, spinning webs of intricate sound in his rendering of the tune 'Get Happy'.

Raymond Cossell, Carol thinks to herself. Is this episode the matter that Lorraine had refused to discuss during her lifetime? Is this memory what Lorraine had never felt confident in divulging? For Carol, the name Raymond Cossell is unfamiliar.

The guard removes a key ring from a second holster, this one on his right hip. *You're aware of his crimes,* he tells the teenaged Lorraine, while he juggles for the correct key.

Crimes?

Is Carol mistaken, or has the temperature risen yet another degree or two? She is certain she can feel sweat in her armpits and beneath her brassiere.

You can escape, though, Carol tells herself. *Just open your eyes. Stand up. Say thank you for the opportunity to Andreas. And leave the house and don't return.* One of the central tenets of Carol's (and Lorraine's former) profession is to keep yourself safe; to execute a swift departure at the earliest glimpse of personal risk.

Aware of her heart's arrhythmia, Carol examines the inside of the room in front of them.

He's been good for nearly two weeks, the guard offers. *This usually means we're due for an episode. Do not approach him. The line you don't cross is where the wooden floor ends and his carpet begins. Do you understand me, Miss? He can only . . .*

". . . step four feet from his bed," Carol whispers, raising her eyelids; "*but he's got long arms. Are you ready?*"

Andreas has ceased playing his piano; Carol is not sure when this caesura took place, so wrapped up has she been in her former friend's dreads of an instance in the long-ago past.

The feeling that Carol experiences is close to waking up after a refreshing nap. Although the room's temperature remains far too high, her heartrate has almost returned to something normal.

"It wasn't true," Carol says to the European.

"What wasn't?"

Having cracked wide the spine of Lorraine's book, it seems easy, now, for her friend to riffle swiftly through the story's pages.

"What the hell's going on, Andreas?"

"*A bene placito,*" is the European's cloaked response.

Within Carol a tussle ensues: between fighting Andreas for meaning and endeavouring to piece together clues that she knows have always been ready for her.

A bene placito.

She has heard this before: again, in Octaves.

"At the discretion of the performer," Carol interprets.

"Close enough," Andreas tells her through a patient smile.

In an abrupt motion, Carol sits forwards on the sofa. "I'm thirsty! You haven't even offered me a refreshment since I arrived!" Though her tone is mocking, her thirst is real.

"What did you mean when you said it wasn't true? *What* wasn't?"

Carol stands up from the upholstered cushions. By itself this feels like an act of assertion, or even of defiance. She tells herself that this divorce is real.

"I want a drink before I say anymore, Andreas. You might explore your awareness of manners while you're at it. Unless you'd rather I did the honours."

Carol waits on the threshold between rooms. Only later does she fathom that she had lingered on additional thresholds at precisely the same time – not least of them, the emotional and the psychological.

When Andreas smirks, Carol is not shocked at the sense of recognition that jolts through her upper body. In the European's facial expression is a vibrant visual echo of the boy who had entered the room in Lorraine's false memory – the room that she now understands to be a psychiatric care space – and the face of the guard who had unlocked the door.

The boy. The guard. The musician.

The same features . . . though separated by a generation apiece.

"I'm going to help myself to a vodka," Carol announces. "Call out your order if you want one while I'm up." She turns her back and takes a few steps away from the music room. Over her shoulder she calls: "You were playing 'Get Happy' by Art Tatum."

*

Not even in the kitchen – because Carol has not reached the kitchen – but in the downstairs loo, where she pauses for a break, Carol perches for a moment of reflection. Micturition being but a simple somatic undertaking, she leans ahead slightly on the yoke; she allows the false memory of what Lorraine had hoped to show her to rinse through her conscious and unconscious.

The most significant problem is that nothing makes sense. Using the entry into Raymond Cossell's room, Carol accepts the flow of information from either direction: Carol sees and hears what had happened to Lorraine on the build-up to that particular day. The atmosphere is a clogged drain of repressed desire and para-generational confusion. Something as sour as a violation spoils the air, changing the atmosphere yet further. Though Carol appreciates that she has no right to a perfect projective identification – certainly not from a dead woman – what she observes is both vague and disturbing. She knows that Lorraine's companion is called Lucas. Through the fantasy's membrane, she is even able to read the name of the asylum's guard as Officer Lovell.

But none of it, she is certain, is what *actually occurred*.

Using the same gentle manner of shaking her head as she had used before (fearful of spilling too much too wide), Carol attempts to turn in the other direction: to see what was thought to have happened *after* Lorraine and Lucas had visited Raymond Cossell.

More transparent the picture in this second direction might be; but it strikes Carol, in this instant, that she is reading the thoughts of the eight year-old boy himself. The vision is young and cartoonish. She sees a chase that could never have happened in real life, with Lucas and Cossell being pursued on foot onto something like a business park. There is no way that they would have escaped the psychiatric hospital, let alone got so far on foot. The pursuit is like something from *The Benny Hill Show*, Carol thinks. Someone would have tackled them before they had made it into the paper mill. Even the name of the business – WHITE AND DALEY, PAPER PRODUCTION – sounds oddly youthful; the word *Production* is surely something that a child might have invented.

Carol stands up and flushes the toilet. She pulls up her underwear and straightens her skirt. Is she ready to face Andreas yet? She asks herself this question with great sincerity, weighing the moment. At the same time, she recalls the sensation she'd had of waking up inside his piano. She feels something like the sensation she experiences on a plane's take-off or descent: a tugging at her belly, and nausea stronger than thirst.

Sadness and confusion are alive and well and living in her head. Why on earth is she seeing through the inaccurate memories of a young boy?

*

"What is it, I wonder, that excites us to turn our back on a good thing and destroy the comfortable status quo. What is *the driver*?" Andreas asks.

Carol ignores the question. "I forgot to mention – I brought you a present," she tells her benefactor. "It's a rare recording." Feeling self-conscious at holding out the gift-wrapped CD, Carol lays it on top of the piano.

"An interesting word – *present*," Andreas offers, "as in gift. It's also the midpoint between the past and the future." Briefly he looks at Carol. "Some say it doesn't even exist – as a temporal frame of reference. The present. But I know differently, Lamella: I've lived through *scores* of presents."

Thinking back on what she had learned from Scottish Tony at Crosstown Trainer, Carol attempts to change the subject. If today is to be their last time together, she would at least appreciate learning a few answers. She plunges.

"Do you ever wear a beard, Andreas? Specifically a *purple* beard?"

She expects to be asked why she wants to know the answer to this question, or what makes her ask it, or who she has been talking to; but instead, Andreas measures his response.

"A beard makes me another man, if only for a short while. What we try to bury," the European says, "has an unfortunate tendency to wriggle to the surface and break free."

"I'm not sure what you're telling me, Andreas."

"I think you are. You are simply not listening to yourself. You're denying your own *character!* In fact, I think you were writing the script earlier than I gave you credit for."

More riddles! More nonsense. Carol's temper simmers like soup in a saucepan.

"The *script?*" Carol repeats. Something inside her grows angry at the way she has been treated. The Stravinsky recording is rare: it cost her eighty pounds and she would like some recognition of the fact – not simply the financial outlay (for she is not short of readies these days), but the time it took her to conduct her research and to discuss her options with Darryl Carbrini. She sits in an armchair by the bay window. By crossing her legs at the knees, she turns her torso ninety degrees away from Andreas, in a gesture that appears dismissive. Had she left the pose like this for a few more seconds (she thinks in retrospect), she might have engineered some emotional leverage; unfortunately, however, she is unable to resist the bait that Andreas has dropped into her waters.

"What *script?*" she demands.

"You imagined I wouldn't find out about your conversations with Darryl," Andreas replies. "But you didn't consider the very same network that you have said in the past is your source of information."

Carol is surprised to experience surprise. For a while – perhaps still under the anaesthetic of Lorraine's death – she has felt incapable of registering much of anything new. The fact that Andreas's words have surprised her is a further surprise, and something of a relief. It means that she is not numb.

"I don't suppose it will help if I act incredulous at this point," says Carol.

"You could try, but not really. I shouldn't wish to waste your time as well as my own."

"You're disappointed, Andreas – I can see that."

"No, Lamella. I'm *disappointed* when I take an egg from the boiling water on the stove and I haven't timed it quite right. It's either too albumen-tastic or it's like a grenade."

"Okay, *worse* than disappointed." Aware that she has been caught out in what Andreas will regard as the equivalent of an adultery (which is ironic, considering her occupation), Carol fights with her instinct to defend herself. Even more compounded surprise has elbowed its way into her consciousness: she is now surprised that she hates herself for having hurt this man who has only ever tried to support her, and only asked for one (massive) commitment in return.

Andreas plays a few bars on the piano. So immediate and pulsing is the moment that Carol will recall the music in subsequent days and will wonder where first she had heard it. It will be another week before she joins dots and quavers and understands that the music is from the very Stravinski CD that she left on the top of the instrument for Andreas's inattention. Without playing the disc on his stereo – indeed, without so much as touching the box – Andreas has started to recite some of the second movement contained therein. Carol had played some of the CD before handing the gift over to Andreas, simply to ensure that the sound quality was sharp.

The music stops. Into the silence Carol says, "Would it help if I said sorry? Or tried to explain?"

Still refusing to look her way, Andreas speaks directly to the keys before him – or perhaps to the knuckles of the hands that hover above them.

"The animals went in two by two," he says. "As a child, did that ever strike you as preposterous? Why didn't the lions eat the antelope?"

Bible stories? Noah's Ark?

"Who said they didn't? The story works on the level of metaphor," Carol answers.

"I'm not sure it works at all. Any intelligent schoolchild can pick a hole in it."

"Did you imagine us as the two-by-two, Andreas? The patriarch and the matriarch, strolling up the gangplank to find oceans safe from the Flood?"

The European does not respond to Carol's question.

"The Ark has to reach its destination as well. I feel it sometimes. It pushes the waves ahead of itself. It is a boat with veins."

Even by Andreas's standards, the *boat with veins* business is beyond puzzling. She knows that she should cross the room and stand beside him. Perhaps she should earn her keep (her tongue wets her lips in an unconscious gesture). However, she feels reluctant to move a muscle. Moments pass as delicately (she will later think) as insects crossing a single line of spider web.

One false move, as they say . . .

Andreas rises to his feet. "Do you ever feel like someone is controlling what you think?" Then he moves towards Carol.

At this precise second, she has no way of knowing if he intends to kiss her or to kill her.

"All the time," she answers. "What are you saying the feeling signifies?"

He stands beside her. He looks down into the well of her face.

"I'm not saying it signifies anything at all. I wanted to check on solidarity."

"Consider it a consensus," Carol informs him. "What else happens? What's the score?"

"I sense your impatience. Perhaps I should play your gift now."

"I hope you will. I really gave it some thought."

Andreas sighs. "And yet, you still betrayed me."

Something tightens in Carol's chest. "And yet, I still betrayed you," she admits. "The problem with scum like me is, we never really know when something good is happening. It makes us doubt ourselves. But for what it's worth, I'm sorry, Andreas."

"But you don't really want me to forgive you, Lamella." Andreas smiles.

"Don't I?"

"No, I don't think so. My forgiveness gives you a relief from the pain."

"And I'd rather stay in agony?" Carol suggests.

"I could not have put it better myself. Now I think the best option would be for you to leave. I'll have your gift as something to remember you by."

"Okay, I will; but before I do, may I ask a question? How did you find out about me and Darryl?"

Andreas sighs. "From the *boy's own lips*, of course!"

"You *know* Darryl Carbrini?"

"Do I know my own son? Certainly I know Darryl! I paid the boy a visit only to find him with skin the colour of ash. It turns out he's been using heroin for the last few months, with a young woman named *Jemima Sange*. Does that name mean anything to you, Lamella?"

"I can't say it does. Who is she?"

"As best I can see, she's one of Louise Reardon's little helpers."

"And who is Louise Reardon when she's at home?"

"The twin sister of a good man," Andreas answers. "A man I pretend to hate but secretly love like a brother of my own." Another sigh drifts through his words.

Carol says: "I need to tell you something, Andreas."

"I know . . . Carol. But humour me. The intentions behind your visit here tonight notwithstanding, you'd better prepare us more refreshments and then come and sit down. I have a few things you should hear from me before you hear them elsewhere."

*

"I have much in common with Lorraine," Andreas tells Carol. "She and I inhabited the same playground, you might say. *One* day I'll compose a symphony about the experience."

"What playground?" Carol asks. Her opinion is that Andreas must have bought Lorraine's services. The aroma of jealousy is at the bottom of the glass that she raises, now, to her lips.

"We both enjoyed a particular game."

"Oh yes?"

"Involving a particular group of people."

"Oh *yes*?"

"You sound perturbed."

"That would be one way of putting it, Andreas. Do you know what I think? I think you've played me as well as you play that piano. I've been an instrument. But do let me know what you meant by the same playground."

"Our paths would cross from time to time."

"Yours and Lorraine's?" Carol waits – and forces herself not to slap the grinning face of the man who has paid her way for the previous months. She teaches herself a lesson. "Do you mean where the *homeless* people gather?"

"Well, it's a gathering of *interested minds*," Andreas corrects her. "*I'm* certainly not homeless and neither was Lorraine. Some of the party were probably without fixed abodes, but we met in the open air, on building sites, behind the train station – the venues changed from time to time."

"The debasement was part of the attraction."

"For some – yes, I would say so. Nothing focuses the mind like having nothing much else to think about, even if it's for a little while."

Carol nods her head. "So you *did* know Lorraine."

"Well, in a sense, I suppose. For me at least, I would go there to hear ideas and debate. The actual *person* you grappled with was only part of the draw. If I knew her, I don't really remember her; sorry. Which is more or less the same thing, mightn't we say?"

"You have a purple beard when you go there," Carol says.

"I get into character – yes." Quickly Andreas adds: "I don't think I've explained myself terribly well. I would ask you not to judge me when I say, I *simply enjoy* the company of what many people think of as homeless groups: just like Lorraine did." He chuckles. "*It's fun!* Don't knock it!"

"Till I've tried it?"

"No; *ever*. Don't knock it at all. I've been good enough not to judge you; I would simply ask you to show me the same courtesy."

Carol's mouth drops open. "Andreas, you judged me the very first second you saw me! To such an extent," she says, "you tried to buy me an exit from my profession. Which is one of the reasons I am here today." Her chest heaves with a combination of nerves and pride. "I'm sorry; but I don't want to go on like this."

Andreas nods his head. "I was fairly certain you had something like emancipation on your mind . . . Carol. You are of course free to go with my full blessing," he tells her. "You can refund the money I've spent on you, less what you think reasonable for the very nice gifts you've given me, by cash, cheque or bank transfer, as you prefer."

Again, Carol's jaw descends at the sound of Andreas's audacity.

"You want me to *pay you back*?"

"But of course! We had a *deal*, Carol. You have chosen to alter the arrangement and therefore we must revert to our original terms."

Seized by a sudden panic, Carol feels her body temperature climb rapidly. While it is not the case that she has been irresponsible with the money that Andreas has given her, she has not scrimped either – and she has not serviced any other fee-paying customers. She is not sure where she will find the funds; and yet . . . this would seem to be the best and only option.

"I'll get you your money," she replies. "Shall we settle on a precise figure? And would you give me a week to move a few things around?"

When Andreas laughs, it is with the sudden aggression of petrol catching light. His hearty guffaws ignite the room . . . Meanwhile, Carol had once read that being doused in petrol is an icy-cold experience; this is exactly how she feels right now.

"Oh, your *face*, Carol! I'm joking, my darling. Keep everything. I'm a wealthy man and I have no real interest in money other than to get what I want," Andreas says, "and to keep my son in the lifestyle he enjoys, of course."

Able to speak again after a few seconds of recovery, Carol sticks to learning more facts. If she can leave Andreas on civil terms, it will be for the best, surely.

"You help him out financially?" she asks.

Andreas shrugs. "From time to time. He works in a music shop – he doesn't earn a fortune."

"Neither do you, Andreas."

"Ah! But I've lived a long time. Money went a lot further in times gone by."

Has Andreas handed her a segue? "I was going to ask you about that," she tells him. "But I have a feeling that it's all connected, in your head."

Appearing puzzled, Andreas asks: "You have a feeling *what's* all connected, in my head?"

"The visions I've had. This Jemima girl you've mentioned. Lorraine. A nine year-old boy. Raymond Cossell . . . whoever *he* might be. And I want to know what you meant when you threw in references to knowing Sigmund Freud; and being a muse to Mahler and the Shost. If I ever meant anything to you, Andreas, all I'm asking is to understand. If this is likely to be our last day together, please help me understand what's in your mind."

Andreas the European grins. "A pretty speech."

"Thank you."

"And *so* predictable!"

The fear and the sense of impotence that had curled just under Carol's skin are now gone. Now, she is furious, pure and simple.

"Or perhaps I should leave," she suggests.

"And *even more* predictable!" Andreas sounds overjoyed. "My predictions coming true is like having my birthday and Christmas on the same day."

Carol has started to feel unwell. Powerlessness has been known to have this effect on her. She recalls a gobbet of advice that Lorraine had once provided her and Robbie.

If someone is toxic, the toxicity isn't always obvious. Some poison acts slowly. But if you're certain, Lorraine had said, *don't try to be* more *toxic. Don't even attempt to create an antidote. Just get yourself out of there.*

Good advice, Carol concludes. It's been an adventure. As she rises to her feet, she offers Andreas a farewell that she hopes will sound more melancholy than bitter. She does not storm out. He will not be offered the treat of witnessing one final hissy fit; no such show of emotion will be provided. Although her heart is beating too quickly, she refuses to sour the atmosphere any more than she needs to.

At the doorway, however, she turns.

"If I'm predictable, Andreas, it's because you've got into my head – and because you've studied the evidence I've given you," she tells him slowly. "Which suggests I've been your project – and your experiment – from the start. Your mention of Jemima and Louise would seem to confirm this idea. So, just remember one thing. When I'm gone, you'll have no one to compose music for. You'll be making up your own results for a while. One question if I may – not about me."

"Fire away!"

"If you found your son at death's door, why aren't you angry with Jemima?"

"Who said I wasn't?"

"You seem more intent on proving a point with me. And I could help you, Andreas."

"How?"

"By rustling up some revenge on your behalf," Carol tells him. "But only if you tell me everything first. I'm not joking. I mean *everything*."

2

Unusually, Chaz Bruce-Sange has lost track of time. She is surprised when a client arrives for a therapy hour appointment ten minutes early.

What Kieran had told her remains *a shock* – and not only because she and the perpetrator had once shared a bed and a menu of dreams for the future. She would have been shocked if a sentenced offender – at a failed parole hearing, for example – had boasted of similar murderous urges. The astonishing factor is not necessarily the *person*: it's the malice aforethought. Now that Chaz has had an opportunity to hold back thoughts about Lorraine and Carol, it is time to focus on her ex.

However, on reflection, Chaz is not sure that she wants to know. She resents her ex-husband for having brought the news to her – and (to the best of her knowledge) her alone. Why could he not have told *someone else*? On the other hand, who would that someone else have been?

I need a holiday, Chaz tells herself. *When this is over, I'll catch a train east . . .*

Stop.

Just stop a minute, won't you?

Kieran had confided in *her* – which meant that he had intended for her to do something; even if that *doing something* was to feel sick or denounce his actions. Confessions are rarely made *solely* to make the confessor feel better; at best, such a transmission is a risky bet. What if no psyche is there to catch the emotional bouquet? The confessor feels worse than ever.

A confession is made to change the world of the one listening.

Chaz exhales through her nostrils. Her fingertips send words to her laptop screen; her brain, unfortunately, seems not to recognise them, individually or in sentences. In addition, it would seem that now is not the right time for typing. Chaz's concentration is cracked by the sound of the doorbell. Her thoughts about her ex-husband will have to remain on hold.

*

Towards the end of the therapy hour, amid a conversation about a bullying line manager that will last another three sessions, Chaz remembers the policewoman at Lorraine's cremation. The trigger is her patient's mention of *a cathedral of incivility*. Unbidden, a memory pipes up.

Outside, after Cecilia Hatton had dismissed the congregation, small talk had ensued on the lawn. As Chaz remembers it, even this episode – usually cathartic, in other memorial services – had felt stiff. Lorraine had known those on opposing sides of the law; and a representative for the law itself – WPC Sharon Bark – had also attended. The demographic had been *unprecedented*.

Chaz opens a hardback book that stays on her desk. This, her record of phone numbers and addresses, has lived with her for most of her adult life. Not once in the intervening years has she ever expunged an entry. Her contacts book – she imagines – is something of an historical piece. One that she uses now to locate a number.

A woman's voice answers the call.

"Keys and Heeling!"

Chaz had known that Robbie tended to hide behind the key-cutting business façade. The greeting is no great obstacle – but neither was Chaz in any mood for nonsense.

"I'm looking for Roberta. She has the building above and behind the key-cutting, shoe-heeling business, okay? *Roberta.* I appreciate you can't hook me up without checking with her, so please pass on my best wishes and my request."

"What's the request?"

"It's about Lorraine, darling. Lorraine who *died*. All I want is a way of contacting WPC Sharon Bark. I don't particularly wish to go through the switchboard."

"You'd like me to get the contact details and pass them to you."

"That would do nicely."

*

Before she telephones Sharon Bark, Chaz attempts to check in on Jemima: she has not heard from her daughter in the last few days. Such is Jemima's independent spirit (or reckless nature), it is hardly a concern if a few days have passed with radio silence between them; but sometimes it is nice to take a breather, phone Jemima, become disappointed or excited about something the girl says, and then move back to whatever task is at hand to execute, vowing to keep her cool better next time.

At the sound of Jemima's recorded voice, Chaz is readying a cookie-cut response (something about her intention to try again at the weekend) when she notices that her daughter's message has changed. Jemima has included a reference to going away somewhere. Chaz ends the call on the word *while* and uses the speed-dial again to listen properly this time.

Hello, you have reached the voicemail of Jemima Sange. (Considerably more formal than the message that has been attached to the service for at least a year.) *And whatever I've done to make you phone me, I'm truly sorry.* (What?) *Now I'm going away for a little while. I don't know if I'll be back, or when – I've got a few things to run away from. I hope you don't hate me any more than I deserve,* Jemima's voice concludes.

"The hell's going on?" Chaz asks her empty office. Next, she calls the phone number for the house that Jemima shares with Lucas. The response is Lucas's recorded voice. *Leave a message and we'll get back to you when we can.* "Darling, it's Mum. Please could you ring me when you get home. Thank you," she says, hoping that no suggestion of panic had ridden her words. In fact, she is suddenly so het-up that she can feel tendons in her neck stretch, and when she sighs her lips flap.

Chaz does not have phone numbers for any of Jemima's friends or fellow students – apart from one. While she considers making the call, the phone on her desk rings.

"Dr Chaz Bruce-Sange?" she sing-songs into the old-fashioned receiver.

"This is Lily from Keys and Heeling? About the number you asked for? Robbie says it's okay to give it to you. Are you ready?"

Chaz jots down the number that Lily provides. She then reads it back and once it's been confirmed, she says thank you – and wonders what to do next. Phone WPC Sharon Bark or phone Billy Alfreth, to see if *he* can shed any light on Jemima's worrying voicemail message.

She's flighty, Chaz tells herself. *Always has been – always will be.*

This is true; but the uncertainty persists – truthfully (she accepts), the *fear* persists. And why? Changes in behaviour are rarely without a provocation . . . or a purpose.

"Where *are* you, Jemima?"

Chaz stands and paces the floor, not least to rid her inner thighs of a tingle that has been her companion in times of stress since she'd sat her Finals.

Meanwhile, at the back of her mind is Louise's recent visit – and Louise staggers into her consciousness now. Chaz shakes her head. Given everything else on the horizon, Chaz is certain that she does not want to think about Louise right now. It feels like storm clouds have gathered.

Billy will know.

Before she can think any further, she reaches for her book and taps in the number – it is not in her list of pre-programmed numbers.

"Hello?"

"This is Chaz – Jemima's mother. I don't suppose she's with you, is she?"

"Ah, hello, Chaz. No, she's not – sorry. We've had a bit of a parting of the ways, to be honest," Billy answers. "I know she called me a couple of days ago, but I didn't want to speak to her."

"Your argument with Jemima is none of my business. I just want to make sure she's okay. Her mobile has a really strange voice mail message."

As quickly as she can, she explains.

Billy tells her: "I know she left at least one message but I didn't want to hear it. I haven't played it. I'm tired of the strife; I just want to get on with my work. And my life."

"I understand; but will you play the message, Billy? And then call me back?"

In the space between hanging up the phone and Billy's returning the call, Chaz encourages herself to focus and to type up the notes of her most recent consultation. She manoeuvres herself into the zone: *bullying. What are my observations? What are my interpretations?* But she cannot think further than a cut-out image of Jemima – and a silent movie of Louise, in these very rooms. She had never really established what Louise had wanted; not *really*. Chaz had half expected a declaration of ill-health from Louise, or of Louise having committed a serious crime for which she had sought absolution. Throughout the late night and early morning that Louise had been with her, there had been a sense of her lingering on the ledge of a decision. She had *wanted* to say something (Chaz is certain of this) but had not found the space to conjure up a full confession.

Chaz stares at Sharon Bark's number on the notepad. She feels uneasy – is it because she does not want to make the call? Is she uneasy about Louise's unexpected (and unexplained) visit?

No; I am scared to death that Jemima has done something really stupid this time.

There is also something peculiar about Sharon Bark's phone number. Chaz has spent most of her working life digging subtly for clues and spotting patterns. Why does this number seem familiar? There is no time to probe: the phone rings again. It is Billy Alfreth.

"Chaz," he says, "this is scary. She said she was leaving her piano teacher's place and she wasn't sure if he was dead or alive."

"Breathe, Billy – take a breath."

"So I looked him up online and called him. No answer. I left a message for him to call me back. I'm tempted to go there right now."

"You know his address?" Chaz asks, confused.

"I went there once. Long story – I was trying to do something romantic for Jem. Surprise her."

"Are you aware of anything new in Jemima's life?"

"She's started using heroin."

*

Halfway through the next fifty minutes, Chaz says to her client, "I'm very sorry, I'll have to end the session here. I received some bad news very shortly before you arrived and I can't pay full attention to what you're saying. There won't be a charge for this session, of course."

Once the visitor has exited (having taken the news in a positive spirit), Chaz sets about firming up a plan of action. She leaves a message on Kieran's work landline and his mobile phone. Without much hope, she tries Jemima's mobile again: it's the same message. Then she calls Lucas again, realising that he will be at work at the flower shop. Can she call him there? Closing her eyes for a few seconds, she pictures the front of the shop but she cannot bring the business's name to mind; and she will need the name to look up a number in an online directory.

No; she has called Lucas twice, and left messages. He will pick them up when he can. She consults her appointments diary and calls the number for her final client of the day. Postponing the session takes a few minutes due to the traffic noise at the other end of the line.

Then she calls Billy Alfreth. To her relief, he answers.

"My head is a little bit clearer now," Chaz tells Billy.

"Mine isn't," Billy replies; and then adds (to the psychoanalyst's surprise), "I'm suffering from hallucinations."

Unfair, Chaz opines; *one problem at a time.* Now is not the occasion to offer her daughter's on-off boyfriend / affair a free therapeutic consultation.

Ignoring what Billy has said, Chaz asks: "Do you know where she gets it?"

"I do. And I've called him. She's not there – or so he says, anyway."

"What's his name?"

"Terry Bates. I worked with him at Coronet Confectionaries until recently," Billy explains.

"And now he's gone?"

"He was invited to leave."

"Okay. Let me ask you how far you've got with trying to find Jemima."

"I haven't got anywhere, Chaz; it's not worth it. It's made me ill! I don't know if you heard me a second ago but I've had hallucinations – and I'm sure Jemima is partly to blame."

"Yes, I heard your self-diagnosis, Billy, but I'd like to track my daughter down, if it's all the same to you. I'd be happy to book you in for an introductory meeting if you'd like that. In the meantime, I have some calls to make. Are you happy to share the phone numbers of anyone in your phone who might know her?"

Billy sighs before making a decision.

"I can share the numbers with you, Chaz, but honestly – I've learned – if she doesn't want to be found, she won't be found. The last time I saw her (I swear this is true) was in a jacuzzi with her friend, who owns a *brothel*."

Chaz thinks back to conversations with both Lorraine and Carol. "Was this friend's name Roberta, by any chance?" she asks.

"Yes, it was! Does everyone know her apart from me?"

"I don't *know* her exactly." *But I know how to find her, through Carol Hayes.* It's a lead at least. "Can I urge you, Billy, to speak to anyone you know who knows her. Just ask her to get in touch."

"With me or with you? Because I'm not that keen on speaking to her, Chaz, to be honest. There's something wrong with my brain at the moment. I'm *seeing* things."

Chaz recalls an accusation that Billy had made. "And you think Jemima's to blame?"

"Yes, I can't help but think that."

"I'll use the word hallucination because you've already used it. Have you ever experienced hallucinations in the past?" Chaz asks.

Billy's response is rather slow in arriving. "Yes, once; a long time ago. I don't know if Jem ever mentioned it, but I went to prison."

"Lord Christ, this just gets better and better!"

"I was a different man back then."

"Yes, I'm sure you were. You were a man who had to say *sir* and wait for a set hour for recreation and meals. I've read a lot about prisons, Billy. So what makes you think Jemima has anything to do with what you experience now?"

"Because until I met her a year ago, my brain had been clean a long time," Billy answers.

"I'm afraid that's flimsy," Chaz tells him; then she shivers again. A sense of professionalism entices her to delve further. Although the man hasn't asked for her help, he *has* asked for her help – he just doesn't *know* that he has! "Explore what might have changed in your life in the time before you experienced your first hallucination. Have you been playing 'let's remember' with Jemima, for example? Have you re-discovered something together that might have confused you?"

This time, the pause in which Billy dunks Chaz lasts longer – and it makes Chaz feel even colder. When finally he speaks, he asks a question.

"Could it be the *diary*?" he says.

"What diary would that be?"

"When I started my course at the university last year, I started a diary," says Billy. "I didn't keep it up long, but the important thing is, I told Jem about it a couple of months ago, when I started at Coronet Confectionaries. She was amused. Or so I thought, anyway. In retrospect, Chaz, maybe I mistook her amusement for her pleasure in seeing another way to mess me up."

Knowing that there is no point in defending her daughter's honour, Chaz thinks for a moment and asks: "Did Jemima see the diary?"

"I read to her from it," Billy answers. "It was supposed to chronicle my days as a BA student. As I say, I didn't keep it going for–"

"Don't get wistful on me, Billy. Did she *see* the diary? Did she have *access* to the diary? Forget about your presence; exclude yourself from the picture."

"Yes, Chaz. She knew where I kept it. She could have read it."

"And what about added to it? Could she have done that?"

"Added to my *diary*? I don't understand, Chaz."

"Read your diary again, Billy: my best advice for now. See if it's the same as you remember it," Chaz instructs. "I promise you I'll keep thinking but for now it's the best I've got. There is always a source for a trauma, of whatever stripe. I'm not saying you've found it, but it's a thought."

"Okay, I'll do that. Meanwhile, I've made a decision."

Impatient for movement, Chaz takes a bite from Billy's silence. "Would you care to share your insight with me, Billy, I'm kind of pressed for time." And once more her gaze swerves across to the notepad on which she has scrawled Sharon Bark's phone number. Although the digits blur, Chaz believes that she has found a foothold.

"I'm going out in the field," Billy tells her. "I'll help you – but I'm also helping myself. I'll go to Lucas; I'll throw my net wide, Chaz. I'll find her if you don't and you'll find her if *I* don't. Deal?"

For a second or two, Chaz waits.

"Probably the best I can give you," she says, "is a promise I won't get in your way. And I *do* give you that, Billy. It feels like we're in the grip of group hysteria; but I don't know the reason. I've cancelled the rest of my working day. I'll help, after my own fashion. First step being Terry Bates. I want to hear that bastard's voice myself."

"And then?"

Chaz picks up the notepad. The number for WPC Sharon Bark, she is certain, is the same as the phone number for Dr Louise Reardon. She remembers it in the same way as we recall a great meal.

"Then I'm going on a treasure hunt," Chaz tells Billy.

*

A mile and a half away, Billy walks from Coronet Confectionaries to the security cabin at the mouth of the business park. He has left the office a half hour early, pleading toothache and a dental appointment. He wonders if he will complete his work placement year anyway. He's had enough of everything. Walking over to the cabin feels like saying *adios.*

Are you coming home? he will demand of Jemima in the never-future-never.

I'm not even certain what that question means anymore, Jemima will tell him. *Where's home, for me, Billy? For that matter,* what's *home?*

A safer place than here, at least.

Are you sure of that? Jemima will plead.

Or a warmer one, anyway.

That's no so tempting. I liked the idea of safety.

"Can I come inside, please, Danny?" Billy asks. "I'm supposed to be going to the dentist. I don't want to be seen by anyone."

Once Danny has admitted him into the cabin, via a door around the back, Billy takes the seat that he is invited to take. Danny asks him what's going on.

"I have a number of problems," Billy admits, "and right now I'm checking my grip on reality. I'm being serious . . . No thanks," he adds, seeing Danny lift a cup, which stands for an offer of a drink of something.

Danny is already seated in a chair near the window that visitors approach in order to gain access to the business park; but he has turned away from the slidable pane of transparent plastic. He has a cup of tea on the go; now he raises it to his lips, while contemplating an appropriate response.

Over the time since they both started work on the business park, a bond has been forged between them. Although he is not sure that he possesses the requisite tools, Danny does wish to help his friend.

"What's on your mind, Billy?"

Billy pauses for a moment before plunging.

"What happened when I hadn't worked at Coronet Confectionaries long?"

"What do you mean: *what happened?* To you at work?"

"I'm testing my reality, Danny; I don't want to steer you. Something that affected us both."

"You mean the dog," says Danny.

"I do. I mean the dog. Please say it out loud."

"Okay. There was a dog in a car, parked in the far corner, all by itself. We were worried about it . . . I broke a window to let the dog out. Then I had a shitty time explaining myself and had to agree to pay to get the glass fixed to stop the owner reporting me to the police."

The sense of relief that Billy feels is communicated to Danny; and yet, Billy has further questions that feel less like an interview than a trap.

"The owner of what?"

"The owner of the *car*, Billy. The dog belonged to a homeless guy and it's now in a dog rescue centre. A policewoman told me."

"And how did the dog *get* in the car?"

"We can only guess, even now. The car-owner calmed down a bit when he understood there really *had* been a dog in his car. But we're no clearer on how it got in there."

Billy sips air through his lips; it is like air escaping from a punctured tyre.

"When we were smoking in Cancer Cottage one time, Danny – or more than one time, actually – you mentioned you'd stared at a man pointing a gun at you."

"I try not to think about it much, but yes – I did say that."

"You were underground, you said."

Danny frowns. "Billy, where's this leading?"

"Please humour me. It's been a rough time. You chased a boy and his uncle from a secure psychiatric facility to a paper merchant's warehouse."

"Well remembered: exactly that. I can hardly believe it happened, but we chased this boy and his uncle down a hill and onto this very business park, where we sit today. They went into a paper warehouse, more or less where Coronet Confectionaries is today. They went in. Then the uncle fiddled with some bricks in a wall and it opened up a chute, and down they went!"

"And you followed them," Billy adds.

Danny nods his head.

"Is it *possible*," he is asked, "you don't believe it because it couldn't have happened the way you remember it?"

"I ask myself the same question often," Danny replies. "But I remember the boy and his uncle in that chamber under the ground. I remember the *Ark* – they called it. Then the uncle showed me a sawn-off shotgun – I swear I was never so frightened. He pointed it over my left shoulder and fired a warning shot across my bows. When he asked me my first name, I was convinced I was a goner – it'd be an old-style execution. But he let me off. Then the uncle and Lucas went into their Ark."

Muscles in Billy's shoulders crimp.

"The boy's name was Lucas?" The smile he offers as he thinks of Jemima and her husband is a mixture of bitter and appeased. "But of course it was. Danny. There is no easy way to say what I'm about to say. Since we saw the dog trapped in the car I have thought of it often – the dog, I mean. I've imagined the dog talking to me. I'm seeing things that aren't there. I'm *panicking*, mate."

Again, Danny nods his head. No word does he proffer.

"So I'll ask you again. Is it possible we've been tricked somehow? Is there any way of checking what happened all those years ago? Were there witnesses?"

Danny sips from his cup, his eyebrows squeezed together as he contemplates. Eventually, he stretches his neck (to an audible click) and says, "Let me tell you a story."

*

"When I was a child, I had a fountain pen my granny gave me when I was seven. She used to encourage me to write down my feelings – or what I was doing at school – or anything at all. She thought I was destined to be a writer."

Danny laughs.

"It was one of the only things she got totally wrong, but there you go. The point of the story is the pen. Granny died unexpectedly and we were all gutted . . . but I felt I still had her with me in some way because I could write with the pen she'd given me – and when I wrote with the pen, I was talking to her in some way. There was a link.

"Well, one day I lost the pen. I turned my bedroom upside-down looking for it but I couldn't find it anywhere. Dad said he'd get me another pen just like it, and he meant well, I know he did. I was frantic with nerves. I felt sick all the time. And Dad's offer was like poison! Losing the pen was ... somehow letting go of Granny. But *replacing* the pen was too horrible to bear.

"To cut a long story short, the pen's disappearance sent me to a very dark place."

"How old were you, by the way?"

"Nine years and six months," Danny answers without a beat of hesitation.

Billy smiles. "That's pretty specific."

"It was the worst thing that had ever happened to me at the time. Even worse than Granny's stroke. The school wanted to see my parents to make sure things were okay at home. I imagine I was about this close to a full-scale psychiatric evaluation . . . when I found the pen."

"Where was it?"

"Of all silly things, I'd slipped it into my swimming bag, in one of the little pockets on the side, along with some cartridge refills. Mum started huffing and puffing about the white laundry wash being spoiled. The towel I used for swimming – somehow – had a fountain pen cartridge hidden in it. That's the bit that's still weird, to this day. The pen and some other cartridges were in a separate pocket on the bag; yet *one cartridge* got tangled up with my towel."

"And leaked in the washing machine?"

"Exactly. Blue smudges on my towel, and Dad's work shirts – that kind of thing. Well. As soon as Mum complained, I saw what I'd done, it was like a film. I'd put the pen and the spare ink in the bag – and crucially, I'd added one spare into the *main part* of the bag. I could see myself doing it, but not knowing why."

Billy frowns. Unbidden and wanted, the memory of a prison psychiatrist has entered his mind; and while he can shoo away her face, he is incapable of expunging what this particular professional had told him, more than once – the essence of which he now relates to Danny. As he speaks, he also thinks of Jemima's mother, Chaz Bruce-Sange, a psychoanalyst seemingly never off-duty, who had chosen the occasion of her daughter's wedding celebrations to instruct Billy with a message very similar to what he had learned at Dellacotte, all those years earlier.

"It's like you were planting a clue for yourself," Billy says; "a way of defending yourself against a future failure of memory."

He can hear the voice of Chaz Bruce-Sange in his own.

"You put the pen in the bag's pocket, with no conscious memory of doing any such thing. You wanted to take her with you, swimming. You wanted to make her proud of your front crawl. But the space – the bag's pocket – was tight, so unconsciously (again, unconsciously) you were mimicking your grandmother in her small box in the ground. You were learning to say goodbye: burying her in the pocket with some of her favourite items – the spare cartridges. But your unconscious also wanted there to be cancellation clause, of sorts."

"The other spare, to mess up the laundry," Danny interprets. "To keep her with me."

Billy shrugs. "That's how I read it, anyway. What happened when you were reconnected with your nan?"

"Sorry?"

"When you found the pen."

"I started writing to her. I told her everything. And then, little by little as these things will, I wrote less and then less, until I almost stopped altogether. But do you know, to this day, on four days a year, I still pick up that pen and write to her. On her birthday. On *my* birthday. On Christmas Day. And on the anniversary of the most frightening day I've ever experienced – the day I met a boy called Lucas and *his* nanny, as in *au pair*, when I worked as a security guard in a psychiatric hospital."

Billy waits for a few seconds.

"Please tell me you've still got those diaries," he says.

"I'm the very model of a hoarder," is Danny's answer.

3

Once, and not so long ago, he had been the Biscuit Inspector. Later, he had become Sir Biscuits, and later still, Lord Biscuits. He had been important. He'd earned himself stature.

How the mighty have fallen.

Kieran Sange is at work, though not at his desk. A man on a mission for which he never signed up, he moves through teams at Coronet Confectionaries, asking after the whereabouts of Billy Alfreth. Once he is in the office of the team managed by Pat Kelly, a woman with tears in her eyes suggests he tries the smoking area outside.

"Thank you – I will," Kieran tells her. "Are you okay?" A hyphenated word on an envelope on this colleague's desk reminds Kieran of her name. In his current confusion, her name has slipped his mind. "Anne-Marie." *Delivered By Hand* is also written on the envelope, in the top left corner, in a handwriting familiar to him.

"I got a letter from Lorraine, my half-sister," Anne-Marie tells Kieran. "It seems like no one's told her she's supposed to have died. I mean, who would want to play a cruel trick like that on me? Aren't I grieving enough for the sick bastard?"

A knot appears in Kieran's stomach: it is something like a sea of indigestion, which fans clouds of nausea through the sky of his upper body, aiming for the north star of his epiglottis. If he is not careful, he'll be five breaths from throwing up. Perhaps he should race pell-mell for the vomitorium, as a pre-emptive strike. Kieran pictures Lorraine, as he had once known her (or known *of* her: on the street, in the group). He can even smell her scent.

At the sight of Lorraine's handwriting, the letter that he had received from the dead woman returns to the forefront of his consciousness. What had started as a terrible day had just got worse. Such a degradation had scarcely seemed feasible when Kieran had read his first text of the morning: the text that had made him want to speak to Billy Alfreth as soon as he'd arrived at work. Now that his brain feels crammed with matters with which he will have to deal, the sensation of nausea intensifies. A pain in Kieran's throat feels like a burn. A sudden attack of indigestion invades the cosmos of his torso.

It is more than a case of basic manners that compels Kieran Sange to ask Anne-Marie: "What did she write? If you don't mind my asking, of course."

"I don't mind at all," Anne-Marie responds. "But weren't you looking for Billy Alfreth? I got the impression you had something important to discuss. You seem jittery."

"My daughter is missing." Kieran blurts out the source of his panic before he can guess how the message will land. He leans slightly closer, attempting to avoid being overheard. In the office are two men named Malcolm; Kieran can never remember how to tell them apart. One of them is typing; the other stands by the photocopier.

Having lowered his voice, Kieran elaborates on his theme.

"She sent me a text last night to say she's worried she's killed her piano teacher. So far this morning I've phoned her husband repeatedly and now I'm trying to question Billy."

"Kieran! A word if I may," comes a voice from the end of the shared office.

"What's Billy got to do with anything?" Anne-Marie wants to know in a raspy whisper.

Kieran turns his head to take in Pat Kelly, who is standing on the threshold between the shared office and his one private space.

"Billy's my daughter's boyfriend – or one of them at any rate," Kieran replies. "Please tell me if you know anything about Jemima that might help me."

"Kieran, mate – now, please!" Pat Kelly calls. "A syllable or two in your shell-like."

Kieran shows Anne-Marie the palms of his two hands. Then he raises the first two fingers of his right hand. The intention is to show his colleague five fingers plus five fingers plus two, adding up to twelve. Kieran hopes that she will infer he hopes to meet her at noon.

With an effort Kieran is able to display a wide grin. He winks at Anne-Marie as he leaves her desk-side; the wink is entirely for show.

"How goes it, Pat?" Kieran asks. "What progress the Zinger?"

"Fuck the Zinger. Get your arse in here now, Kieran."

In the office, Kieran asks Pat if he's seen Billy Alfreth this morning.

"Yes, he's here, Kieran. I sent him to Procurement – the air around him was stale. But do you know what, mate? Do you know what's in the God's seats of my particular theatre, looking down at the stage? It's got nothing to do with Billy Alfreth."

"It should have."

Pat Kelly pulls at the hairs of his moustache with energetic fingertips. Kieran is put in mind of the feelers on a deep-sea diving fish.

"The thing on my mind isn't Billy, mate. The thing on my mind is a policewoman named Sharon Bark. Who suggests something rather fanciful. Something that turned my stomach, truth be told."

"Pat, my daughter Jemima is not at home and nowhere to be found. Billy is a current boyfriend. Don't ask. I'm looking for him because I can't reach Jemima. My ex-wife is panicked silly. *I'm* panicked silly. She's not at the house she shares with her husband, or answering her phone."

"Kieran. Did you know I used to go out with Lorraine, when she was a teenager?"

"Your personal life, Kieran, is not really any of my business."

"I received a letter from her," Pat replies. "Any idea where I might be going with this?"

Kieran leaves it a fraction too long before answering: "No, not really."

"I don't believe you, *Lord Biscuits*."

Kieran's lips push together so hard that he feels pain – but he has no idea that his mouth has turned white. He watches Pat Kelly pinch one side of his moustache. Although the latter has an authority over the Biscuit Inspector's work grade, he is not his line manager. Kieran is within his rights to disregard the other man's accusations – if that's what they are.

"Quite honestly, Pat, I don't care what you believe or don't believe." Kieran rises to his feet. "Your selective hearing seems to have edited out the part about my daughter being missing."

Pat Kelly sighs. "Sit down again, Kieran. The world's bigger than your immediate concerns."

"And what's *that* supposed to mean?"

"It's supposed to *mean* I think I know something about your daughter. So I repeat. Sit *down,* you arrogant bastard, and put your listening ears on, once and for all."

*

Partway through the conversation that follows, Anne-Marie enters Pat Kelly's office with a cup of coffee in either hand. Not a word does she utter; and it is not until she is most of the way back out into the wider office that Pat says "Thank you" and Kieran understands that people can be invisible. Although it is unlikely that Anne-Marie *intended* to be invisible, she has managed to slip in, deposit two drinks and leave, without two grown men, engrossed in their own conflict, noticing her until the last possible moment.

Returning to her desk via the snacks machine, Anne-Marie allows herself to be engulfed in a swathe of depressive thinking.

No one will ever ask her opinion – she is certain of this – but she believes she can help the greater good with one key piece of information.

That policewoman Sharon Bark has been present more than Anne-Marie might have thought necessary. Why is that woman still attending court at Coronet Confectionaries, from time to time?

Why was Sharon Bark here this morning? The morning when Anne-Marie had returned to her desk to find a letter from Lorraine.

*

"If I say I'm saying this is as a friend, you understand what I mean, don't you?"

"Yes. It means we're not friends in the slightest, but we're somehow appropriating the conventions of friendship," Kieran says, "for the sake of passing on information that's uncomfortable."

"Well put. Now, with that in mind: your daughter. You won't like it."

"I don't doubt it for a second. But as I'm getting more anxious by the second, why don't you climb down off your camel and start being a human being. *What the fuck* are you talking about, Pat?"

"I have a good idea where she is. Do you know the name Louise Reardon?"

"I don't think so."

"She's an academic – and a prize-winning troublemaker. I think she's controlling Jemima."

Kieran sniffs and laughs at the same time. "Then she's doing better than anyone else has ever managed! My daughter's not one for taking advice, to put it mildly."

"I'm not joking, Kieran. Your daughter's in danger."

Kieran thinks about offering a response like *She's* always *in danger*; but instead he listens to the rumours circulating in his own nervous system.

"Who is she?" he asks seriously. "How do you know her?"

"Through an ex-girlfriend, twenty-five years ago." Pat appears to experience distress: the memory would seem to be sending barbs into the inside of his skull. "A woman whose name you know. Lorraine."

An instant passes; once again, Kieran forces himself not to jump at a stock phrase. His first reaction is to say something about coincidences, and to mention Anne-Marie's half-sister.

"Lorraine who died on the High Street," is what he settles for.

Pat nods his head. "Anne-Marie's half-sister. It was twenty-five years ago. We were going out together and she got a babysitting job with Louise and Robert. The boy's name was Lucas – he was eight, nine, and a real handful. A *difficult child* might be one way of putting it. A *special child* might be another. Well. There were four male influences in Lucas's life. His dad was weak but he was one of them. Then he had an uncle called Raymond who he adored. A guy from Europe – a piano player, *obsessed* with music. And a guy called Derek."

Although Kieran feels twitchy, he does not want to interrupt Pat's flow. He notices a mug in front of him; steam climbs out of it. How long has it been there? In his mind, Lorraine's face has morphed into Anne-Marie's. Kieran thinks of his army as he reaches for his drink.

"Well, because the boy had a few issues, there were problems at school, and problems in general. The four men I mentioned – and a bit later on, me as well – got involved in discussions about how to protect the boy. How to raise him safely."

"Protect him from what?" Kieran asks.

"From life in general! They were obsessive – and heated. They tried to *teach* Lucas things, but things a boy doesn't need to know at such a young age. Jazz music, for example."

The cup is a hand's-breadth from Kieran's lips, and there it hovers. "Wait a minute," Kieran says, "I've just realised what you're saying. The *boy* Lucas is Jemima's *husband* Lucas?"

"The very same: a quarter of a century on."

"Well, he ended up okay. He's got some quirks, there's no doubt about that, but he's basically a decent feller. Goes to work every day. Rarely ill. Puts up with my daughter's embarrassing shenanigans."

"Let me ask you a question, Kieran. Who asked who to marry?"

"Do you mean Jemima and Lucas?"

"No, I mean Popeye and Olive Oyl. Did Lucas ask Jemima or was it the other way around?"

"I have no idea," Kieran tells him. "What does it matter?"

"I'm willing to bet Jemima asked Lucas. And why? Because of Louise, I reckon. She's keeping an eye on all six of us, even now. And she'll publish her findings in academic journals or a book that'll gather dust in a university library in the Midlands."

"At the risk of provoking your *ire* again, Pat, allow me to make an interpretation or two, if you would. Are you saying this Louise woman influenced my daughter to propose marriage to her son?"

Pat picks up his own mug from the desk. "I think it's likely."

"Well, *I* don't think it's likely. Who *is* she, this Louise?"

"A very bitter ethnographer, to put it bluntly. Her entire working life is about finding her place among the subjects she's either interviewing or influencing."

"But what's that got to do with Jemima?"

"Here's where I'm hazy. I can only guess, but I think Jemima's her newish recruit. I don't think even a psychopathic nutbag like Louise can keep all of the plates spinning in a way she'd like, especially when she's got a job in the north. She needs someone on the ground, as it were."

"And that's Jemima."

"That's my guess. And I think that's where she's gone – to see Louise. I have a feeling we're going to see more and more of her."

"Who? Jemima or Louise?"

"They'll become the same person, I reckon. Louise isn't getting any younger, after all. She'll want someone to pass the reins to. Someone suitably unpredictable and erratic. No offence."

"Oh, none taken, I'm sure," Kieran replies sourly, frowning his way into a headache. "The letters," he adds. "Did you get a letter from Lorraine?"

"Lorraine's dead, remember?"

"I *know* Lorraine's dead, Pat – that's not what I asked."

"No, I didn't receive a letter from Lorraine. I actually feel left out. *You* obviously did."

Kieran nods his head. "So did Anne-Marie. Maybe others. But who's to say it was Lorraine who delivered them, right? Because she can't. But *Jemima* could have."

"Yes; or the policewoman could have. WPC Sharon Bark. She's been here a few times." Pat drinks from his mug. "Someone would have let someone in a police uniform gain access. And if it was your daughter, maybe Billy Alfreth let her in if she said she was here to see her dad."

Their boats drift into a still and silent harbour.

Pat places his mug on the desk and starts fiddling with his moustache again. Kieran is *this close* to telling him to knock it off, but resists the temptation. It is clear that Pat has not finished his speech.

"Some of the conversations were dark in tone, Kieran," Pat continues. "The four men – despite Louise's protests – were adamant they had to keep Lucas away from anything negative. He was smothered. Molly-coddled – as if he was a *patient*. Well, I'm sure you can guess what happened in due course."

"No I can't, as a matter of fact."

"Basically, he exploded." Pat winces and screws his eyes shut. "That's a terrible word to choose, for reasons you'll hear in a minute. I'll go back. Once I was part of the group, so to speak, only because of Lorraine's positive influence on Lucas, we got involved in conversations about fighting fire with fire. The logic was: if negativity exists all around us, the only way to get rid of it is by brute strength and ignorance. Letters to the council and the government weren't getting anywhere, so it was only a matter of time before we started talking about taking more direct confrontational action. It was round about then we started to talk about bombs."

"Christ. I didn't see *that* coming," says Kieran.

"Neither did any of the victims."

"Are you being serious? People were hurt?"

By failing to offer either a nod or a shake of the head, Pat keeps his story-cards close to his chest. For this semblance of confidentiality, so late in the confessional day, the Biscuit Inspector – or Lord Biscuits, no less – hates the man with a passion that's stronger than fate.

"We decided to disrupt – not to maim innocent people," says Pat. "If nothing else, at least I'd like you to believe our *intentions* were good. We were *agents provocateur*. Not terrorists." This seems like a routine that Pat has performed before. "Emphatically not terrorists."

"Not-terrorists but setting off bombs," Kieran summarises.

"I know it sounds antithetical, Kieran. It was a long time ago; and maybe I've forgotten important parts of the rationale. But it made sense to us at the time. We'd scare the establishment into taking us seriously. No one was supposed to be hurt."

"But they were?"

This time, Pat's body language is sufficient to send a flare across the still and silent surface of the sea between them. Kieran knows what Pat is going to say before he opens his mouth.

"We placed a device in the council offices. It was deliberately timed to go off overnight. But what we didn't know was, they cleaned the offices overnight. A cleaner suffered flesh wounds."

"You were lucky you didn't go to prison, the lot of you."

"Yes, we were. The point being: while *we* were making our plans about the futility of resistance, we took our eyes off Lucas. And nobody knew – I don't think – how much he was being stifled and suppressed. Well, as I said (it's too late to unsay it), the boy exploded. He was trapped in an over-cautious and over-loved environment: he was *bound* to rebel."

"What did he do?" Kieran asks.

"He got into his Uncle Raymond's files and made his own bomb."

"How old was he?"

"Nine. He put the family dog – Narna – into the family car. Then blew it up. The dog was killed but the car got through its next M.O.T. Don't talk to me about fairness."

"And this is Lucas. Just so I'm clear. The man who married my daughter exploded a dog."

"I *think* the dog died of a heart attack. But yes, in essence."

"Christ. And I just called him normal."

"Well, that's the point," says Pat. "He *is* normal – now. But he wasn't. It was at this point Louise took it upon herself to control the boy's thinking. She made herself the boss. She basically called bullshit on everything that had happened up to then. She was going to teach him the values and beliefs she wanted him to adhere to. She made him forget."

Kieran exhales. "She brainwashed him, you mean."

"I think that's the money."

"Until *now*? All these years?"

"Well, that I simply can't know. All I *do* know is this. Louise was incredibly jealous of her husband and especially her twin brother Raymond's influence on Lucas. Her anger was forged in the fire, there and then. It's like a branding she's worn on her skin ever since."

"I see. And do you have a contact number for this Louise? What was her surname?"

"Reardon. I looked her up on her university's website. She's easy to find."

Kieran cocks his head to one side. "That's *something* at least," he offers, bitterly.

*

But no one will ever ask her, she types, *and that's the pity.*

Dr Louise Reardon stares at the words on her screen, seeking footholds on how to climb what seems to be the sheer face of the penultimate third draft chapter. She is nearly there: she is inching closer, possessed by the right frame of mind – and with victory cheering in her cerebral cortex.

Earlier, she had answered a few emails on the subject of the exam board scheduled for next week. Partly because of this, and partly because it's late in the working day and Louise is tired, she answers her phone without looking at the screen. Although she does not say her name, as she sometimes does when she answers the mobile, she says "Hello?" in a querying tone.

At the other end of the line, the caller asks: "Am I speaking to WPC Sharon Bark?"

"Yes, you are," Louise busks.

"No I'm not, Louise," the caller tells her. "I'm talking to Super-Supe. What's going on?"

In her car in the car lot that serves the business park, Louise dips her head. Something that feels like victory nests at the back of her skull. She knows that she has been discovered, and she is fine with that analysis. After all, it has been a quarter of a century coming.

"If you don't mind offering an explanation," says Chaz, "I'd be happy to hear what you've thought through with reference to Sharon Bark."

"She's my eyes on the prize," says Louise.

"With the prize being what exactly?"

Louise pauses before responding. "The prize is a relief from the constant attritional *boredom*."

"I'll bear that in mind. Are you at home?"

"No. I've just been inside Coronet Confectionaries. I'm invisible. Nobody *sees* me. It's depressing. I've waited twenty-five years for someone to notice me; still nothing."

"How about *I* see you, Louise? How about right now?"

Not exactly answering the question, Louise says, "I'm so tired, Chaz. I thought I'd be caught a long time ago. Believe me: it's getting harder and harder not to be noticed."

"Well, *I've* noticed you, Louise. And I think it's time you stopped."

4

Later, Billy is at home, in bed and in the dark. Although it is not time to go to sleep, he feels depressed and has slipped fully dressed under the duvet. His bodily requirements have been met but his mind is in turmoil. There is too much in his brain. Any thought-filtration facility that he used to deploy is clearly on the blink tonight. Images, words – some from his memory, some invented – wash around inside his head, creating a bad dream before he has closed his eyes.

The thought of going to work tomorrow is like a very black tunnel. In fact, Billy realises that he can only define himself by using negatives; by saying what he does *not* want to do. He does not want to watch the television. He does not want to read. He does not want to do anything but rest. He has had some toast and is not hungry. Half a can of lager is on his night-stand, unwanted. He cannot be bothered to go outside to smoke a cigarette. Most of all he wishes to avoid his phone and laptop; he has embarked on a journey of digital detoxification.

Instead of thinking about Jemima and Terry Bates and a talking dog, Billy tries to locate his housemates by any noises being made. But it's odd: although the time cannot be later than eight p.m., there is no sound in the house – not even heavy metal from Metal Mickey's room. Where is everyone? From downstairs, in the kitchen, no audible evidence of a meal being prepared or washing-up being done. There is no distant throb of the washing machine or tumble drier. No television chatter from anywhere in the building; no conversations to eavesdrop on. Were it not for the fact that Billy can hear his own heart pounding too quickly and hear the roar of blood in his skull, he might even imagine that he's gone deaf.

Billy falls back on a tried and tested method of relaxation – one he'd used many times during some of the longer nights of imprisonment at Dellacotte Young Offenders. He pictures sheep. He thinks of them running down a slope towards him. Whistles from an unseen shepherd's lips flute merrily on the air. (These whistles come from Billy's nostrils: he has started to drift off and is gently snoring.) The scene is restful and rural: while in jail he had watched *Countryfile* and *One Man and His Dog* with a fervour all-but religious. He had used these programmes to source fantasies of a better life: an existence in the countryside, maybe working on a farm in the hills.

The sheep in Billy's dream are running closer; and now, for the first time, the dreamer is able to see the shepherd's dog. It is not a traditional sheepdog: the breed is Labradoodle. In fact, the dog is the dog that was trapped in the car; the same dog that had talked to Billy on the pavement on the Bank Holiday Monday. When the sheep move past Billy's mind's eye, the dog stops to talk.

We're in this together, Billy, the dog informs him; *but you ask the wrong questions of the wrong people.*

Will you help me work it out? Billy asks. *Who should I talk to?*

Slowly, in close-up, the Labradoodle closes his eyes, and answers: *The man with this voice.*

Billy raises his eyelids. Not certain if he is awake or dreaming, he thinks of the voice that had said *The man with this voice* – and Pat Kelly's face fills his mind.

Pat is one more person whom Billy will need to speak to. But not first.

The first person he wants to speak to is Lucas. Although he knows it is unlikely to be an easy conversation, Billy is sure that Lucas must know something about Jemima's disappearance.

On so deciding, Billy can relax. Once again, he closes his eyes, and waits.

*

The next morning is a Thursday. For no reason that he understands, Billy is acutely aware that he has worked at Coronet Confectionaries for four months and six days.

Four months is approximately one hundred and twenty days. Therefore, for one hundred and twenty-six days, Billy has reported for work without taking so much as one sick day. He has only been late twice (because of bus problems); he feels justified at calling in ill. He leaves a message on Anne-Marie's voicemail, and then – just to be on the safe side – he emails Pat Kelly with a similar message. By typing "a bit under the weather" he keeps the matter vague.

The house feels no more occupied than it had the evening before. Billy considers slamming a door or two, just for the pleasure of hearing a complaint. This, however, he does not do. Instead, he plods downstairs, on the hunt for housemates. He finds Holier Than seated at the kitchen table, nibbling the crusts from around a slice of toast. A cup of something hot steams near his left elbow.

"All right, Holier?" Billy offers.

"What have you done to upset Mercy and Ross?" asks the other man.

"What? Nothing, as far as I know. What do you mean?"

"They want you to leave."

"Who do? You mean *leave the house*?"

"That's exactly what I mean. Floored Masterpiece played in The Anchor again last night and Mercy was on the vodka martinis, rarely enough. She was not quite *complimentary* about you, Bill."

Billy already has a long list of tasks to execute today. He has not expected to add *domestic strife* to this same list. But he feels hurt. Why wasn't he invited to The Anchor to see the band, as he had been the last time? The fact that he hadn't much enjoyed the previous experience is not relevant.

What have I done? How have annoyed them?

"Why are they cross?"

Holier Than Thou lays down the remains of his slice of toast. Taking his time about it, he picks up a tea towel and wipes his fingertips clean while he chews a mouthful.

"Billy? You're a right pain in the arse sometimes. You know that."

Billy has not moved far from the threshold between the kitchen and the hallway. Now he moves over to the sink and feels the side of the kettle. It is warm but not hot. He flicks the switch to boil the water inside it again.

"As a matter of fact, Holier, I didn't."

"My name's *Joshua*, Billy. That's item one on the pain-in-the-arse catalogue. Whoever said you could change my name? I never gave you *permission*."

"It's banter!" Billy retorts. "I didn't think I *needed* your permission."

"Well, you did." Thou rises to his feet. "My personal problem with you, if you're interested, is you're scruffy. You're *dirty*. You leave plates in the sink. Your personal hygiene is questionable. And you're aloof to a degree I can't find amusing."

To the monotone whisper of water boiling in the kettle, Joshua Thou exits the kitchen. He leaves behind a panicked Billy – and a *furious* Billy, at that. It is probably too early to demand an explanation; and anyway, perhaps Thou has got his facts wrong.

Billy prepares his first coffee of the day. Nothing should stop him, today of all days, from undertaking his multiple meetings. The fact that he has learned he is not popular in the house should not deter him from these plans. You don't throw a sicky every day, after all.

Although he sits at the table and sips his coffee, no one joins Billy: there is no opportunity either to apologise or seek an explanation. Billy gets it into his head that Mercy, Ross and Metal Mickey must be avoiding him; but is that conclusion fair? Eventually, he gives up; he ascends the staircase to shower and then dress. There's unpaid work to execute today.

*

As he enters the premises, Billy reflects that the number of times in his whole life he has entered a similar florist's shop could be counted on the fingers of his two hands. Which shake.

Scared as fuck, he thinks – as an electronic security feature alerts the staff to the entrance of a potential visitor.

Bee-boo.

Billy lets go of the door; behind his back as he walks towards the counter, the door closes slowly on hydraulic hinges.

The air is as thick with condensed floral odour as a jungle would be. In the past, Billy has wished that he understood more about plants and blooms, but this thought is not on his mind right now. Instead, he showers under the rain of memories that soaks him. Although he is not visiting Jemima (and would that he could!), he is visiting the person that he believes is closest to her. For this reason, among others, the thought of Jemima is loud in Billy's head. Camouflaged though she might be, he can see his girlfriend in the bouquets; he can smell her scent above all else.

Months have passed since Billy and Lucas have spoken. When Lucas steps out from the back to take his place behind the counter, he regards his visitor with what Billy interprets as momentary panic – but not surprise. There is no surprise on show, as Lucas's first comment seems to confirm.

"I was wondering when I'd see you," Lucas tells Billy.

When, Billy notes – not *if*. "Has she been in touch?"

Lucas shakes his head. He lays his hands on the counter, leans forwards slightly as the result of his shoulders sagging with apparent weariness, and sighs comprehensively.

"And you don't know where she's gone?" Billy presses. "You have no idea."

"Genuinely. I have no idea, Billy. She could be anywhere."

"She could be dead," Billy adds, and Lucas nods his head.

While both parties silently hope for a customer to enter the shop – or for the phone to ring – Billy casts an eye over his heavily-scented surroundings. Flowers of every hue are crammed into buckets that climb decorative metal scaffolds. Wedding day arrangements and arrangements for other occasions are framed on pallets, encircled by fake grass that looks like green hair.

Billy breathes deeply. "Do you sell nightshade?"

Baffled by the question, Lucas frowns. "No. There's not much call for it, Billy. Try Central or South America. Australia or Africa at a push."

Billy tries to look Lucas in the eye. "Have you any idea why I would ask?"

Tapping his fingertips on the counter, Lucas waits; he leads Billy to believe that the man is seeking divine inspiration – a whisper behind a cupped hand from the Man Upstairs Himself.

"Shall I give you a clue, Lucas? Nightshade is used to make certain drugs."

"Yes I know. What of it? It's used to make burandanga."

"It is. Or its other name is *scopolamine*." Billy stresses the word slowly, reminding himself briefly of the difficulty that Narna the Labradoodle had had with articulating the English language. "The drug that's said to remove a person's free will."

Again, Lucas shrugs. "It's not new. It breaks down psychological barriers and makes people susceptible. I don't understand the point you're making."

"The point I'm making is, I think Jemima's been drugging me for *months*."

"With *scopolamine*?"

"Or something like it. She's given me drugs and suggestions and watched me invent my own saga. I thought I was losing my mind! I was hallucinating in broad daylight."

Lucas cocks his head to one side: the gesture is alarmingly canine. "What did you see?" he asks, not without a trace of awe in his words.

"Well, for example: I saw a man I worked with tell me he'd made a sign to hang up in the loos at work. Then later he denied he'd made or said any such thing. At the time I thought he had to be high; but now I understand it was *me*. *I* was the one under the influence. Even worse – I might never have sussed it out if I hadn't kept a diary when I started university a year or so ago. Did Jemima ever mention my diary?"

"Why would she?"

"I went back and read some of the entries from my first year – even if it made me feel sick. I found Jemima's annotations on the paper. Tiny words and phrases here and there I hadn't noticed before. So small in some cases they looked like my crossings-out. All *influencing* me, one way or another, hand in hand with whatever drug she was feeding me."

"But to what end? I can't deny it sounds like something Jemima might get it into her head to do, but why bother?" Lucas asks.

He hasn't asked where Jemima might have got the drug, Billy tells himself. *What else does he know? What's he not telling me?*

"Because I'm her experiment," Billy answers. "She made me believe a dog could talk to me. She put the word *sapor* in my head, so it echoed."

"Sapor?"

"It means a vile taste."

Lucas nods his head. "I go back to my earlier comment. Why? I'm not doubting you, Billy – I just don't *get* it."

"I don't either. But what does it suggest if she's buying drugs and trying to twist my mind? Possibly the minds of others?"

"I don't *know*. What *does* it suggest?"

Ignoring the question, Billy poses one of his own. "How does a student afford the heroin, for one thing?" he asks.

"Someone's supporting her."

"That's right, Lucas. Specifically: your *mother* is supporting her. Her name is written in small font all the way through the diary. *Louise Reardon.* She's played me for a fool for at least a year."

"And *me*, it would appear. One of the many problems with our mutually thankless marriage is that I torture her by not showing an iota of interest in a single thing she says. She tortures me in turn with her flings and casual affairs – and now, of course, with a penchant for Grade A narcotics."

"But why would you want to torture each other at all?" Billy asks.

"It's the air we breathe."

"Where does she live? I'm going to visit her."

"I have the address at home. I can't remember off the top of my head. Why?"

"Why what? Why do I want the address? Because I think Jemima's there."

"At my *mother's*? They don't even get on!"

"She's either there or hanging out with the rough sleepers," says Billy. "That seems to be fashionable these days."

"Or what about a hotel?" asks Lucas. "Let's imagine she's gone old school."

"I don't see it, do you? It's too *comfortable*."

Lucas sighs. "I think you might have a point," he admits.

*

The train is twelve minutes late leaving the station this mid-morning, but mostly empty.

Billy finds four seats around a table and claims two of them with his body and his rucksack. From the bag he pulls out his laptop, a notebook and the diary. Now that he knows Jemima has spiked the diary, he is drawn to it; he wants to examine in detail what his ex-girlfriend had deposited for him to excavate at a later date.

After fifteen minutes, a railway employee begins his journey down the aisle.

"Tickets, please, ladies and gentlemen!" says Derek Latham.

On the latter's arrival at the table, Billy produces his ticket. The two of them do not know each other, and yet both feel a spark of inexplicable recognition.

"Is there a drinks trolley on this service?" Billy asks.

"Yes, sir. Hot and cold drinks and light refreshments. Service commences in about five minutes. Do enjoy your journey."

"Thank you – I'll try," Billy answers, without any conviction.

*

For today's occasion Billy Alfreth has donned the suit that he wears for work at Coronet Confectionaries. Just in case he is being watched from inside the house, he raises his left hand closer to his line of sight and makes a show of reading what is displayed on his phone, as if checking an address. In his right hand and clutched to his torso by the positioning of his right arm, are two bunches of flowers. The bunch he holds in his hand are white lilies; the bunch against his body, red roses. He strolls up the short driveway to the house.

He need not have gone through the mime of checking the address: from the time it takes for the door to be opened it is plain that no one has caught sight of him or his floral offerings. Nor would anyone inside have expected him.

The woman who answers is in her mid-fifties, attractive (thinks Billy); her grey hair is short and stylish. Even within her own home she has dressed smartly, the only concession to utilitarian comfort being (perhaps) the Pokemon slippers on her tiny feet. At the sight of the flowers her eyes widen in what

Billy takes to be pleased surprise.

"I have a bouquet for Dr Louise Reardon," Billy begins.

"So I see. Lucky I'm working from home today. I'm writing."

"And a bouquet for Tamara Reardon as well."

Billy hands over both; the transparent wrapping crackles against Louise's bosom.

"I can't see a card in either of them," Louise states.

"The lilies are a condolence offering, following the shocking death of your ex-husband, Dr Finley Reardon. The roses are a late congratulation present to Tamara, for her twenty-first birthday."

Louise looks puzzled. "Why no flowers for Algernon, I wonder?" she offers Billy through a smile that the recipient struggles to read.

"Pardon me?"

"Nothing. A silly joke on my part," Louise answers. "But who are they *from*?"

Billy takes a beat and gives her an answer that bleaches her attractive face of much of its colour. "Emeritus Professor Raymond Cossell," he says. "Your twin brother, Louise."

Expressionlessly, Louise closes the door.

The Prof's not dead then, he thinks. Louise's reaction is not appropriate for a sister who lost her brother a quarter of a century earlier. Lucas had told Billy that his Uncle Raymond was "probably passed on by now"; the man had lost everything and had been forced to make a new home for himself on the streets. Jemima had written Cossell's name in Billy's diary but had not committed to whether the man was alive or dead. Instead, she had deposited tiny clues like: *twins, too much jealousy.*

Billy waits in the front garden. Sounding the doorbell again will seem pushy, he is certain. Has the train journey been in vain?

The door opens again.

"You're Billy Alfreth, aren't you?" Louise asks.

"You know perfectly well I am. Is Jemima in there with you to identify me?"

"Not right now. But come inside, Billy. You might say I've waited twenty-five years to be confronted. Why shouldn't I be happy, now it's happened?"

Billy approaches the front door.

"The flowers were a nice touch, I must admit," Louise Reardon tells him.

*

"They were obsessed with protecting the boy," Louise tells them. "Obsessed in the original – I think original – sense of it being a daily occurrence."

"But protecting him from what?" Billy asks. "They must've imagined he was threatened."

"Where do I start? Protect him from the world," Louise answers. "Protect him from nameless dread, in the Bionic sense – after Wilfred Bion. You name it. Their goal was to save this beautiful boy from the rigours of a normal life."

"I must admit I'm struggling with this a bit. What you're suggesting they did as a wrong thing sounds pretty laudable to me. Protecting a child."

"In theory, yes – I agree. But how about the opposing view? That children should be allowed to make their mistakes and find their own answers – without adult intervention."

It takes no more than a second for Billy to recall a few of the events of his own childhood. This memory gives way to a close-angle shot of the cell in which he had lived during his time at Her Majesty's Pleasure, in Dellacotte Young Offenders, which had started before Billy had so much as reached his second decade of his planetary span.

"I might have to disagree with you there, Louise. For reasons I can't really go into, I ended up getting into trouble with the law – precisely because of the absence of a realistic father figure."

"*Realistic* is an interesting word here, Billy."

"Are you going to make notes? Put me in a book?"

"I might at that." Louise smiles. "Perhaps you're in one already."

Fudging has its time and place. "Do you know where Jemima is?" Billy asks.

"Yes; but she's asked me not to reveal her whereabouts. And I'll respect that."

Billy acknowledges the point made. "Will she stay here with you?"

"That's a matter for *her* to consider."

"Yes it is. But you can tell me – as her new employer."

"Well done, Billy. I feel genuinely relieved. It's so *delicious* being found out."

"I'm delighted to hear you say that, Louise. You're in for a good afternoon, I must say. What I'm about to say will leave you cosy and wosey ...Do you remember Danny Lovell?"

"Of course I remember Danny," Louise answers. "The guard at the psychiatric facility my son was admitted to. Not that he knows it."

"Not that *who* knows it? Lucas or Danny?"

"I meant Lucas – but maybe both of them."

"Have you followed the man's career progression?" Billy asks.

"I follow everything," Louise replies with robust sincerity.

The response is enough to make Billy smile. "I suppose I might have expected that," he tells his interlocutor. "Just out of interest, don't you find it exhausting?"

"More than you will ever know, Billy. What were you going to say about Danny Lovell?"

"I read his diaries. Or some of them. From twenty-five years ago."

Louise makes a pert face that suggests intense fascination. "Oh, do tell," she says.

"Danny worked security in the hospital. He knew Lucas."

"Oh, I know *that*. I thought you'd say something new."

"All right then. How about this? Your son set off a bomb with his dog Narna the Third inside the car. Lucas killed your pet and had a nervous breakdown, of sorts. He was invited into the hospital. Became the confidante of Danny Lovell. Is *that* specific enough?"

Louise smiles. "You're getting there, at least."

"The man's broken," Billy adds.

"I'm pleased to hear it."

"Why? What's he ever done to you?"

"Nothing. Do you honestly think my satisfaction is based on others' sense of *wellbeing*? No, of course not. Grow up, if so."

"Your son tried to shoot him."

"I know. My idiot brother took him a gun. To a hospital! It was the final straw, to be honest with you. I knew he and I weren't destined to be together when I learned about the gun. Doesn't matter if you're twins or what you are. You don't turn your back on stupidity, do you?"

Ever since the madness that he endured at Dellacotte Young Offenders, Billy Alfreth has made it a point of principle not to dwell on those times. But now, in Louise's company, they swim into his inner vision. They demand his attention.

"No," he responds at length; "you don't turn your back on stupidity. Why did your brother take Lucas a gun?"

"I'm certain you think I'm something of a risk-taker. I'm *nothing* compared with Raymond and his coterie, believe me. If they'd had *their* way, they would've blown up Parliament or something!"

Although Billy is sure that Louise is fishing for a response, he declines the invitation.

Louise says, "I should be a *heroine*!"

"A Freudian choice of word, if I may be so bold."

"Oh, *please*, Billy! What does an old prison lag know about *Freud*?"

If no other proof is needed, this remark would indicate that Jemima and Louise have been in contact; that Jemima has been something of a blabbermouth, in fact.

"It might surprise you to know, you're allowed to read in prison. As you'll discover in due course," Billy adds.

"Oh, don't threaten me, Billy – not in my own home. It makes me even wearier."

Billy's return smile is no more than a flicker.

"Talk me through the decision to make Jemima a drug addict," he says.

"Simplicity itself. I did no such thing."

"You introduced her to hard drugs. Via Terry Bates."

"Don't be naïve, Billy. You know what she's like – she would've found heroin if it was what she wanted to find. Don't overestimate my own importance in all of this. The fact she's in the company – right now – of a group of homeless people should be testament to my lack of involvement in her drug-taking ways. It's none of my business. And she asked me not to tell you. Sorry."

"Where do they gather?"

"I'll give you directions when we're finished. Is that really all you wanted to ask?"

"You sound disappointed."

"I've waited a quarter of a century, Billy. I thought you might *bust* me. I've given everyone enough clues, for Christ's sake. So yes, if you're not going to indulge, you could say I'm disappointed in you. I can go *that far*. I've spent a fortune on procuring drugs and travelling south – I've even had to buy a policewoman's uniform to be Sharon Bark – and no one has had the *simple courtesy* to look intrigued at this old gal still treading water at the rank of WPC."

Louise is racing into her theme. "So *yes*. You could say I'd hoped for a more dramatic final scene. I am very *very* tired of being *ordinary*."

Torn between asking about Jemima and asking about Louise herself, Billy plumps for what he regards as the middle ground. Her work.

"I need to use your toilet, please, Louise," he states.

"Turn left at the top of the stairs. I'm going to fix a drink. Would you like one?"

"I could murder a beer."

"Ready when you've washed your hands and returned."

Wasting no time whatsoever, Billy slopes into the room that Louise obviously uses as her office. One wall is crammed with books. Facing the window is a computer. Billy knows that he has no hope of cracking a password, but his assumption based on Louise's age and occupation bears fruit. The stack of A4 pages to the left of the machine is indeed the work in progress.

Billy picks up the manuscript. It must be six hundred printed pages so far and weighs the same as a bag of potatoes. On the front sheet is a stab at what will be the title.

Ethnographic Work in Progress: a MS in search of a name and home.

In the bathroom, Billy pees while reading the Acknowledgements page at the front. To Billy it seems like a valediction, the fact that Louise has thanked Jemima Sange in the relevant paragraph.

He descends the stairs to claim his lager in the front room.

"I *thought* you might be going for the book," Louise tells him. "If you're thinking of threatening me with destroying it – just a word to the wise – it's backed up on the cloud and in my email."

"I wasn't thinking of destroying a damn thing," Billy tells her. "I was showing interest."

"You could have done that without bringing it down, but thank you. Your interest is noted."

"I'm so interested, in fact," Billy continues, "I have the idea I'll pass these ideas off as my own. I'm going to contact a publisher as soon as I get home. Make it clear you've plagiarised my work."

"Unless I do what?"

"Unless you do nothing at all. I'm not *haggling*, Louise. It's what I'm going to do."

"I see. Destroy my academic reputation."

"At least *question* it. Have you *heard* of the Ethics Board? You might or might not know I'm a student myself. Mature student: second year, on work placement for a year."

"Yes, I know about academic ethics," Louise replies.

"You've disobeyed the Board, Louise. Now, I'll make it my business to ruin your reputation. Just as you've wanted for twenty-five years. I'm your knight. I'll make it all work *wrong* for you, don't worry."

"In this defining moment, I'm not quite sure how to react."

"React to this. Jemima will betray you; it's in her genes."

"I know she'll betray me. It's been in my book notes and working draft for years."

"She's probably poisoning you right now."

"I know that as well," Louise answers. "And I think I'm ready."

Billy takes a sip from his bottle of lager and stands up. He does not wait for a thank you. He does not wait for anything. He only pauses at the front door to remember Louise's scent.

ACKNOWLEDGEMENTS

A version of an early chapter of this novel was published under the title 'The Biscuit Inspector' in the *Fresh Anthology,* edited by Zachary Amendt and published by Montag in 2017.

In these pages, a (fictional) disgraced academic quotes from *Crowds and Power* by Elias Canetti. The scene takes as its reading the chapter entitled 'The Pack's Determination' – page 136 onwards in the (real-life) Penguin edition.

A psychoanalyst quotes from Chapter 1 of Jessica Benjamin's *Beyond Doer and Done To.* The sentences appear on page 39 of the Routledge edition. The same psychoanalyst paraphrases the opinion of Juan-David Nasio, on the subject of jealousy. The opinion is offered in *A Psychoanalyst on the Couch*, page 34 of the SUNY edition.

Early support for the section entitled 'Then' was offered by Dr Alan Bainbridge, Dr Elizabeth Chapman Hoult and Professor Linden West, along with the audience to whom I read at Canterbury Christ Church University in 2016.

My respect to Steven Stapleton, Stephen Thrower, Boredoms and John Zorn, for musical inspiration during the drafting of this book. The typing-up of this manuscript was completed to the sounds of *Ghosteen* by Nick Cave and the Bad Seeds, *Total Eclipse* by Billy Cobham, *Bend Sinister* by The Fall, *The Swinging Reflective* by Nurse With Wound, *Wraith* by Teeth of the Sea, and *A Nickel if Your Dick's This Big* by The Residents, in the weeks surrounding my 48th birthday, in November 2019.

Incredibly late in the day, an astonishing album by Misha Mullov-Abbado came my way, via BBC Radio 3 on a Saturday afternoon. Not only did *Cross-Platform Interchange* occupy my attention creatively, it also inspired the name of a gym in this book over which I had dithered for weeks.

Mostly I owe this choppy voyage to Charlie Franco, and one day I'd like to buy him a ticket on an equivalent cruise. From the bottom of my heart, thank you, Charlie.

www.ingramcontent.com/pod-product-compliance
Lightning Source LLC
Chambersburg PA
CBHW031109030726
47496CB00002BA/465